GW01458030

RAGEBORN

THE WITCH QUEEN SAGA BOOK 1

SIMON SHUGAR

Copyright © 2024 Simon Shugar
All rights reserved

The characters and events portrayed in this book are
fictitious. Any similarity to real persons, living or dead, is
coincidental and not intended by the author.

No part of this book may be reproduced, or stored in a
retrieval system, or transmitted in any form or by any
means, electronic, mechanical, photocopying, recording,
or otherwise, without express written permission of the
publisher.

ASIN: B0DBR5FXX2

DEDICATION

To my friends, you know who you are.

Chapters

ACKNOWLEDGMENTS

My father, who he himself, has helped me survive through some of the toughest times of my life. You will always have my gratitude and love.

The readers whom I know each and every one of you have experienced hardship. Thank you for reading and I hope this helps you escape and see there is always light at the end of the tunnel.

Chapter 0 - Forsaken

The sky bled out the last of its light as we moved, a ghostly procession beneath the thinning light of the moon. My lungs filled with the sharp tang of pine, the crisp prelude to snow, whispering through the trees like a promised secret. Their paws, a symphony of thuds against the soft earth, kept a rhythm primal and true.

They were a relentless tide of silhouettes, shadows woven into the fabric of the night. Each form, from the smallest pup to the hardened veterans, melded into a single, formidable force. The forest shuddered at their passage, the air thrummed with the raw power of their collective spirit. They were warriors, conquers, they were my children, my pack.

But the seasons turned, as they always do. The fierce snarls that once tore through the silence of night softened into laughter. Bonds formed, not of blood and battle but of playful tussles and lazy afternoons. The wildness that once defined them, tamed by a peace I never sought.

I found myself adrift, a forgotten relic of a bloodier age, my snarls fading echoes in their harmonious new world. Where once I stood a deviant among beasts, they forsook me.

How dare they FORSAKE ME!

When the last ember threatened to die, I lingered, a shadow bound to the frail heartbeat of a runt. Karn, he named himself—Karn, with eyes too bright for one so small, a spirit that refused to yield as his kin once had.

"And so," I growled into the night, the forest listening in on my solitary pact, "this is not the end but the beginning. Karn's tale is yet to be sung. His fire will burn through the complacency, rekindle the wild that sleeps within. Watch him as he becomes the legend they forgot they could be."

Chapter 1 - The Ashen

The morning air held a crisp chill, flowing down from the snow-dusted peaks and weaving through our village. Thatched roofs, rough and wild like untamed hair, crowned the wooden homes that clung to the edge of the encroaching wilderness. My village, a tiny speck cradled by craggy mountain faces and dense pine forests, buzzed with the sounds of daybreak chores. I stood apart from the bustle, my gaze fixed upward, tracing the majestic Titan's Crest that towered above us.

Mother called them the Guardian Peaks—these mountains, steadfast sentries of our village. Her voice sliced through the morning's mist, snapping me from my reverie. "Leif, come."

I joined the other children, who had gathered in a loose circle on the frosted grass, my boots pressed shallow imprints into the earth. We convened at the edge of the woods where the land began to rise, and the mountains loomed like silent sentinels over us.

"Listen," my mother, the villagers' sole Wisewalker, began, her eyes reflecting the grey sky, "the mountains are the soul of The Ashen. They protect us, yes, but they teach us too." Her hand gestured expansively towards the rugged slopes. "They remind us to be strong, resilient."

She scooped a handful of soil, letting the dark grains filter through her fingers. "Every plant, every creature here has a role, a purpose. As do you," she said as her gaze swept over us, but I could feel it linger upon me. I straightened, feeling the weight of her words.

"Why do they call them the Guardian Peaks?" I piped up, my voice tinged with the eagerness that often earned me simpers or sighs from the adults.

"Because," she paused, a small smile played on her lips as she encouraged my curiosity, "just as I protect and support you all, the mountains support the land. They are our strength, our guardians against the world beyond."

Harlan, the blacksmith's son, stood a little apart from the main group with his friends, his broad shoulders and thick arms already showing the promise of his future trade. I could never imagine myself working a forge—too dirty, too much work.

He frowned, his dark eyes narrowed as he asked, "If the mountains are so strong, why do their peaks crumble when a storm hits? Doesn't seem all that strong to me."

Mother's gaze turned to him, her expression patient yet firm. "The mountains, like us, endure. They may be weathered by storms, but they stand tall, providing shelter and strength. It's the weak ones that think strength is never bending or breaking. I would think a blacksmith's son should know that. Real strength knows how to weather a storm and still stand tall afterward."

Harlan's face reddened, a hint of embarrassment flashed across his features. He glanced around, noticing a few of the other children smirking at his question. His jaw tightened, and he looked away, the moment seeding a grudge in his mind.

I just nodded, absorbing her metaphor, picturing the mountains as giant, stony spines. My sister, Liv, with her spirited green eyes and freckled cheeks, elbowed me gently. "He's always full of boyish questions, that one," she teased, tossing her long, chestnut braid over her shoulder. The statement was like a fan to the kiln of Harlan's face which only glowed all the brighter.

A boy to the left of Harlan, the miller's son—Torin—snickered. "Yeah, but at least they're good ones. Better than asking why the sky's blue for the hundredth time, Liv" He said, obviously trying to quench the flames.

"Do not!" replied Liv.

Feeling the tension thick in the air, I decided to break it with yet another question. I grinned, then pointed to a hawk circling above, its wings slicing through the air. "What's it looking for?" I asked, squinting against the light.

"Opportunity," Mother replied swiftly, then pointed to a bush near us. "Just as you should always look for opportunities to learn. Like this," she reached out, plucking a leaf, "Sagebrush. Used for toothaches or wounds. Remember that."

I took the leaf, rolling it between my fingers, the scent sharp and clean. Torin smirked, still eyeing my sister. "Does it cure stupidity?" he asked, nodding towards Liv.

Heat prickled at the back of my neck. "Watch it," I snapped before I took a step in front of her.

Mother's eyes flicked between us with a sly smile, that softened her stern features. "Only silence cures foolishness," she interjected with mock severity, quelling the simmering tension and drawing a round of chuckles from the group. But her smile faded into seriousness again as she swept her arm towards the mountains. "Respect these teachings. The mountain's roots are deep, their wisdom ancient. You must be willing to climb, to struggle, to reach the heights of understanding."

Mother dismissed us with a wave of her hand, the cool morning air seeming to sharpen her words as they floated over to us. "Remember what we discussed about willow bark yesterday? It's time to put that knowledge to good use," she called out, her gaze swept over the cluster of us with an instructive gleam. "You need to find the willows by the stream. Look for the trees with the long, slender leaves and the rough bark. That's where you'll get what we need."

Liv and I exchanged a quick glance, her eyebrows raised in mock seriousness. We threaded our way through the group, the other children's chatter and laughter fading as we veered off toward the familiar path that led to the stream.

"And remember," Mother's voice followed us, strong and clear, "the inner bark is what you're after. Carefully peel it back. It's valuable for its medicinal properties — can reduce fever and relieve pain. Be mindful not to harm the tree more than necessary."

As we moved away from Mother's instructive presence and deeper into the grove, the topic of our conversation shifted from the practical to the personal.

"Torin's a prat," I muttered, brushing a low branch aside for Liv.

She laughed lightly, the sound mingling with the rustle of leaves. "He's just a boy. Maybe he teases because he likes me."

I snorted, surveying the brush for the telltale slender branches. "If that's his way of showing affection, remind me to stay on his bad side."

Liv nudged me with her elbow, her eyes sparkling with mischief. "Afraid you might start liking him too?"

I made a face, and she laughed again, a genuine sound that made the chilly air feel just that bit warmer.

We crouched by the water, the reflection of the clouds overhead dappled by the gentle flow. As Liv pulled her belt knife to cut a few strips of bark, a voice sliced through the quiet.

"Look, the runt and his keeper," sneered a voice I knew too well — Harlan, flanked by his usual lackeys, which included Torin.

"Your turn," Liv whispered to me.

I straightened, my hands balling into fists. "Leave us be, Harlan."

Harlan, a head taller with arms like an anvil, stepped closer. "What? Not happy to see us?" His eyes flicked to Liv, "or maybe you need your sister to save you again?"

Heat pricked behind my eyes, a slow, simmering anger building with each beat of my heart. The edges of my vision tinted, the world taking on a reddish hue.

Liv stood, placing herself in front of me. "Leave us alone, Harlan. We're just here for the willow bark."

"Yeah? Me too," Harlan said, snatching the bark from Liv's hand with a roughness that made her flinch. He was faster than his size befitted.

My anger surged, a deep growl built in my throat unbidden. Harlan laughed, turning his attention back to me. "What, you gonna cry now runt?"

"No, but you might!" I shot back as I stepped around Liv. I didn't see the punch coming until it was too late, Harlan's fist connected with my cheek and sent a shock of pain through my skull. I imagine that's how his hammer felt when it met the anvil.

The heat in my eyes blazed, the world a blur of red and shadow. I lunged forward, driven more by instinct than thought, my own fist swinging wildly. More of a windmill than any real punch.

Liv caught my arm, pulling me back. "Leif, no!" Her voice was sharp, a command that sliced through the fog of rage.

Torin also stepped forward, his face conflicted as he glanced at Liv. "Harlan, that's enough," he said, his voice firm as he attempted to grab at the larger boy's arm. "Come on, let's go."

Harlan, ready to retaliate, paused, his eyes darting between Torin's intervention and my heaving chest.

"Come on," Liv urged, her grip firm on my hand. "He's not worth it."

I allowed her to pull me away, the warmth behind my eyes slowly receded leaving a dull throb of humiliation and simmering anger. As Liv and I walked back from the stream, the tension from the confrontation slowly unwound, she shot me a sly glance with a hint of a smirk playing upon her lips.

"You know, if Torin's way of showing he likes me is by teasing, maybe Harlan actually fancies you," she quipped, her eyes twinkling with mischief.

I scoffed, rubbing the sore spot on my cheek. "Yeah, right. He punches like he's courting me, then." My voice dripped with sarcasm.

She chuckled, nudging me gently with her elbow. "It's a love tap, clearly. You know, the rough beginnings of a beautiful friendship."

I rolled my eyes, the corners of my mouth twitched despite the ache. "Let's stick to making friends who don't leave bruises, yeah?"

Liv laughed, her laughter lightening the mood as we continued our way back. "Deal. But just so you know, I'm keeping an eye on Torin, just in case he decides to start showing his affection with something sharper than words."

I shook my head, a small smile finally breaking through. "Just make sure he knows you punch back."

As Liv and I made our way back to the clearing, Mother emerged from behind a gnarled oak, stepping into our path. Her tall, willowy frame was accentuated by the flowing hair the colour of autumn leaves that gathered at her nape. She had a presence that warranted attention, yet her eyes, full of reprimand, softened slightly as we approached. Faint lines framed her gaze, hinting at wisdom and weariness, while still vibrant and sharp. The air around us cooled, heavy with her unspoken disappointment.

"I saw what happened," she began, her voice low and even, forcing each word to carry its full weight. The disappointment was blatant, her gaze shifting from Liv to me with a deep, knowing look.

Trying to defend our actions, I started, "Mother, ever since Da—"

"Leif," she interrupted firmly, her tone brooking no excuses. "I understand your reasons, but reacting with fists is not our way."

Liv and I exchanged a quick, guilty glance, accepting the rebuke.

"You must learn to master your emotions," Mother continued, her expression softened as she stepped closer. "Anger is a quick spark, easy to ignite but difficult to extinguish. Remember, you are both capable of more."

"How do we hold back when pushed so far?" Liv's voice cracked slightly, her usual resolve wavering.

Mother's shoulders slumped, just a little, as her breath escaped in a gentle sigh, her eyes reflecting our own emotions. "By practising control. Let me show you." She stood between us, her presence grounding. "When you feel that surge of heat, that rush of blood that presages anger, take three deep breaths. With each breath, imagine drawing in the calm of the earth and casting out your fury."

She demonstrated, inhaling deeply, her chest rising, and exhaling slowly, her features smoothing into calm. Liv and I followed, the rhythmic breathing helping to leach away the remnants of our earlier tension. If I had the sense back then I might have realised that we may have been the reason my mother knew those techniques. Then again she was the Wisewalker.

"Feel the peace you draw in," Mother advised as we opened our eyes, "and let it temper the storm within. This is how we uphold the tranquillity of our tribe."

She then placed a hand on each of our shoulders, her touch reassuring. "Embrace peace, my children. It is not merely the absence of conflict, but the active presence of calm. Your father believed in this, as do I. We must be the calm in the storm, the stillness that can withstand the winds."

Mother's eyes narrowed ever so slightly as we reached the edge of the clearing, where the other children had already gathered, their voices mingled with the rustling of the leaves. "I'll be having a word with Harlan's father about this," she murmured, her tone firm, a hint of steel underlying her usually calm demeanour.

Liv caught her arm, her fingers tightening as she said, "please don't. It'll just make things worse." Her voice was low, but the plea was clear.

Mother paused, considering Liv's words, then gave a slight nod, her features mellowing. "Very well, for now."

We joined the circle of children, all sitting cross-legged on the ground. Their curious eyes flicked to my bruised cheek, then away. Our mother, the Wisewalker, cleared her throat, drawing the attention of her pupils. "Let's continue," she said, holding up a piece of bark she'd collected. "This is willow bark. It contains a substance that can relieve pain and reduce fevers. You can chew it directly, or brew it into a tea. It's nature's remedy, and knowing how to use it can aid not just yourself but others. It can ease pain, yes, but also teaches resilience. It bends in the wind, yet remains strong—much like we must be." She glanced at me briefly with a meaningful look. "Now, for tonight's Harvest Moon Festival. We celebrate our strength and unity. Together."

The children nodded, some taking notes, others whispering amongst themselves about the uses of the bark.

"As we prepare for the Festival," The Wisewalker continued, her voice lifting with a hint of excitement, "remember that our connection to the land and its gifts is what sustains us. Now, off you go. Prepare well, there is much to be done."

The group dispersed quickly, the prospect of the celebration ignited a buzz of energy. Liv and I lingered for a moment, watching as the other children ran off, their laughter echoing back through the trees.

Together, with Mother leading the way, we started the walk back to the village. The path was familiar, edged with the gold and crimson of early autumn leaves. The air was crisp, and the distant sounds of the village preparing for the festival drifted toward us, blending with the scent of pine and the cool earth underfoot.

"Tonight will be a good night," Mother said, more to herself than to us, a smile touching corners of her lips.

Liv squeezed my hand, her earlier tension eased as the promise of the festival lightened her mood. "Let's make the best of it," she said, a spark of mischief returning to her eyes.

I nodded, the earlier anger and hurt from the confrontation with Harlan slowly melting away, replaced by an anticipation of the festivities. That night, under the glow of the Harvest Moon, the village would come together, and for a few hours, all would be right.

The sun dipped low, casting a warm, amber glow over the village. Lanterns hung from every post, swaying gently in the evening breeze. The air buzzed with laughter and the sweet scent of spiced cider. Stalls lined the main square, their tables overflowing with harvest fruits, breads, and crafts. The Harvest Moon Festival had begun.

Liv dashed off, her braid bouncing as she joined a group of friends near the bonfire. Mother gave me a quick hug before heading toward a cluster of women, their heads bent together in animated conversation. I was left alone to explore.

I wandered through the crowd, the crunch of leaves underfoot mingling with the music of flutes and drums. Other children darted past, chasing each other with wild abandon, their faces painted in bright, festive colours. The decorations were simple yet vibrant— garlands of autumn leaves, pumpkins carved with grinning faces, and cornucopias spilling over with the season's bounty.

Near the centre of the square, a group of elders sat in a semicircle, their stories of past harvests captivating a wide-eyed audience. The firelight danced on their weathered faces, highlighting the deep lines etched by years of toil and joy.

I spotted Torin near a games booth, his usually smug expression softened as he spoke with Liv. They were tossing small sacks into a wooden target, laughing as they tried to outdo each other. Liv's eyes sparkled with excitement, her earlier worries forgotten in the festival's embrace.

A smile tugged at my lips. Maybe Liv was right about Torin. He didn't seem so bad when he wasn't being a little prick. As I watched them, a feeling of contentment settled over me. Despite the challenges, the village was united, and on that night, we celebrated our resilience and the bounty of our land.

I rounded a corner and found myself face-to-face with my own tormenter, Harlan. He stood in front of a stall, a blacksmith's game of skill and strength. An awkward silence stretched between us, the air thick with the remnants of our earlier conflict.

Harlan shifted, his eyes darting to the ground. "Leif, I... I'm sorry." His voice was rough, unsteady. I noticed he was hiding his right hand, a fresh lash mark barely concealed under a cloth wrap.

I frowned, concern overriding my anger. "What happened to your hand?"

Harlan glanced at it, then back at me. "Torin told my father about the fight. The rotten rat," he muttered, shaking his head. "But... I deserved it. My da says it's the way of the young, but we should learn to control our anger."

I nodded slowly, feeling a strange kinship in his words. "My Ma said the same thing," I replied.

We stood there for a moment, the tension between us easing. Harlan offered a tentative smile. "Do you want to play? It's not too hard once you get the hang of it."

I hesitated, then nodded. "Sure."

Harlan stepped up to the game, a contraption of iron and wood with targets set at varying heights. He grabbed a heavy mallet, demonstrating. "You have to hit the lever just right to send the weight up to ring the bell."

He swung the mallet with practised ease, the weight soaring upward to clang against the bell with a satisfying ring. With a confident grin, Harlan handed me the mallet. "Your turn."

I gripped the handle, feeling its weight. With a deep breath, I swung, hitting the lever. The weight shot up, falling just short of the bell. Harlan clapped me on the back, his smile broadening, still tinged with a hint of superiority. "Not bad for a first try."

I laughed, the sound surprising even I. "Thanks," I managed, shaking my head at his barely concealed pride.

We spent the next few minutes taking turns, the game bridging the gap between us. As the bell rang out again and again, the remnants of our earlier fight faded into the background, replaced by the simple camaraderie of two boys finding common ground.

Harlan's father returned not long after. His arrival was marked by a heavy silence, his formidable presence filled the space. Broad shoulders strained against his worn shirt, and callused hands bore testament to years at the forge. Each step he took was a quiet display of strength. I watched him, feeling the weight of his quiet solidity, so unlike Harlan's boisterousness.

Harlan glanced up, his expression tightening. "Da, can I go explore with Leif?" he asked, his voice carried a hopeful note.

His father studied us for a moment, his gaze piercing yet not unkind, then gave a single nod of approval.

Clearly grateful for the permission, Harlan turned to me with a relieved grin. "Let's go then," he said, and we continued to weave our way through the festival.

Harlan and I wandered through the crowd as the festival thrummed with life, our earlier animosity replaced by a budding friendship. We played more games, our laughter blending with the festive noise. Liv joined us, teasing Harlan mercilessly when he missed a shot at a ring toss. He took it in stride, a good-natured grin on his face.

Mother found us near the food stalls, her gaze lingered our way with a mixture of relief and mild concern as she noted our companion. Her eyes briefly caught the bandage on Harlan's hand, a silent question in her glance, but she said nothing about it. Instead, she handed us each a warm pastry, the aroma of spiced apples wafted up inviting us to take a bite.

"Enjoy the festival," she said, her eyes twinkling with a mirth that seemed to light up the dimming evening. "But stay close, alright?"

We roamed the stalls, the air vibrant with the scents of roasted meats and freshly baked bread. As the sky darkened, the lanterns strung between booths and trees started to glow like clusters of fireflies, casting a soft, flickering light that made the festive decorations sparkle. Liv, caught up in the excitement, joined the other children by the musicians. She danced with abandon, her braid whipped around as she spun with Torin, her laughter rang out clear and joyful.

Harlan and I stood on the sidelines, swapping stories about our fathers and the lessons they'd taught us. Our shared losses created a silent understanding between us, deepening our newfound friendship. As Liv danced closer, Harlan's eyes narrowed at the sight of Torin, and his fist clenched without him realising it. I placed a hand on his shoulder, a quiet reminder of our earlier conversation, and he relaxed, letting out a slow breath.

18

Around us, the evening buzzed with activity. Couples strolled hand in hand, my friends darted between adults playing lively games, and the elderly recounted tales of festivals past, their voices woven with nostalgia and wisdom. The community's laughter and chatter created a symphony of joyous noise, underscored by the rhythmic strumming of guitars and the melodic flutes that played traditional tunes.

It was an evening of lively celebration, the community bound together in a shared revelry that seemed to momentarily lift the burdens of everyday life. As we moved through the crowd, the warmth of the festival enveloped us, its pulse echoed our own beating hearts, full of life and the promise of a memorable evening.

As night fell, the villagers gathered around a massive bonfire in the centre of the square. The flames reached high, casting dancing shadows on our faces. The elders led us in song, their voices strong and clear:

"To the mountains, to the sea,
Where the wild roam free,
By the fire's gentle glow,
Ancient secrets we must know.

Deviants whisper in the night,
Guardians of our hidden light,
Resonance in hearts so strong,
Peaceful spirits, our true song.

Hold your fury, still your hand,
Strength is found in calm command,
In the darkness, light shall lead,
Through the storm, we plant the seed.

Mountain roots and ocean's call,
Teach us to stand tall, never fall,
In the fire's warming grace,
We find our place, we find our pace."

As the song swelled around us, I was swept up in a profound sense of unity and belonging. Liv stood close beside me, her eyes shimmering with the reflection of the flickering flames, her hand firm in mine. Harlan, to my other side, had dropped his usual bravado, his features moulded into a sombre expression but his eyes alight with the warmth of the fire.

The air was suddenly charged, a cold prickle ran down my spine, cutting through the warmth of the night. The festive clamour dimmed, as if muffled under a heavy blanket, and a low, menacing whisper slithered into my mind, chilling my blood.

They're here.

My muscles tensed, my breath caught in my throat. I surveyed the crowd frantically, but the faces around me remained blissfully unaware, caught up in the joy of the moment. The whisper in my head turned into a commanding growl.

Prepare yourself.

A scream—sharp, terrifying, and full of pain—suddenly ripped through the fabric of the night. The music stumbled to a stop, and a hush fell over the crowd, broken only by the crackling of the bonfire. The festival's heart skipped a beat, and then panic bloomed as another scream echoed, closer this time, more desperate.

The unity of the song shattered into chaos as the village plunged into a nightmare.

Chapter 2 - Nightmare

The last scream faded, leaving a heavy silence draped over the village like a suffocating blanket. The night seemed to swallow the light from the lanterns and flames, plunging us into a darkness that was more than just the absence of light—it was oppressive, unnatural.

I found myself gripping Liv's hand tighter, my breath shallow as I skimmed the crowd for Mother. Harlan had already disappeared into the shadowed outline of his father's sturdy form.

"There," Liv whispered, relief flooded her voice as she pointed toward Mother standing by the well, her figure a beacon in the wavering light.

We pushed through the stunned villagers, reaching her side. Mother's face was etched with worry, her eyes scrutinised the area as if she could will away the impending danger by sheer force of will.

Before any of us could speak, a chilling melody sliced through the stillness. It was unlike any song I'd heard before—a series of high, piercing notes that seemed to claw at the very air. The melody twisted and turned, diving into deep, mournful wails that scraped against my ears like jagged rocks. It felt as if the night itself had started to sing a dreadful lullaby.

"What is that!?" Liv's voice trembled, barely above a whisper.

Mother's brow furrowed, her lips pressed into a thin line. "I don't know, but stay close," she murmured, pulling us in tight against her.

The song wove through the village, a haunting presence that seemed to linger just out of sight, sending shivers down my spine. It was as if some great and terrible creature from the old tales had descended upon us, its voice a harbinger of doom.

My skin crawled as the shrill notes penetrated the night, each tone slicing through the air like a blade. The sound seemed to vibrate in my chest, a resonating fear that pulsed with my heartbeat. My eyes darted around, half expecting to see phantoms emerge from the shadows that flickered at the edge of the torchlight.

"Make it stop," I pleaded under my breath, not knowing to whom I was speaking. The song seemed to seep into my bones, a cold dread that made my heart race and my thoughts scatter.

Mother held us close, her arms a reassuring fortress in the chilling darkness. But even she could not shield us from the eerie song that continued to echo, a spectral melody that promised nothing but despair. As the operatic shrieks escalated, the unsettling sensation grew, making my stomach churn and my knees weaken as if the very ground beneath me might give way.

As the dreadful song clawed at the night, more screams tore through the eerie quiet. From the darkness, shapes coalesced—twisted, shadowy figures that moved with unnatural fluidity, as if made of smoke. One by one, villagers fell prey to the spectral assailants, their bodies impaled by what looked like tendrils of pure shadow.

The village square, once a beacon of light and laughter, became a scene of horror. Villagers scrambled in all directions, their faces twisted in terror. The flames from the bonfire cast grotesque silhouettes, making friends look like foes and adding to the panic. The horrific song continued to weave through the chaos, its melody now a sinister lullaby to the unfolding nightmare.

I gripped Mother's hand as my other held onto Liv's, as we tried to make sense of the madness. My heart hammered, each beat syncing with the shrill peaks of the haunting melody. Then I saw him—Torin, not far from us, trying to pull a younger child to safety. A shadow swept over him, and in an instant, he was on the ground, a dark form retracting from his chest. Blood spread quickly across his tunic, stark and bright against the fabric. Liv's scream pierced the night, a sound of raw agony that mirrored the sharp pain in my own chest at the sight.

"No, no, no!" Liv sobbed, her tears flowed freely as she struggled to move toward him, but Mother held her back, her own face pale with shock.

All around us, the shadows moved relentlessly. I watched, frozen with horror, as a woman tried to fend off one of the figures with a burning torch. But it passed right through the shadow like mist, the woman's cry cut short as she fell, her life extinguished as quickly as a snuffed candle.

The air was thick with the smell of blood and burning, the crackle of flames now a menacing undertone to the screams and the omnipresent song. The ground felt unstable under my feet, as if the very earth was recoiling from the horror it had to bear, the blood it had to soak up.

"This can't be real," I murmured, my voice lost in the cacophony. Every shadow seemed to hide a monster, every sound was a potential death knell. The festive lights that had earlier illuminated the square now seemed to mock us, their glow harsh against the nightmarish scene.

Mother's grip tightened, her knuckles white. "Stay close," she hissed, her eyes darting around, assessing each threat even as she shielded us with her body.

But there was no safety to be found. The shadows were everywhere, and so was the song, its eerie high notes now a grotesque dirge for the dying. The stark reality of death, so brutal and sudden, was nothing like the tales of heroism and peaceful passings into the other world that I had heard of. It was ugly, it was terrifying, and it was all around us.

Mother's hand was firm around my own as she pulled us
through the chaos, her eyes sought a path to safety. The village,
once so familiar, was now a labyrinth of fire and shadows. Flames
licked at the wooden structures, the heat intensifying as the fire
devoured everything in its path, blocking exits and creating a deadly
barrier that kept pushing us back toward the centre of the village.

"Over here!" Mother shouted, pointing toward what looked like
a clear way out. But as we moved, a sudden explosion of sparks
and flames erupted from a nearby hut, sending villagers screaming
in the opposite direction. The heat was overwhelming, the smoke
blurred my vision and seared my throat.

Amidst the smoke, I caught sight of Harlan, his face set in
determination as he climbed over a fallen log. But then, one of the
shadowy figures in darkness lunged at him from behind. There was
a brief struggle—a spike of shadows—and Harlan fell, his body
crumpling to the ground in a heap. A scream of pure fury erupted
from the blacksmith, Harlan's father, who had seen everything
from his position by the forge.

His massive frame shook as he picked up his hammer, his eyes
suddenly glowing a fierce red. With a roar, he charged at the
armoured figure, the intensity of his anger seeming to clear the air
around him. The nightmarish miasma that had cloaked our
attackers lifted like fog under the morning sun, revealing them not
as demons but as men—men in black armour, their faces obscured
by dark helmets.

The eerie song continued, now clearly coming from a group of
cloaked women standing protected behind a line of these black-
garbed soldiers. They sang without ceasing, their voices high and
haunting, but their melody no longer held any sway. The fear it

once inspired was gone, replaced by a smouldering anger that bubbled up from within my fellow villagers.

As the blacksmith swung his hammer, it connected with the soldier's chest with a sickening crunch. The soldier fell, his armour doing little to protect him from the blacksmith's rage-fueled strength. More villagers' eyes began to glow red, a wave of fury swept over them as they took up whatever weapons they could find—pitchforks, axes, even stones—and turned on the invaders.

The transformation of our enemies from spectral assailants to mortal men did little to lessen the horror of the night, but it shifted something within us. What was once paralysing terror became a righteous anger, driving the villagers to defend their homes and loved ones with newfound ferocity.

Mother kept us close, her eyes now reflecting the same red fire that blazed in the eyes of the blacksmith. "Stay behind me," she commanded, her voice rough with smoke and determination. We moved as one, Liv clinging to my other hand, her sobs muffled against my shoulder as we navigated through the battlefield that our village had become.

The clamour of battle surged around us, punctuated by the sharp clanging of metal and the desperate cries of villagers. Amid the chaos, a distant, haunting howl sliced through the night air, sending a shiver down my spine. It was neither wolf nor human—a sound that seemed to stir the very air with unease.

Mother's grip tightened on my hand, her eyes now glowing a deep, fiery red, reflecting the savage determination that had overtaken her. Once a serene Wisewalker, she transformed before my eyes into a fierce warrior. Her every move was swift and decisive as she manoeuvred us through the melee, her usual calm demeanour replaced by a raw, primal intensity. It scared even me.

Just as we neared what looked like a safer path out of the village, a black-armoured soldier blocked our way, his sword drawn and face hidden behind a dark visor. Mother pushed us behind her, stepping forward to confront him. The soldier lunged, and she parried with a staff she had snatched from the ground, moving with a speed and agility that belied her gentle nature.

The clash was brutal. Mother struck the soldier with ferocious precision, but not before his blade sliced across her arm, drawing blood. Despite her injury, her resolve didn't waver; she fought with a feral determination, each strike fueled by a mother's need to protect her children.

"Run, Leif, Run Liv!" she yelled over the clash of weapons, her voice strained but unwavering. "Get to safety, now!"

Liv and I hesitated, torn, but the urgency in Mother's tone propelled us forward. As we ran, I heard her let out a battle cry, a sound so fierce and desperate it echoed in my ears long after we had turned away.

We dashed through the smoke and flames, dodging falling debris and frantic villagers. Liv, who ran just ahead of me, suddenly cried out as a shadow darted in front of her. Before I could react, she was on the ground and a dark figure stood over her. My heart stopped, a scream lodged in my throat.

I lunged forward, reaching for Liv, but the world suddenly lurched as the ground shook violently. A wall of a nearby burning building groaned ominously and then, with a deafening crash, collapsed onto us. I felt a searing pain and then nothing but overwhelming darkness as unconsciousness claimed me, the last sounds I heard were the continuing battle cries and that distant, mysterious howl echoing through the chaos.

Chapter 3 - Trapped

Sunlight pierced my eyelids, dragging me back into a world I no longer recognized. A high-pitched ringing filled my ears, drowning out any other sound, while pain—sharp and insistent—throbbed through every part of my body. I tried to move, but agony flared with each attempt, pinning me under an invisible weight.

The realisation hit me slowly, as if seeping through the fog of my dazed mind: I was trapped, the heavy, unyielding pressure of rubble pinned me down. Panic clawed at my throat, each breath a laboured gasp as I struggled against the debris.

My eyes adjusted to the light, focusing with excruciating slowness. Then I saw her. Liv. Just inches from my face, her eyes— once vibrant and full of mischief—now stared blankly at the roof of our cairn. Our burial place. Her chest was still, too still, and a dark stain marred her favourite green tunic, the one with the embroidery she was so proud of.

A sob tore from my chest, raw and uncontrolled. "Liv," I choked out, my voice breaking, the sound muffled by the rubble and the relentless ringing in my ears. My sister, my confidant, gone—her life snuffed out like a candle in the wind. The unfairness of it, the brutal, senseless cruelty, filled me with a grief so profound that for a moment, it overshadowed even the physical pain.

Tears streamed down my face, soaking the dust and grime that coated my skin. I reached out, fingers trembling, desperate to touch her, to feel some part of her still warm, still alive. But cold met my touch, the chilling finality of death that no wishful thinking could deny.

"Liv, please," I muttered, my voice a broken whisper, my mind recoiling from the truth before me. "Not you, please not you." But no plea could bring back the dead, no tears could wash away the horror of that moment.

Trapped, unable to turn away, I lay there, forced to gaze into the lifeless eyes of my little sister, each second an eternity of despair.

As my sobs subsided into shuddering breaths, the incessant ringing in my ears began to fade, replaced by the more immediate sounds of the world outside my cramped prison of debris. Voices, low and gruff, carried over the shuffle of boots against the scorched earth, creeping closer with each passing second.

Fear, cold and sharp, speared through me. My heart pounded against my ribcage, each beat a thunderous echo in my own head. I dared not move; the slightest shift could draw attention. Lying amidst the rubble, I forced my body into stillness, though I was scarcely able to move under the weight that pinned me.

The voices grew louder, clearer. "What was that?" one voice asked—a question tinged with suspicion.

"I'll check on it," another replied, closer now, almost directly above me.

Through a narrow gap in the debris, sunlight filtered in, casting a beam across my hiding place. A shadow fell across the light, and then, blocking out the sun, a soldier appeared. He bent over the rubble, his face coming into view. A black helm framed discerning green eyes, which surveyed the debris briefly before they fixed directly on me.

My breath hitched, frozen in my throat. His eyes locked onto mine, and for a moment, the world seemed to pause—just a boy and a soldier staring each other down amidst the chaos. I was shaking, each tremor uncontrollable, betraying my terror. The soldier's gaze was intense, searching, but then his expression changed subtly, a decision made. He straightened up, breaking eye contact.

"It's nothing," he called out to someone behind him, his voice loud and clear. "Just a rat."

His footsteps receded, and I was left alone once more, shrouded in the dubious safety of his lie. Relief flooded through me, tinged with confusion and a lingering dread. Why had he spared me? In the pit of my stomach, a knot of suspicion twisted—what did it mean for my fate that he had let me live?

For a long time, I lay there, silent and still, listening to the retreating sounds of the soldiers, my mind racing. Each second that stretched, filled with the echo of what had just passed and the fear of what was to come.

Time lost its meaning as I lay there, each moment blended into the next, tangled in a web of exhaustion and fear. The heavy scent of smoke hung in the air, mingling with the iron tang of blood that seemed to coat the back of my throat. My mind was a whirlpool, thoughts spinning too quickly to grasp, each one slipping away before I could make sense of what had happened, of what I had lost.

The judgement of Liv's dead stare grew unbearable, her lifeless eyes a constant reminder of the nightmare that had torn through our lives. With a shuddering breath, I knew I couldn't lie there any longer, couldn't let her glassy gaze be the last image I held of her. Gritting my teeth against the pain, I began to shuffle away, each movement a torment of both body and soul. Gravel and debris pressed against my skin, but the physical discomfort was nothing compared to the ache in my heart.

I crawled inch by painful inch, distancing myself from her, from the sister I couldn't save. Finally breaking free from the worst of the rubble, I paused, panting from the effort, the fresh air felt like fire in my lungs.

Cautiously, I peered out from my partial cover. The early morning light cast a stark glow on the devastation around me. Buildings that once stood proud and inviting were now charred skeletons, their structures weakened and crumbling, a few still caught in the throes of lingering flames. The village that had been alive with light and laughter the night before was now a smouldering ruin, the smoke rose to the sky like the final breaths of what had been.

Silence hung over the scene, a haunting absence of life where there should have been the start of a new day. The stillness was unsettling, as if the earth itself was holding its breath, waiting for the next horror to unfold.

From my vantage point beneath the remnants of what had once been a vibrant marketplace, I watched in horror as the black-clad soldiers methodically moved through the village. Their movements were precise, almost ritualistic, as they plunged their swords into the bodies strewn across the ground, ensuring death had claimed those who might still cling to life. Each thrust was a blow to my chest, each victim not just a fallen villager but a friend, a neighbour, a face that had smiled in the morning sun.

Among them, I saw old Marn, the baker, his jolly laugh forever silenced; young Elia, who had danced at the festival, now motionless in the dirt. The soldiers treated them all with the same cold indifference, their boots slipped in the still-wet blood as they continued their gruesome task.

Anger flared within me, a fiery heat that threatened to consume my composure. I felt it behind my eyes, a burning that edged toward an uncontrollable blaze. But then my mother's voice echoed in my mind, her calm, steady instructions on how to breathe, how to hold back the storm of emotions that could so easily rage out of control. Inhale. Hold. Exhale. Each breath was a struggle, but slowly, the fire within dimmed to a smouldering ember. I couldn't afford to lose myself, not now, not when every moment mattered.

My attention was drawn back to the grotesque actions of the soldiers as they began a new and horrifying task. They started checking the eyes of the dead, I had no idea what they were doing at first. Then, with gruesome efficiency; they dug out the eyes of those they found, collecting them with a chilling reverence in small, dark bags at their belts. Each pair they dug out still had the red glow, hot like a dying ember. The sound of sobbing was mine, though I scarcely heard it over the pounding of my heart.

I watched, hidden and helpless, as the sun climbed higher and then began its descent, marking the passage of a day that felt as long as a lifetime. The soldiers eventually began to disperse, their bags heavier, their steps as unburdened by guilt as when they had started their day's work.

When the last of them had vanished from sight, leaving only the smoking ruins and the ravaged dead behind, I finally allowed myself to move. My body ached with every inch I gained as I crawled from the shadows of my broken refuge, the image of the soldiers' brutality etched forever in my mind.

As the silence stretched, I edged forward, the gravel beneath my hands shifting with a soft scrape that sounded thunderous in the quiet. Each movement was a gamble, each pause filled with the listening dread that another pair of boots would appear. But none came, and the smouldering ruins around me seemed empty, abandoned by both ally and enemy. Gritting my teeth, I pulled myself from the crumbling shelter of the broken building, the body of my sister behind me a weight on my soul I could not bear to face again.

Just as I was about to haul myself into the open, black boots filled my vision. Frozen, I could only stare as the world suddenly flipped. Strong hands gripped me, yanking me out with an efficiency that left me gasping. A rough hand clamped over my mouth stifled my cries, the smell of metal and sweat assaulted my senses.

The soldier, clad in black and silver plate, dragged me upright. His armour was harshly ridged, giving him a sharp, angular appearance that seemed designed to intimidate. His grip was iron, unyielding, as he turned me to face another—this one adorned in black and gold, his protective shell even more elaborate with ornate decorations that glinted cruelly in the sunlight, his presence commanding.

"I found one alive, my lord," the soldier in black and silver reported, his voice betraying a hint of satisfaction.
"Good," the lord responded, his voice cool and detached. "We can use him."
Rage, deep and blistering, flared within me at his words. Use me? No. The red heat behind my eyes burst forth, a fury unleashed.

Kill him, rip his throat out. A voice growled from within me. I could feel the wicked snarl almost like a smile of sinister delight.

With a sudden surge of strength, I slammed my head against the soldier's nose. The crunch was satisfying, his blood warm and wet against my forehead as his grip loosened in shock.

Free, I swung wildly, fists pounded against his plate. Each hit was a release, a scream of grief and anger given form. The sharp ridges of his armour cut into my hands, the pain barely registering over the rush of adrenaline. But the lord acted quickly, stepping forward with a gauntleted fist that crashed into the back of my head. The world spun, stars burst across my vision, and then darkness claimed me, once again, swallowing the rage and the light alike.

Chapter 4 - Call me Karn

Consciousness returned slowly, dragging me out of the depths with a series of jolts and rattles that confused my senses. My eyes fluttered open to darkness, dense and unyielding, pressing against me from all sides. The world seemed to sway, and it took a moment for my sluggish thoughts as they struggled to catch up with the rolling movement beneath me. As I shifted, trying to find some orientation, the smell of damp wood and iron filled my nostrils, confirming my fears—I was on the move. The realisation was a dull thud in my chest, each bump of the wagon's wheels on the uneven ground a harsh reminder of my captivity.

My body ached in protest as I shifted, trying to orient myself, only to feel the harsh bite of ropes around my wrists and ankles. A rag was tightly stuffed into my mouth, silencing the instinctive scream that bubbled up from the pit of my stomach. Panic fluttered like a trapped bird in my chest, every instinct screamed at me to fight or to flee, but the bindings held me cruelly still.

Outside the confines of my dark prison, the world was alive with movement. The rhythmic thudding of horse hooves paired with the creaking of wooden wheels rolling over uneven ground filled the air. Amidst these sounds, the muffled voices of men drifted into the wagon—rough, casual tones that belied the earlier chaos. The clanking of armour punctuated their conversations, it spoke of men at arms just beyond my flimsy barrier.

The truth crashed down on me, each laugh and bootfall from the soldiers outside a brutal reminder. I was a captive, their casual banter a twist of the knife to my grief. What did they want with me after they had turned my home, my family, to ashes?

Pressed against the rough wooden floor of the wagon, I strained to catch fragments of the conversations from the soldiers outside. Their laughter cut through the stifling air like a blade, sharp and intrusive, accompanied by the jarring symphony of clinking armour and the relentless drumbeat of marching boots.

"They reckon we'll be home by the frost," one voice boasted, a rough chuckle following his words. "First thing I'm doing is finding my way into a warm bed, and I don't care whose it is."

"Aye, that's if your wife hasn't taken up with the smithy," another retorted, laughter erupting among the group.

Their words twisted a knot in my stomach. They spoke of homecomings and warm beds as if the world hadn't just crumbled around me. The conversation turned, the tone sobering a fraction as they recounted that very event on the previous night.

"Didn't sit right, did it? Burning that village..." one voice murmured, almost too low to catch.

"Orders are orders," another replied sharply. "Don't start doubting now. Not when the Witch Queen's eyes could be anywhere."

The mention of this figure I'd never heard of, the Witch Queen tightened the cold grip on my heart. "Witches," someone hissed, a note of fear thread through the word. "Cloaked in black, singing like death itself was coming down. I still struggle to sleep at night when I'm on tour with them."

"You joined up with the Black Guard," the other said as if that was an answer to the unspoken question.

A shiver ran through me as the eerie melody resurfaced in my mind, each ghostly note curling around my thoughts like icy chains, binding me in a fear that seeped deep into my bones.

Days and nights blurred together in the suffocating darkness of the wagon, my world reduced to a cramped, damp cage stinking of iron and hopelessness. Humiliation struck as my bladder finally gave in and I felt the warmth spread and then cool, shifting away from the wet patch, misery settling in like an unwanted friend

My lips split painfully, and my throat felt like sandpaper, each breath a torturous reminder of my helplessness. Time lost all meaning, days marked only by the shifting light through the wagon slats, as I lay bound and gagged, silent tears cut clean tracks through the grime on my face accompanied by muffled sobs.

Amidst the camp's settling murmur, a faint rustle outside the wagon stood out, the flap lifted to reveal familiar green eyes. The soldier, a shadow in black and silver armour, moved with a deliberate stealth, every motion precise and quiet.

Silently, he leaned in and gently loosened the gag, my cracked lips parting painfully as I inhaled the cool night air, a momentary relief from the oppressive heat inside the wagon. He handed me a flask and bread, his stern gaze leaving no room for refusal. "Drink, eat," he whispered urgently. "But stay silent, or they'll kill you."

I nodded, too weary and desperate to question his unexpected kindness. The water was a balm to my parched throat, the bread coarse but satisfying against my hunger. As I sipped and chewed slowly, the soldier watched the wagon's entrance, his body tense, ready to act at the slightest sign of discovery.

This clandestine routine repeated for two more nights. Each visit was a brief respite from the relentless misery of captivity, but with the soldier's departure, the hopelessness settled back in. Thoughts of escape flickered through my mind like distant fireflies—visible, yet beyond grasp. The ropes binding my wrists were tight and unforgiving, the skin beneath rubbed raw and bled, the bruises from the collapse throbbing with persistent pain.

During the long hours of solitude, my body ached from the cramped space. The injuries from the village's destruction made their presence known more with each passing moment. A deep, throbbing pain suggested something broken somewhere in my ribcage, at least that is what each breath told me. The wagon's hard floor offered no comfort, no relief. Sometimes, the pain overwhelmed, drawing silent tears that tracked clean lines down my dirt-streaked face.

Gradually, the relentless din of the army—hooves pounding, metal clanking, voices shouting—faded into a quiet murmur, and then to nothing at all. The wagon trundled on, the only sounds now the creaking of the wooden wheels and the distant calls of birds that seemed indifferent to the sorrow of a boy. I lay still, absorbing the eerie solitude, my mind skirting around the edges of thoughts about my mother and sister, thoughts I wasn't ready to face. Instead, I listened to the wind whispering through leaves, a cruel imitation of peace.

Without warning, the wagon ceased its motion. The abrupt stop jolted my bruised body, drawing a muffled grunt of pain. Silence enveloped the space for a lingering moment before the curtain at the back of the wagon was yanked back, flooding the dark interior with the soft glow of evening light. My eyes, accustomed to the shadows, squinted against the brightness, taking in the silhouette of a man.

The green-eyed soldier, now without his imposing black and silver armour, looked more like an ordinary man. His eyes, still sharp, scanned me with a hint of authority. Climbing into the wagon, he moved with a swift precision, his grip firm as he reached for me, a reminder of the power he held over my fate.

"Quiet now, you're safe," he murmured, his tone low but firm as he grasped my arms to help me out. His grip was strong but not harsh, pulling me gently but with undeniable authority from the confines of the wagon.

As my feet hit the soft earth outside, the freshness of the evening air felt like a slap, shockingly cold compared to the stale, foetid atmosphere I'd grown accustomed to in the wagon. He steadied me with a hand on my shoulder while he surveyed the area briefly as if to ensure no unwanted eyes were looking or ears listening.

"Stay close, and keep your voice down," he instructed, his gaze locking with mine, an intensity in his green eyes that commanded obedience.

The green-eyed soldier, his grip unyielding, ushered me across the uneven ground, my steps faltering as weakness from the days in captivity took its toll. The open air was a brief respite, but the reality of my situation bore down relentlessly as he led me towards a large, looming house. Larger than any singular building that claimed home to my village. Despite my feeble attempts to wriggle free from his grasp, my body, drained and tightly bound, betrayed me, rendering my efforts futile. With a sigh that felt like resignation, he scooped me up with ease, carrying me into the house as if I weighed nothing.

Inside, the air was cooler, the dim light a stark contrast to the fading evening outside. He navigated through a narrow hallway, his footsteps echoed softly on the wooden floor, until he reached a room adorned with modest furnishings. There, he gently set me down on a soft bed, the mattress yielding under my weight.

Moments later, the older man in the black and gold armour entered the room. With a deliberate motion, he lifted his helm off, revealing a head of peppered hair, his face marked with lines of experience and authority. His gaze met mine, searching, perhaps for signs of the fight left in me.

The green-eyed soldier moved closer, his expression serious.

"We're going to take the gag off now," he stated, his tone indicating no room for argument. "But you mustn't scream. Can you do that?" His question hung in the air, weighted with an expectation of compliance.

I nodded, not trusting my voice, the rawness of my throat a reminder of my vulnerability. Carefully, he reached behind my head and loosened the gag, the fabric pulling away from my mouth with a tenderness that contrasted sharply with the brutal context of our meeting. The relief of being able to open my mouth fully was immediate, but so was the overwhelming urge to cry out.

A raw, guttural scream tore through the silence of the room, fueled by days of pent-up fear and anguish. It was a sound that echoed off the walls, stark and desperate. Almost immediately, the fabric was thrust back against my mouth, silencing me with a roughness that contrasted sharply with the previous careful touch.

The older man stepped forward, his expression hardened into a grim mask. "I'm not as patient as Banar," he said, his voice low and threatening. "If you scream again, I will hurt you. Do you understand?" His hand rested ominously on the hilt of his sword, a silent but unequivocal promise of pain.

I nodded hastily, the seriousness of his threat clear and terrifying. With a reluctant gesture, he signalled to the green-eyed soldier.

Once more, the gag was removed, more gently this time. The soldier, his eyes holding a hint of sympathy, spoke softly, "My name is Banar." He gestured toward the older man, adding simply, "This is my lord, Lord Caine." Banar then leaned closer, his voice gentle yet firm. "And what is your name?"

Taking a moment to gather the saliva to moisten my parched throat, I whispered hoarsely, "L...Leif." My voice cracked, the name sounding foreign on my lips after the silence of captivity. The questions that burned inside me spilled out in a raspy, urgent whisper, "My mother, my sister... what happened to them?"

Banar exchanged a glance with his lord, a silent communication passing between them before he turned back to me, his face sombre. "We will talk about that," he assured, his tone suggesting this was not the moment for such revelations. The underlying message was clear: first, trust needed to be established.

Lord Caine's voice was steady, each word measured as he began to explain. "We were under direct orders from the Witch Queen," he said, his gaze firm yet not without a trace of regret. "None of us wanted to bring harm to your family or your village. But we must follow commands, or we face consequences far worse than what you've seen."

He paused, allowing the gravity of his words to sink in. "I understand your anger, your need for answers. I'd feel the same in your place," he continued, his tone a mix of authority and an attempt at empathy. "But know this—if we disobeyed, it would have been our families facing the sword next. We are soldiers, and sometimes our hands are forced."

As he spoke, a sharp sting of betrayal mixed with the grief already simmering inside me. The mention of the Witch Queen, the very name, a curse that had shattered my world, ignited a fierce, blinding anger that coursed through my veins like fire.

With a sudden surge of adrenaline, I twisted against the ropes binding my wrists. The fibres bit into my skin as I fought against them, fueled by a primal need to fight, to avenge. To my own surprise, they gave way under the strain, fraying and snapping, freeing my hands. In a fluid, almost instinctual motion, I lunged at the older man, my fingers clawing out, driven by a deep-seated rage.

Both soldiers reacted swiftly, their training evident as they moved to subdue me. Banar caught my arms, pulling them behind me in a firm, controlled grip, while the older man stepped back, his hand on his sword but not drawing it yet, his eyes cold and hard. "Enough!" he barked, his voice commanding and sharp.

It took both of them to hold me down, my body shook with uncontrollable rage and exertion. "Calm yourself, boy," the older man growled, a stern warning laced through his tone. "This won't bring them back, and it won't help you."

Lying there, held firm by hands that had both freed and fought me, the red mist of rage began to clear, leaving behind a hollow, aching fatigue. My chest heaved as I struggled to regain control, the reality of my powerlessness washing over me in cruel waves.

As I lay there, panting and subdued, Banar knelt beside me, his expression sombre yet gentle. "Leif," he started, his voice soft, catching my attention amidst my turmoil. "I understand your pain more than you might think. The Witch Queen took from me as well—my first wife and our children. They were not spared her wrath."

His words, heavy with sorrow, pierced the veil of my anger, drawing a sharp breath from me. He continued, the pain evident in his voice, "What happened to your village, to your family... it's a cycle of terror that will continue unless we stand to end it. More families, more innocent lives will be lost if we do nothing."

The weight of his shared loss, his shared vulnerability, dampened the fiery rage within me, cooling it to a hard, determined ember. He reached down and cut the bindings on my legs, the ropes falling away from my raw, chafed skin. "I'm showing you trust now, Leif," Banar said firmly. "And I'm asking for trust in return."

The older man, the lord, stood by the doorway, his voice carrying a tone of command mixed with a hint of warning. "You must learn to master that rage of yours," he declared. "If you're discovered, not just you, but all of us connected to you, face grave danger from the Witch Queen." He paused, then added, "Will you trust us? Will you work with us to avenge your village?"

My mind swirled with the enormity of everything—grief, rage, and now a deceptive calm imposed by necessity. I didn't truly care about their plans or intentions at that moment; my heart was still raw, every beat a reminder of what I had lost. Yet, I nodded, agreeing to their terms silently, planning to bide my time, to find a way to escape or seek my own form of justice later.

Banar stood, his stance protective as he looked down at me. "I'll take you in as my adopted son. My cousin recently passed and I'll claim you were his boy. It's safer for you, and it gives us a chance to plan without raising suspicions."

Lord Caine gave a curt nod, satisfied. "Good. Remember, you must control your rage and learn to fight. Banar and his wife are good people, and they will take care of you."

I nodded again, outwardly compliant, but my mind was already plotting. I would play along for now, but I would find a way to escape and avenge my family on my own terms.

The lord, standing tall with an air of authority, glanced down at me with a critical eye. "You'll need a new name," he said, his voice firm. "Leif is clearly northern."

I flinched inwardly at the mention of my name, the one my mother had given me. It was a tether to a life that now seemed impossibly distant. Lord Caine continued, listing names with no difficulty, "Blaanid, Orry, Aalin..."

I cut him off, my voice unexpectedly steady as I said, "Call me Karn."

He raised an eyebrow at that. "Karn... is an interesting choice but should suit for our purposes. You'll need to keep up appearances, Karn. I'll drop by from time to time to check on you."

A low, rumbling voice echoed in my mind, a primal agreement. *It is a good name.*

The lord's gaze softened, though it did little to ease the knot of distrust in my chest. "Banar and his new wife are good people. They will take care of you." Lord Caine repeated.

Banar flinched at the usage of new wife. That did more to persuade me than anything else. Yet, I didn't respond, my mind too clouded with anger and grief to consider trusting anyone. Lord Caine turned to leave, pausing at the doorway. "I'll return when the time comes," he said, a final note of authority in his voice, he then nodded to Banar, who returned the gesture.

As the door closed behind him, Banar stepped closer, his expression gentle but probing. "Why did you choose Karn?"

The question hung in the air, heavy with unspoken pain. I swallowed hard, forcing the words past the lump in my throat. "I left my sister under a cairn of rubble. It felt like a part of me died there too, with her."

Banar nodded slowly, a flicker of understanding in his green eyes. In that moment, the fragile thread of connection between us tightened, a shared grief that spoke louder than words. The chapter of my life as Leif had ended; now, as Karn, I would have to find a way to survive and make sense of this new, fractured existence.

Chapter 5 - Gilded Cage

Banar stood at the door, pausing before he left. "I'll send servants to see to your needs," he said, his voice carrying a mix of authority and concern. "Rest and recover, Karn"

As his footsteps faded down the hallway, a knock on the door announced the arrival of the servants. Three of them entered, carrying a copper bath between them. Their faces were a mask of practised indifference, though I caught a flicker of sympathy in the eyes of one.

They set the bath down and began to fill it with steaming water. "Strip," one of the servants said, her voice flat and unemotional. I hesitated, but their stern looks left no room for argument. As they peeled away the tattered remnants of my clothes, the air stung my exposed skin, still raw and bruised from the past days.

Two of them lifted me into the bath, the hot water biting into the cuts and scrapes, making me wince. "Hold still," one instructed, scrubbing my skin with a rough cloth. The scrubbing felt like sandpaper against my tender flesh, each stroke igniting a fresh wave of pain. I clenched my teeth, suppressing the urge to cry out.

"Can't imagine what you've been through," the young woman muttered as she worked, her tone softer than the others. The other servants ignored us both, focused solely on their tasks. One servant, a lanky man, picked up my discarded clothes, his nose wrinkled in distaste. "We'll burn these," he said to another young woman.

The young woman winced at the smell of my clothes as she took them from him, following the man's orders. "Guess you'll be needing new ones," she added, more to herself than to me.

I focused on the sensations—the hot water, the rough cloth, the sting of soap in my wounds. It was better than thinking about anything else. Better than thinking about Liv, about the village, about what lay ahead.

When they were done, the servants helped me out of the bath and into a plain robe. I felt cleaner, lighter, but the hollow ache inside remained. They left me alone in the room, the copper bath cooling as the door clicked shut behind them. I sat on the bed, staring at the hearth, the fire cast flickering shadows on the stone walls.

Banar had said I was safe now, but I couldn't shake the feeling of being a prisoner in a gilded cage. My mind raced with questions and doubts, but for now, I had to play along. I had to heal. I had to survive.

After the servants left, I stared at the closed door. As I sat on the bed, I stared at the flickering flames in the hearth, trying to make sense of Banar's position. He spoke to the other man with deference, yet his clothes and manner suggested he held power too. The pieces didn't fit, and the more I thought about it, the tighter the knot in my stomach grew.

To occupy my mind I took the opportunity to look around the room. The hearth dominated one wall, its flames cast flickering shadows across the stone. The heat felt good, seeping into my bones. Above the hearth hung an ornate tapestry, depicting a hunting scene with wolves and stags, the colours rich and vibrant. Near the hearth stood a heavy wooden desk, cluttered with parchment and ink. A sturdy chair, worn smooth by years of use, sat in front of it.

The bed I had been lying on was large, its posts intricately carved with twisting vines and leaves, the blankets thick and warm. Beside it, a small table held a polished silver basin and a matching pitcher, their surfaces reflected the firelight. On the other side of the room, a tall wardrobe, its doors inlaid with intricate patterns, loomed against the wall. I imagined it filled with fine clothes and linens, though it felt out of place in a room meant for a guest.

I got up, the robe rustling around me, and wandered over to the desk. The parchment was filled with notes and diagrams I couldn't understand. I ran my fingers over the smooth surface, feeling the grooves and notches. Beside the desk, a bookshelf stretched from floor to ceiling, crammed with volumes of varying sizes and colours, their spines cracked and worn.

Eitherside of the hearth was a small window, high on the wall, let in a sliver of evening light, illuminating dust motes that danced in the air. The windows were much too small to climb out of, more a portal to let light in than an escape route. The windows were framed with heavy curtains, dark and plush, that could be drawn to shut out the world completely.

Curiosity pulled me to the door. I tried the handle, my heart sank when it didn't budge. Locked. I was still a prisoner, despite the comforts of this room. I pounded the door with my fist, a dull thud that echoed in the silence. No one answered.

I pounded on the door once more, a futile gesture, before slumping back to the bed. Each step felt heavier than the last, the locked door taunting me with my helplessness. Sitting on the edge, I stared at the flames in the hearth, their dance mocking my entrapment. A beautifully crafted game set with little soldiers, archers and knights, its pieces carved from bone and ebony, caught my eye on a low table near the window. The luxurious surroundings couldn't mask the reality—I was trapped. The rage simmered beneath the surface, mingling with the grief and uncertainty that had become my constant companions.

Over the next few days, the routine was the same. The servants brought me food—simple but hearty meals—and watered-down wine. Each bite and sip helped me feel a little stronger, though my body still ached from the bruises and raw wounds. The solitude gave me too much time to think, to remember, and to rage quietly within the confines of my mind.

One afternoon, a knock on the door preceded the entrance of a woman carrying string to measure and fabric swatches. She was tall and thin, with a face that bore the marks of both kindness and years of experience. She smiled gently as she approached.

"Let's see what we can do about getting you some proper clothes," she said, her voice soothing. "Stand up straight for me, please."

I obeyed, feeling awkward as she measured my shoulders, chest, waist, and inseam. Her hands were quick and efficient, cutting the string at each measuring point to have a record of my size.

"How old are you, child?" she asked, glancing up from her notes.

"Thirteen winters," I replied, my voice hoarse.

She nodded, making a few more mental notes. "I'll leave some room to grow, then. We wouldn't want you outgrowing your clothes too quickly."

I watched her work, her focus intent on her task. She tried to make small talk, asking where I was from and how I liked the room, but I kept my answers brief. I didn't know what I should say, and the memories of my village were still too fresh, too painful.

"You're lucky, you know," she said, not looking up from her work. "To be adopted by the Lord and his Lady Elara. Such good folks they are. They do well for the people of Eldewood. Though, I do wish they'd take care of the deviant of the forest."

I blinked, having never heard that word before, "the deviant?"

She nodded, a flicker of something—fear, maybe—crossed her features. "Aye, the wild beast that prowls the woods. Been causing trouble for years, they say. But don't you worry about that now. Do you have any favourite colours?" she asked, trying to coax more out of me.

"Blue," I said finally, thinking of the sky over the mountains.

She smiled, tucking her notepad away. "Blue it is, then. Though Lord Fayle's colours are typically a darker shade of blue. I'll make sure you get something nice. You'll feel better once you're in proper clothes."

She paused at the door, giving me one last look. "You're in good hands here, child. Remember that."

I nodded, though I wasn't sure anything could make me feel better right now. She gave me a final, sympathetic look before gathering her things and leaving the room. The door clicked shut behind her, the lock turning once more, sealing me in my gilded cage.

Banar's visits became the only consistent part of my days, a routine that brought both comfort and a constant reminder of my captivity. Each day, he'd enter with a nod, his expression unreadable, settling into the chair by the hearth as if bracing himself for a difficult conversation.

One morning, as he sat in the chair, I asked, "Why do you call the other man 'lord'? Aren't you one too?"

Banar sighed, leaning back. "I serve as an officer in the Black Guard, a vassal to the man you met. My status isn't as high as his, but I have my own household and responsibilities. Once, I was just a soldier in an army that fought against the Witch Queen. We lost, and those of us who survived swore fealty to her or faced death."

I leaned forward, my curiosity piqued despite myself. "What happened to your army?"

"We were outnumbered and outmatched," Banar said, his tone grave. "The Witch Queen's forces were ruthless, their strategies unlike anything we'd ever faced. You saw them too... the resonance witches." His expression grew blank, his eyes distant, as if recalling a nightmare.

I wanted to ask about the witches, but the very thought of them sent a shiver down my spine, my heart pounding with fear. Their eerie song, the way it had seeped into my bones, filled me with a terror I could hardly bear to remember.

Eventually, Banar snapped out of it. "We fought hard, but it wasn't enough."

"Did anyone else in the village survive?" I asked, my voice barely above a whisper.

Banar's eyes softened, and he shook his head. "No, you were the only one we found alive."

The words hit me like a physical blow, and I looked away, fighting the sting of tears. "I saw men taking the eyes of my kin. Why, why would they do that?"

Banar hesitated, then answered, "I don't know. The order came from another lord. It's not something I understand, but it was a directive we had to follow."

I stared at the floor, the rage bubbling just beneath the surface. "Why is my door locked?"

Banar leaned forward, his gaze steady. "For your safety. Once you're fully healed and can move about, you'll be free to go as you please."

His words rang hollow, the locked door standing as a stark reminder of my reality. I glanced at it again, feeling the cold iron of the lock binding me as surely as any chain.

"What if I never heal?" I asked, my voice hard. It was a stupid question I'll admit but it was born out of frustration and I was still a child.

"You will," Banar said firmly. "You're strong, Karn. Stronger than you know."

Days passed, blending into one another yet Banar came each day. He talked about his life, his losses, and his reasons for fighting. In return, I asked questions, trying to piece together the world I had been thrust into.

One afternoon, I gathered the courage to ask, "Why did you choose serve the Witch Queen?"

Banar's face darkened. "I had no choice. The land and lords I served are now dead or scattered. Swearing fealty was the only way to survive."

"Do you regret it?" I asked.

"Every day," he replied quietly.

Our conversations continued, each one revealing more about the man who had become both my captor and, oddly, a reluctant confidant. Banar was tall and broad-shouldered, his frame strong from years of battle. His green eyes, which might have been bright once, were now shadowed by countless memories of war and loss. His face bore the marks of his past—a scar running from his left temple to his jawline, a reminder of a close call with death.

He had a rough, weathered look about him, his hair cropped short and flecked with grey, betraying his years. His hands, calloused and scarred, spoke of a life spent wielding a sword, and yet there was a gentleness in his touch when he checked my wounds. Despite his gruff exterior, there was an undeniable sadness in his eyes, a vulnerability that made it hard to see him as just my captor.

I still didn't trust him, but his honesty was a small comfort in the midst of my confusion and grief. He spoke with a straightforwardness that left little room for deceit, answering my questions with a sincerity that was rare in these dark times. Each answer he gave, though often painful to hear, built a fragile bridge between us.

The more I learned, the more I realised how entangled we both were in the Witch Queen's web. Banar had once been a soldier like any other, fighting for his land and people. Now, he was bound by the same chains of fear and obedience that held me. He spoke of loyalty and duty, of the necessity to serve and survive, but I couldn't shake the feeling that he was as much a prisoner as I.

His eyes would sometimes drift to the window, as if longing for a freedom he had long since abandoned. It was in those moments of silence, when the weight of our shared captivity hung heavy in the air, that I saw the depth of his own struggles. We were both caught in the same storm, and though I yearned to escape, I began to understand that Banar's own chains were forged from a different kind of despair.

A week later, I received new clothes: three sets in total. Two were simple, sturdy garments for everyday tasks, and one finer set, rich blue fabric with silver embroidery, clearly meant for special occasions. Each set bore an emblem embroidered on it—a stag's antlers surrounded by a circle of silver stars, a fitting representation of Banar's fierce and protective nature. The clothes fit well, the woman who took my measurements having left room for me to grow. I felt a strange mix of gratitude and a peculiar draw towards the emblem, its design stirred something deep within me.

Banar entered my room, his presence as commanding as ever. "Time for a tour," he said, his tone matter-of-fact. "Let's start with the basics."

He led me down the corridor, the sound of our footsteps echoing off the stone walls. The first stop was the privy. "You'll need this often enough," he remarked with a hint of dry humour. "Better to know where it is."

Next was the baths, a large room with a sunken stone tub. The walls were lined with shelves holding soaps and towels, and the floor was covered in smooth, polished stones. "You can clean up here whenever you need," he said. "Hot water is brought in every morning."

We moved on to the kitchen, the air filled with the scent of baking bread and roasting meat. The cook, a stout woman with a stern face, barely glanced at us as she barked orders to the scurrying kitchen staff. Pots clanged, and the fire roared in the hearth. "Don't bother the cook," Banar advised. "She's good at what she does but has little patience for interruptions."

Then, he showed me the drill hall, a wide-open space with weapon racks lining the walls. Swords, spears, and shields hung neatly in place, their polished surfaces gleamed in the light streaming through high windows. "This is where you'll learn to fight," he said, a serious note in his voice. "I'll tutor you in the martial arts. It's essential for you to know how to defend yourself."

We made our way to the stables, the smell of hay and horses strong in the air. The stable boys were busy grooming the horses, their coats shining. "Do you know how to ride?" Banar asked.
I shook my head. "No."
"We'll change that," he replied. "Riding is a valuable skill, and you'll need to learn."

The tour continued to the gardens, a peaceful area overlooking the fields and the village below. Flowers and herbs were meticulously tended, and the air was filled with their fragrance. "This is my holding," Banar said, a note of pride in his voice. "It's small, mainly farmers, but it's still a holding. I'm good to the people, and they respect that."

I scanned the horizon, noting the dense forests beyond the fields. An escape route, perhaps. Banar seemed to read my thoughts. "I know what you're thinking, Karn. Don't try it. The forest is dense and easy to get lost in."

He paused, then added, "There are also rumours of deviants in those woods. Best to stay clear."

We re-entered the house, Banar pointing out the different wings—the servants' wing, the family wing, and the guest wing where I was staying. The hallways were lined with tapestries and lit by oil lamps, casting a warm glow. Finally, he stopped at a large wooden door. "This is my study," he said. "You're not to enter unless invited. Understood?"

I nodded, noting the seriousness in his eyes.

"Good," he said, his tone softening. "Now, it's time for supper. Follow me."

He led me to the family hall, a spacious room with a long wooden table set for a meal. The walls were adorned with even more tapestries depicting hunting scenes and landscapes, and a large fireplace that crackled, breathing life into one end of the room. Banar's wife and step-daughter were already seated. His wife, a young woman with kind eyes and soft features, smiled warmly at me. The step-daughter, just a bit older than me, regarded me with a cool detachment, her posture rigid and her gaze sharp.

"Everyone, this is Karn," Banar introduced. "Karn, this is my wife, Elara, and my step-daughter, Serah."

"Hello, Karn," Elara said kindly. She had soft, kind eyes that seemed to carry the warmth of summer, her brown hair neatly pinned back, framing a face that was both welcoming and serene.

Serah just nodded, her expression unreadable, her lips a thin line. She had a striking presence, with dark, piercing eyes that seemed to see right through me. Her long, black hair fell in waves over her shoulders, contrasting sharply with her pale skin. There was a coldness to her, a guardedness that made me wary.

Banar sat at the head of the table, gesturing for me to sit. "They know why you're here, Karn," he said, his tone firm but not unkind. "But let's keep those conversations private. We'll talk more about it in my study."

I nodded, feeling the weight of their gazes on me. Dinner was a quiet affair, the clinking of cutlery the only sound that broke the silence. The food was delicious—roast meat, seasoned vegetables, and fresh bread—but I ate mechanically, my mind elsewhere.

Halfway through the meal, Elara looked at me with a thoughtful expression. "Karn, can you read?"

I shook my head, feeling a pang of embarrassment. "No."

Serah scoffed under her breath, her disdain obvious. "Figures."

Banar shot her a stern look. "Serah, enough." He turned back to me, his tone softening. "Elara will be helping you with your academics, reading included."

Elara smiled reassuringly. "We'll start with the basics and go from there. You'll be reading in no time."

I nodded, feeling a mix of gratitude and frustration. In my village, we didn't really learn to read. We learned to count and understood basic symbols, but most knowledge was passed down through trade and the teachings of our Wisewalker—my mother. The idea of learning to read seemed daunting, a mountain too high to climb.

Elara glanced at Serah, then back at me. "Serah is an excellent equestrian. She'll actually be the one teaching you to ride."

Serah's eyes widened, a look of surprise and irritation flashed across her face. "I will?"

Banar nodded, a hint of amusement in his eyes. "Yes, you will. You're the best rider here, and Karn needs to learn."

Serah huffed, crossing her arms. "Fine. But don't expect me to go easy on you."

I met her gaze, my determination hardening. "I don't expect you to."

Banar chuckled, breaking the tension. "Good. Now, let's finish dinner."

I kept my eyes down and I continued to eat. I hungrily devoured the roast meat and vegetables, my stomach still growling even as I chewed. Each bite was a reminder of how weak and fragile my body felt, the lingering pain in my ribs a constant companion. Around me the family continued to converse.

Elara smiled and turned back to Banar. "I heard from the merchants today that there's been trouble in Dúnmara again. More unrest among the guilds."

Banar nodded, chewing thoughtfully. "Yes, I heard the same. The capital's always simmering with something. We need to keep an eye on it. It affects trade and, inevitably, us."

Serah rolled her eyes. "The capital is always in trouble. Why should we care?"

Elara shot her a look. "Because, Serah, what happens in Dúnmara can have a ripple effect. The more unstable things are there, the harder it is for us here. Prices rise, supplies dwindle."

Banar added, "And it's not just trade. Political shifts can change allegiances and power dynamics. We need to be aware of these things, even if they seem distant."

Elara nodded. "Exactly. It's all interconnected. Even here, in our small corner, we're not immune to the currents of change. Though I suppose we might be immune to good weather."

We continued eating, the conversation flowing around me. I listened, trying to piece together this new world I was thrust into. The atmosphere was a mix of tension and reluctant acceptance, but the talk of village affairs and the capital gave me a glimpse into their lives, their concerns.

As the meal came to an end, Serah spoke up again, her tone cut through the chatter like a knife. "So, Karn, what tragic story brought you here? Lose your family too?"

The question hit me like a punch to the gut. Memories of the attack, the screams, and the sight of Liv's lifeless eyes flooded back, choking me.

Banar shot her a warning look. "Serah, show some tact."

She shrugged, looking unapologetic. "What? It's not like I was going to ask about the weather."

Banar excused me from the table and a servant guided me back to my room. My fists clenched and unclenched as we walked through the corridors, nails digging into my palms as Serah's words echoed in my mind. The memory of Liv's lifeless eyes flashed before me, and I forced myself to take deep, steadying breaths to keep from shaking. When the servant left, I tried the door again, finding it locked. My cage, no matter how gilded, remained just that, a cage.

Chapter 6 - The Path

The next morning I was awoken abruptly by the sound of my door as it creaked open. The room was cloaked in darkness, the thin slivers of morning light peeking through the narrow slit windows unable to penetrate the shadows. Banar loomed in the doorway, his form outlined by the faint glow from the corridor. "Time to rise, Karn," his voice gruff but not unkind.

I groaned softly, my body stiff from yesterday's unaccustomed activity. The chill of the morning air bit at my skin as I swung my legs off the bed, the stone floor cold against my bare feet. I shuffled across the room, splashing water on my face from the basin beside my bed. The cold shock of it jolted me awake, chasing away the last vestiges of sleep.

I dressed quickly, pulling on the sturdy clothes laid out for me the night before. The fabric was new, stiff, and smelled faintly of lavender, likely from the wash. My new boots were a snug fit, their leather stiff and unyielding, moulding slowly to my feet as I laced them tight.

Banar waited patiently by the door, watching as I gathered myself. "We've much to do," he said, a hint of anticipation in his tone. He turned and led the way, his steps echoed down the stone corridor.

The drill hall was a short walk from my quarters, but the air outside was even more brisk, the dawn light now stretched across the sky, painting everything with hues of pink and orange. I followed Banar's broad back, the rhythm of his walk steady and sure as any soldier.

As we approached the hall, I could see my breath misting in the cold air, each exhale a cloud of vapour. Banar pushed open the heavy wooden door, and the smell of oil and metal greeted us.

"Here we are," Banar announced, stepping inside. The vastness of the drill hall came into view, its high ceilings and wide-open space filled with racks of weapons and padded training mats. I stepped in behind him, the door closing with a thud that seemed to seal us in this world of martial discipline.

Banar walked over to stand in the centre of the drill hall, his broad frame casting a long shadow in the dim light of dawn. He stretched his arms over his head, muscles rippling under his tunic. "First things first, we start with stretches. Flexibility and strength are as important as skill with a blade. Can't have you pulling a muscle in the middle of a fight."

I mimicked his movements, feeling the strain in my limbs as I reached upwards. The morning chill seeped into my bones, making the stretches feel both necessary and painful. "Banar, you said we have a lot to do, what exactly are we going to be doing?" I asked, curiosity getting the better of me.

Banar shifted into a deeper stretch, touching his toes with ease. "We're going to test your fitness and martial knowledge. That means fighting techniques, handling weapons, understanding war, strategy, and tactics. All the essentials."

I frowned, trying to keep up with his movements. "My people didn't learn those things. We were peaceful. We focused on mindfulness and calm exercises, staying connected with nature."

Banar paused, his eyes narrowing with interest. "Mindfulness, you say? Now that's intriguing. You'll have to teach me some of those exercises someday. But for now, we need to make sure you can protect yourself. The world outside your village is far from peaceful."

I nodded, my mind flashing back to my mother's teachings, her calm voice guiding me through meditations and breathing exercises. It seemed a lifetime ago, yet it had only been a week.

Banar switched to a lunge, his leg muscles taut. "Why are we doing all these stretches again?" I asked, struggling to match his flexibility.

A grin spread across Banar's face, a rare moment of levity. "Because I'm old and stiff, Karn. Keeps me from creaking like a rusty door. Besides, you don't want to be as brittle as a dried twig when you finally get to swinging a sword."

Banar stood in the centre of the drill hall, watching me with a critical eye. "Alright, Karn. Let's see what you're made of. Start by running laps around the hall. Keep moving until I say stop."

I nodded, setting off at a brisk pace. The cold air bit at my lungs, and my breath came in frosty puffs. My feet pounded against the hard ground, each step echoed in the vast space. Banar's voice called out encouragement and corrections as I ran. "Keep your back straight! Breathe through your nose! Push harder!"

After what felt like an eternity, he finally called out, "Stop!" I staggered to a halt, panting heavily, my legs feeling like jelly.

"Not bad," Banar said, nodding approvingly. "Now drop and give me twenty push-ups."

I hesitated, unsure. "What's a push-up?" I asked, feeling suddenly foolish.

Banar stared at me, disbelief etched in his features. "You don't know what a push-up is?" He shook his head, then dropped to the ground beside me, his movements fluid and precise. "Watch closely," he instructed. He placed his hands flat on the ground, shoulder-width apart, and straightened his body into a plank. "Keep your body straight, push down until your chest is near the ground, and then push yourself back up. That's one."

I mimicked his position, feeling awkward and stiff. As I lowered myself down, my arms shook under the strain, and pushing back up felt like moving a boulder. Banar watched, nodding as I struggled through the motion. "That's it," he encouraged. "Keep going. This is to build your upper body strength. You'll need it if you are to wield a sword properly."

After a series of gruelling push-ups, he stood and led me to the rack of swords. My arms were trembling, but my excitement surged at the sight of the gleaming steel and intricate hilts. Banar, however, tempered my enthusiasm quickly. "Pick one up, hold it for a moment, then put it back. We're not fighting yet."

I lifted each sword, the weight felt substantial in my fatigued hands. I savoured the brief moments they were in my grasp, feeling a connection to the steel—though more than likely that was just boyish glee at a new toy, before reluctantly placing them back on the rack as instructed.

Once the exercises were over, I was left drenched in sweat, my muscles burned with the unfamiliar strain. Banar nodded, a hint of approval in his eyes.

"Good," he said, his voice gruff. "You're not completely hopeless. Now, take this."

He handed me a wooden sword, its surface worn smooth from countless hands before mine.

"We're just getting started boy," he said with a smile.

Then he drew his own sword, and it was like nothing I'd ever seen. The blade was a blend of menace and art, a single sharp edge on one side and a straight, robust back on the other. It wasn't overly long, more a short sword than the towering weapons I'd imagined from tales. The hilt was adorned with a wolf's head, its eyes set with small, dark stones that seemed to glint with a life of their own. The hand guard was square, simple yet solid, framing the grip in a way that spoke of practicality and protection. My guess is that it was for a man that liked to keep all of his fingers.

"We're going to go through some drills," Banar explained as he balanced the weight of the sword in his hand, the blade caught the morning light with every subtle movement. "These are basic forms that teach you the movements and techniques you'll need in a fight."

I held the wooden sword, feeling suddenly childish with my simple, blunt replica. But as Banar positioned himself parallel to me, the sword in his hand seemed less a weapon and more an extension of his will, something forged from necessity and honed by years of discipline. I tried to adopt his stance, aware of every awkward shift in my own posture, my eyes fixed on the gleaming steel that had known real battles.

He began to move, the sword cutting through the air with precision. I tried my best to mimic his movements, but it was clumsy at first. Banar's form was fluid, each motion seamless and efficient. I felt like a clumsy child, my wooden sword wobbling with each attempt.
"Focus on the big moves first," Banar instructed. "Get the basics right, and then we'll fine-tune the details."

We repeated the first five moves over and over again. My muscles burned, and sweat dripped down my face, but I kept going. As I began to get the hang of the larger moves, Banar's scrutiny intensified. He stepped closer, correcting the angle of my sword, adjusting my stance. "This is why we do these drills," he explained. "Each movement has a purpose. This one," he demonstrated a quick thrust, "is to deflect an incoming blow. And this," he shifted into a defensive stance, "is to protect your vital areas."
He repeated the drill once again, "did you know your muscles have memory? Each time you repeat the drill you ingrain it into

your very fibres until it becomes second nature," he continued to explain.

I listened intently, absorbing his words and the reasoning behind each motion. Slowly, my frustration gave way to a growing sense of competence. I wasn't just swinging a sword; I was learning to fight. At least I hoped I was. Each correction, each adjustment, brought me closer to understanding.

By the end of the session, my body felt like it had been put through a grinder, but there was a flicker of pride in Banar's eyes. "Good work today, Karn," he said. "You're starting to get it. We'll keep at it until it's second nature."

After the strenuous morning, Banar led me back to the family hall where breakfast was already laid out. The table was less formal than dinner had been, yet it bore a welcoming spread: steaming bowls of porridge, fresh bread with butter and honey, slices of cold ham, and a pitcher of milk. Elara and Serah were seated, engaging in a muted conversation that paused as we entered.

"Good morning, Karn," Elara greeted warmly, gesturing to the seat beside her. "I hope you're hungry."

I nodded, my stomach rumbling in response as I took my place at the table. Banar joined us, filling his plate, his earlier severity replaced by a more relaxed demeanour.

Serah, her expression somewhat contrite yet still reserved, cleared her throat. "Karn, about last night—I'm sorry if I was out of line." Her apology hung in the air, feeling more like a formality than genuine remorse

"Thank you," I managed to say, keeping my tone neutral while scooping porridge onto my plate.

"How did the training go this morning?" Elara asked Banar, her voice carried a note of genuine interest.

Banar chuckled, taking a sip of his milk. "Karn's a quick learner.

He's already showing promise, even if he did complain about the stretches."

"Why can't I learn to use a sword too?" Serah suddenly blurted out, her frustration evident.

Elara turned to her daughter with a measured look. "You have your own studies, Serah. If we are to prepare you for The Forge."

This mention of 'The Forge' piqued my curiosity, but no further details came, as Serah simply huffed and focused on her breakfast, clearly not satisfied with the explanation.

After our morning meal, Elara led me to her study, a room filled with shelves of books and scrolls, her desk cluttered with maps and various documents. The air was thick with the scent of ink and parchment.

"Let's start with the basics," Elara began as she pulled a small stack of books from a shelf. "Reading and writing are fundamental. You'll need these skills not just for daily life here but also to fulfil your role."

She sat down opposite me at her desk and opened a book, pointing to the letters. "This is the alphabet. Each symbol represents a sound. Together, they form words, and words convey meaning."

She spoke to me as if I were a child and I guess back then I was. I followed her finger as it traced the shapes, but they made little sense to me. "Why do I need to know all this?" I asked, frustration crept into my voice.

"You're taking on the role of Banar's adopted son, the son of Banar's late cousin. He was the first born of a soldier rising through the ranks, and you'll need to fit that part convincingly," Elara explained. She leaned back, her eyes assessing me. "Knowing your history, understanding the economy, politics, and the houses of Eirithia—it's all part of the masquerade."

I sighed, rubbing my temples. "In my village, the Wisewalkers, like my mother, taught us about the land and how to live in peace. After learning the basics, we apprenticed under a master to learn a trade. It was much easier and more fun."

Elara nodded, understanding lit her eyes. "Here, those of lower birth often don't learn to read or write, similar to your people. But those in power, like us, must be well-versed in these skills."

She returned to the symbols, guiding me through each painstakingly. "This is 'A,' as in 'ash,' and this is 'B,' as in 'barrow.' Let's try to form these with a quill."

The quill felt awkward in my hand, and the ink blotted on the parchment as I tried to mimic the shapes. Frustration mounted with each clumsy attempt. It made the next hour a struggle. My mind rebelled against the confinement of letters and words, yearning for the open skies and the straightforward lessons of nature.

As we worked, Elara called for lunch to be brought into the study. We ate quietly, a map of the kingdom spread out between us on the desk. She used the opportunity to explain more about the world beyond my mountains.

"The Kingdom of Eirithia, ruled by the Witch Queen, is just south of your Northern Highlands, though the rest of the continent would still call our domain the north," she explained, pointing to various regions on the map. "Here, in Eldewood, we're somewhat insulated, but we're still under her rule. The capital, Dúnmara, is here," she tapped the map, "known for its grand palace and the seat of the Witch Queen's power, it's alive with political manoeuvring and courtly intrigue."

I listened, absorbing her words while munching on bread and cheese. The map was a swirl of names and places, each holding stories of power and struggle that my young mind didn't quite understand.

"Your village, The Ashen, is nestled here in the Northern Highlands," Elara began, her finger tracing the craggy mountain ranges on the map that shielded my home. "Its seclusion has preserved your people's unique culture, away from prying eyes and the grasp of greater powers."

"It didn't save them though, did it?" I said.

"No, I am sorry for that. The Witch Queen has something planned and I think your village is merely the start." Elara replied.

I hated it, felt the sorrow swirl within me.

She continued, her eyes locked on mine, her voice dropping to a more serious tone. "Grasping these dynamics—the alliances, the conflicts—it's vital, Karn. Understanding this will be key as you navigate the complexities of the kingdom, especially if you are to convincingly pass as Banar's kin."

The words stirred a storm within me, and I slammed my fist down on the desk, the echo of the impact bouncing off the walls. "My people are gone, massacred by soldiers—Banar's soldiers!" My voice cracked under the strain of grief and fury.

Elara maintained her composure, her gaze unwavering and intense. "Yes, and tragically so. But remember, it was the Witch Queen who commanded them. Banar, like you, was a victim of her cruelty; he lost his own family to her madness," she said, her voice a mix of gentleness and steel.

"How can any of this be right? How does learning this," I gestured to the maps and books around us, "bring back what was lost?" I demanded, my voice raw.

Elara leaned forward, her expression resolute. "It doesn't bring them back. But it gives us the power to fight, to not let their deaths be in vain. We're arming you with knowledge, Karn, for when the time comes to strike back at the Witch Queen. That is how we avenge them."

"And just how are we supposed to do that?" I asked, the weight of scepticism heavy in my tone.

"That's all to come," she assured me, her voice firm with a promise. "For now, we build your understanding, we forge your abilities. When the time is right, you'll be ready to act, to make a difference. Revenge requires preparation and patience."

The session ended with my mind swirling with names and places, each a thread in the complex tapestry of politics and power. My heart weighed heavy with the realities of my new role—a burden cloaked as an opportunity. Elara's teaching was patient and her manner gentle, yet each fact she imparted felt like another link in the chain of destiny I had not chosen.

As I stepped out of her study, the map's intricate lines and colours haunted me, a stark reminder of the vast world that sprawled beyond the secluded valleys of my mountain home. A world I was now intricately part of, whether I desired it or not, each step forward entwining me deeper into its sprawling conflicts and hidden alliances.

In the afternoon, I was to join Serah for horse riding lessons. The musky scent of hay and horse in the stables was strangely comforting after the morning's intense discussions and drills. Following a servant through the barn, my boots scuffed the dirt floor, my fists clenched at my sides as the earlier conversation with Elara continued to simmer in the back of my mind.

Serah, in the centre of the paddock, skillfully guided a chestnut mare through a complex routine. She rode with the confidence and grace of someone who had spent countless hours in the saddle. Each of her movements was fluid, a seamless dance between rider and horse. As she completed a particularly intricate manoeuvre, she dismounted with a flourish, her boots kicking up a cloud of dust that caught the light of the afternoon sun.

Leading the mare over, Serah wore a smirk that seemed to say she'd anticipated my unease.

"This is Sable," she introduced, her tone carrying a subtle challenge. She stroked the horse's neck affectionately; Sable responded with a soft nuzzle against Serah's hand before turning to investigate me. As I tentatively extended my hand, the mare's velvety muzzle brushed against my palm. The gentle contact, a contrast to the morning's frustrations, momentarily softened the edge of my anger.

"First rule—always let a horse get to know you—let her smell you." Serah instructed with a hint of reluctance. She demonstrated the proper way to hold the reins, her movements precise and sure. "And this is how you mount," she continued, gracefully swinging her leg over without startling Sable. "Be smooth, don't kick her side, or she'll bolt."

I acted out her instructions, my attempts clumsy. As I hoisted myself onto Sable's back, my grip on the reins was slick with perspiration, my entire body taut with the novelty and tension of the act.

"Just relax and sink into the saddle," Serah directed, circling to adjust my position. Her impatience was thinly veiled as she tweaked my foot in the stirrup. "You're not climbing a mountain, remember—it's just a horse."

Her offhand remark about my origins stung, tempting me to retort. Yet, I swallowed the sharp words, focusing instead on the rhythm of Sable's breathing beneath me, feeling the power and potential in the animal's restrained energy. I tried to ease my stiffness, to meld with the motion and spirit of the horse, seeking harmony over conflict.

Serah's eyes twinkled with an impish gleam that I entirely

missed, so focused was I on the massive creature before me. "Go on then, show us what you've got," she taunted. As I hesitated, she delivered a sharp slap to Sable's hindquarters. With a startled snort, the mare lurched forward into a full gallop.

Panic gripped me as the stable yard became a whirlwind of shifting colours—green grass and brown earth blending into a dizzying torrent. I clung to the saddle, my fingers knotted in Sable's mane, but my efforts were futile against the sheer power of the horse's movement. My grip slipped, and the earth came rushing up to meet me. I hit the ground with a wet thud, the smell of fresh manure assaulted my senses as I landed squarely in its midst.

Peals of laughter echoed from where Serah stood, doubled over with mirth. "Oh, look! The mountain boy can't even stay on a horse! How does it feel to be swimming in shit?" she crowed, pointing at my sorry state.

Fury and humiliation burned through me as I pushed myself up, dung clung to my hair and clothes. I squinted through the grime that smeared my face, my eyes finding Serah's figure blurred by my indignation and the tears that frustration had brought to my eyes. The fall had wounded more than my flesh—it was an insult to my very competence, a stark declaration of my novice status in this new, unforgiving world.

With my pride thoroughly trampled and my clothes disgracefully soiled, the riding lesson came to an abrupt halt. A servant, younger than me but with an air of practised deference, appeared at Serah's nod. He led me away from the stables, casting sympathetic glances my way as we walked toward the bathhouse. The walk was a silent procession, my steps squelching unpleasantly with every movement.

At the bathhouse, the servant gestured to a sunken stone bath, steam rising invitingly from its surface. With a grimace, I stripped off my dung-covered clothes, my skin crawling from the filth. The servant gathered the soiled garments with a wrinkled nose. "I'll bring the master's spare clothes and wash these," he said, his voice carrying a slight tremor of disgust—or perhaps it was empathy.

"Thank you," I muttered, feeling an odd twinge of discomfort at being waited on. The servant nodded and hurried away, leaving me to my solitude.

Stepping into the hot water, I submerged myself, letting the heat seep into my aching muscles. The bath's warmth enveloped me, a stark contrast to the cool derision I'd felt under Serah's mocking gaze. I scrubbed at my skin, the dirt and manure washing away, but the sting of humiliation lingered. With each stroke, I tried to cleanse not just my body but my spirit, grappling with the day's trials—both physical and mental.

The more I soaked, the more I questioned the path laid before me. Why endure this training, these lessons, this new life thrust upon me without my consent? Each thought circled back to an uncomfortable realisation: I was far from the mountains, far from the life I knew, yet here I was.

After what felt like an eternity, the servant returned, his arms laden with clean clothing. He placed them neatly on a bench near the bath, his manner brisk but not unkind. "Do you need anything else, sir?" he asked, pausing at the doorway.

I shook my head, dismissing any further needs. With a nod, the servant departed, leaving the door ajar. My eyes widened at the sight—an open, unlocked door. It wasn't merely a gap in the doorway; it was an opportunity, a rare lapse in the tight schedule and control of the day. For a moment, I simply stared, the steam curling around me like whispers of possibility.

The significance of this small oversight wasn't lost on me. Here lay a sliver of freedom, stark against the backdrop of commands and expectations that had defined my time in this strange place. As the servant's footsteps faded into silence, the open door stood as a quiet invitation to escape, to reclaim a choice that had been wrested from me upon my arrival.

Chapter 7 - Escape to the Forest

I hoisted myself out of the bath, my limbs trembling, not just from the cold but from the thrill of the open door at the far end of the room. An escape, a sliver of freedom momentarily unguarded. The coarse fabric of the towel barely dried my skin before I yanked my clothes on, my movements quick, jerky, driven by a rising tide of excitement. Each garment felt like armour, cloaking my intentions.

Approaching the door, I paused, my ear pressed against the cool wood. Silence. My heart thudded against my ribcage, a drum of war in the quiet of the manor. A quick glance through the gap confirmed it—no one in sight. My breath came out in a controlled exhale, and I stepped into the hallway, the air chilled the damp spots on my shirt.

The manor was a labyrinth, but hunger sharpened my memory. I skulked through the corridors, the soft carpets swallowing the sounds of my hurried steps. My goal: the kitchen, a vault of smells and sounds even this late in the day. As I neared, the aroma of stewing meat and baking bread wafted toward me, a siren call.

Peeking around the corner, I spotted the cook, her back turned, singing softly to herself as she chopped vegetables. A perfect moment of distraction. I slipped into the room, keeping low, and slid behind the long table covered in flour and dough. Her tune was a lullaby, perhaps meant for the bread rising under cloths.

Timing my movements with her song, I edged along the table. When she reached the chorus, her voice swelling with pride, I snatched a loaf of bread from the counter. Cheese next, then a strip of dried meat hanging above. My hands, though shaking, were deft, each item disappearing into the sack like the tricks I'd seen from the long tooth elder of our village.

By the time the cook turned to the oven, the sack was heavy with provisions. My exit was silent, a ghost flitting from a feast, heart pounding not just from the thrill of theft, but from the burgeoning adventure that awaited beyond the manor's stone walls.

I pressed my back against the wall as I crept down the hallway, the sack of provisions slung over my shoulder making a soft thud against the stones. My boots were muffled by the rich carpets, but each heartbeat felt like a drum in my ears. As I rounded a corner, the sound of a solitary voice halted me.

Elara.

She approached, her voice not educating me of academics but rather humming a tune, soft and melodic. Panic surged, hot and prickly, under my skin. Spotting a tapestry depicting a great hunt, I slipped behind it just as her silhouette cast long shadows against the wall. My body was tight against the rough fabric, the scent of dust and age filled my nose.

The leisurely tap of Elara's footsteps echoed down the hallway, harmonising subtly with her humming. I held my breath, counted to ten, and waited for the quiet to reclaim the space. Peeking out, I saw the hallway now empty, her presence lingering only as a fading note in the air.

I darted from behind the tapestry, my steps swift and silent across the cool stone floor. Ahead, the manor's back door stood ajar, a sliver of the outside world beckoning. I nudged it wider with a cautious hand, and a breath of cool evening air swept across my face, crisp and invigorating.

Stepping into the courtyard, the dwindling light cast long

shadows that twisted and turned as if alive, playing over the cobbles. Torches mounted on the walls flickered, their flames danced erratically in the gentle breeze, throwing patches of light that briefly illuminated the path ahead.

Crossing the threshold, the weight of the manor's stone walls fell away. I stepped into the open, the ground beneath my feet crunched softly on gravel, then yielding to the soft earth of the fields beyond. The wide sky, painted in strokes of orange and purple by the sinking sun, stretched endlessly above, a dome of freedom.

Farmers dotted the fields, their backs bent, collecting the last of their day's bounty. They moved with a rhythmic certainty, tools swinging, sacks filling with the earth's offering. None spared a glance for the lone boy crossing their land; they were the last brushstrokes on a canvas of fading day.

My boots sank with each step, mud clung to them. The scent of turned earth and fresh harvest filled the air, a sharp contrast to the sterile opulence of my gilded cage. As the boundary of the manor's influence faded with each step, the fields whispered promises, each stalk of wheat that brushed against my legs a soft caress, urging me onward. The horizon called, the forest line dark against the twilight, an edge of the world yet to be explored.

The forest edge loomed before me, a jagged line where the cultivated fields gave way to untamed nature. The last rays of daylight faded, surrendering to the creeping tendrils of twilight that seemed to emanate from the woods themselves. With each step, the shadows grew, swallowing the path that wound deeper into the forest. The air cooled rapidly, the earthy scent of decay and growth mingled in a breath that was both inviting and warning.

As I ventured deeper, the canopy thickened, blotting out the weakening sky. Twigs snapped underfoot, their cracks sharp in the hush that enveloped the woods. Leaves rustled, whispered secrets of the forest, their sound a soft backdrop to my hurried steps.Then, a voice, deep and commanding, sliced through the silence of the forest, filling my head.

What's your plan, runt?

I froze, my heart slamming against my ribs. The voice was familiar, a distant echo that had always lingered in the back of my mind but never fully emerged.

"Who are you?" I called out, feeling small and exposed in the expansive darkness of the woods.

You know me, it replied, a rumble more felt than heard. *You've always known. You are mine, boy. No pack but this.*

"I have no pack, no family," I countered, spinning slowly in the dark, every shadow seeming alive. "They're gone."

The voice laughed, a sound as cold as cracking ice. *And what will you do for them? Mourn forever? Or will you rise and avenge?*

A spark of anger ignited within me, my confusion fusing with a sudden, sharp clarity. "What do you want from me?"

The forest seemed to exhale, the air around me tightening. *Remember who you are. Choose. Will you squander your life in the shadows or will you forge it in the flames?*

My fists clenched, frustration boiling over. "I... I don't know," I confessed, the admission tasting of ash.

Then know this, the voice thundered, the resonance sharp and enticing as it wrapped around every word, pulling me deeper into its command. *The path to power, real power, to revenge—it leads back. Return, learn their secrets, sharpen your fangs. Then go for the throat.*

Chills raced down my spine, realisation dawning not just from the cold but from the unyielding truth in its words. Without another thought, my feet turned back toward the manor, leaves crunching resolutely underfoot.

"ok," I murmured, though the voice had already faded, leaving me with nothing but the echo of its decree and the certainty of my next steps.

Turning, I made my way back through the forest, each step lighter, almost guided. Then, a scream pierced the night, shrill and desperate, shattering the calm. My breath caught; every instinct screamed to flee from the sound, from the danger it heralded.

But I ran towards it.

My legs moved on their own, propelling me through the underbrush, each branch that whipped against my face and arms urging me faster. The girl's scream echoed again, sharpening the cold dread that pierced my chest. It was a sound from a nightmare, eerily reminiscent of Liv's last cries—desperate and terrified.

Breaking into the clearing, I found Serah crumpled on the ground, her riding trousers stained dark with blood. Her eyes, wide with fear, met mine as she tried to scramble away from an invisible tormentor. "Karn, help me!" Her voice cracked, the words sliced by another wail of pain as a fresh cut appeared on her leg, blood welling from thin air.

"Stay still!" I commanded, more to calm my own panic than to reassure her. I dropped to her side, my eyes watched the empty air that seemed to lash out at her from nowhere. My hand brushed against her arm, feeling the tremor of her fear.

As I shielded her with my body, a sharp pain lashed across my back, the sensation startlingly cold—like the kiss of a blade. I grunted, the sound muffled by the thumping of my heart in my ears. Serah screamed again, her body jerking with another unseen strike.

Grabbing the torch from the ground where it had fallen, I

waved it frantically, the flames slicing through the darkness. "Come on then!" I shouted into the trees, my voice edged with fury and fear.

The air shifted, a subtle rustle of leaves the only warning before a searing pain cut across my cheek. Instinctively, I swung the torch at the disturbance—a desperate, angry arc. The flame connected with something solid, a brief resistance before passing through. A cat-like cry pierced the air, high and pained, retreating into the underbrush.

A hunt—good, kill it! My inner voice growled, its ferocity resonating with my own rising anger. My grip tightened around the torch, its wood warm and solid in my hand, a stark contrast to the cold fear in my veins.

Just as I lowered the torch, thinking the menace had retreated for good, a searing pain slashed across my forearm—a clear message that it wasn't over yet. My anger, a smouldering ember all evening, flared into a roaring blaze.

At that moment, the darkness retreated like a scorned animal, pulling back in a manner that eerily mirrored how the shadows had dissolved around the attackers on that fateful night my village was assaulted. Now, it wasn't fear that vanished but the concealing gloom around the creature, revealed by the stuttering torchlight. Before me stood an animal, its body like a cat but larger and muscular under a coat of slick fur, long ears tufted at the tips, twitching with alertness. Its eyes were like twin moons, capable of pulling the very light into their depths, radiating nothing but cold malice.

Serah's voice, high and sharp, cut through the tension. "It's a deviant caracal!" she cried.

With no time to ponder what that meant, I thrust the torch forward, the flames catching the beast's tail. The creature hissed—a sound like boiling oil—and then turned, fleeing into the underbrush. Its tail, now a fiery beacon, marked our brief triumph as it disappeared into the dark.

As the creature retreated, Serah staggered to her feet, clutching at me for support. Her gaze locked onto mine, and she faltered, her pupils widening. "Your eyes... they're red." Her voice trembled, like she was looking into the glow of a fire just before it consumed everything. "Like—like sunset on a bloody horizon."

I looked away, unable to hold her gaze, unable to face the shock reflected in her eyes.

Gripping her arm, I steered us out of the dark embrace of the woods. "What's a deviant?" I asked as we cleared the tree line, my voice rough with unspent adrenaline.

"They're creatures," Serah said, her breaths quick and shallow, "connected to Resonance, not unlike the witches that attacked your village. But these are more wild, intertwined deeply with the elements of nature."

"Resonance?" I echoed, the word unfamiliar yet ringing with an obscure significance.

"It's... there's a lot to it," she said, turning her own gaze away, the shadows of the trees flickering across her face. "Too much to explain right now."

Under a cloak of deep night, Serah and I limped back across the manor's expansive grounds. Each step was laborious, our shadows merging and stretching eerily on the grass as the moon cast its silvery glow overhead. The imposing walls of the estate rose before us, dark silhouettes against the starlit sky, a sight that made me feel relief with a tinge of dread.

Banar and Elara stood at the entrance with a handful of

servants, their figures stiff and silhouetted by the flickering torchlight that framed the doorway. As we approached, their postures shifted—a tableau of relief at our safe return, tempered by the stern set of their brows, ready to reprimand.

"What were you thinking boy, running off like that?" Banar's voice thundered across the courtyard, echoing off the manor's stone walls as he confronted us with visible ire in the moonlit air.

Serah, leaning on me for support, straightened as much as her injuries allowed. Her voice, though weary, carried a firm resolve. "He didn't run off. We encountered a deviant in the forest. I would be dead if not for him. He even managed to wound it."

At this revelation, Elara rushed forward, her earlier sternness melting into concern. "Wounded? Let me see those injuries at once. This needs immediate attention," she insisted as she began to examine our cuts and bruises with a practised eye.

Banar's expression softened, his gaze shifting from stern to thoughtful as he took in Serah's battered state and my defensive stance. "You shouldn't have been out there at all," Banar chastised gently, though his eyes briefly met mine with what seemed like grateful acknowledgement.

As we began walking towards the manor, Serah leaned closer and whispered, her voice barely audible over the crunch of gravel underfoot. "In truth I thought you had run away... because of what I did earlier. It was a stupid prank. I'm sorry, really." Her eyes searched mine, seeking forgiveness.

"It's alright," I murmured back, a small smile breaking through the tension. "We're past that now."

Banar cleared his throat, signalling an end to the immediate crisis and pulling our attention to him. "Let's not have any more such foolishness," he grumbled, though the edge in his voice had softened.

As Elara guided Serah gently toward the manor, a retinue of concerned servants quickly enveloped them, their murmurs blending with the rustle of leaves in the night air. The lanterns cast a warm glow against the cool moonlight, painting a scene of urgent care as they disappeared into the archway.

Meanwhile, Banar and I lingered outside for a moment longer. His tall frame was silhouetted against the dimly lit courtyard, his posture rigid yet expectant. Turning to face him squarely, the gravel crunching underfoot, I steadied my voice. "You don't need to lock my door anymore," I declared, the moonlight casting long shadows behind us. "I've made my decision—I'll stay, learn, and fight with you."

Banar's gaze, usually so piercing and quick to judge, softened as he studied me. His eyes, reflecting the starlight, seemed to reassess the man I was becoming rather than the boy he had kidnapped. After a moment, a smile cracked his currently stern demeanour. "Good," he finally said, the gravelly timbre of his voice blending with the night sounds. "Let's get you cleaned up. Training starts at dawn."

Turning together, we walked toward the manor, our footsteps synchronised. The tall, imposing doors of the estate loomed before us, swinging open to engulf us in its shadowed interior. As we crossed the threshold, the warmth from the hearth fought off the evening chill, promising not just physical warmth but a forging of something new. The shared ordeal in the forest had not just tested our mettle—it had started to weave the threads of camaraderie between Serah and me, a bond unspoken yet palpably present in our exchanged glances.

Chapter 8 - Bonds and Identities

The days melded into a relentless cycle, starting before dawn broke over the horizon. Each morning began the same—waking in the grey pre-dawn light, the chill of the room bit at me as I dressed in silence.

Training with Banar was a arduous ordeal. We started each session with the Plough drill, a sequence of fifty eight precise movements that left my muscles screaming. The first time I completed it, chest heaving, I thought surely we would move on to actual sparring. But Banar just laughed—a deep, rumbling chuckle that echoed off the stone walls of the training hall. "That's just warming up," he said, and my heart sank as he began demonstrating Sickle Form.

Frustration gnawed at me, but as the weeks passed, I could not deny the transformation in my body. I grew leaner, stronger, more balanced. My movements became confident, each step sure, each gesture deliberate—unless the ache of new muscles betrayed me.

After the morning's exertions, breakfast was a quieter affair, sometimes it was just Banar and I, sometimes the whole family but more often than not Banar had business to see too and on one or two occasions was called to serve in an official capacity as an officer, though there had been no more true fighting since my village was decimated.

Belly full, I'd join Elera in her study. We'd sit at the long wooden desk, and I'd try to keep up as she discussed politics, history, and something she called economics. Maths was a particular torture; I never thought I'd need to know more than counting goats, but Elara insisted it was essential. Sometimes I ate alone when she busied herself with the household accounts—

apparently, even minor lords left their coffers in their wives' capable hands.

The afternoons brought a change of pace and a breath of fresh air—literally. Riding with Serah began as another trial; the horses seemed as tall and intimidating as the towering trees that bordered the estate. But the rush of wind, the sense of speed, the sheer freedom of galloping through the fields—it was exhilarating. Gradually, I found joy in the rides, and in my conversations with Serah. She had thawed somewhat since our encounter with the deviant, her sharp wit now edged with a playful sarcasm that I learned to parry with my own.

Each day, as the sun began to dip below the treeline, casting long shadows over the grounds of the manor, I reflected on these changes. From the structured discipline of sword forms to the laughter and lightness of a horseback ride, I was not the same person who had first crossed the threshold of this estate. Each night, I fell into bed not just exhausted but grateful, the smouldering anger that once fueled me now banked into a steady, burning resolve.

As dawn broke the next morning, heralding the start of a new day, that resolve would be tested. The room was cloaked in shadow, dim despite the morning sun blazing outside. Candles flickered weakly around the edges, casting trembling pools of light that barely reached the centre of the space. Today marked the culmination of countless gruelling days, each one a step on the path to this moment.

My opponent wasn't made of flesh and steel, but the challenge felt just as daunting. My hands trembled not from exhaustion but from the weight of what I was about to undertake. I reached forward, my fingers closed around the weapon that might seal my fate. It was lighter than a sword, slender and delicate, yet it carried a weight all its own. The quill, dark and sharp, was my tool today, and the ink was my ally.

With a steadying breath, I dipped the quill into the inkwell, the black liquid clinging to its tip like blood to a blade. Then, cautiously, I brought it down to the parchment spread before me like a battlefield awaiting the clash of armies. Each letter I formed was a careful manoeuvre, my name—Karn Fayle—taking shape with every deliberate stroke. The script was uneven, a testament to my inexperience in this particular form of combat, but legible nonetheless.

Beside me, Elara watched, her expression composed yet expectant. As I finished, she gave a slight nod, her approval quiet but sincere. "Well done," she murmured, and the simple praise felt like a victory.

Across the table, the scribe and notary, a stern woman named Onora with grey hair tightly bound in a practical ponytail, leaned over the document. Her eyes, sharp behind thin spectacles, scrutinised each letter as if searching for enemies hidden within the curves and lines. Finally, she nodded, her hand moving swiftly as she added her own name to the parchment, a witness to the act.

"That is that, then, Lord Fayle," she declared, her voice carrying a formal edge as she addressed Banar. Around us, the quiet murmur of those gathered acknowledged the title, their voices a soft cloak of sound in the dim room.

Banar, standing tall and imposing as ever, offered me a not so rare, broad smile. "Congratulations, son," he said, his hand came down firmly on my shoulder in a warrior's congratulation.

The weight of his approval, the finality of the quill's work, and the new name bound to me now more tightly than armour felt like a knighthood in its own right. As we stepped from the dim room into the glare of the day, the snow outside sparkled under a sun that seemed to herald a new beginning.

Stepping into the heart of Eldewood village, the change from the manor's structured quiet to the lively chatter and clatter of daily life was immediate. People nodded respectfully as Banar passed, their murmurs of "Lord Fayle" weaving through the air like a binding spell of reverence and familiarity. I trailed beside him, my eyes wide, drinking in the sights not so foreign from my own village—the neatly thatched roofs, the well-worn paths seething with traders, and children darting between stalls with an energy that seemed to fuel the very air.

We ventured into the Silver Stag Tavern, a cosy establishment that felt like the heart of Eldewood. Warmth spilled from the hearth, challenging the chill that had started to seep into my bones. The air was rich with the smell of roasted meat and freshly baked bread, mingling with the tang of spilled ale. Behind the bar, the barkeep—a burly man with a mane of salt rock hair and a laugh as deep as a barrel—poured drinks with a deft hand, his eyes twinkling beneath bushy eyebrows as he swapped stories and jokes with the regulars. Banar ordered rounds of watered-down ale for the table—a kindness to my unaccustomed palate, served with a nod and a knowing smile from the barkeep.

At a nearby table, a group of villagers huddled over a wooden board, pieces clinked softly as they moved them across marked spaces. My curiosity piqued, I nodded towards them. "What's that they're playing?"

Banar followed my gaze, a small smile played at his lips. "Ah, that's Skirmish. A game of strategy—each player commands a 'battalion' trying to capture the opponent's 'flag'. The rules shift slightly depending on the region. Makes it a fresh challenge each time you play in a new town."

Elara leaned back in her chair, her eyes twinkling with a mixture of challenge and amusement. "Banar, when was the last time you actually won a game of Skirmish against me?"

Banar raised an eyebrow, his voice rich with mock offence. "My dear, are you suggesting I'm losing my touch? I'll have you know I've been practising in secret."

"Oh, practising, is it?" Elara's laugh was light, teasing. "Well then, perhaps it's time to test these secret strategies of yours. What say you, Lord Fayle? Care to defend your honour in a public match?"

Banar's grin widened as he stood, extending his hand to her with a flourish. "Lady Elara, it would be my utmost pleasure to accept your challenge. Let's give these fine people a show they won't soon forget."

As Elara and Banar arranged their pieces on the Skirmish board, the tavern quieted, the crowd leaning in. Serah nudged me, a mischievous glint in her eyes. "Keep your eyes peeled, Karn," she whispered, her tone teasing yet instructive as she gestured toward the game. "Skirmish is less about the clashing of swords and more about the clashing of wits."

She pointed to the board—a grid marked with alternating coloured squares, larger than a typical checkerboard. Each player had a set of pieces: small carved figures, some shaped like foot soldiers, others like knights and archers, each with distinct moves. "Foot soldiers plod along one square at a time, knights hop around in L-shapes, and archers? They snipe from a distance, straight lines only."

At the centre of each player's territory lays a small flag. "The whole game," Serah explained, her voice tinged with enthusiasm as she watched Elara's intense focus, "is about capturing your opponent's flag. You can bluff, sacrifice pieces, set traps. Watch mother—her archers are readying an ambush, but I'll bet my last copper she'll throw a knight into the mix just to spice things up."

Banar's strategy unfolded with a protective stance, advancing slowly, building a shielded formation around his flag. His moves were thoughtful, designed to outlast Elara's more aggressive tactics.

As the game deepened, Elara executed a risky manoeuvre, her knight sweeping across the board in a bold thrust that broke through Banar's lines. The tavern held its breath, then let it out in a collective gasp of surprise. Banar responded quickly, sacrificing two of his pieces to fortify a weak point in his defence.

"Every piece matters, like subjects in a kingdom," Serah said, her tone half-teasing as she glanced at me to make sure I was keeping up. "Knowing their strengths and weaknesses? That's what wins wars—or at least tavern games."

The match culminated in a surprising twist, Elara's feint paying off as she diverted Banar's attention and snuck a soldier through to snatch his flag. The tavern erupted in applause, Banar's laugh booming above the cheers.

Elara, with a graceful smile, turned to Banar, her eyes sparkling with triumph. "Well, my lord, it seems this time the cunning of the fox has outmatched the strength of the bear."

Banar chuckled, his voice rich with amusement and pride. "Indeed, my lady. I must admit, you've outplayed me thoroughly today. Your strategies grow more devious by the day."

Elara's smile widened, her tone light but filled with affection. "Perhaps you could use a refresher on the subtleties of the game, my dear. It's all in the details."

"Ah, that must be it," Banar replied, nodding in mock seriousness. "Or perhaps it's just the brilliance of my opponent that dazzles me so." He took her hand, raising it to his lips for a brief, respectful kiss, which drew a few more cheers from the onlookers.

Banar then turned my way. "Every game's a lesson, Karn," Banar said, clapping me on the shoulder as he conceded victory to Elara. "And the best lessons often come from unexpected quarters."

Serah, raising her ale with a sly smile, quipped, "That's why you never underestimate a quiet opponent—or a diluted ale. Both can surprise you when you least expect it."

Their laughter mingled with the smoky air, and the warmth of camaraderie and simple joy was a stark contrast to the cold strategy of Skirmish. I realised, perhaps for the first time, that here in this village, amidst games and tales, I might just find another kind of family. Though the same thought filled me with shame and guilt.

We stepped out of the Silver Stag Tavern into the crisp afternoon air, the village of Eldewood settling into a peaceful twilight. Banar paused to exchange farewells, his voice boomed across the square as he clapped backs and shook hands with his denizens, leaving smiles in his wake.

"Until next time," he called, a final wave dismissing the last of the lingering crowd. Elara waited by the carriage, wrapped in a heavy cloak. She and Banar exchanged a nod, and then she climbed gracefully inside.

Serah tugged at my sleeve, pulling me towards the horses tethered a few steps away. "Let's make this interesting, Karn," she grinned, her eyes gleaming with mischief. "Race you back to the manor."

Elara's voice floated from the carriage window, tinged with amusement and warning. "Be careful, both of you. The paths are slick with snow."

"Best no harm come to my Granite, Karn," Banar added, referring the horse I rode, his horse.

Ignoring the caution, Serah vaulted onto her horse with

practised ease. "What's life without a little risk?" she called over her shoulder as she spurred her mount forward.

I mounted more cautiously, feeling the horse's warmth seep through the saddle. The thrill of the challenge ignited a fire in my veins. We set off at a moderate pace, navigating the narrow streets of the village. The cold air nipped at my face as we trotted past villagers who stepped aside, nodding respectfully.

Serah glanced over, a sly grin on her lips. "What's the matter, Karn? Afraid of a little snow?" she teased, her voice carrying just enough edge to spur me on.

I narrowed my eyes, a competitive spark flaring. "Just making sure I don't trample any innocent village folk," I shot back.

We kept the pace steady until we reached the village gates. The path ahead lay clear, a blanket of white stretching towards the dark line of the forest. Serah, always the instigator, leaned forward and gave her horse a gentle nudge. "Ready to eat my dust?"

Without waiting for my reply, she took off, her horse leaping into a gallop. The controlled trot of the village streets transformed into a wild dash, hooves pounding against the snow-packed road. I spurred my horse, feeling the adrenaline surge as we sped up, chasing her trail.

Serah was a natural, her movements fluid and confident. She seemed to meld with her horse, a single entity moving with grace and precision. I pushed harder, leaning into the horse's rhythm, but she kept gaining ground.

"Is that all you've got?" Serah's voice floated back, teasing and triumphant.

Determined, I urged my horse faster, the cold wind biting harder. We tore through the open fields, snow spraying up from beneath the hooves. The world narrowed to the sound of our racing breaths and the thundering of our mounts.

Just as we approached a bend in the path, the ground shifted treacherously beneath us. My horse stumbled, hooves slipping on an icy patch hidden beneath the snow. I fought to regain control, but it was too late. I tumbled, landing in a deep, soft drift of snow, the cold biting through my clothes instantly.

Lying there, I stared up at the sky for a moment, the absurdity of it striking me. Laughter bubbled up, and I heard Serah's voice above me, filled with amusement.

"At least it's not a pile of shit this time, right?" She peered down, her smirk evident even through the falling snowflakes.

I pushed myself up, brushing the snow from my clothes, still chuckling. "There's always a bright side with you, isn't there?"

We rode back at a more sedate pace, reaching the stables as the last light faded. Serah swung down from her horse and patted its neck. "I'll leave you to the care of these beasts," she said, thrusting the reins into my hands. "Consider it part of your training."

Caring for the horses brought a sense of peace, a reminder of simpler days in my own village. I brushed down their coats, filled their troughs, and checked their hooves, each task grounding me in the present.

As I was finishing, the sound of carriage wheels crunched on the gravel outside. Banar and Elara alighted, their faces flushed from the cold. Banar spotted me and gestured towards the manor's stout wooden doors.

"Meet me in the drill hall once you're done here, Karn. Training isn't over for the day," he called, his tone firm yet encouraging.

I nodded, watching them disappear inside before turning back to the stables. With a final pat for the horses, I grabbed an apple from the feed bin and headed towards the drill hall, ready for whatever lesson Banar had planned next.

Chapter 9 - Control

I entered the drill hall, the scent of sweat and old wood greeted me. Banar stood in the centre, a wooden sword in hand. He tossed me a similar weapon, its weight familiar in my grip. I couldn't resist a rare attempt at humour. "So, does this mean I have to call you Lord Fayle, Lord Father? From now on?" Rare because I was never good at it, when I did try I ended up just copying other people which made me look more the fool.

Banar chuckled, shaking his head. "Lord Fayle and only in public, Karn. Here, you can still call me Banar."

From the corner, Serah's voice cut through with a playful lilt. "Yeah, only my mother gets to call him Daddy."

I blushed, and Banar shot her a stern look, though a smile tugged at his lips. "Serah, behave," he said, though there was warmth in his tone.

We squared off, and I took a deep breath, readying myself. I felt strong, my muscles honed from weeks of training. Banar stood with an air of ease, his wooden sword held lightly, as if it were an extension of his arm. I mirrored his stance, swinging my sword with confidence.

"Ready?" Banar asked, his voice steady.
I nodded, tightening my grip on the hilt. "Ready."

We began, circling each other. Banar moved with a fluidity that belied his size, his steps almost silent on the wooden floor. He feinted left, then swung right. I blocked, the impact reverberating up my arm. I swung back, aiming for his midsection, but he parried with ease, deflecting my attack and stepping back smoothly.

Banar's own strikes were precise, each one calculated to test my defences. I barely blocked an assault to my side, my arm jarred by the force. Before I could recover, his next hit landed on my upper arm, a sharp sting spread from the welt it left behind.

I bit back a growl of frustration, focusing on my breathing, trying to steady the anger that bubbled up. Each inhale and exhale became a tether, grounding me. I shifted my stance, trying to anticipate his next move, but Banar was always one step ahead. He moved like a predator, circling, waiting for the perfect moment to strike.

Our wooden swords clashed repeatedly, the sound echoed through the hall. Banar pressed his advantage, his strikes coming faster, more relentless. I swung wide, hoping to catch him off guard, but he ducked under my attack and countered with a swift blow to my ribs. Pain flared, but I kept my footing, determined not to show weakness.

"Keep your guard up, Karn," Banar instructed, his voice calm despite the intensity of the exchange.
I nodded, gritting my teeth. "I know!"

Banar's eyes flickered with something—respect, maybe?—before he launched another series of attacks. I blocked high, low, then high again, my arms aching from the effort. Banar's wooden sword came down hard on my left shoulder, and I hissed in pain.
From the side, Serah's voice rang out, sharp and biting. "Come on, Karn! Is that all you've got? No wonder your village couldn't defend itself!"

My grip tightened on the sword, knuckles white. The insult struck deep, dredging up painful memories. I struggled to keep my breathing steady, my vision narrowing as anger flared. Banar's eyes never left mine, gauging my reaction.
Another insult from Serah, this one even more cutting. "They must have been weak if they produced a runt like you!"

The anger roared inside, a beast straining at its leash. I felt a surge of strength, raw and unrefined. Banar swung again, aiming for my midsection. I parried with a fierce shout, knocking his sword aside. Banar's eyes widened, the first sign of surprise I'd seen from him.

I pressed my advantage, swinging with everything I had. Banar blocked, but my strength pushed him back. He stumbled, and with a final, desperate strike, I knocked his sword from his hand. Banar hit the ground with a thud, breathless and disarmed.

Breathing heavily, I stood over him, the sword poised for another thrust. Banar raised his hand, his voice calm and authoritative. "Enough, Karn. Enough."

I froze, the reality of the situation crashing over me. My chest heaved, each breath burning as I tried to rein in the anger that still simmered beneath the surface. Slowly, I lowered the sword, my fingers ached from the tight grip, and stepped back.

Banar rose from the ground, his composed demeanour cracking. He dusted himself off, eyes wide before narrowing them, studying me intently. His jaw tightened, and his breath quickened. His fingers flexed, as if unsure whether to reach for his weapon again. The intensity in his gaze spoke volumes—shock, and maybe even fear.

"The purpose wasn't just to spar, Karn," he said, his voice steady despite the recent struggle. "We needed to see if you could control your anger, even under provocation."

I glanced at Serah, who looked at me apologetic. My gaze hardened, a fierce look aimed at her. Banar stepped between us, raising a hand. "Don't blame her, Karn. This was my doing."

I kept my eyes on Serah, but my attention shifted to Banar's words. "What do you mean?" I asked, my voice still rough with unspent adrenaline.

Banar's expression softened, the shock giving way to a look of approval. "We needed to test your control. The Witch Queen has sent orders and placed a bounty on anyone seen with red eyes. They fear what you represent."

My heart skipped a beat. "Are they looking for me?"

Banar shook his head. "No, not specifically. Not everyone would have been in your village that day. But anyone with the abilities your people have is a threat to them. It's why you must learn to control your anger, to hide it until the time is right."

I nodded, still trying to catch my breath, the rage subsiding into a smouldering resolve. The room seemed to close in around me, the weight of the lesson settling like a stone in my gut. "I understand," I said quietly, the words almost lost in my heavy breath. The enormity of what had just happened, what I had nearly done, sank in. My hands still shook, not from exhaustion, but from the remnants of the anger that had threatened to consume me.

Banar's expression softened, the shock giving way to a look of approval. "You did well, Karn. Better than I expected. Controlling that kind of rage is not easy, but it's necessary."

Banar stepped forward, his eyes still locked on mine. "Your next opponent," he said, his voice steady, "will be Serah."

I struggled to control the remnants of my anger, my voice coming out more harshly than intended. "Why? She doesn't know how to use a sword."

Banar shook his head. "No, but she knows how to fight. Hand to hand."

I frowned, glancing at Serah. "You want me to fight a girl?"

Serah rolled her eyes, her tone dripping with sarcasm. "Oh, don't worry, Karn. I promise you won't break a nail."

Reluctantly, I placed the wooden sword on the rack and walked to the centre of the drill hall. Serah stood there, her posture relaxed yet ready. Despite being a year older, she was smaller than me. *This should be easy*, I thought.

We squared off, and Banar gave the signal to begin. I smiled, confident in my size advantage, and moved forward. Serah's hand flashed out, and before I knew it, a sharp sting spread across my cheek. She had slapped me. Hard.

I blinked, more surprised than hurt. Serah smirked. "Watch my feet and eyes, Karn. Not just my hands."

Banar's voice echoed her advice. "Raise your fists, Karn. Stay focused."

I raised my fists, feeling the heat of embarrassment mix with the simmering anger. I lunged at Serah, but she dodged, her hand connecting with my other cheek. Another sting, another surge of anger.

"Keep your guard up," Banar instructed, his tone calm.

Serah moved around me, quick and nimble. Her slaps continued, each one a sharp reminder of my lack of control. My frustration grew, my breathing heavy as I tried to anticipate her movements.

"Is that all you've got?" she taunted, her voice edged with sarcasm.

I swung wildly, but she ducked and slapped me again, the sting sharper this time. The anger boiled, rising from the pit of my stomach to the back of my skull. My fists clenched, and I could feel the rage threatening to take over.

Finally, with a swift move, Serah knocked my legs out from under me, and I hit the floor hard. I lay there, breathing heavily, the anger pulsing behind my eyes.

Serah extended a hand, her expression softened. "Sorry, Karn. Maybe next time you'll get a hit in."

I hesitated, then took her hand, letting her help me up. The apology helped deflate the anger, just a little.

Banar stepped forward. "We'll continue training like this, both physically and mentally, until you can control your emotions."

I nodded, shame replacing with the lingering anger. "I understand," I said quietly.

Serah handed me a book, her eyes earnest and a bit softer than usual. "My mother found this for you. It's written by a scholar who studied the mindfulness techniques of the Ashen. It might help you."

I took the book, running my fingers over the worn cover. "The Seeker's Guide," I read aloud, then added, "To Self Control." The title wasn't familiar, the techniques were though. "Your mother found this?" I asked, looking up at Serah.

She nodded. "Yeah, she thought it might be useful. She knows how hard you've been working."

I glanced over at Elara, who was watching us from the other side of the hall. She gave me a small, encouraging nod. "Thank you," I said, my voice steady. "I appreciate it."

Serah smirked, her usual edge returning. "Don't get all sappy on me now. Just read it and try not to let me knock you down so easily next time."

I couldn't help but smile. "I'll do my best."

Banar stepped closer, his presence a grounding force. "This is just another part of your training, Karn. It's not just about strength and skill, but control. If you can master these techniques, you'll be able to harness your anger, not be consumed by it."

I nodded, the weight of the book in my hands a tangible reminder of the path ahead. "I understand," I said quietly. "I know it's not going to be easy, but I'll do whatever it takes."

Elara approached, her expression kind but serious. "We believe in you, Karn. You're capable of more than you realise. This book is a tool, but the real work comes from within you."

I looked at each of them in turn, feeling a mix of gratitude and determination. "Thank you all. I won't let you down."

After a bath to wash away the grime of the day, I sat at my desk under the dim flicker of candlelight. The Seeker's Guide Serah handed me lay open before me, its pages filled with the wisdom of the Ashen, my people, but I had never heard of the Seekers or their guild, just who were they? The shadows danced across the parchment as I read about three breaths, mindful listening, and self-awareness.

The three breaths were familiar, a technique my mother had drilled into me from a young age. Inhale, hold, exhale—each breath a step toward calm. But the other techniques were less familiar, their nuances eluding me as I tried to grasp their full meaning.

Mindful listening, the act of truly hearing and understanding, not just the words but the emotions behind them. Self-awareness, the deep understanding of one's thoughts, feelings, and actions. As I read, I could feel the teachings sink into my bones, a quiet strength building within me.

You think this will help? A dark, snarling voice echoed in my mind, full of rage and mockery. *Pathetic. Breathing won't save you when the time comes. It didn't save your pack, did it?*

I tensed, the familiar yet unsettling presence of the voice clawing at the edges of my consciousness. It rarely spoke, but when it did, it was always with venom and scorn. I had never told anyone about it, fearing they'd think me insane, possessed, or worse, weak.

Focusing on the book, trying to drown out the voice with the scholar's teachings. Three breaths—inhale, hold, exhale. The words blurred as the voice continued its tirade.

Listening to whispers won't make you stronger. Knowing your thoughts won't stop your enemies. You need power, not this drivel.

The candle flame wavered as my frustration grew. I clenched my fists, nails digging into my palms. The voice was relentless, a constant reminder of the anger simmering beneath the surface.

"Shut up," I hissed out loud, the words laced with a defiant edge. "Just shut up".

For a moment, silence. The voice retreated, its presence fading into the recesses of my mind. I took a deep breath, focusing on the rhythm, feeling the calm it brought.

I closed the book, my eyes straining from the flickering candlelight. The room felt stifling, my thoughts too loud. I needed a break. I slipped out of my room, the cool hallway air a welcome change from the stuffy confines of my quarters.

The kitchen was quiet, save for the occasional clatter of pots. The cook, a burly woman with arms like tree trunks, was tidying up. Her back was turned, giving me the perfect opportunity to sneak a snack. I reached for a loaf of bread, my fingers just grazing the crust when her voice cut through the silence.

"Boy, what do you think you're doing?" She spun around, hands on her hips, eyes narrowed. "You know better than to be skulking around here at this hour."

I shrugged, trying to look innocent. "Just hungry, is all."

She huffed, waving a ladle at me. "Supper will be ready in a bit. You can wait like everyone else. Now get out of my kitchen."

I sighed, my stomach growling in protest, but I left the kitchen empty-handed. The hallway stretched before me, and instead of returning to my room, I turned towards Banar's study. The door was slightly ajar, an invitation I couldn't resist. I peeked inside— empty. Perfect.

Slipping in, I closed the door behind me. The room smelled of old leather and ink. Books lined the shelves, each one a potential treasure trove of information. I moved to the desk, scanning the scattered papers. My heart raced, the thrill of potential discovery pushed me forward.

Ever since I had learned to read, I had made it a habit to sneak in, hoping to uncover something about Lord Caine or Banar himself. So far, Banar had proven to be a good man, but I couldn't shake the need to know more.

I rifled through the papers, careful not to disturb their order too much. Among the documents, I found letters that caught my eye— personal correspondence between Banar and someone named Elena. As I read, the words painted a picture of a man who had loved deeply and lost painfully. Even as a boy I understood that.

"My dearest Elena,

Not a day passes that I don't think of our son. His laughter haunts these halls, and your absence is a wound that never heals. I see him in every corner of this place, in the way the light filters through the windows, in the echoes of footsteps down the corridors. I still hear his voice, calling out for you, for me. It is a ghost that I carry with me, a burden I can never set down.

Your sister, Elara, has been a pillar of strength. She shoulders the responsibilities of this household with a grace that never ceases to amaze me. She is a balm to my weary soul, her presence a constant reminder that life goes on, even when it feels like the world has ended. We keep each other sane, find solace in shared silences and whispered confessions in the dead of night. She has brought warmth back into this cold, empty house, a flicker of hope that I cling to.

And yet, I feel a profound guilt, Elena. Loving her as I once loved you feels like a betrayal. I catch myself comparing her to you, in the way she smiles, in the way she cares for the children. It is unfair to her, and it is unfair to you. But I cannot help it. You were my first, my deepest love, and no one can ever take your place. Elara understands this, I think. She knows the depth of my sorrow, and she carries her own, though she never speaks of it. We are two broken people trying to make something whole again.

Sometimes, in the quiet moments before dawn, I imagine what our lives would have been like if you were still here, if our son had lived. I picture us as a family, whole and unbroken. It is a bittersweet fantasy, one that brings both comfort and pain.

I miss you, Elena. I miss the life we were supposed to have. I promise to honour your memory, to keep our son's spirit alive in my heart. And I will protect this household, this family, with every breath I have left.

Yours always,
Banar"

A previous wife and a dead son, a grief that permeated Banar's life. Was I as much a replacement as Elara was? Shame washed over me for reading such intimate thoughts, but I couldn't stop. Each word revealed a layer of Banar I hadn't seen before—a man of strength, yes, but also of profound sorrow and deep, lingering love.

I carefully replaced the letters, the weight of what I'd read settling heavily on my shoulders. Banar's pain was a private thing, something he didn't show to the world. It made me respect him more, knowing the burdens he carried silently. The way he wrote about Elara, his conflicted feelings of guilt and love, showed a complexity I hadn't appreciated. Banar wasn't just a warrior; he was a man trying to piece together a shattered life, finding moments of solace in the arms of a new love while still mourning the old.

The realisation made my own struggles seem smaller, my anger and grief more manageable. If Banar could carry on with such a heavy heart, perhaps I could too.

As I stepped back from the desk, a sound pierced the quiet—a haunting melody, eerily familiar, like the echoes of my village's final moments. My heart skipped a beat. The sound twisted my gut, a chorus of dread and dark memories. I left Banar's study, the unsettling tune pulling me down the hallway toward Serah's room.

Fear prickled under my skin, not the hot, angry kind but the cold, paralysing kind that makes you want to run but roots you to the spot. My breath was shallow as I gently nudged her door open. The door creaked, revealing Serah standing in the centre of the room, her voice carrying the same eerie resonance I'd heard before.

"What are you doing?" The words tumbled out, tinged with fear and anger, a raw edge in my voice.

She turned, her singing faltering. Candlelight flickered, casting long shadows on the walls. "Singing," she said simply, like it was the most natural thing in the world. Her eyes held a strange mix of determination and sadness.

"It's the same... the same as the cloaked women," I said, my voice barely a whisper, eyes wide with the realisation.

Serah met my gaze, her expression serious. "It's called resonance singing. I have to learn it." Her voice was steady, but there was a tension in her posture, a silent plea for understanding.

"Why?" The question was sharp, filled with confusion and a hint of betrayal. I took a step closer, my fists clenched at my sides, trying to control the rising tide of emotions.

A shadow loomed behind me, and Banar stepped into the room, his presence commanding. "Because she too is part of the plan," he said, his voice calm, deliberate. "Another weapon against the Queen. She's not training to become a soldier, Karn. She's training to become a Witch."

Chapter 10 - Skirmish

The days dragged on, each more grinding than the last. The dull thud of our training echoed through the courtyard, every insult from Serah's lips sliced deeper than the last. My skin would prickle, a flush of heat rising unbidden as her words struck. It wasn't just the sting of her sarcasm that got to me—it was the melody of that damned song, its notes winding through my thoughts, a haunting reminder of those witches.

Banar's shouts snapped me back, his voice a rough bark across the training ground. "Focus, Karn!" But my focus was shattered, splintered into fragments of fear and frustration that I couldn't stitch back together.

Serah squared off against me, her stance loose, almost mocking in its casualness. My hands clenched at my sides, every instinct screaming to engage, to fight back against the invisible chains her voice wrapped around me. But as she advanced, a simple feint to the left that I should have seen coming, my body froze. It wasn't anger that held me—it was sheer, unadulterated fear. Her presence, tied to that chilling melody, paralyzed me.

I dodged a punch, barely, my movements sluggish, driven by the icy dread that filled my veins rather than any real skill. "I haven't been trained for this," I spat out the excuse as soon as Banar's scowl deepened.

"That's a poor excuse!" Banar retorted, his disappointment clear. "These drills aren't just about swords or spears—they're about preparing you to use anything. A fist, a shovel, hell, even your head if need be."

I nodded though it was a hollow gesture that didn't reach my clouded eyes. Each session ended with me stepping aside, sucking down breaths that did little to cool the burn of humiliation. Serah's gaze flickered to mine, a flash of concern there that only deepened the knot in my stomach. I looked away, unable to meet her eyes, unable to admit the truth.

The cycle repeated each day, a relentless loop of dread and evasion. My nights were restless, haunted by the echo of that song and the image of Serah as something other than the friend I thought I'd gained. The revelation of her training gnawed at me, an open wound that refused to heal.

The hours spent with Elara in her study were an oasis in the desert of my daily frustrations. As she unfolded the parchment detailing the political structure of the kingdom, I leaned in, absorbing each name and title with an eager, almost desperate focus. "At the top," Elara began as her finger traced the intricate lines of the diagram, "sits the Witch Queen, ruling over all. Beneath her are the Great Houses: the House of Thorn, masters of the northern forests; the House of Sable, guardians of the central plains; and the House of Marrow, the stoic rulers of the mountainous east."

"Directly below the Great Houses," she continued, pointing to another tier on the parchment, "are the Sovereign Wardens, key figures like Lord Caine, who govern large territories under the Queen's banner, acting as her direct enforcers and overseers."

"Below them," her voice a steady cadence, "are the Vassal Lords, those who have sworn fealty to maintain their lands and titles. They govern the lesser regions, the borders, and the outlying towns, much like Lord Fayle here in Eldewood."

The names and titles danced in my mind, forming a hierarchy as rigid and daunting as the walls of the manor. The structure of power was a tangled web, each strand woven with precision and purpose, designed to uphold the rule of the Witch Queen and her iron grip on the kingdom.

When the weight of the sparring sessions grew too heavy, when I could no longer bear the sight of Serah without hearing that cursed song, I found myself avoiding our afternoon rides. Instead, I lingered in the study, pouring over texts and maps until Elara, with a gentle yet firm insistence, would send me out, claiming the need to attend to her own duties.

With nowhere else to turn, I took my refuge in Eldewood's tavern, clutching "The Seeker's Guide" like a shield. The tavern, with its dim lighting and the constant hum of low conversations, was a balm to my frayed nerves. The patrons, accustomed to their own routines, paid little heed to the lord's adopted son turning up each day. They served me ale, always watered down, a subtle nod to my youth and inexperience with the stronger spirits.

Day after day, I found a corner table where the light was just enough to read by. The book opened to pages on mindfulness and self-awareness, the words a stark contrast to the internal turmoil I felt. As I read, the voice inside my head—dark and taunting— would sometimes sneer at the techniques, mocking their promise of peace and control.

But here, in the familiar, almost home-like atmosphere of the tavern, surrounded by the soft clatter of tankards and the occasional burst of laughter, I found a semblance of peace. It was here, in this unlikely sanctuary, that I could momentarily escape the complexities of my training and my senseless fear of Serah.

The hum of conversation in the tavern often lulled me into a sense of belonging that the manor never did. I'd sit back, letting the ebb and flow of village gossip wash over me, a comforting murmur punctuated by bursts of laughter or the clinking of ale mugs. Today, a snippet caught my ear, a villager musing about how the deviant attacks had dwindled. "Must've been poachers stirring up trouble," another agreed, shaking his head with a certainty that left no room for doubt.

But it was the game of Skirmish that truly captured my attention. It was played often here, the clatter of wooden pieces on the board punctuating the tavern's usual noise. Curiosity piqued, I approached a table where two elderly gentlemen were resetting their pieces for a new game.

"Mind if I watch?" I asked, leaning in. "Maybe you can show me how to play?"

One of them looked up, his eyes crinkled with a mix of amusement and caution. "Oh, young master, we'd hate to embarrass you. This game takes a keen strategy, something us old folks have had years to refine."

"I don't even know the rules," I admitted, trying to keep my tone light. "I'm not looking to challenge, just learn."

The other chuckled, rubbing his beard thoughtfully before replying, "Well, it's kind of you to say, Young Lord, but we wouldn't want to bore you with our slow pace."

I frowned, sensing their reluctance wasn't just about my status or their pace. "I'm really interested. It's just a game, right?"

They exchanged a glance, the unspoken words hung between them. Finally, the first man sighed, setting down his piece with exaggerated care. "It's not just a game to us, my lord. It's... well, it's something of an old man's pastime. We're afraid we couldn't keep up with your youthful energy."

The excuses felt thin, almost rehearsed, and I stepped back, nodding my understanding even as disappointment tugged at me. "I see. Well, thank you anyway."

As I stood there, stewing in my frustration, a new figure approached the table, cutting through the tavern's smoky haze with an ease that caught my attention. His hair was a tangled mess, falling over a face marked by a narrow nose and crowned with a mischievous smile that seemed to know more jokes than it told. He wore a long, dark coat that brushed against the floor with each step, and his hat—a peculiar thing with a brash red feather—bobbed amusingly as he walked.

"Seems like you could use a friend in this game," he said, his voice smooth and inviting. "I'll teach you. These old timers just don't want to admit they're scared of fresh competition."
The elderly gentlemen scoffed, but their eyes twinkled with a blend of irritation and amusement as they watched us.

"Deal," I replied eagerly, feeling a spark of gratitude for the interruption. "And I'll buy a round or two for your trouble."
Banar had provided me with a stipend that I had yet to use, this seemed as good as an opportunity as any.

We moved to a vacant table, where he deftly pulled a folded game board and a bag of pieces from his coat, setting them up in a formation as if by habit. "I'm Lucas," he introduced himself as he arranged the pieces with care. "A travelling merchant. Seen more games of Skirmish played than I have towns."

"Karn," I returned the introduction, watching him work. His hands moved with a grace that belied their rough appearance, each piece placed with a deliberate purpose that hinted at a mind well-versed in strategy.

Lucas's eyes sparkled as he caught my gaze on his hat. "Like the feather? Picked it up in a little shop down south. Makes for a good conversation starter." As he spoke, he hummed a light, catchy tune, the melody floating through the air and adding a layer of comfort to the atmosphere. It was strangely soothing, smoothing the edge of my nerves.

I chuckled, nodding, my earlier irritation ebbing away under his easy demeanour. "It certainly caught my eye. So, how do you play this game?" His humming continued softly, a pleasant backdrop as we dove into the intricacies of Skirmish.

As Lucas arranged the game pieces on the board, his voice took on a didactic tone. "So, what do you know about Skirmish?"

I rubbed the back of my neck, trying to recall Serah's explanation. "Well, it's about commanding a battalion, right? Trying to capture the opponent's flag while defending your own."

"Exactly," Lucas nodded, his fingers deftly setting up the pieces. "But here in Eirithia, we use the witch piece. In my homeland, Verdanis, we play with the Spy. Each kingdom has its quirks."

Intrigued, I leaned closer, surveying the array of pieces spread across the board—foot soldiers, knights, archers, each poised for a silent battle. "So, how does each piece move?"

Lucas pointed to the small wooden figures. "Foot soldiers are your basic unit; they move one square in any direction. Knights," he placed one on the board, "move in an L-shape,."

"And the archers?" I asked, picking up a piece with a finely carved bow.

"They move any number of squares but only in straight lines. Can't jump over other pieces," he explained, then grabbed a more ornate piece. "Cavalry—they can move up to three squares straight and jump over one piece in their path."

I nodded, absorbing the rules as he continued with the siege engines and the unique earthworks. "And the Witch?" I pointed to the piece that replaced the Spy in Eirithia.

"The Witch," Lucas grinned, setting it beside his flag, "moves one square in any direction and can cast a spell once per game to immobilise an adjacent enemy piece for one turn. Very handy for breaking through or stalling an attack."

As we started the game, Lucas's strategy became clear. He used his pieces not just for attack but as part of a layered defence, constantly adjusting to my moves. "Remember, each piece captures by occupying the square of the opponent's piece, except the siege engine. It destroys an adjacent piece without moving."

The game progressed, and as Lucas arranged his pieces— earthworks shielding a vital path, archers positioned for long-range threats—he casually probed, "So, Karn, what brings you to this corner of the realm?"

"Family, I'm learning how to be in one again," I said, focusing on moving my knight to a more strategic position. Which technically wasn't a lie. "I'm the adopted son of Lord Fayle. My father, his cousin, passed away recently."

He raised an eyebrow at that, "you don't sound too cut up about it…" he replied brazenly.

"I… I'm still coping with it, which is another reason I needed to get out of the house," I replied clumsily.

Lucas nodded thoughtfully as he captured one of my knights with a well-placed archer, chuckling softly. "Always watch for archers; they change the game from afar. And never forget—the game ends when the flag is captured, no matter how many pieces you have left."

I responded with a tight smile, shifting uncomfortably under his gaze. The game was indeed more than a pastime; it was a dance of minds, a battle wrought not by swords but by sharp wits and cunning moves. As Lucas manoeuvred his witch to block my cavalry, I realised I was learning more than just a game—I was learning how to think several moves ahead, to anticipate and counter.

"Adopted, you say? That's quite the tale," Lucas observed, setting up a siege engine with a calculating glance. "Must be a heavy mantle to carry, stepping into such a role."

"Yeah, it's... a lot," I admitted, adjusting a foot soldier defensively. "Trying to make sense of it all, really."

Lucas smiled, the gesture tinged with an enigmatic quality as he surveyed the board. "Well, every piece has its role, just like in life. Knowing where you stand can make all the difference in both games and reality, don't you think?"

I nodded, absorbing his words along with the strategy unfolding on the board. This casual conversation was threading through our moves, a subtle duel of its own, probing for openings and understanding, just as we strategized with the pieces before us.

"Good move," Lucas praised as I used my own archer to pin his knight, following his earlier advice. "You're getting the hang of it. Remember, Skirmish is about predicting your opponent's moves and sometimes about bluffing them into mistakes."

The tavern's dim light flickered over the board, casting long shadows as we played into the evening, the clinking of mugs and the low murmur of conversations around us. Lucas's guidance turned the game into a lesson, not just in strategy but in understanding the depth of tactical warfare, a mirror of the larger battles beyond the board.

As the game drew to a close, with both our flags perilously close to capture, I leaned back, my mind buzzing with strategies and possibilities. "Thanks, Lucas," I said genuinely, "this is more than just a game, isn't it?"

He smiled, collecting the pieces. "Every game is a reflection of life, Karn. How you play on the board could very well be how you play in life. Always be a step ahead, and keep your strategies close."

Over the next few days, I found myself gravitating back to the tavern to sit across from Lucas, the board between us cluttered with pieces poised in strategic confrontation. The man had a way about him, a lightness in his demeanour that made conversation flow as easily as the ale from the tavern's taps. He was always smiling, humming a tune that seemed to soften the clinks and murmurs of the crowded room.

"So, Karn, what else do you do when you're not losing at Skirmish?" Lucas teased, capturing one of my foot soldiers with his knight.

I laughed, shrugging nonchalantly. "There's the training... horse riding, mostly. Just the usual lordly education," I said, careful to skirt around the edges of the truth.

"I tell you, Karn," Lucas said one afternoon as he set up the board, "travelling opens your eyes to more than just new sights. It's the people, the stories—they change you."

I nodded, arranging my pieces. Talking to Lucas was easy, like stepping into a stream that was moving just at the right pace. "I can only imagine. Training and horse riding are about as far as I've ventured into the world."

Lucas chuckled, pushing a knight forward. "Ah, but even knights have their journeys, right? Each piece on this board has seen more battles than most men."

His casual wisdom, interspersed with tales of distant lands, made the hours slip by unnoticed. As he continued to hum, the melody seemed to wrap around my thoughts, smoothing the edges of my caution.

Today, though, as we played, Lucas's curiosity veered into new territory. "I've noticed you never choose to play the Witch," he remarked, his tone light but probing. "A powerful piece, yet you avoid it. Why is that?"

I hesitated, moving a foot soldier. "I think they're unnatural," I confessed, keeping my gaze on the board. Trying not to let my fear show.

Lucas's expression turned reflective, the casual humour faded into a more thoughtful demeanour. "Unnatural, or simply another form of power? Magic—or resonance, as we call it—varies widely across the kingdoms," he mused quietly. "Take the Western Peaks of Rhudoria, for example; they tattoo symbols on their skin, which toughens it like leather. Harder to cut, yet they still bleed."

I blinked in surprise, processing the bizarre nature of such practices. Lucas's grin reappeared, though now tinged with a hint of seriousness. "And then there's Seraphel on the southern coast. Women there weave spells with their fans that make men lust after them—a different kind of weapon."

My eyes widened with the imagination of a boy on the cusp of manhood. Lucas caught my astonished look and chuckled. "Trust me, Karn, it's not so bad," he teased, his voice dropping to a conspiratorial whisper. "Being the focus of such attention can be... quite enjoyable."

The uneasy shuffling of nearby patrons underscored the tension such topics stirred in the tavern. Lucas leaned closer, his tone earnest yet filled with an undertone of caution. "It's just another tool, my friend," he explained. "Here in Eirithia, it's wielded as a weapon. But everywhere else, it's all about how you wield it."

Curiosity piqued, I leaned forward, my voice low. "How do you know so much about all these things?" I asked, eyeing Lucas with a mix of awe and suspicion.

Lucas simply hummed a response, his smile broadening as he arranged his pieces on the board. "Didn't I mention? You learn a lot as a travelling merchant," he said, his tone light but his eyes twinkling with secrets untold. "Every city, every village has its stories. You just have to listen."

The next day, I returned to the tavern, eager for another round of Skirmish with Lucas, but he was nowhere to be found. I approached the bar, where an old man with a ponytail white as salt rock wiped down the counter.

"Seen Lucas around today?" I asked, my voice betraying a hint of disappointment.

The barkeep shrugged without looking up from his glass polishing. "That merchant? Lucas? Comes and goes like the wind. Could be anywhere by now," he muttered, setting the glass aside with a finality that seemed to seal the uncertainty of my new friend's whereabouts.

With a resigned sigh, I left the tavern. The familiar weight of solitude settled over me as I made my way back to the manor, the road quieter than usual, echoing the hollowness of my mood.

As I neared the manor, deep in thought about Lucas's tales and strategies, Banar's imposing figure suddenly blocked my path. His face was stern, and the lines around his eyes seemed etched deeper by disapproval.

Banar's call halted me in my tracks, his tone sharp enough to slice through the chilly air. "Karn, we need to talk. You've been avoiding your responsibilities, training, and Serah," he declared all in one go, his voice cut deeper than the brisk wind.

Before I could muster a response, his firm hand clamped on my shoulder, guiding me forcibly toward his study. The room felt as cold and formal as his greeting. Serah and Elara were already there, seated like jurors in a trial I didn't know I was facing. Their expressions—a cocktail of concern and frustration—only tightened the knot in my stomach.

Banar closed the door with a solemn thud and faced me squarely, wasting no time. "This tension between you two is senseless," he began, his voice firm, echoing off the study's austere walls. "You're both here for the same purpose—to be of use in our fight against the Witch Queen."

His gaze was unwavering, and I felt the weight of his disappointment. I looked towards Serah; her eyes were cast down, unable to meet mine, her fingers nervously twisting a strand of hair. Beside her, Elara's face was etched with concern, her hands clasped tightly in her lap.

Banar's voice brought me back. "Serah's training as a witch is just as vital as your swordplay. The song... it's something that affects everyone differently. Even without Resonance, it induces fear."

I looked at him, curiosity piqued. "You've felt it too?"

Banar nodded, his expression serious. "It took me a long time to not fear the song. It can be mastered, but it requires more than just strength. It takes time, control, and resilience."

"Is that even possible?" I asked, the disbelief clear in my voice.

Banar's lips curved into a knowing smile. "You'll see. For now, we need her power just as much as we need yours."

Those words ignited a storm of resentment and a sharp spike of curiosity within me. Lucas's lessons echoed in my mind, his talks about the diverse manifestations of power. Silence engulfed me as the room's tense atmosphere seemed to constrict tighter around us. Understanding Banar's rationale did nothing to soothe the raw, seething anger festering within me—the witches' magic hadn't just touched my life; it had ravaged my village, massacred those I loved. This burning desire for vengeance solidified my resolve, painting my perception of all witches with a broad, unforgiving stroke. Yet, somewhere deep, a reluctant part of me acknowledged that Serah, despite her training, did not belong to the same nightmares from my past..

Somewhere deep within me, the seldom-heard voice that lurked in the shadows of my mind found a moment to speak, its tone dripping with dark satisfaction. *Good,* it whispered, a sibilant echo in the confines of my skull.

I nodded slowly, my acknowledgment directed more inward than to the expectant faces before me. "I understand," I spoke, my voice low and grudgingly resigned. "It's necessary, even if I don't fully embrace it."

Banar's expression softened slightly, as if a formidable barrier had been partially dismantled. "Good," he said, a trace of relief in his voice. "Elara suggested that Serah teach you to play Skirmish, Karn. You've shown an interest, after all."

I felt a twinge of annoyance at the idea of spending more time with Serah, but I couldn't deny the appeal of the game. "I already know how to play," I admitted, my voice steady. "I've been learning from a merchant in town."

Banar raised an eyebrow, intrigued. "Is that so? Well then, let's see what you've learned." He motioned to a table already set up with the game board and pieces. "Why don't you and Serah have a match?"

Serah's eyes narrowed, but she nodded, moving to the table with a determined air. I joined her, my hands grew steady as I began arranging my pieces. The weight of our earlier conflicts hung between us, but the familiar challenge of Skirmish brought a strange sense of calm.

We started the game in silence, the only sounds were the soft clicks of wooden pieces as they moved across the board. Serah's strategy was aggressive, pushing her knights and archers forward with precision. I countered with a more defensive approach, fortifying my flag with earthworks and placing my cavalry in strategic positions.

The tension in the room shifted as we played, our focus narrowing to the game. Each move became a conversation, a challenge met with a counter, a threat neutralised with a careful defence.

"Not bad," Serah murmured as I captured one of her knights with an archer, her voice holding a grudging respect.

"Thanks," I replied, a small smile tugging at my lips. "You're not too bad yourself."

The game drew on, each of us pressing forward, adapting to the other's tactics. In the end, it was a stalemate—neither of us could make a legal move without risking our flag. We sat back, breathless and frustrated, but there was a sense of mutual respect.

"Draw," Banar announced, a hint of pride in his voice. "Well done, both of you."

I turned to Serah, the words forming before I could stop them. "I'm sorry," I said quietly. "For avoiding you, for the tension."

Serah met my gaze, her expression softening. "I'm sorry too," she replied, her voice sincere. "Let's start over."

Banar nodded approvingly. "Each night after supper, we'll all play. It's good for strategy, and it'll help you two work together."

I glanced at Serah, feeling the weight of our shared past lift, if only just a bit. The road ahead was still fraught with challenges, but for the first time in days, I felt a flicker of hope. "Agreed," I said, it felt like a step forward.

Chapter 11 - The Hunt

The morning air was brisk as I splashed cold water on my face, feeling it shock the sleep from my eyes. I dressed quickly, the fabric of my shirt pulling tight across my shoulders—a reminder that my new set of clothes couldn't come soon enough. As I buckled the belt around my waist, I lifted the weighty, blunted sword Banar had insisted I carry. It was more a slab of iron than a weapon, cumbersome and dull, designed to make a true sword feel like a feather when the time came. It was like training with stones in your pockets, only to find yourself bounding across the fields once they were removed.

Two years had sharpened me in more ways than one. I had grown, not just in stature but in spirit. The door creaked as I pulled it open, and there was Serah, striding down the hallway. Time had stretched her too, pulled her up past my own height, which irked me more than I cared to admit. We were the same age, but she was just days away from her sixteenth name day.

She had a striking presence, with dark, piercing eyes that seemed to see right through me. Her long, black hair fell in waves over her shoulders, contrasting sharply with her pale skin. The coldness, the guardedness that once made me wary, was still there but had softened slightly with time. Yet, as we locked eyes, there was an understanding—a shared journey in the countless hours of training that had forged between us a bond as strong as steel.

"Morning, Karn," she called out, a smirk tugging at the corners of her lips, fully aware of our silent race to see who could pluck the highest apples.

"Morning," I grumbled back, adjusting the sword at my side as I fell into step beside her. "Banar wants to see us in his study," Serah said, her tone a mix of curiosity and annoyance. "Sent me to come get you."

"Of course he did," I replied with a sigh, falling into step beside her. "Any idea what he wants?"

"Maybe to tell you how bad you still are with that oversized club you call a sword," she teased, the smirk still tugging at her lips.

"Very funny," I shot back, rolling my eyes. "At least I don't sing like a dying cat."

She snorted. "My singing improved, thank you very much. Besides, Banar says it's crucial for my training."

"Yeah, well, it's crucial for my headaches too," I muttered, earning a chuckle from her.

We walked down the hallway, the corridor seemed smaller now, the tapestries less grand. The patterns and colours were still intricate, but they didn't hold the same awe.

"So, do you think it's about another training exercise?" Serah asked, glancing at me.

"Probably," I replied. "Or maybe he's finally going to tell us what we've been training for."

"Wouldn't that be nice," she said dryly.

We reached Banar's study, the door ajar. Inside, Banar stood by the window, the morning light casting a halo around him. He turned as we entered wearing a knowing smile.

"Good, you're both here. No training today," he began, his tone serious but warm. "You've both come a long way, and it's time to put you to the test."

Serah raised an eyebrow, her curiosity piqued. "And what grand test do you have for us, Father?"

He crossed his arms, leaning against the desk. "There have been signs of game going missing in the forest. The local hunters are blaming the deviants. I want you two to track it down."

Serah's sarcasm was sharp. "If the local gamekeeper can't find it, how do you expect us to?"

Banar's expression didn't waver. "The gamekeeper's son will be joining you. He's in training too. Consider it a test for all of you."

I glanced at Serah, seeing the same mix of doubt and excitement in her eyes. This was more than just a task; it was a chance to prove ourselves.

"Karn," Banar said, his tone growing serious, "you must keep your abilities under wraps. The apprentice hunter must not find out about you. Understood?"

I nodded. "Understood."

Serah's eyebrows knitted together, but she said nothing. She had yet to learn anything of resonance, her training still focused on combat and that infernal singing. It was a small comfort to me, though I still couldn't stand the sound.

"All right," Banar said, clapping his hands together. "Get your gear and meet in the courtyard. The gamekeeper and his son are waiting."

As we left the study, I felt the weight of the task ahead settle over me, heavier than the blunt sword at my side. This was more than just a hunt—it was a test of everything we'd been training for.

"So," Serah said, breaking the silence as we walked. "Ready to play the hero and save the day?"

I snorted. "I just hope I don't trip over my own feet."

"Don't worry," she said with a grin. "I'll be there to pick you up."

Banar led us to the courtyard where the morning sun cast long shadows over the cobblestones. The gamekeeper stood there, a tall man with bright blonde hair that seemed almost white in the sunlight. Beside him was his son, who shared his father's striking hair but had a youthful, eager look in his eyes. He was a bit older than Serah and me, his frame lean and athletic, a bow slung casually over his shoulder.

Banar gestured toward us. "Karn, Serah, meet Fynn."

"Thank you Lord Fayle," the young man said bowing to Banar and then turned to us. "Pleasure," Fynn said, his eyes lingering on Serah with a smile that was just a bit too charming. "Looking forward to working with you."

"Likewise," Serah replied, her tone light but not dismissive. I watched them interact, a strange mix of jealousy and protectiveness stirred within me. Was he flirting? And why did it bother me so much? Serah was my adopted sister, wasn't she?

Banar handed me a short sword to replace my weighted training blade. It felt balanced and sharp in my hand, the hilt wrapped in leather for a firm grip. The blade gleamed with a cold, efficient edge.

Serah was given a long stave, sturdy and worn, perfect for close combat. She twirled it experimentally, nodding in satisfaction. Fynn, already equipped with his bow and a dagger at his side, seemed ready for anything.

"Remember, Karn," Banar said, his voice low and serious, "keep your abilities under wraps. No one must know."

I nodded, gripping the sword tighter. "Understood."

We said our goodbyes, Banar's eyes lingering on us with a mix of pride and worry. As we turned to leave, Fynn fell into step beside Serah, his easy smile never faltering.

"So, Serah," he began, his tone casual, "ever been on a real hunt before?"

"Plenty of times," she replied with a hint of a smirk. "But never with someone who looks like they belong on a tapestry."

Fynn laughed, a sound that grated on my nerves more than it should have. "I'll take that as a compliment."

Fynn led the way with an air of confidence, the underbrush

crunching under his boots as he moved through the forest. He chatted easily with Serah, his tone light and playful, while occasionally throwing a comment my way. Mostly, though, he seemed to enjoy making Serah laugh, and it irked me more than I cared to admit.

"So, Serah," Fynn said, flashing her a grin, "what's the most dangerous thing you've ever fought?"

She smirked. "You're looking at him."

Fynn laughed, the sound echoed through the trees. "Well, I hope you don't need to save me from anything more dangerous than Karn."

"Shouldn't we be quiet during a hunt?" I said not being able to help myself.

Fynn chuckled, not missing a beat. "We need to find where the creature is first. To do that, we look for its last kill."

Half a day passed in a blur of foliage and shadows. The sheer expanse of the land amazed me. It was vast, stretching far beyond what I had imagined. Banar's domain was immense, each step revealing more of the responsibility he carried. The deeper we went, the thicker the forest became, the air heavy with the scent of pine and earth.

Eventually, we stumbled upon a grisly scene—a deer, its carcass torn apart. Fynn knelt by the remains, his expression serious. "Strange," he muttered, examining the wounds. "It could be one creature, but I've heard deviants can work together as a pack."

Serah's brow furrowed. "You mean, more than one might be hunting together?"

Fynn nodded, standing up. "It's possible. We need to be careful."

We continued our trek, the forest grew dense, the light dimmed as the sun dipped lower. The underbrush thickened, branches clawing at our clothes as we pushed forward. The air was cool, filled with the earthy scent of damp leaves and pine.

Suddenly, Fynn froze, his eyes narrowed as he scanned the ground. He moved with a predator's grace, his bow coming up in a fluid motion. I followed his gaze and spotted a rabbit, its ears twitching nervously. Fynn released his arrow, the shaft cutting through the air with a soft whistle before striking its target with a quiet thud.

"Dinner," he announced with a satisfied grin, his eyes gleaming with pride.

Serah, who had been watching closely, nodded appreciatively. "Nice shot," she said, her tone genuinely impressed.

Fynn's grin widened. "Thanks. Years of practice, you know." He retrieved the rabbit with swift, practised movements, and slung it over his shoulder. "We'll eat well tonight."

We carried on, the forest growing darker as the sun continued to sink. The shadows lengthened, casting eerie shapes across our path. The canopy overhead thickened, blotting out the last of the twilight. The sense of isolation deepened, every rustle and snap of a twig echoed ominously in the stillness.

Eventually, Fynn found a suitable spot to make camp, a small clearing surrounded by dense trees. The air was cooler here, the smell of pine mingling with the scent of the damp earth. As we set up camp, the sky turned a deep indigo, the first stars peek through the gaps in the foliage.

I gathered firewood, the rough bark bit into my hands. The rhythmic thud of wood splitting was a comforting, steady sound. Serah set up the tents and I smiled to myself as I saw her patience wane as she fiddled with the poles. Fynn, meanwhile, worked on preparing the rabbit, his hands moving deftly as he skinned and cleaned it.

Serah watched him for a moment, then smiled. "Looks like you've done this a few times."

Fynn chuckled, his eyes meeting hers. "More times than I can count. My father always said a good hunter respects the land and the life it gives. Preparing the game is just as important as the hunt."

As he worked, Fynn glanced up at Serah, a playful glint in his eyes. "You ever skinned an animal before, Serah?"

She shook her head, her expression thoughtful. "No, can't say I have. Seems like it requires a lot of skill and patience."

Fynn nodded, his tone becoming more serious. "It does. But it's also about understanding the animal, knowing where to make the cuts, and being ready to handle the mess."

Serah raised an eyebrow, a hint of a smile playing on her lips. "Handling the mess, huh? Sounds like a job for someone else."

Fynn chuckled, shaking his head. "It's all part of the process. You'd be surprised how much you can learn from it."

Karn, listening to their banter, couldn't help but feel a twinge of annoyance mixed with curiosity. "So, you're saying there's more to hunting than just shooting and hoping for the best?"

Fynn grinned, finishing his task. "Exactly. It's about respect for the animal and the land. Maybe one day you'll give it a try, Karn. It might teach you a thing or two."

As the rabbit roasted over the fire, its aroma filled the clearing, mingling with the crisp night air. The fire crackled and popped, casting flickering shadows on our faces. We sat around the fire, the rabbit stew bubbling in a pot, its aroma mixed with the smoky scent of burning wood. The warmth of the fire contrasted with the cool night air, wrapping us in a cocoon of light and heat. The stew tasted rich and gamey but edible none the less.

"So, do you play Skirmish?" I asked Fynn, trying to stir the conversation towards something familiar and comforting.

Fynn snorted, shaking his head. "Childish games. Out here, it's real skills that matter. Tracking, hunting, surviving. Not pushing pieces around a board."

His dismissive tone irked me, but I bit my tongue. "It's more than that," I muttered, mostly to myself. "It's strategy."

Serah threw me a sympathetic glance but didn't comment. The conversation drifted to other topics—local gossip, recent hunts, and the latest news from nearby villages. I stayed mostly quiet, lost in my thoughts, the firelight flickering in my eyes.

As the night deepened, we retreated to our tents. Fynn and I shared one, Serah in another. The sounds of the forest crept in, rustling leaves and distant animal calls, creating an eerie backdrop to the night.

Sometime later, I heard Fynn stirring. His movements were stealthy, but I wasn't asleep. I grabbed his arm as he tried to slip out. "Where are you going?"

He scowled, yanking his arm free. "For a piss, Karn. Or do you need to come hold it for me?"

I sighed, letting him go. My suspicion gnawed at me, but I lay back down, staring at the tent ceiling. Moments later, I heard a scuffle, a hushed commotion outside. I tensed, ready to leap up, but then I heard Fynn's voice, low and apologetic. Whatever had happened, it didn't seem urgent. Sareh could handle herself. I closed my eyes, trying to force sleep.

My dreams were vivid, unsettling. A wolf with crimson fur prowled through my snowy mountain home, each paw print it left behind blossoming into a pool of blood, staining the pristine snow. Its eyes glowed with a fierce, knowing light, and its presence filled me with a strange mix of fear and anger.

I saw the familiar faces of my past—my mother, her gentle eyes now wide with terror; Liv, my sister, clutching her doll as she backed away from the spreading blood; Torin, the mischievous boy always up for an adventure, now frozen in fear; and Harlan, the blacksmith's son, his hands usually so steady, now trembling. The wolf's blood-red fur seemed to ripple and shimmer in the moonlight, its gaze piercing through the cold night, locking onto mine with a predatory intensity.

Every step it took was deliberate, each pawprint a reminder of the carnage that had torn through our village. The snow, once a symbol of purity and peace, was now a canvas of horror. The air was thick with the metallic scent of blood, mingling with the crisp, cold air of the mountains. The wolf's growl reverberated through the stillness, a sound that spoke of untold destruction and a promise of more to come.

I woke with a start, the images still fresh in my mind. The tent was empty. I crawled out, the early morning light cast long shadows across the camp. Serah and Fynn were by the fire, preparing breakfast. Fynn looked sheepish, a fresh black eye marring his face.

I couldn't help but smile. Walking over to Serah, I asked, "Sleep well?"

She shot me a wry grin. "Better than some, it seems."

I chuckled, glancing at Fynn. "Looks like you had a rough night."

Fynn muttered something under his breath, his gaze avoiding mine. Serah's eyes twinkled with mischief as she stirred the pot.

We packed up camp, the morning air still cool and crisp. My breath fogged in front of me, each exhale a reminder of the chill that clung to the forest. The memory of the crimson wolf was vivid and unsettling, its presence a dark shadow in my mind. Every step I took felt charged, as if the dream had ignited something deep within me, a simmering energy that I couldn't shake.

We moved through the forest, Fynn leading the way with a hunter's confidence. The ground was damp with dew, and the forest floor was a mosaic of fallen leaves and tangled roots. Fynn paused, crouching to examine some tracks, his fingers brushed lightly over the disturbed earth. "More dead game," he murmured, his eyes narrowing in concentration.

We followed the trail, winding deeper into the woods. The trees loomed tall around us, their branches forming a dense canopy that filtered the sunlight into dappled patterns on the ground. Suddenly, Fynn motioned for us to hide. We ducked into a thick bush, peering through the foliage with bated breath.

Three men stood in a clearing, their rough clothing and furtive glances marked them as outlaws. Their faces were weathered, hardened by a life of taking what wasn't theirs. "Poachers," Fynn hissed, his voice barely a whisper.

Serah frowned, her brows knitting together in concern. "We should return to Lord Fayle and get his guard."

Fynn shook his head, a glint of determination in his eyes. "We can take them."

Surprisingly, I found myself agreeing, the thought of a fight stirred a dark excitement within me. "Yeah, let's do it."

But Serah's voice cut through my eagerness, sharp and decisive. "No, it's too risky. We need to be smart about this."

As we began to retreat, a twig snapped underfoot. The sharp crack echoed in the quiet forest, and one of the poachers' heads snapped up. "Who's there?" he barked, his voice rough and suspicious.

The poachers spotted us, their eyes narrowing as they recognized just who we were. "Young lordlings," one sneered, drawing a blade that glinted menacingly in the dim light. "We'll need to slit their throats, or they'll go running back to their lord and tattle on us."

The three men advanced, their intentions clear. We readied ourselves, the tension clear in the air. My heart pounded in my chest, the adrenaline surging through my veins. The thrill of combat, the promise of violence, surged through me once more. The fight erupted like a thunderclap. I drew my sword, the weight familiar and reassuring in my grip. One of the men notched an arrow and let it fly. It whistled past my ear, embedding itself in the tree behind me.

Fynn's bow twanged in response. His arrow found its mark, sinking into the arm of one of the poachers. The man howled in pain, clutching his bleeding limb. Fynn had no time to savour the hit; another man charged at him. He dropped his bow and pulled out his dagger, his face set in grim determination.

Serah sprang forward, her stave a blur as she aimed for the injured outlaw. Her movements were fluid, precise, her stave cracking against the man's ribs with a satisfying thud. The poacher stumbled back, his face contorted in pain.

That left me with the last one, a hulking brute with an axe. He swung wildly, the blade carving through the air with a menacing hiss. I danced back, easily evading his clumsy attacks. Each missed swing fueled my exhilaration.

He roared in frustration, swinging again with all his might. I sidestepped so the axe bit into the ground where I had stood moments before. His wild eyes locked onto mine, filled with rage and desperation. I knew those feelings.

I kept my movements controlled, measured, trying not to let the thrill of the fight consume me. The weight of my sword felt perfect, the balance just right. I ducked another swing, letting the blade glide past me harmlessly.

"You're too slow," I taunted, a smirk tugged at my lips like it was some kind of game.

He snarled, charging again. I waited until the last possible moment before stepping aside, tripping him with a swift kick to the back of his knee. He fell forward, crashing to the ground in a heap. I stood over him, my sword at the ready.

End him! The voice whispered.

He looked up, fear now mixed with the anger in his eyes. But I didn't strike. I kept my breathing steady, my grip firm. This was control. This was my fight.

Serah swung her stave with precision, taking down the injured man with a sharp crack to his head. "Lay down your arms!" she commanded, her voice strong and unyielding.

The poachers didn't listen. The injured man on the ground made a desperate move, lunging forward to trip Serah which sent her sprawling to the ground. I saw the momentary flash of panic in her eyes as the attacker jumped on top of her.

Enough playing around.

The man on his back in front of me grabbed his axe, swinging it up with renewed determination. I parried the blow with a swift motion, the clash of metal ringing in my ears. With a decisive thrust, I drove my sword through his chest, feeling the resistance give way as the blade sank deep. He gasped, eyes wide, then crumpled to the ground. My heart pounded, anger rising like a dark tide within me. I tried to control it, remembering the breathing exercises. Inhale, count to three. Exhale, count to three.

I turned, adrenaline surging, to see Serah kicking her attacker off with a powerful blow. Without thinking, I rushed forward, sword in hand, and impaled the man before he could regain his footing. His eyes went wide with shock, then glazed over as he collapsed.

Serah stared at me, breathless. "Why did you do that?"

For a moment, I was frozen, the reality crashed over me like a tidal wave. This wasn't training. I had killed a man. No, two men. The blood pooled on the ground, eerily similar to the crimson in my dreams. My breath hitched, and I felt a strange mix of horror and grim satisfaction.

My anger still simmered, threatening to boil over. I closed my eyes, forcing myself to breathe again. Inhale, count to three. Exhale, count to three. The anger ebbed slightly, replaced by a hollow feeling in my chest.

A shout pulled me from my daze. Fynn was still locked in combat, both he and his opponent sporting fresh wounds. The remaining poacher, seeing his comrades fallen, hesitated. With three of us against him, he dropped his weapon and raised his hands in surrender.

"I give up," he muttered.

"Bind him," Serah ordered, her voice steady despite the chaos.

I took the rope from my pack, my hands trembling as I tied the man's hands behind his back. His rough breathing matched my own, both of us acutely aware of the blood-soaked ground beneath our feet. The fight was over, but the memory of it lingered, searing itself into my mind. I glanced at Serah, her expression unreadable, and felt a pang of regret.

The voice inside me murmured its approval, a dark whisper that I tried to silence with more breaths. Inhale, count to three. Exhale, count to three. The anger was a part of me, but I would not let it control me. Not now, not ever.

We walked back through the forest in a heavy silence, the weight of the day pressed down on us. Each step felt like a lifetime, and my thoughts circled around the men I had killed. The vivid image of their lifeless bodies, the blood pooling on the ground, stayed with me, gnawing at the edges of my mind.

When we reached the manor, I noticed a second carriage next to Banar's, more horses tethered at the stable. It seemed we had visitors, but I pushed the thought aside, focusing on the task at hand.

We brought the captured poacher to Banar and the Gameskeeper. The man, now resigned, admitted freely to their poaching activities. "We've been at it for a while," he muttered, eyes downcast.

Banar turned to Fynn, his eyes probing. "What about the deviant? Any sign of it?"

Fynn shook his head. "No, my lord. I think it was the poachers all along, spreading fear to keep the hunters at bay."

I knew that wasn't the truth; for Serah and I had fought off the deviant two years ago but I kept quiet about it, so did Serah.

The Gameskeeper's face was etched with guilt. "My lord, I apologise. I should have seen them, should have stopped them."

Banar shook his head, his expression stern but not unkind. "There's no need for apologies. They've been dealt with, and that's what matters."

He turned to Fynn, a rare smile breaking through his usual stern demeanour. "You did well, Fynn. You'll make a fine hunter."

Fynn straightened, pride evident in his stance. "Thank you, my lord, I am honoured."

Fynn turned to us, a hint of a smile playing on his lips. "Goodbye, Karn. Serah. Thanks for the adventure."

He shifted awkwardly, glancing at Serah. "Serah, about last night—"

Serah cut him off, her tone light but firm. "Don't worry about it, Fynn. It's forgotten."

Relieved, Fynn nodded. "Karn, you fight well."

"You too," I nodded back, but my mind was still tangled with the images of the men I had killed. The weight of those deaths clung to me, a dark cloud that I couldn't shake.

Fynn gave a nod to his father, and together they headed off, the weight of their future resting on Fynn's shoulders.

Banar watched them go, then turned to us. "You both did a good job," he said, his voice steady. "Now, come to my study. We have a visitor."

I wanted to talk to him about what had happened in the forest—the killing, the blood, the way it had all felt too real. But Banar was already striding away, his steps quick and purposeful. "Banar, wait," I called out, my voice a little too desperate.

He didn't slow down, just looked back briefly. "We'll talk later, Karn. This is important."

Frustration and confusion gnawed at me as we hurried through the halls. Serah shot me a glance, her expression unreadable.

When we reached the study, Banar pushed the door open, and there, sitting in the chair, was Lord Caine. His presence filled the room, a mix of authority and something darker, something that made my skin prickle.

Lord Caine looked up, his eyes pierced through the dim light, thought me.

Chapter 12 - Preparations and Promises

Lord Caine sat in Banar's chair, his salt-and-peppered hair adding to the sternness of his strong features. His eyes, piercing and cold, seemed to see right through us. I felt a chill run down my spine as he turned his gaze on me and Serah.

"I'm surprised by how much you've both grown," he said, his tone as sharp as his features. His eyes lingered on Serah. "Especially you, Serah. You're taking after your father."

I noticed she stiffened at the mention of her father. "Yes, my Lord," she replied, her voice respectful and subdued. It was strange to hear her speak this way, especially when she never used that title for Banar.

Lord Caine shifted his gaze to me, his expression unreadable. "I understand you took on a challenge recently? Hunting a deviant, a Caracal, was it?"

I nodded, swallowing hard. "Yes, though we didn't find it. It has the ability to hide in shadows."

He leaned back in the chair, fingers steepled. "Do you know what deviant are?"

I hesitated before answering. "Animals that have turned into monsters?"

He shook his head slowly, a hint of a smile on his lips. "No, creatures that have learned to use Resonance. A normal Caracal cannot hide itself, but a deviant uses Resonance to do it. Like a person. Interesting, right?" His eyes glinted with a hint of dark amusement. "You'll find out more in the future, I hope, from experts much more knowledgeable than I."

I took a deep breath, forcing the words out. "We didn't find the deviants. Instead, we found poachers. I... I killed two of them."

The room seemed to close in around me as I spoke. Banar, always the steady rock, looked genuinely shocked.

Serah averted her eyes, her usual bravado gone. Lord Caine, however, remained impassive, his gaze fixed on me. "Your first kill?" he asked, almost clinically. "Did you hide your abilities?"

I nodded, a knot tightening in my stomach. Two men dead, and all he cared about was the secret. "Yes, my Lord."

"Good," Lord Caine said, his tone approving. "You've progressed well in your training, both of you. It is time to put that to good use."

At this, both Serah and I perked up, curiosity and a bit of dread mixing in my gut. Banar, however, stepped forward, his face a mask of concern. "They still need more time to train, my Lord. The time isn't right."

Lord Caine's eyes flashed, silencing Banar with a look. "The Witch Queen is on the move. Now is the right time. They've had plenty of training, and their recent success proves it."

I swallowed hard, forcing the words out. "What do you want from us?"

Lord Caine's gaze shifted between us, his voice unwavering and calm, an icy edge to his words. "In a few days, you will travel to just outside of Dúnmara and join The Forge. It's the only academy in Eirithia where both lords and common soldiers train to become officers in the Witch Queen's army."

I felt my jaw drop. Serah, beside me, looked equally stunned. I'd never heard of The Forge before, and the name alone conjured images of fire, steel, and relentless training.

Banar stepped forward again, concern deepened the lines on his face. "My Lord, they still need more time. They aren't ready."

Lord Caine cut him off with a sharp glance. "Quiet, my friend. Both you and I attended at a younger age. They are ready." His tone was calm, collected, and carried an air of deadly certainty that sent a shiver down my spine.

"But we had more training," Banar insisted, his voice edged with desperation.

Caine dismissed Banar's concern with a wave of his hand, the gesture as dismissive as it was final. "They are ready," he repeated, turning his piercing gaze on us. "Aren't you?"

Serah, to my surprise, nodded immediately, her eyes burning with determination. I found myself nodding as well, though my mind raced with doubts and questions. If Serah believed we were ready, maybe we were.

Banar's shoulders slumped, a sign of his resignation. He gave a reluctant nod, stepping back into the shadow of Caine's authority.

Lord Caine's expression softened just a fraction. "Good. You will both do well. Prepare yourselves. This is the path to reclaiming what has been lost. This is the beginning of our revenge."

His words hung in the air, heavy with promise and foreboding. The room seemed to grow colder, the weight of our future pressed down on my shoulders. Caine's presence was like a storm on the horizon—unavoidable, unstoppable, and fraught with danger. As I looked into his eyes, I saw a depth of resolve and a chilling readiness to do whatever it took to achieve his goals. It made my blood run cold, yet ignited a fire within me at the same time.

We had to be ready.

Lord Caine stood, moving with a fluid grace that belied his age. He picked up a small, ornate box from Banar's desk and handed it to Serah. "It's your name's day in a few days, right? This is for you. Wear it well."

Serah took the box, her fingers trembling. She opened it to reveal a dark cloak adorned with the emblem of House Fayle—a silver set of stag antlers surrounded by stars. The fabric shimmered under the room's dim light, catching the flicker of the candles.

"Thank you, my Lord," Serah said, her voice steady but her eyes glistening with a mix of pride and emotion.

Caine nodded, his gaze shifting between us. "After your name's day, you and Karn will travel to the capital and enrol. Serah, you will finally become a resonance user. I'll expect written reports on the process. I need to know more about it."

Serah's eyes widened slightly, but she nodded, determination replacing her surprise.

"Karn," Caine continued, turning his piercing gaze on me. "Your job is to rise through the ranks and become an officer. Eventually, an officer in the Black Guard, like Banar and I. Those who guard the witches. It's not guaranteed, and you'll have to work for it."

I swallowed hard, the weight of his words settling heavily on my shoulders. "I understand, my Lord."

"Also," Caine added, his tone dropping to a deadly seriousness, "I expect you to keep those red eyes of yours in check and hidden. No one must know. Understand?"

I nodded, feeling the gravity of his command. "Yes, my Lord."

Caine's eyes bore into mine, searching for any sign of doubt. "Do you think you're up to the task?" he asked, his voice cold and unyielding.

"I am," I replied, my voice firm.

"So am I," Serah added, her voice strong and clear.

"Good," Caine said, a thin smile curved his lips. "Then we will have our revenge. Leave us now. Your adopted father and I have much to discuss."

Banar stepped forward, placing a hand on each of our shoulders. "I'll speak to both of you later," he said, his voice warm but edged with a hint of sadness.

We nodded and turned to leave, burdened with new responsibilities that we did not know the full extent of, yet. As we walked down the hallway, I felt a mix of emotions—fear, determination, and a burning desire for vengeance. This was just the beginning.

We left the study, the heavy door closing behind us with a definitive thud. The hallway stretched before us, dimly lit by torches mounted on the walls. Our footsteps echoed in the silence, a stark contrast to the storm of emotions that raged inside me. Each step felt heavier than the last, the weight of Lord Caine's words pressing down on me.

As we walked, the images of the dead men flashed in my mind—their lifeless eyes, the blood staining my hands. The reality of what I had done hit me like a wave, and I stumbled, my vision blurring with unshed tears. I stopped, unable to go any further, and felt the hot tears spill over, streaming down my cheeks.

Serah turned, her expression softening as she saw my distress. Without a word, she stepped closer, her arms encircling me. Her embrace was firm yet gentle, and she began to stroke my hair, her touch soothing. The comfort of her presence broke the dam inside me, and I sobbed against her shoulder, the anguish pouring out in broken murmurs.

"I killed them, Serah," I choked out between sobs. "I killed those men."

She held me tight, her voice a quiet murmur in my ear. "I'm here, Karn. It's going to be okay. You did what you had to do."

For a few moments, we stood like that, her presence grounding me as I let the tears flow. The hallway around us seemed to fade, the only reality was the grief and comfort shared between us.

Eventually, she pulled back, her hands resting on my shoulders. "We've got to stay strong, Karn. This is just the next step. We need to be strong to keep climbing."

I looked into her eyes, seeing the determination there, the resilience that had grown in her over the years. Her words resonated with me, pulling me back from the edge of despair. I nodded, wiping my face with the back of my hand. "You're right. We have to be strong."

Serah gave me a small, encouraging smile. "We're in this together. Always."

I managed a shaky smile in return, a newfound respect for her settling in my heart. We continued down the hallway, side by side, ready to face whatever came next.

Over the next few days, I threw myself into preparation, trying to distract my mind from the gnawing guilt of the killings. My new set of clothes arrived, fitting perfectly and giving me a semblance of the nobility I was supposed to embody. They were darker, with fine stitching and the emblem of House Fayle subtly embroidered on the cuffs. The fabric was sturdy yet comfortable, ready for both court and combat.

I sought out Banar one afternoon, the weight of my actions still heavy on my shoulders. He found me first, his expression softer than usual, but still holding that stern edge.

"Banar," I began, my voice trembling, "about what happened... those men..."

He placed a hand on my shoulder, his grip firm but reassuring. "Karn, you did what you had to do. They were poachers, breaking the law, and they attacked you. It was self-defence. The man we brought back will face justice. He will be hanged, but only after we return from the capital."

I was taken aback. "You're taking us there?"

A rare smile tugged at the corners of Banar's lips. "Technically, I am your father now. It's my duty to enrol you both. Besides, it's a significant step in your training."

I nodded, processing his words. Lord Caine had departed immediately after giving his orders. I had expected him to stay, at least for Serah's name day, but he left abruptly, leaving a strange tension in his wake.

Serah seemed unfazed by his departure, but I couldn't shake the feeling that there was more between them than she let on.

The days passed in a blur of packing and preparation. On one of those days I took a trip into Eldewood, hoping to find Lucas and explain why I wouldn't be able to continue our games of Skirmish. The barkeep, an older man with the ponytail, shook his head when I asked about Lucas.

"Haven't seen him in a while, lad. He comes and goes as he pleases, you know that, your lordship" the barkeep said with a shrug.

Disappointed, I left the tavern, feeling a pang of loss. Lucas had been a strange but intriguing presence in my life, and now, like many things, he was just another fleeting memory.

Back at the manor, the atmosphere was charged with anticipation. Serah's name day was approaching, and soon after, we would be leaving for the capital. The weight of our future responsibilities loomed large, but for now, we had a moment to breathe before the storm.

Serah's name day dawned bright and clear, the spring sun casting a warm, golden glow over the village below. We climbed the hill overlooking Eldewood, a blanket of wildflowers spread beneath our feet, painting the scene in vibrant hues of yellow, purple, and blue. The air was alive with the scent of blooming flora and the distant hum of bees.

We set up our picnic under a sprawling oak tree, its branches swayed gently in the breeze. Banar, Elara, Serah, and I sat on a large blanket, laden with food—fresh bread, cheese, fruits, and a pitcher of cool spring water. It was a simple but hearty feast, fitting for the occasion.

Banar was the first to present his gift. He handed Serah a long, slender package wrapped in cloth. Her eyes lit up as she unwrapped it to reveal a new stave, the metal caps gleaming in the sunlight.

"Thank you, Banar," she said, examining the weapon with a keen eye. "It's perfect."

Elara followed, handing Serah a beautifully decorated box. "Open it," she said, a knowing smile on her lips.

Serah lifted the lid to reveal a set of tarocchi cards, each card intricately illustrated with scenes of magic and mystery. She gasped, running her fingers lightly over the cards. "They're beautiful,."

"Let me show you how they work," Elara said, taking the cards and shuffling them with adept skill. "These are popular with the ladies of Dúnmara. Each card has a meaning and can tell a story about your future."

I watched as Elara dealt out a few cards. "This one," Elara pointed to a card depicting a woman with a sword, "is the Lady of Blades. She represents strength and determination. And this one," she flipped over another card showing a moonlit forest, "is the Enchanted Woods, symbolising mystery and the unknown."

Serah's eyes sparkled with fascination. "What about this one?" she asked, picking up a card that showed a bird of flame rising from the ashes of a fire.

"Ah, the Phoenix," Elara said with a nod. "It stands for rebirth and transformation. A powerful symbol."

"Can you teach me to read them?" Serah asked eagerly.

138

"Of course," Elara replied, placing the cards back in Serah's hands. "It takes time, but you'll get the hang of it. Each card tells a part of a larger story, just like our lives."

Serah grinned. "I can't wait to start learning. Thank you, Mother."

Elara smiled warmly. "You're welcome, Serah. I thought you'd appreciate something that's both beautiful and meaningful."

I watched the exchange, feeling the warmth of their connection. The joy in Serah's eyes as she explored the cards was a welcome sight after the recent trials we'd faced. The moment felt peaceful, a calm before the storm of our upcoming journey.

Finally, it was my turn. I handed Serah a neatly bound book, its cover plain but sturdy, with a touch of elegance in the simplicity.

"Happy name day, Serah," I said, a hint of anticipation in my voice.

She took the book, her fingers tracing the edges before she opened it and read the title aloud, "The Seeker's Guide." She looked up, eyes wide. "You wrote this for me?"

I chuckled. "Well I commissioned it, Onora,did the work. But it means a lot to me, so I thought you might appreciate it too."

Serah's expression softened, a mix of surprise and gratitude playing across her features. "This is... unexpected, Karn. Thank you."

I smirked, trying to lighten the moment. "Maybe it'll cool your temper too."

She shot me a playful glare. "I'll remember that next time you need a sparring partner."

We both laughed. It felt good to share something personal with her, something that represented the growth we'd both experienced.

We all laughed, the tension of the past few days melting away in the warmth of our shared celebration. As the day wore on, we ate, talked, and basked in the simple joy of each other's company. The sun began to set, casting a fiery glow over the horizon. The sky blazed with shades of orange, pink, and purple, a breathtaking backdrop to our little gathering.

As the last light of day faded, we sat in comfortable silence, watching the stars emerge one by one. Serah's laughter still echoed in my ears, and I felt a sense of peace, knowing we were all together, if only for a brief moment longer. On the morrow', we would begin the next step of our adventure, but tonight, we celebrated Serah turning sixteen, marking the end of one chapter and the beginning of another.

Chapter 13 - Brightridge

I stepped out of the manor, the morning air crisp, it felt refreshing like a new beginning. Banar's carriage stood out front, sturdy and practical. It's dark wood was polished but not ornate, reflecting Banar's status as a minor lord. Two guards, enlisted from the local militia, flanked the carriage. They wore simple leather armour, their spears resting against the side of the wagon. Banar couldn't afford actual guards of his own; he relied on the town's garrison when needed.

I dragged my trunk over, the wooden wheels of the wagon creaking under the weight as a servant hoisted it into the back. As I watched the guards, a thought crossed my mind. Could I take them in a fight? They didn't have the same rigorous training Serah and I had undergone, but they had experience. Or did they? Banar had mentioned that the militia fought for the Witch Queen when the armies were mustered, but I had never seen them in action. Their rough demeanour suggested some level of combat readiness, but appearances could be deceiving. The boldness of youth had me thinking, I could take them.

Serah emerged next, a rare smile lit up her face. She practically radiated excitement, an unusual sight. "What's got you so chipper?" I asked, unable to hide my curiosity.

She rolled her eyes, but the smile didn't fade. "Getting away from Eldewood, finally. Doesn't travel excite you?"

I paused, the question lingered in my mind. Travel? It wasn't something I had considered much. My focus had been singular: training, revenge, all that good stuff. But then I thought of Lucas and his stories. The tales he told of distant places and different people had ignited a flicker of curiosity in me. What would it be like to see the world beyond Eldewood? "I suppose it could be interesting," I admitted, thinking back to those conversations with Lucas.

She nodded, a rare sincerity in her eyes. "Trust me, there's a whole world out there."

Banar stepped out of the manor, flanked by two servants. His appearance was as impeccable as ever—clean-shaven, with a crisp tunic and boots polished to a shine. There was no hint of the disapproval I suspected he harboured about Lord Caine's decision to send us to The Forge. His expression was composed, betraying nothing.

"Ready for the journey?" Banar asked, his voice carrying the weight of authority mixed with a hint of encouragement.

Serah and I both nodded, the anticipation of the unknown tightening in my chest. "Yes," we answered in unison.

"Good. Go saddle up the horses, and we'll be on our way," Banar instructed, turning to check the straps on the carriage.

Serah headed off towards the stables to get Sable, her steps light with the excitement she tried to mask. I hesitated, looking at Banar. "But I don't have a horse. I've just been riding Granite."

Banar's smile broadened, a rare flash of mischief in his eyes. "Go look."

My curiosity turned into excitement, and I bolted toward the stables, barely noticing Serah's amused glance as I passed her. Inside the stable, the familiar scent of hay and leather filled the air. My eyes scanned the stalls until they landed on a magnificent black stallion. The horse stood tall and proud, its coat gleamed like polished obsidian.

Banar and Serah followed me inside, watching my reaction.

Serah leaned against the stable door, her arms crossed, a smirk on her lips. "I convinced Banar it was time you had your own mount," she said. "You ride well enough now. Besides, you couldn't well be holding onto your father's waist all the way to the capital, could you?"

Her teasing made my cheeks flush, but I couldn't hide my grin. "He's... perfect."

Banar nodded approvingly. "He's a young stallion, strong and spirited. I expect you to take good care of him."

Serah added, "I wanted you to have more time to bond, but he only arrived yesterday."

Banar's tone was firm but kind. "This was all a bit unexpected. You'll need to name him."

I approached the stallion, feeling a connection form already. "I'll need a moment to think on it. You have to know an animal first to name it."

I took an apple from the feed box, offering my hand for the horse to smell before giving him the treat. The stallion eyed me warily at first but soon took the apple from my hand. Banar nodded in approval. "We'll meet you outside."

I saddled the horse, following the steps Serah had taught me. First, I brushed down his sleek coat as I talked to him in soothing tones to build trust. The horse's dark eyes watched me, gradually softening. I carefully checked the saddle blanket, ensuring there were no wrinkles that might cause discomfort. Lifting the saddle onto his back, I took my time adjusting the straps, making sure they were tight but not too constricting. Each buckle was fastened with precision, the methodical process calming my nerves.

Once I was done, I led the stallion outside, feeling a sense of pride and responsibility. The sunlight glinted off his glossy black coat as he pranced a little, testing his boundaries. I placed my foot in the stirrup and swung myself up, settling into the saddle. For a moment, he resisted, his muscles tensing under me. But I gently guided him with the reins, speaking softly. He settled, and I felt a rush of triumph. This was my horse, and together, we were ready for whatever lay ahead.

"Thought of a name?" Banar asked.

I thought for a moment, the name coming to me naturally. It reminded me of home, my own language but not to foreign that people would question it, I hoped. "Sköll."

Banar hesitated, then nodded. "A good name. Fitting."

With that, the servants climbed into the carriage; Banar and Serah mounted their horses, and the two militia men positioned themselves behind the wagon.

We set off with the horses at a slow walk, the carriage creaking behind us as it was pulled by two sturdy mules. The morning air was crisp, filled with the earthy scent of dew-soaked grass. We passed through Eldewood and hit the main road, mingling with travellers heading to and from the village.

As we rode, I couldn't help but admire the fields and rolling hills around us. The landscape was a patchwork of greens and golds, dotted with wildflowers swaying gently in the breeze.

"Enjoying the view?" Serah asked, her tone light but genuinely curious.

"Yeah," I replied, a bit wistfully. "I never had the chance when I first came to the manor, what with being tied up and thrown in the back of a wagon."

Banar laughed nervously, the memory clearly unsettled him, as it did me. "Well, it's good to see you appreciating it now," he said, and we all managed to share a laugh together.

We continued to ride slowly down the country roads, exchanging idle chatter. The odd merchant passed by, their wagons heavy with goods. The air was filled with the sounds of nature—birds chirping, leaves rustling, and the occasional distant call of a hawk. The farms and hamlets we passed were bustling with life, farmers tending to their fields and children playing near the edges of the forest. It was much different from my mountain home, especially in the full bloom of spring.

During the journey, I bonded more with Sköll. I petted his sleek black mane and talked to him in low, soothing tones, just as Serah had taught me. The stallion seemed to respond well, his ears flicking back to listen, his steps becoming more assured.

As the sun began to set, casting long shadows across the path, we reached the village of Brightridge. The dusk painted the sky in hues of orange and purple, a serene end to our day.

We entered the village and Banar led us toward the Brightridge Inn. The place exuded warmth, with golden lights glowing in the windows and the lively sound of music spilling out into the cobblestone street. The inn was a two-story building with a thatched roof and ivy that climbed up its stone walls, giving it a rustic charm that seemed to invite travellers in from the cold.

"Won't we be staying with the village's Lord?" I asked, curious about the change from the manor's usual accommodations.
Banar shook his head. "Most villages don't have Lords. The only reason I'm in Eldewood is because of my family's long history there. Tonight, we're staying at the inn."

We took the horses and carriage to the stables. The stablehand, a grizzled man with a weathered face and a kind smile, took the reins with a nod. Inside the inn, the air was thick with the scent of roasting meat and fresh bread, mixed with the tang of spilled ale. Laughter and music created a lively atmosphere, the sounds of a lute and a fiddle harmonising in a joyful tune.

Banar approached the barkeep, a burly man with a salt-and-pepper beard, speaking in low tones. He then turned to Serah and

I. "Find us a table, and get another one for the guards and servants."

The inn was packed, with people crowded around tables and a roaring fire in the large hearth casting a flickering glow across the room. It took some manoeuvring, but we managed to pull two tables close together without being too obvious. The patrons were a mix of villagers and travellers, their faces flushed with drink and cheer. Some were swaying to the music, while others engaged in animated conversations.

I scanned the room for anyone playing Skirmish, but to my disappointment, there was no sign of the game. Instead, the focus seemed to be on merrymaking and enjoying the evening.

We sat down, and Banar soon joined us with a look of mild irritation plain on his face. "Got us rooms for the night," he announced, his voice barely audible over the din. "But someone already booked the state room. The servants will have to sleep in the carriage, and the guards in the hay of the stables."

He sighed, taking a moment to let his annoyance fade. "Lively, isn't it?" Banar remarked, gesturing to the lively inn. The barkeep had already brought over a round of ales, frothy and inviting.

I nodded, taking in the scene. The inn's wooden beams were adorned with dried herbs and lanterns, casting a warm, inviting light. Serah was tapping her fingers to the rhythm of the music, a look of contentment on her face. The atmosphere was infectious, and despite the day's travel, I felt a surge of energy in the lively inn. The noise, the music, the smell of food—it all created a comforting cacophony that felt like a world away from the quiet corridors of the manor.

Not long after we had settled, a girl, of similar age to my own, came over, balancing seven mugs of ale spread between her two hands with an impressive ease. Her auburn hair was tied back in a loose ponytail, and she wore a low-cut blouse that revealed more than a hint of cleavage. Her figure was curvaceous and confident, and she moved with grace.

As she deposited a mug on the servants' table, I couldn't help but admire her... skill. When she came to our table, she gave me a warm smile, her green eyes twinkling with mischief. "Here you go, my lords and lady," she said, her gaze shifting to Serah. She handed me my mug with a cheeky wink that sent a wave of heat rushing to my cheeks.

Serah, always quick to notice, grinned. "Looks like someone's got an admirer," she teased, her voice low enough for only me to hear.
"Shut up," I muttered, trying to hide my embarrassment by taking a long drink of ale.

We continued to drink, the mood lightening with each passing moment. Banar leaned in, his voice carrying a note of seriousness. "We'll be on the road for a few days. Our next major stop is Ironhold, a larger town with a military garrison. It's owned by a different Warden than Lord Caine."
Serah frowned. "Isn't it strange that the garrison is on the border between their domains?"
Banar's eyes darted around the room before he replied, "Best not to talk about that here."

From the other table, I could hear the guardsmen boasting loudly about their exploits, their voices rising above the din. Their laughter was infectious, adding to the lively atmosphere of the inn.

As we settled into our seats, Banar took a deep breath and

began to speak. "The academy is not going to be easy. It's all about discipline, rigorous training, and pushing yourselves beyond your limits," he said, his tone serious.

Serah nodded, her attention fixed on Banar. "What kind of training are we talking about?"

"Physical, mental, and strategic," Banar replied. "You'll be tested in ways you can't even imagine."

I tried to focus, but my eyes kept drifting to the serving girl. She returned with bowls of stew, bread, and butter, placing them before us with a practised flourish. Her playful glances and subtle winks made it hard to keep my mind on the conversation.

Banar continued, "You'll need to be ready for anything. The instructors will push you hard. They'll expect nothing but the best."

Serah nudged me with her elbow, catching my wandering gaze. "Eyes on the prize, Karn," she whispered, smirking. "And I don't mean the ale."

I flushed, trying to refocus. "Yeah, yeah, I know. It's just... she's distracting."

Serah laughed softly. "Just wait until the academy. You'll have plenty of distractions there, too."

Banar cleared his throat, drawing both mine and Serah's attention back. "As I was saying, The Forge will demand everything from you. You'll need to work together, support each other, and rise to every challenge."

I nodded, forcing myself to concentrate. "Got it. Work hard, stay focused."

Serah added, "And don't let the distractions get to you."

Banar's expression softened a bit. "You'll both do fine. Just remember why you're there and what you're fighting for."

The serving girl passed by again, her smile lingering as she looked my way. I felt the heat rise in my cheeks, but this time I managed to keep my attention on Banar. "We're ready," I said, more to convince myself than anyone else.

Serah's eyes sparkled with a mix of amusement and determination. "Ready for anything."

I chuckled, trying to push the serving girl from my mind and refocus on the conversation at hand.

The ale kept coming, more than I was used too, and I could feel the heat of it coursing through my veins. The room seemed to grow louder, the clatter of mugs and laughter merging into a heady mix. I tried to keep up with the conversation, but my focus kept slipping, drawn away by the tavern's many diversions.

One such disturbed occurred at the servants' table. One of the militia guards from Eldewood was arm wrestling a burly villager. The tension was obvious, the table creaked under their strain.

Banar noticed too as his expression darkened, disappointment etched into his features. He rubbed his palm against his face in frustration. "This is not what we need right now," he muttered.

As Banar began to rise, the guard won, slamming the villager's hand down with a triumphant grin. The local blacksmith, his arms thick and muscular, looked furious. Without warning, he lunged at the guard, and the inn erupted into chaos.

I stood up, ready to intervene, but before I could move, a man in a familiar black coat and a red hat with a feather stepped between the two men. His presence seemed to defuse the situation instantly, the combatants backing down, their anger ebbing away.

I blinked in surprise. "Lucas?"

He turned, a smile spread across his face. "Well, well, if it isn't young Karn. Pleasant surprise to see you here. We haven't had a chance to play in a while."

Banar was already scolding his men, his voice a low growl. Meanwhile, I introduced Lucas to Serah. "Serah, this is Lucas, the travelling merchant I mentioned. Lucas, this is Serah."

Lucas gave Serah a charming bow, his smile never wavering. "A pleasure to meet you, Serah."

She returned his smile, her curiosity piqued. "Likewise, Lucas. Karn's told me about your games of Skirmish."

Lucas chuckled. "He's quite the quick learner. Perhaps we'll have a chance for another game soon."

"I'd like that. Why don't you join us, Lucas?" I suggested, motioning to the empty seat at our table. Lucas hesitated for a moment, his eyes flicking between Serah and me, then nodded, taking the seat with a casual grace.

As he settled in, I leaned closer, excitement bubbling up. "We're heading to Dúnmara, to join The Forge. It's a training academy."

Lucas's eyebrows shot up. "The Forge, huh? That place is legendary. Heard it's tough as nails."

Serah grinned, her eyes bright. "We're ready for it."

Lucas chuckled, a hint of admiration in his eyes. "I'm sure you both will do great. The Forge shapes strong leaders, apparently. Just keep your wits about you."

We continued to talk, the conversation flowing easily. Serah seemed to enjoy Lucas's company as much as I did, her laughter ringing out often. Lucas had a way of drawing people in, making them feel comfortable and at ease.

Banar returned, his expression serious but softening slightly as he saw us. "Everything's sorted," he said. Then he noticed Lucas. I gestured. "This is Lucas, Lucas, Lord Fayle,"

Banar waved his hand as if dismissing his title. "Just call me Banar," he said as he took his seat. Banar then extended his hand, his grip firm. "Thanks for settling that dispute earlier. Much appreciated."

Lucas took his hand, their grips firm, a silent challenge sparking between them. "No problem at all. I've got a knack for defusing situations. Besides, why ruin good ale over a petty squabble?"

Banar nodded his agreement.

I chimed in, eager to share. "Lucas taught me how to play Skirmish."

Banar raised an eyebrow. "Did he now?" He looked back at Lucas, a glint of curiosity in his eyes. "It's surprising I've never seen you in Eldewood."

Lucas shrugged, his smile easy. "As a peddler, I travel a lot. Not often in the company of lords."

Banar nodded. "Well, you managed to find time to play with one young lord. Fancy a game?"

A grin spread across Lucas's face, his eyes lit up with the challenge. "I'd love to."

Lucas produced his set of Skirmish pieces, the same set we had used, each one worn with use yet meticulously cared for. The board was placed on the table, and Lucas's hands moved swiftly, setting up the familiar grid. Banar watched intently, his eyes narrowing with interest.

They each chose their pieces, Lucas opting for the Spy, while Banar selected a special piece I hadn't seen before called the Sentinel from the collection Lucas held out. The game began with an intensity that drew the immediate attention of those around them.

"Been playing long?" Banar asked, moving his foot soldiers forward.

Lucas flashed a charming smile. "Long enough to know how to keep things interesting," he replied, advancing his knights with a flourish.

Banar's eyes glinted with a competitive spark. "We'll see about that."

As the game progressed, their strategies unfolded, each move calculated and deliberate. The room's atmosphere shifted, the lively chatter dimming as more patrons gathered to watch. The serving girl, her earlier flirtation with me now a distant memory, stood nearby, her attention captured by the unfolding battle.

I watched in awe, realising that both men were playing at a level I had never seen before. Their pieces danced across the board with precision and purpose.

Serah leaned in close, whispering, "Think they went easy on you?"

"Definitely," I muttered, my eyes glued to the board.

The tension built as the game neared its climax. Banar's forces pushed forward, cornering Lucas's defences. But Lucas, with a knowing smile, manoeuvred his Spy into position, executing a series of moves that left Banar's flag exposed.

With a final, decisive move, Lucas claimed victory. Banar leaned back, a mixture of surprise and admiration on his face. "Your Spy was well-played. I didn't see that coming."

Lucas nodded, his smile widening. "A little misdirection goes a long way, my friend. You played a strong game."

Banar signalled the barkeep. "Drinks are on me tonight, Lucas. You earned it."

Lucas inclined his head gracefully. "Thank you, Banar. But I must turn in. Long day of travelling ahead, and I wouldn't want to overstay my welcome." He turned to me and Serah, his eyes full of mirth. "It was a pleasure, truly. Until next time."

As he tipped his hat to the crowd and made his way upstairs, the room buzzed with whispers of his skill and, from some of the ladies, his charm. Enough to be envious of.

Banar, looking annoyed, turned to me and Serah. "Alright, you two, don't stay up too late. We have a long day's ride on the morrow'."

Serah and I stayed up, the warmth of the ale loosening our

tongues and lightening our spirits. We watched as first the servants and then the guards retired to their beds—or in the guards' case, the stables. The inn's lively atmosphere had mellowed, the music now a soft backdrop to the murmured conversations.

"So, Karn," Serah said, leaning back in her chair, a mischievous glint in her eye. "How does it feel to have a serving girl wink at you? Finally getting some attention from the fairer sex?"

I rolled my eyes, feeling the heat rise to my cheeks again. "Attention? Please. What about you? When did you become such an expert on men?"

She laughed, a genuine sound that echoed in the quieting room. "Touché. I guess neither of us is exactly winning any romantic battles."

We chuckled, the ease of our laughter dissolving any lingering tension from the day. We continued to talk, the conversation meandering from our upcoming journey to Dúnmara, to the game of Skirmish we had just witnessed, to memories of training under Banar's watchful eye.

"So," I said, my tone more serious, "do you think we're ready for the Forge?"

Serah looked thoughtful, swirling the ale in her mug. "Ready or not, we're going. And honestly, I'm excited. It's a chance to prove ourselves, to show what we're made of."

I nodded, feeling the same mixture of excitement and apprehension. "Yeah. It's a big step."

An awkward silence fell between us, our hands resting on the table. My fingers brushed against hers, a fleeting touch that sent a jolt through me. We both pulled back slightly, the moment stretching longer than it should have.

Serah cleared her throat, breaking the silence. "Well, we should probably get some sleep. Big day tomorrow."

"Yeah," I agreed, pushing back my chair. "You're right."

We stood, the weight of the day settling on our shoulders. As we headed towards our rooms, I glanced back at Serah, feeling a strange mix of emotions—gratitude for her friendship, admiration for her strength, and something else I couldn't quite define.

"Good night, Serah," I said, pausing at my door.

"Good night, Karn," she replied, her smile soft and genuine.

As I closed the door behind me, I couldn't help but feel that our journey together was just beginning, and whatever lay ahead, we would face it side by side.

Chapter 14 - On The Road

The next morning, I woke with a dull ache in my skull, the remnants of last night's ale lingering. I strapped on my sword, the familiar weight a grounding comfort. As I descended the creaking stairs of the inn, the common room bustled with activity. Banar, Serah, the servants, and the guards were already gathered around a table. The savoury aroma of bacon and bread wafted through the air, mingling with the low murmur of conversations.

As I approached, I caught one of the guards in the middle of recounting the arm-wrestling match from the night before. Banar's tone was firm but not harsh. "Doran here was just telling me how much of a fool he was last night," Banar said with just a hint of a smile. "Come join us for some breakfast, Karn."

I pulled out a chair and sat down, the wooden legs scraping against the floorboards. The inn was alive with movement: patrons nursing mugs of steaming tea, servants weaving between tables with trays of food, and the clatter of dishes blended with the hum of morning conversations. "Have you seen Lucas this morning?" I asked as my eyes searched the room as it came to life.

Banar shook his head. "No sign of him yet. He's a travelling man; maybe he's already on the road."

A servant placed a plate in front of me—milk, bacon, a slab of bread, and a jar of honey. I tore into the food, wolfed it down, the rich flavours woke me up more than anything else could.

"Eat up, you'll need your strength," Banar said, his voice carried the authority of his title. "Today's journey won't be any easier."

Serah leaned over. "Try not to let the food escape your mouth, Karn."

I chuckled, my mouth full. "I'll try my best, Serah."

Banar's expression softened as he watched the exchange. "Good to see you two in high spirits. We've got a long road ahead, and it's best we tackle it with clear heads and full stomachs."

After breakfast, we gathered outside the inn, the cool morning air sharp and invigorating. The inn's stableboy had already brought the horses and carriages around, their hooves clopped against the cobblestones, filling the air with a rhythmic sound.

As I adjusted my saddle, another horse trotted over, its rider familiar. Lucas rode up on a sleek chestnut, a large backpack and saddle bags strapped to the sides. He tipped his hat, a charming grin plastered upon his face.

"Good morning!" Lucas called out with a bright smile. "Mind if I join you for a bit? Safer in numbers and all that."

Before Banar could reply, I blurted out, "Not at all!"

Banar shot me a look, and I quickly corrected myself. "I mean, my apologies, my lord." I felt a flush of embarrassment creep up my cheeks, remembering the importance of decorum.

Banar's stern gaze softened, and he nodded. "Lucas, you're welcome to join us."

Lucas grinned with a tip of his hat. "Much appreciated, my lord."

With that, we started off, the horses moving at a steady pace, the sound of hooves and wheels joining with the morning birdsong. The road stretched out before us, less crowded than the day before. The absence of merchants and travellers gave our journey an eerie stillness.

Banar rode silently, his eyes constantly focusing on the horizon. Lucas, however, filled the silence with stories. "Did I ever tell you about the time I bartered with the Sultans of Merak?" he began, his tone light and engaging. "Exotic spices and silks, unlike anything you've ever seen."

Serah leaned in, her eyes sparkling with curiosity. "Really? What are they like?"

"Opulent," Lucas said, his smile almost wistful. "Golden palaces, vibrant markets. The air is thick with the scent of incense and the sounds of music."

"No magic carpet rides?" Serah smirked and Lucas just laughed. I couldn't help but be drawn in. "What about the people?"

"Warm, if you know how to speak their language," Lucas chuckled. "Though the language of trade is universal."

Banar, always cautious, finally spoke. "You travel light for a merchant, don't you?"

Lucas shrugged, his grin never fading. "I carry everything I need in these saddle bags. I trade in exotic goods—light and valuable. No need for heavy carts or wagons."

I could see the scepticism in Banar's eyes, but he let it drop. As the day stretched on, Lucas's tales became a welcome distraction from the monotony of the road. He spoke of desert caravans, mountain fortresses, and flourishing port cities. Each story more vivid than the last, painting pictures in our minds of places we'd never seen.

Serah asked endless questions, her excitement pretty obvious. "Did you ever get into trouble?"

"Oh, plenty of times," Lucas laughed. "Once, I found myself in a tavern brawl in Dorsain. Let's just say, it didn't end well for the other guy."

Banar's eyes narrowed slightly, but he remained silent. I could tell he was trying to figure Lucas out, weighing the risk of letting this charismatic stranger travel with us.

I asked, "What's the strangest thing you've ever traded?"

Lucas thought for a moment, a mischievous glint in his eye. "A live peacock for a ship's passage. The captain's face when I handed it over was priceless."

Serah and I laughed, the image of a bewildered captain with a peacock on his deck too ridiculous not to.

Despite Banar's quiet vigilance, Lucas's stories brought a sense of adventure to our journey. It was hard not to be caught up in his world, even if only for a little while.

We travelled down the dusty road, the sun casting long shadows as it climbed higher in the sky. The gentle clop of hooves and the creak of the carriage wheels were the only sounds that accompanied us. As we rounded a bend, a broken-down merchant wagon came into view, its wooden frame leaned precariously to one side.

Serah pointed at it, a hint of concern in her voice. "Should we be worried?"

Lucas shook his head with a reassuring smile. "That old wreck? It's been there for years. I've seen it on my travels many times. Just another relic of a failed venture."

Banar wasn't as easily convinced. He nodded to one of the guards. "Stay alert, just in case."

We continued past the wagon, the afternoon sun beat down on us. I took a sip from my waterskin, trying to shake off the remnants of last night's ale. My head still felt heavy, and my mouth was dry despite the water.

Lucas, always on the know, pulled a flask from his saddlebag and offered it to me. "Here, a little hair of the dog. Works wonders for a hangover."

I hesitated, reaching for the flask, but Banar's stern voice cut in. "Better not, Karn. We can't afford to be sluggish. Let's be cautious on the road."

Lucas nodded, his easy going nature never faltering. "Of course, Lord Fayle. Just trying to help. Your Lord father is right. We need our wits about us."

I handed the flask back, a bit of a scowl on my face. "Fine," I muttered, annoyed but knowing Banar was probably right. The road ahead seemed to stretch on forever, and we couldn't afford any more distractions.

As we rode on, the sun began its slow descent, casting a warm, golden glow over the landscape. I could feel the heat from the sunburned road rising up in waves, and every now and then, a breeze would bring a momentary respite from the unnatural spring warmth. The day dragged on, each hour feeling longer than the last.

Lucas kept the mood light with more tales from his travels, his voice animated and full of life. He had a way of making even the dullest stories seem fascinating.

"And then," Lucas continued, "I found myself bartering for a rare herb in the markets of Saphir. The merchant thought he could outsmart me, but a little charm and a lot of patience go a long way."

Serah laughed, her eyes bright with amusement. "I bet you could charm the scales off a snake, Lucas."

Lucas winked at her. "Only if the snake is a lady, not coiled to strike."

Banar remained silent, his gaze fixed ahead, ever vigilant. Despite his quiet demeanour, I could sense his unease. He didn't trust easily, and Lucas's smooth words did little to reassure him.

As the sun dipped below the horizon, painting the sky with hues of orange and purple, we pulled off the road toward a river. The sound of the water rushing over rocks was a soothing backdrop after the long day's journey.

Banar dismounted first, stretching his legs. "Gather wood and rocks for a fire," he instructed the servants, who nodded and quickly set to work. From the carriage, Banar pulled out our travel rations, a mix of dried strips of beef and a few preserved apples from the previous winter. "I make a mean road stew," he said with a rare smile. "This'll warm us up."

Lucas, who I was working out was an opportunist, grabbed his fishing rod from his saddlebag. "I'm heading to the river to try my luck with the fish," he said, a mischievous glint in his eye.

Banar raised an eyebrow. "Fishing at dusk? You think that's wise?"

Lucas chuckled. "Best time, my lord. They're just about to settle down for the night, easy pickings."

Feeling the need to stretch my legs and clear my head, I spoke up. "I'll join you, Lucas."

Serah waved her hand at me as I glanced in her direction. "I'll help Banar with the stew. You two go on."

I found Lucas perched on a rock, chewing on a blade of grass, his long black coat flowing around him and the feather in his hat swaying gently with the evening breeze. He was fiddling with a fishing rod he'd somehow produced from his seemingly bottomless saddlebags. I wondered briefly where he stored all his gear but pushed the thought aside as he patted the rock beside him.

"Have a seat, Karn," he said, still humming a tune I couldn't quite place.

I settled next to him, the cool rock biting through my trousers. The sound of the river mixed with Lucas's humming created an oddly calming atmosphere. We sat in silence for a few moments, the only sound the gentle splash of the river and the occasional rustle of leaves.

"That was some game last night," I said finally, breaking the silence. "I've never seen anyone beat Banar like that."

Lucas chuckled, his eyes twinkling under the brim of his hat. "Banar's a formidable player. He's strategic, but sometimes too straightforward. It's not a bad thing, just a different style."

I nodded, feeling a sense of camaraderie with Lucas. "Do you think we could play tonight?"

Lucas shook his head, his eyes focused on the water. "Not

tonight, Karn. Tonight is for fishing and stories, not games."

Before I could respond, the line on Lucas's rod went taut. In a swift, fluid motion, he thrust it into my hands. "Here, pull!" he urged, his voice brimming with excitement.

Panic surged through me as I grabbed the rod, my grip clumsy. The fish on the other end fought fiercely, and I struggled to hold on, my heart racing. Lucas moved quickly, guiding my hands and showing me how to reel it in. The rod jerked and strained in my grasp, the line whizzing as the fish fought back.

"Like this," Lucas coached, his hands steadying mine. I mimicked his movements, my breath coming in short gasps.

After a few intense moments, we landed our first catch: a beautiful rainbow trout, its scales glistening in the sunlight.

"Impressive," I said, genuinely awed, still catching my breath. Lucas grinned. "Want to learn how to catch more?"

For the next half hour, Lucas taught me to fish. He showed me how to cast the line, how to feel for the bite, and how to reel in the catch. We landed three more fish, each one a little easier than the last as I got the hang of it.

"Now comes the not-so-fun part," Lucas said.

He pulled out a small knife and started showing me how to clean and gut the fish. The sight and smell of the blood made my stomach churn, vivid memories of the men I had killed and the destruction of my village flashed through my mind. I swallowed back the bile that had risen in my throat. It burned.

I tried to focus on Lucas's instructions, but the images wouldn't leave. "I hate this part," I admitted quietly.

Lucas's eyes were hard as he looked at me. "It's necessary, Karn. Not everything we have to do in life is pleasant, but it's part of survival."

I nodded, swallowing hard and forcing myself to follow his lead.

The task was gruesome, but Lucas's calm and steady presence made it bearable. Once we finished, we carried the cleaned fish back to camp, ready to contribute to the night's meal.

Lucas and I returned to the camp with four sizable fish dangling from a makeshift stringer. The smell of Banar's stew wafted through the air, making my stomach growl. Serah was sitting by the fire, her stave propped against a log, engrossed in the book I had given her.

"Have fun?" she asked without looking up but I saw the smirk.
I nodded, holding up the fish. "We brought dinner."
Serah glanced at the fish, then back at me, leaning in to whisper. "You're making Banar jealous, you know."
I frowned, confused. "Jealous? Why?"
Before she could elaborate, Banar's voice cut through. "Throw those into the pot. Fresh fish beats dried rations any day."

I handed the fish to Banar, who deftly added them to the bubbling stew. As the fish cooked, the smell became even more enticing. We settled around the fire, the warmth of the flames pushing back the chill of the evening.
"So, Lucas," Banar said, stirring the pot. "What brings you on the road this time?"
Lucas leaned back, the firelight casting shadows on his face. "Oh, the usual. Seeking out rare goods, trading stories, avoiding trouble. You know how it is."
Banar grunted, not entirely convinced. "And you found us. Quite the coincidence."
Lucas smiled, a glint of mischief in his eyes. "The road's full of surprises. Besides, I couldn't resist the company of such fine folks."
Serah rolled her eyes. "Charming, Lucas."
Lucas chuckled. "I do try, Serah."

The conversation flowed easily as we ate. The stew was hearty and rich, the fresh fish added a delicate flavour. Plus having caught them myself I felt a twinge of pride. Well nearly myself, Lucas helped. I found myself relaxing, the camaraderie around the fire a welcome respite from the tensions of our journey.

"Banar, this stew is fantastic," I said, savouring each bite.

"Years of practice," Banar replied, a rare smile on his face. "When on campaign we take turns cooking, even us officers, it teaches you a thing or two."

Serah looked up from her book, eyes twinkling. "Karn, did Lucas teach you how to fish, or did you just watch him do all the work?"

I laughed, shaking my head. "He taught me. Caught a few myself."

Lucas raised his bowl in a mock toast. "To new skills and good company."

We all raised our bowls, clinking them together. The warmth of the food and the fire, coupled with the easy conversation, made the moment feel almost like home.

Settling down around the campfire, the warmth of the flames wrapping around us like a comforting blanket. The night was clear, stars scattered across the sky like tiny shards of glass. Lucas leaned back, his eyes reflecting the firelight, and I could sense a story coming.

"Ever hear the tale of the Raven King and the Fire Maiden?" Lucas began, his voice low and melodic, drawing us in immediately.

I shook my head, intrigued. Serah glanced up from her book, her interest piqued.

"Once upon a time," Lucas started, "in a kingdom far to the north, there was a king named Eldric. He was known as the Raven King because of his dark, piercing eyes and the black feathers he wore. He ruled wisely but was plagued by a curse—a curse that turned his heart cold as stone. No matter how hard he tried, he could not feel joy, nor could he love."

I watched as Banar listened quietly, his usual stern demeanour softened in the flickering firelight.

"One day," Lucas continued, "Eldric heard of a maiden who lived in a hidden valley. She was called the Fire Maiden, for she possessed a heart as warm and bright as the sun. It was said that her mere presence could melt the coldest of hearts. Desperate to break his curse, Eldric set out on a journey to find her."

I found myself leaning forward, captivated by the story. I could almost see the Raven King, his cloak billowing as he travelled through icy landscapes in search of warmth.

"After many trials and tribulations," Lucas went on, "Eldric found the hidden valley and the Fire Maiden. She was indeed as radiant as the tales described, her eyes like embers and her smile like the dawn. Eldric pleaded with her to break his curse, to share her warmth with him. The Fire Maiden agreed, but only on one condition."

Serah shifted, her eyes never leaving Lucas. "What was the condition?"

Lucas smiled, clearly enjoying the suspense. "She asked Eldric to show her his true self. Not the king, not the warrior, but the man beneath the crown. Eldric hesitated, for he had hidden behind his titles and his curse for so long. But seeing no other way, he removed his cloak, his armour, and stood before her as just a man, vulnerable, exposed and stark naked."

I swear I saw Serah blush at that description. That made me grin and I think she saw it for she grinned back. Yet, I felt a pang of empathy for Eldric. The idea of revealing one's true self, stripped of all defences, was terrifying. I wondered if I could do the same.

"The Fire Maiden saw Eldric for who he truly was," Lucas said, his voice softer now. "She saw his pain, his loneliness, and his strength. She took his hand and placed it over her heart. The warmth flowed from her to him, melting the ice that had encased his heart for so long. Eldric felt emotions he had forgotten—joy, love, hope. They returned to his kingdom together, ruling side by side, their combined warmth spreading throughout the land."

There was a moment of silence as Lucas finished, the crackling of the fire the only sound. I could feel the weight of the story settling over us, its message lingering in the air.

"That's a beautiful story," Serah said softly, her usual sarcasm absent. "Thank you, Lucas."

Banar nodded, a look of approval on his face. "Yes, thank you. It's a tale worth remembering."

I couldn't help but wonder about my own heart, hardened by the last two years of training and the quest for revenge. Could there be warmth for me too, somewhere down the line? The thought was both comforting and unsettling.

As we prepared to sleep, I continued to find myself thinking about the Raven King and the Fire Maiden, their story a beacon in the night. I glanced at Serah, who was carefully putting her book away, and at Banar, who was checking his sword one last time. Maybe, just maybe, there was hope for us all. The fire's warmth began to fade, and the night air grew cooler.

After the story, we all headed to our cloaks, the lingering warmth of the fire a fleeting comfort in the cool night air. Banar instructed the guards to take shifts, letting the servants use the carriage. He, Serah, and I opted to remain under the stars. There was something comforting about the vast sky above, despite the unknown dangers.

Lucas, ever prepared, pulled out a small hide tent from his saddlebags. With effortless grace, he tied a piece of rope between two sturdy trees and draped the hide over it, securing the edges with wooden pegs. "Good evening," he said with a nod before retreating into his makeshift shelter.

I settled onto my cloak, exhaustion quickly pulling me into slumber. My dreams were vivid and pleasant—scenes of the serving girl from Brightridge intertwining with images of the Fire Maiden from Lucas's tale. The serving girl's playful wink and teasing smile melted seamlessly into the Fire Maiden's fiery gaze and her warm, enchanting presence. Her eyes were like embers, glowing with a secret warmth, and her smile was the dawn, promising new beginnings. It was an intoxicating mix, a tantalising escape from the weight of reality, filled with the blush of stolen glances and the heat of imagined touches.

But then, a voice inside my head growled with urgency, *Runt, wake up!*

My eyes snapped open, the remnants of my dream evaporating instantly. I saw Doran, the guard on watch, his eyes wide with shock, as a blade slid across his throat. Blood sprayed, and he crumpled to the ground.

"Ambush!" I shouted, the word burst from me with desperate urgency. I scrambled to my feet and took hold of my sword, the familiar weight a cold comfort in my hand.

Banar was already up, his sword—a hand-and-a-half blade— gleaming in the moonlight. His face was a mask of determination, every inch the seasoned warrior I aspired to be.

From the shadows around our camp, dark figures emerged, their forms wrapped in black cloth, strange hoods hid their faces, as if they jumped right out of Lucas' stories. They moved with a predatory grace, their intentions clear and deadly. My heart pounded in my chest as I faced the nearest attacker. The adrenaline surged through me, sharpening my senses and steadying my hand.

The fight was upon us, and there was no room for hesitation or fear.

Banar was a blur of motion, rushing forward to cleave through a man poised to kill the other militia guard. With a swift, brutal swing, Banar's sword sliced clean through the attacker's arm, severing it from the shoulder outright. Blood sprayed in a gruesome arc, the man's scream followed the sickening thud of the dismembered limb hitting the ground. The remaining militia member stumbled to his feet, wide-eyed with relief, as Banar's blade sliced through the air with a decisive finality, ending the man's agony.

I turned just in time to see another assailant coming at me, his sword curved like a crescent moon. The unfamiliar weapon was a nightmare to defend against. The clash of steel echoed in the night as I blocked his strikes, the force of each blow vibrating through my arms.

He pushed forward, locking our swords. The sharp tip of his blade inched closer to my throat, and I could feel the cold edge of death creeping in. My heart pounded in my ears, and panic threatened to take over. Once more I had to keep myself calm, my rage hidden. Just as I was about to lose hope, the attacker was yanked back. Serah appeared like a shadow, her stave sweeping his legs out from under him. He hit the ground hard, and before he could recover, she planted her stave firmly in his face, knocking him out cold.

Serah suddenly screamed, "Banar!" I whipped around to see him dispatching another man, ramming his sword into the attacker's belly. Blood spurted, and the man's face contorted in pain as Banar shouldered him aside. But behind Banar, another assailant loomed, ready to strike.

My heart lurched. Banar wouldn't be able to get his sword out in time. I shouted a warning, but before the words fully left my mouth, I saw a flicker of movement.

Two daggers flew through the air, embedding themselves in the third assailant's chest with a harsh thud. The man stumbled, eyes wide with shock, before crumpling to the ground. I turned to see Lucas, his stance poised, another set of knives glinted in his hands as he surveyed the area for more threats.

My breath caught in my throat, the relief and adrenaline mingling into a heady mix. Lucas caught my eye, giving a quick, knowing nod. The man had saved Banar's life in the blink of an eye.

I turned back to Banar, who was catching his breath, pulling his sword free from the fallen attacker. He glanced at Lucas, then at me, a silent acknowledgment of the narrow escape he just had. I felt a strange mix of admiration and unease. Lucas's skills were impressive, but the ease with which he dispatched the attacker was unsettling.

Banar wiped the blood from his sword, his expression unreadable. "Stay sharp," he muttered, voice gruff with lingering tension.

We gathered around the carriage, each of us breathed heavily, well all but Lucas. Banar, Lucas, Serah, the surviving militia man, and the servants who huddled inside the carriage. The night was still and eerie, the only sound our laboured breaths. My heart hammered in my chest as I scanned the surroundings for more threats, but no more came at us.

"Any alive?" Banar's voice was a growl, low and filled with anger.

Serah pointed to the one she had knocked out. As if on cue, the man stirred, blood gushing from his nose as he scrambled to his feet. He took off running, but Lucas moved with deadly precision. A dagger flashed in his hand, and a moment later, it was buried in the man's back. He fell with a final, sickening thud.

Banar turned on Lucas, fury in his eyes. "We needed information man! Just who the hell were they?"

Lucas remained unfazed, crouching beside one of the bodies and rifling through it with not a bother at all. He pulled out a small coin purse, inspecting its contents before glancing up. "Salorain," he said, his tone matter-of-fact. "They're from Salora. Made any enemies to the south, my lord?"

Banar shook his head, still seething. "I've never even been that way."

Lucas stood, dusting off his hands. "It was clear they were after you. Their mistake." He glanced at the bodies, his expression cool and detached.

Banar's face darkened with anger, his jaw clenched tight. "Let's clean up and get moving," he ordered, his voice hard.

As we began to move the bodies, a sense of unease settled over me. The blood, the violence, it all reminded me too much of my village, of the men I had killed. Each time I wiped blood from my hands, the memories resurfaced, a constant gnawing at the back of my mind.

We worked in grim silence, the night air thick with the scent of blood and death. Lucas's efficiency was almost unsettling, his demeanour calm and collected, as if this were just another day for him. I couldn't shake the feeling that there was more to him than he let on.

Banar's anger simmered, clear to me even in the dark. He was a man used to control, and tonight, control had slipped through his

169

fingers. As we gathered the last of the bodies, I glanced at Serah. Her face was set in a hard mask, but her eyes betrayed a flicker of the same unease I felt.

As dawn broke, I helped put the bodies in a pile. More dead. At least not by my hands this time. We lit the bodies on fire using oil from Lucas's bags and wood we had found. Banar said a few words for Doran, the one of our own who died. The second militia man, that to my shame I never learnt his name, cried for his friend, his sobs a stark reminder of the night's toll.

We mounted up and got on our way, a more quiet and subdued journey.

Chapter 15 - Ironhold

Daylight burned my eyes as we left the forest. When they finally adapted, I was given my first view of Ironhold. The sight was something out of a legend. A massive iron fortress that loomed high, its dark, imposing walls standing stark against the sky. Below it lay a large town, its rooftops peeked out like uneven teeth against the landscape. The fortress seemed like a monstrous guardian, a deviant that overlooked the water below, ready to devour any threat.

Ironhold was perched on a cliff split between two rivers. The waters crashed together below, creating a swirling vortex that looked like a mix of liquid earth and rust. The town's buildings, though not as grand as the fortress, had a sturdy, weathered charm, their wooden and stone structures nestled close together as if seeking protection from the behemoth above. The size of it all dwarfed anything I'd ever imagined.

Lucas broke the silence first, his voice carried a note of casual familiarity. "Ironhold got its name from the Ironsand, which only forms where the Tamara and the Redrun meet," he explained, his tone almost reverent. "The water below the fortress is a murky red colour, like that of dried blood."

The thought of the river, thick and red as if flowing with blood, sent a shiver down my spine. My mind drifted to the ambush the night before, the blood, the violence.

I didn't respond to Lucas, and I wasn't surprised no one else did either. The toll of last night's ambush hung over us, a lingering shadow. Lucas, however, seemed immune to the weight, his spirits unhampered as he hummed his tune, his horse trotting ahead of the carriage.

Serah and I rode on either side of Banar, the rhythmic clopping of our mounts a steady backdrop to the tension. Lucas took the lead, his silhouette a jaunty figure against the morning light. Banar suddenly kicked his horse into a faster pace, moving up next to Lucas. The two of them rode ahead, their conversation a muted exchange of words and gestures. I strained to catch any hint of their talk but saw only the occasional tilt of a head or the flick of a hand.

"What do you think they're talking about?" I asked Serah, my curiosity getting the better of me.

Serah shrugged, "what do you think?" she shot back.

She was right, of course. It was pretty obvious what they were talking about. Banar's face was a mask of stern focus when he returned to our side, offering no clues about the conversation. He didn't look like he wanted to discuss it, and I knew better than to press him.

The fortress loomed larger with each step, an iron behemoth that seemed to grow from the hill itself. The town below, flourished with life, clung to the slopes like a determined survivor. Our path wound upwards, the climb steep and demanding. Every hoofbeat echoed the effort, the horses' breaths heavy in the morning air.

As we neared the gates, we dismounted, the cobblestones uneven beneath my boots. The town's entrance was a hive of activity, with groups of people flowing in and out. Merchants with laden carts, travellers like us, and townsfolk mingled in a chaotic dance.

What struck me most were the men in armour, their full plate gleamed dull in the light. They moved with purpose, eyes sharp and vigilant. Their presence was a stark contrast to the relaxed demeanour of the villagers I had known. One man, helmet askew, scratched incessantly beneath his visor, a minor imperfection in an otherwise disciplined facade.

Banar guided us through the gates with a nod to the guards. Lucas's humming had ceased, replaced by a watchful silence. We made it, at the threshold of Ironhold, and the reality of our journey struck me. It was the furthest I'd ever travelled whilst not tied up and blind folded in a back of a wagon.

Once we were in the town proper, Lucas turned to us with a rare moment of seriousness. "This is where we part ways for now, my friends. I believe you are going to Dúnmara? I am heading in the opposite direction."

I frowned, confusion creased my brow. "Didn't we just come from that way?"

Banar answered before Lucas could. "This is the only place for a league where you can get a horse on a boat that goes downriver."

Lucas nodded, a twinkle of amusement in his eyes. "Exactly, my young friend. Convenience over repetition."

Lucas stepped closer, extending his hand. "Good luck at The Forge, Both of you."

I clasped his hand firmly. "If you're ever in town, drop by and we can have a game Lucas."

Lucas glanced at Banar, a fleeting shadow of something unreadable crossing his face. "Unfortunately, young Karn, that is not one of my trade routes. But perhaps one day, we'll meet again in Eldewood."

He said his goodbyes with his usual charm, mounting his horse with a fluid grace. As he rode away, I couldn't shake the feeling of unfinished business, of secrets left unsaid. The road ahead suddenly felt a little emptier without his constant humming and enigmatic presence. It seemed all too sudden.

Banar, Serah, and I stood there for a moment, watching him

disappear into the throng of people and horses, the hum of the town swallowing the silence he left behind. The weight of his departure settled over us briefly, but Banar quickly shifted the reins.

"Alright, let's get to it," Banar instructed, breaking the spell. He directed the servants to take the trunks to the docks and the remaining guard to stay in place and watch the horses. He had a missive to send, something he didn't elaborate on but seemed urgent.

Serah seized the moment. "Banar, please, can we explore a little?"

"No," Banar replied firmly.

"Come on, we're already here," Serah pressed, her eyes sparkling with determination. "Just a quick look around?"

Banar sighed, clearly exasperated. "Fine. But only for an hour. We need to catch our own boat soon. I would have liked to show you Ironhold proper, but we must be on our way."

He pulled Serah and me to the side, his expression serious. "Listen, it's clear that those men last night weren't after us. But I don't want you interacting with Lucas anymore. He's dangerous. We can't afford to get mixed up in his business, nor he in ours. Got it?"

I nodded, though a pang of regret twisted in my chest. Lucas felt like the first friend I'd made on my own, a connection I wasn't ready to sever.

As Banar walked away, I turned to Serah. "What do you think he's hiding?"

Serah shrugged, "something juicy, no doubt. But we have an hour. Let's make the most of it."

I tried to shake off the lingering sense of loss as we ventured into the busy town. The sounds of merchants haggling, the smell of roasting meat, and the sight of vibrant fabrics all around us were a welcome distraction. Yet, the warning about Lucas loomed over my thoughts, casting a shadow on the brief freedom we had.

Afterwards, Banar went on his way, leaving Serah and I to explore the town. Ironhold sprawled before us, a lively maze of market stalls and traders hawked their wares. The air was thick with the scent of roasting meat, fresh bread, and the sharp tang of pickled vegetables. Colourful awnings flapped in the breeze, shading an array of goods that dazzled the eye – bolts of vibrant cloth, intricate jewellery, and iron, lots of iron.

As we wandered through the market, I couldn't help but notice something peculiar about the townspeople. Many had patches of dry, flaky skin, red and irritated, creeping up their arms and necks. It was as if the very air or water here was against them. I stared a little too long, my curiosity getting the better of me.

"Stop gawking, Karn," Serah snapped, though her eyes flickered with the same interest. "It's rude."

I shrugged, pulling my gaze away. "It's just... strange."

"Maybe, but they're still people," she replied, softening her tone, if only slightly. "Come on, let's see what else is here."

We meandered through the narrow alleys, each corner revealing something new. Serah was quickly drawn to a stall displaying ornate staves and wooden carvings. I watched her for a moment, her fingers traced the intricate designs, her face alight with interest. She had always had a keen eye for craftsmanship.

As I turned to explore further on my own, the noise of the market enveloped me. Vendors shouted their prices, children darted through the crowds, and the constant murmur of haggling filled the air. I caught sight of a booth selling weapons, the glint of polished steel catching my eye. With a last glance at Serah, engrossed in her own discoveries, I made my way over, eager to see what this part of Ironhold had to offer.

I wandered further into the market, the din of haggling voices and clinking coins faded as I entered an area dominated by blacksmiths. The air was thick with the scent of iron and coal, and the rhythmic clang of hammers against anvils echoed through the narrow streets. I watched as skilled hands crafted swords, horseshoes, and ornate metalwork, each piece a testament to the craftsmanship of Ironhold.

As I admired a particularly fine sword, its blade gleaming in the mid-morning sun, a commotion nearby drew my attention. A young noble, with emerald green eyes and dark hair that fell in neat waves, stood sneering at a local man. His clothes were of fine quality, made from rich fabrics that caught the light, and the ornate sword at his waist marked him as someone of importance. The hilt of the sword was encrusted with jewels, and the scabbard was adorned with intricate designs, a clear display of wealth and status. I am not so sure I would have displayed my wealth as such though I imagine the guards standing ten feet or so away gave the boy confidence.

"Don't touch me with your filthy hands," the noble spat, his voice dripping with disdain. "You're disgusting."

The local, his skin marked with the same patches I'd noticed earlier, tried to explain as his voice trembled. "It's the water, my lord. It does this to all of us. We can't help it."

The noble glanced at the cup of water in his hand, his lip curling in disgust before he spat it out onto the ground. "Vile. Absolutely vile."

Something inside me churned at the sight. Without thinking, I stepped forward, intending to defuse the situation. "Hey, you shouldn't—" But my words came out awkwardly.

The young lord turned to me, a smug grin spread across his

face. "That's right, you shouldn't touch nobility like that," he said, clearly thinking I was on his side. Before I could correct him, he clapped me on the back. "So, who are you?"

My stomach churned. This wasn't how I wanted things to go. Before I could answer, the noble spat at the local, the disdain in his eyes burned hot. I knew that feeling, for I was trying to keep my own heat and disdain for this young lordling down. It was as if everywhere I went, the world, tried to challenge my emotions.

"Who I am isn't important," I began, but before I could continue, Serah stormed over, her eyes flashing with anger. She had overheard everything and wasn't having any of it.

"You pompous ass," Serah snapped, her voice cut through the air like a whip. "How dare you speak to someone like that? It's not their fault they live here and drink this water."

The lowborn man, seeing his chance, backed away quickly, grateful for the reprieve. He gave Serah a grateful nod before disappearing into the crowd.

The lord's son, now red with anger, turned on Serah. "And who do you think you are to talk to me like that, wench?"

Serah stepped forward, her voice low and dangerous. "Wench? No, I'm a witch," she said, her eyes narrowing. The effect was immediate; the young lord's bravado faltered, and a flicker of fear crossed his face.

I stepped in, trying to steer the conversation. "What she meant is, she'll be training at The Forge to be a witch. We'll both be training there."

The noble's eyes widened a fraction before he regained some composure. "The Forge? Me too," he said, extending a hand to me. "I'm Quisten Cowle. Apologies, lady witch." His voice wavered slightly as he addressed Serah, the earlier arrogance replaced with caution.

I shook his hand, noting the nervous glance he threw at Serah. This wasn't exactly how I'd envisioned making introductions, but at least it was something.

Quisten looked back at the local and sneered, but Serah wasn't having any of it. She stepped forward, her eyes ablaze. "You should apologise to him," she demanded, pointing at the man who looked as if he thought he'd gotten away.

Quisten's eyes flickered with surprise, then annoyance. He hesitated, clearly unused to being challenged. He had never met someone like Serah before. Finally, he muttered, "Fine. I'm sorry." The apology was half-hearted at best, dripping with insincerity.

Before Serah could respond, Banar appeared, his presence commanding immediate respect. Quisten straightened up, and his men, who had been loitering nearby, moved closer.

Quisten quickly introduced himself, his tone changing to one of clearly practised politeness. "Quisten Cowle, son of Warden Cowle."

Banar nodded, his eyes sharp. "Banar Fayle. I served in the same campaign as your father, but under a different lord. This is my son, Karn and daughter, Serah."

Recognition flashed in Quisten's eyes, but before he could respond, one of his men stepped forward. "We must be off, my lord."

Quisten nodded curtly, turning back to Serah and I. "Until we meet again at The Forge." His tone was more measured now, a hint of respect creeping in.

As they departed, Banar turned to us. "We must make haste if we want to catch the next boat." His voice was firm, leaving no room for argument. We fell into step behind him.

Banar glanced back at us as we walked. "Quisten Cowle is a Warden's son," he began, his tone serious. "That's a level of nobility above even my own. He'd make a great ally but a terrible enemy." He shot a pointed look at Serah, who simply shrugged in response.

"He was being a prat," she said, unapologetic.

"A powerful prat," Banar replied. "We can't afford to make enemies, Serah."

We reached the horses, where the carriage and the militia man awaited.

"Stay in town for a few days," Banar instructed. "I'll return once I've finished enrolling Karn and Serah and my business in Dúnmara. Keep an eye on things."

The servants nodded, accepting the extra coin Banar handed them without question. It was clear they were used to his commands. I felt a strange mix of anticipation and dread about what lay ahead. Dúnmara and The Forge loomed large in my mind, a future full of unknown challenges and opportunities.

We followed Banar to the docks, our horses' hooves clopping against the cobblestones as we navigated a winding, sloped path. Merchants and travellers crowded the way, their voices mingling in a chaotic symphony. The path twisted and turned, each curve revealing glimpses of the busy harbour below.

I couldn't keep my eyes off the fortress towering on the cliffs above us. It loomed like a sentinel, casting long shadows over the town. Below it, the waters of the Tamara and the Redrun met, the currents swirling together into a murky red that looked disturbingly like dried blood. Just as Lucas had mentioned.

"Don't worry," Banar said, noticing my fixation. "You'll be back. This is a major trade route and a military garrison. I'm sure you'll be sent here by the masters of The Forge at some point."

I nodded, trying to shake off the unease.

As we descended, the noise of the docks grew louder. The scent of saltwater mixed with the tang of fish and the earthy aroma of the town. I glanced at Serah, who seemed as absorbed in the surroundings as I, her eyes wide with curiosity and determination.

We reached the bottom of the path, and the docks spread out before us, a hive of activity. Ships rocked gently in the water, sailors shouting orders and hauling cargo. The air buzzed with the energy of constant movement.

It took time, but we eventually boarded a large flat-bottomed barge. The deck was already crowded with people, horses, and even a wagon, which surprised me given the swift current of the river. The barge swayed as we settled our mounts, the water below churning and flowing with relentless energy, making the rocking world go round.

The crew moved with practised efficiency, securing the animals to sturdy posts along the sides of the barge. They provided feed and water, ensuring the horses were comfortable for the journey. Buckets of water sloshed over the edge of the barge, flowing into the river below, while the smell of fresh hay mingled with the earthy scent of the river.

I focused on Sköll, my black stallion, who was acting up a little, his eyes wide and nostrils flaring at the unfamiliar surroundings. He stomped his hooves and tossed his head, causing a few of the other passengers to glance our way with mild curiosity.

"Easy, boy," I murmured, stroking his neck in long, calming strokes. "It's just a boat ride."

Sköll snorted, his muscles tense beneath my touch. I made sure his feed bucket was full and adjusted the straps securing him to the post, ensuring they were neither too tight nor too loose. The steady, rhythmic motion of the barge seemed to unsettle him, but I stayed close, whispering soothing words and scratching his favourite spot behind his ear.

The other passengers watched with mild interest as Sköll gradually settled, his nervous energy giving way to a reluctant calm.

One of the crew members nodded approvingly at me. "Got a good handle on him, young lord," he said, tipping his cap.

"Thanks," I replied, continuing to stroke Sköll's neck. "Just need to make sure he's comfortable."

Among the other patrons, I spotted the young lord from earlier, Quisten, surrounded by his retainers. He was not the only one carrying a sword; a few more young men stood with weapons at their sides. Potential recruits for The Forge, I guessed. One of them caught my eye. He looked to be about my age, but unlike the others, his clothes were worn and patched, his boots scuffed and muddy. His dark hair was messy and matched his tanned skin. The boy carried himself with a wary confidence. What really made him stand out was a scar on his right cheek that made it look as if he had been marked by lightning. I wondered who he was and what his story might be.

The boat ride took a day and a night, a journey that would have otherwise taken us two weeks on horseback, Banar explained. The barge cut through hillsides that would have been a nightmare to traverse with our horses. The landscape shifted from dense forests to rolling hills, the river winding its way through the heart of the land.

As the day turned into night, the rhythmic sound of oars slicing through the water and the fluttering of sails filled the air. The crew worked tirelessly, their muscles straining as they navigated the river's currents. I found myself lost in thoughts of what lay ahead. The steady flow of the river and the quiet hum of activity on the barge created a strange, calming rhythm. I couldn't help but glance at the other recruits, wondering what challenges and opportunities The Forge would bring.

When dawn finally broke, we approached the outskirts of Dúnmara. The air was crisp and cool, a gentle breeze rustling through the trees that lined the riverbank. The Forge awaited us, its imposing silhouette visible in the distance. My journey for revenge had only just begun, and I felt a mix of anticipation and anxiety. This was the next step, the path to becoming something more than just a boy from the mountains.

Chapter 16 - Arrival

The spring rains began as we drew closer to The Forge, the downpour melded with the spray of the river. Banar, Serah, and I stood on the barge, our horses shifting restlessly beneath the canvas cover the crew hastily put over the animals when the dark clouds opened; the scent of wet leather and hay mingling with the crisp, rain-soaked air.

Raindrops pattered against the wooden deck, a relentless rhythm that matched the pounding in my chest. The Forge loomed ahead, a complex of dark, brooding buildings shrouded in steam and smoke. The rain sizzled as it hit the rooftops, creating a perpetual fog that rose from the countless furnaces within. The air was thick with the acrid smell of burning coal and molten metal, a bitter tang that clung to the back of my throat.

Banar stood beside me, his cloak pulled tight against the rain, eyes fixed on the imposing structure. Noticing my stare, he broke the silence, his voice steady despite the cacophony of the storm. "The Forge lives up to its name. Most of the iron from Ironhold is transported here, turned into weapons of war."

I looked at him, the question already forming on my lips. "But isn't this the place where we'll be training?"

A smirk played at the corners of his mouth, a rare hint of amusement in his usually stern features. "This is the place where you'll be forged."

Serah leaned over the rail next to me, her hair plastered to her face by the rain. "Dúnmara," she said, pointing beyond The Forge. "The city beyond."

I squinted through the downpour, trying to make out the distant sprawl. "You've been to the capital?"

"Once before," she replied, her voice barely audible over the hiss of rain and steam. "It's massive but spread out, like different kingdoms all stitched together."

I followed her gaze. From a distance, Dúnmara wasn't as cramped as I'd imagined. It sprawled across the landscape, each district distinct, like patchwork on a giant quilt. Lantern lights flickered through the mist, casting an eerie glow.

Banar joined us, his presence a solid anchor against the shifting fog. "You'll get a chance to visit," he said, his voice cut through the elements. "But for now, focus on your training. The challenges ahead will need all your attention."

Serah and I exchanged a look, the weight of his words settling between us. The rain continued to pour, soaking us to the bone, but the promise of the city—and the trials it held—burned hotter than the forges below.

The boat took its time, the rain a relentless companion. When we finally docked at The Forge, other barges were already there, unloading their cargo of iron sand. The bargemen moved swiftly, tying the boat to the moors and then helping unhook the horses.

I led Sköll off the barge, his black coat slick with rain. Serah followed with Sable, Banar with Granite. The crowd moved steadily off the docks and toward the imposing buildings ahead. The air was thick with the smell of wet metal and coal, every breath came with a harsh sting. Stable boys waited, their eyes wide as they took our horses. Sköll snorted, reluctant to leave my side, but a firm pat on his neck settled him.

Banar glanced at us, rain streaming down his face. "Let's go," he said, his voice gruff. The steam from the forges entwined with the smoke, creating an oppressive haze that hung over everything.

Serah adjusted her cloak, her eyes reflecting a mix of determination and apprehension. "Welcome to The Forge," she muttered, more to herself than anyone else.

Banar turned to us, rain dripping from his hood. "Follow me," he said, cutting through the murmur of the crowd.

We trudged through the mud, each step a squelching reminder of the relentless rain. The Forge loomed dark and forbidding, flames licking the sky from various structures. I wasn't sure I liked it. The place felt alive, but in a way that made my skin crawl.

Banar held open a thick wooden door, and we stepped inside, wiping our boots on a worn mat. The heat inside hit like a wall, a stark contrast to the cold rain outside. Banar led us to a man behind a desk, his attention buried in a ledger.

The man didn't look up until Banar cleared his throat with purpose. Recognition flickered in his eyes. He stood, holding up his hand. "Banar... or should I say Lord Fayle? What brings us the pleasure of your company? Looking to relive your glory days? You're a bit past your prime for that, aren't you?"

Banar grinned, letting go of the man's hand. "If only, Rhys. But no, I'm here on business. Got some fresh meat for the grinder."

Rhys's gaze shifted to us, taking in our soaked and bedraggled state. "I see. Fresh recruits, huh? Well, let's hope they last longer than the last batch."

Banar chuckled, a sound more sinister than amused. "These ones have a bit more bite. They'll be fine."

I stood there, dripping wet and restless, watching the exchange with smouldering curiosity, feeling the heat of the forges seeping into my bones.

Banar nodded toward us. "This is my adopted son, Karn Fayle, and my step-daughter, Serah Fayle. They're here to enrol."

Rhys looked us up and down, his gaze sharp and assessing. "Adopted son, you say?" His tone held a hint of scepticism.

"Cousin's boy," Banar replied smoothly. "His father, unfortunately, passed."

Rhys nodded in my direction but then his eyes softened as he shifted his focus to Serah. The flickering torch light illuminated the lines on his weathered face. "And you, lass," he said, his voice gentler. "You probably don't remember me, but I was a friend of your father's. I was sorry to hear of his passing. He was a good man."

I glanced at Serah, intrigued. She rarely spoke about her father, Elara's previous husband, and I knew little about him.

Serah narrowed her eyes, clearly searching her memory. Her wet hair clung to her face, and the room's heat flushed her cheeks. "Didn't you sneak sweets to me when my father wasn't looking?" she quipped, a sly smile tugging at her lips. "Always had a pocketful of licorice sticks, didn't you, Rhys?"

The old man smiled broadly and slapped the desk, the sound echoing in the room. "Good memory, Serah. It's been a while."

Rhys turned back to Banar, his expression softening. "You've done well by these two. Now, let's get the paperwork sorted. You'll need to fill out a few forms."

Banar sighed, a rare crack in his usual stoic demeanour. The sound of the rain outside and the distant roar of the forges filled the silence as Rhys began pulling out the necessary documents. Banar quickly filled out the paperwork, his pen scratching against the rough parchment. He handed it back to Rhys, who then slid a page toward me and another toward Serah.

"Once you sign here," Rhys said, his voice taking on a graver tone, "there's no turning back. This isn't a school. You can and will be hurt, but we'll forge you into something stronger, like your father here.."

I glanced at Serah, then at Banar. His expression was stern, resolute. I took the pen, feeling the weight of the moment, and signed. Beside me, Serah did the same, her hand steady despite the tension in the room.

"Good," Rhys said, nodding approvingly. "Now hand your weapons over to Banar. You won't be needing them here."

I hesitated, my hand instinctively tightening around the hilt of my sword. I looked to Banar for guidance. He gave a slight nod. "Trust me. You'll see."

Reluctantly, I handed over my sword. Serah followed suit, her eyes never leaving Banar's face. Banar set our weapons down with a finality that made my stomach twist.

"This is it," Banar said, his voice carrying the weight of years and unspoken fears. "I hand you off now, and we won't see each other for some time. Not until the half year mark in fall. Do your best, work hard, become strong."

Serah stepped forward, giving Banar a tight hug, her fingers gripping his cloak like she was afraid to let go. She whispered something in his ear, and he nodded, giving her a reassuring squeeze.

Banar then turned to me, holding his hand out. I reached to take it, but he pulled me in close, his grip strong and unyielding. "You are as much a son to me as any blood could be," he murmured. His voice was low, urgent. "Stay alive, come back in one piece."

I stood there, stunned, as he stepped back. The words hung heavy between us. Banar cleared his throat, then said his goodbyes to Rhys.

"Give my love to Elara," Rhys replied, his voice warm with familiarity.

Banar nodded and smiled at the old man. He picked up my sword and Serah's stave, hefting the weight of easily. A clerk hurried to open the doors, the rain outside still coming down in sheets.

With one last look at us, Banar walked out into the storm, the door closing behind him with a solid thud. The room felt suddenly emptier, the sounds of the forges outside now louder in the absence of his presence.

Chapter 17 - The Price of Admission

Serah and I stood in front of Rhys, the room heavy with the sound of rain and the distant clang of metal. Rhys leaned back in his chair, eyeing us with a mixture of expectation and something more calculating.

"I was there when Lord Fayle clawed his way up the ranks," Rhys said, his voice rough, weighed down by memories perhaps. "He set the bar high, and I expect you two to do the same. You carry his name now. Don't make him regret it."

He reached up and pulled two ropes, ringing separate bells next to the doors behind his desk. The left door had an anvil etched into it, the right a hammer. The sound echoed, a sharp reminder of the trials ahead.

The right door, marked with a hammer, creaked open first. A girl stepped out, looking older than Serah but not by much. Pale makeup covered her face, and her black hair was slicked back into a ponytail. Her eyes were cold, calculating. When her gaze landed on me, a shiver ran down my spine—a witch.

Serah turned to me, her eyes reflecting a mix of determination and unease. "Good luck," she whispered, pulling me into a brief, tight hug. The warmth of her embrace did little to dispel the chill left by the witch's stare.

"Luck to you too," I replied, my voice low.

The girl turned without a word, expecting Serah to follow. Serah glanced back at me once, then trailed after her, the door closed behind them with a finality that hit me hard.

Rhys noticed my expression and clapped a hand on my shoulder. "Don't worry son, you'll get to see her at the Autumn's Grace Promenade," he said with a knowing wink. "You might even get to dance with her."

Shortly after, the door on the left, marked with an anvil, creaked open. A young man appeared, tall and lanky, with unruly brown hair and a smirk that suggested he found the whole situation amusing. "New recruit?" he asked, glancing at Rhys.

Rhys rolled his eyes. "Of course, it's a new recruit. Why else would I pull the bell?"

The boy raised an eyebrow, his smirk widening. "Maybe you wanted more sweet tea, Lord Rhys?"

Rhys let out an exasperated sigh. "Off with you, Keird. Show young Karn around and get him set up."

Keird nodded, stepping forward with a hand extended. "Keird. Welcome to the madhouse."

I took his hand, feeling the firm grip of someone who wasn't as careless as he appeared. His eyes were sharp, contrasting with his casual demeanour. He wore a simple tunic and trousers, but there was an air of confidence about him that suggested he knew his way around the place.

"Thanks," I replied, meeting his gaze.

Rhys watched me with a keen eye, "Good luck, Karn," he said, his tone carrying a hint of something that felt almost like genuine concern.

Keird led me through the doorway, the sounds of the forge growing louder as we stepped inside. The door closed behind us, cutting off the last vestiges of familiarity.

Keird led me through dark hallways lit by flickering lanterns. The shadows danced across the stone walls, the air damp and cool.

"Don't let the gloom get to you," Keird said, glancing back with a grin. "It's not always this dark and miserable. Last week felt like spring. Then the rain appeared from nowhere."

I nodded, the smell of wet stone and burning oil filled my nostrils. "Where are you from, anyway?" Keird asked, his voice echoing off the walls.

"Eldewood," I replied.

"Eh, where's that?" he interrupted, not waiting for an answer.

"Small village west—"

"You made it just in time," he cut in again, hardly pausing for breath. "Most of the recruits have arrived already, but we got some stragglers, like you"

I followed him, the constant chatter a strange comfort against the oppressive silence of the halls. The sound of our footsteps echoed, the anticipation of what lay ahead gnawed at my insides.

We continued down the dim corridor, the stone walls closing in around us. The lantern light flickered, casting eerie shadows that danced along our path. Keird's chatter was a constant, a backdrop to the relentless patter of rain outside.

"Gonna have to brave the rain again," Keird said, pushing open a heavy door. The rain hit us instantly, a cold, soaking sheet that made my skin prickle.

We dashed between buildings, boots splashing through puddles. Keird led me to another structure, the door creaking open to reveal a long, narrow room lined with bunks. The smell of damp wood and sweat was thick in the air.

"This is the quarters for Iron Initiates," Keird said, pointing to a pile of trunks and chests stacked haphazardly in a corner. "Your trunk will be over there. Find it and choose a bunk that's not already taken."

I scanned the barracks, already missing my small, cosy room back at the manor. Bunks lined each wall, two hearths placed at either end of the long room. The few free bunks were far from the warmth of the fires.

Keird continued, "Behind the dorm is the Masters' Quarters. Never go there unless it's an emergency, or you'll end up in The Expanse."

I wondered what The Expanse was but didn't get a chance to voice it. The urgency in Keird's tone suggested it was something to avoid at all costs.

191

Keird must have noticed my hesitation. "Don't worry," he said, clapping a hand on my shoulder. "Once you move up in rank, you'll get a better room. Next is a shared, and if you move up again, you'll get one all to yourself."

"What are the ranks?" I asked, curiosity getting the better of me.

"Iron Initiate, Steel Novice, Bronze Adept, Silver Sentinel, and Gold Vanguard," Keird explained. "The higher you go, the better it gets."

I nodded, recalling the sight of Banar in his silver and Lord Caine in gold. Determination flared in my chest as I walked over to the pile of trunks. I found mine near the bottom, the wood slick with rain.

With a deep breath, I dragged it to an empty bunk, far from the warmth of the hearths, and set it down.

My stomach growled loudly, a sharp reminder of how long it had been since I'd eaten. Keird's eyes flicked to me, a grin spread across his face. "Figured you'd be hungry. We'll head to the refectory next," he said, already moving again.

His voice was a constant stream of words as we stepped back into the rain. "Lavs are over there," he pointed to a nearby shack. "Bathhouse next to it. Get soap with the rest of your gear from the quartermaster."

"Where would I find him?" I asked, but he kept talking as if he hadn't heard me. "The forges are over there with the blacksmiths' apprentices. Don't bother them unless a master tells you to."

We crossed a sizable courtyard, the rain relentless. A few other figures dashed between buildings, heads down against the downpour. I noticed a large wall splitting The Forge in two, with two buildings nestled between it, one large and one small.

"What's that?" I asked, pointing.

Keird actually paused, glancing at the wall. "That's the Split. On the other side, the witches become... well, witches. Sometimes you can hear their song at night. Gives me nightmares." He shivered, then shrugged. "You'll find out soon enough."

"And the those buildings?"

Keird pointed to the smaller one. "That's the registry we came out of. The larger one is the grand hall." He didn't elaborate, and his tone suggested I shouldn't ask.

We continued through the rain, my mind churning with questions and unease. The promise of food was the only thing that drove me forward as Keird's chatter filled the oppressive air.

Finally, we reached the refectory. The smell of roasted meat and fresh bread hit me, making my stomach growl even louder. Inside, the place buzzed with noise—clattering plates, laughter, and the murmur of voices. Recruits and other inhabitants of The Forge filled the long tables, their eyes heavy with fatigue but their postures stiff with resolve.

Keird seemed to be a familiar face here. A group of boys waved him over, calling out with easy familiarity. Keird turned to me, his grin never fading. "Instructions start tomorrow morning. Be up with the rest of the boys. Don't tarry, or they'll punish you. You can find your way around now, yeah? Good, see ya around."

Before I could respond, he was off, blending into the crowd with the same effortless energy that had driven him through the halls. I shrugged, watching him go. Keird was an odd mix of lazy and hyperactive, a whirlwind of contradictions that left me both amused and slightly irritated.

I grabbed a wooden tray, a plate, and a bowl, then joined the line of boys waiting for food. Some of them were already in uniform, making it clear that I'd get mine soon enough. The line shuffled forward, and I watched as each boy received a bread roll, a ladle of soup, and slices of meat. When it was my turn, I accepted the food and figured it wasn't a half-bad affair. I filled a cup with water and turned to find a seat among the rows of tables.

As I scanned for a spot, a voice cut through the noise. "Fayle, over here."

I turned to see Quisten, the Warden's son from Ironhold. A flicker of annoyance shot through me. I wanted to turn around and ignore him, but it was too late. He waved, a smug grin on his face.

With a reluctant sigh, I waved back and walked over to him. Quisten sat with a few other boys, still wearing his ornate sword, a symbol of his status. The sword's hilt was encrusted with jewels, and its scabbard bore the intricate emblem of his house: a silver gryphon clutching a golden shield. I sat down, my tray clattering on the wooden table, and forced a smile, ready for whatever Quisten had up his sleeve.

Quisten leaned back, his voice dripped with arrogance. "Fayle, tell them about those horrible scabs in Ironhold. You know, the ones who look like their skin was flaking off?"

I clenched my jaw. "It's Karn. Karn Fayle."

"Sure, Karn." Quisten said dismissively, then continued his grotesque description. "Their skin all cracked and red, like they're constantly peeling. It's disgusting."

One of the other boys grimaced and pushed his plate away. "Come on, Quisten, I'm eating. Do you have to describe something so disgusting while I'm trying to enjoy my meal?"

Quisten turned to him, his eyes cold. "Hugo, if you can't stomach a bit of talk, maybe you're in the wrong place." Hugo looked down, chastised. Quisten turned back to me, a smile curling his lips. "Come, sit with us."

"Quisten I really…" I began.

Before I could say more, Quisten carried on, again. "Karn's father, Lord Fayle, was the hero of the Battle of Black Rock Hollow. Despite his low birth, he was raised to officer. Quite the story, really."

Another boy, tall and lean with piercing blue eyes, extended his hand. "Illiam. Stick with us, Karn. Your sire might be just a vassal, but he's got a reputation. That counts for something around here."

I shook his hand, it didn't feel as soft as I had expected it too. The food on my plate suddenly seemed less appealing, but I forced myself to eat, the noise and banter of the refectory swirled around me. The smell of roasted meat and the heat from the crowded room felt oppressive, adding to the weight of my new reality. I continued eating, half-listening to the chatter around me. Quisten boasted about his father's latest exploits, while Hugo cracked jokes and Illiam watched silently. The room buzzed with noise, a constant hum of voices and clattering cutlery.

Suddenly, the doors to the refectory burst open. A long-haired boy, breathless and wide-eyed, shouted, "The trials are starting!"

Every boy in the room sprang to their feet, food forgotten. Trays clattered as they were abandoned, and the din of conversation turned into a chaotic rush toward the door.

Quisten grabbed my arm, pulling me up. "Come on, Karn, you don't want to miss this."

I glanced longingly at my half-eaten meal but had no choice. I joined the stampede, following the stream of boys as we raced across the courtyard, rain still falling in a steady drizzle.

"What's happening?" I asked, struggling to keep up.

Hugo, running beside me, grinned. "We're going to the arena. They're starting the trials for the lowborn. Hope you've got some coin on you, should make for some good betting."

The swarm of boys swept me along, pulling me into a torrent of movement. My hair slicked to my face, clothes drenched from the rain, I felt like I was being swallowed up and carried by their momentum. We charged through the entrance and into a coliseum-like structure, the roar of the gathered boys echoing off the stone walls, amplifying the chaos.

Other boys made room for Quisten, who motioned for me to join him, Hugo, and Illiam under the only covered area, a cloth banner providing scant shelter. Quisten handed Hugo a handful of coins, and Hugo disappeared into the throng.

"What's happening?" I asked, the excitement around me infectious yet unsettling.

Illiam leaned in, his voice low but clear. "It's the trials. While lordlings like us get admitted to The Forge by blood, they let lowborn in too—those who've proven themselves in combat. But they still have to pass a trial. This trial. Though, honestly, it's more for our entertainment."

Quisten snickered, his eyes gleaming with cruel amusement. "Yeah, watch them scramble. Pathetic, really."

I looked down to see a group of about twenty boys lining up, emerging from a gate. My heart skipped a beat when I recognized one of them—the boy I saw on the barge. The lighting bolt scar on his cheek and messy hair were easily recognizable. He stood there, rain mixed with sweat on his face, looking determined yet wary.

Hugo returned, a grin split his features. "Bets are in. Anyone else want to place one?"

I shook my head, unable to tear my eyes away from the scene below. The tension in the air was thick, charged with the collective anticipation of the crowd. The trials were about to begin, and the atmosphere was electric with the promise of violence and spectacle.

The crowd's roar quieted as a man stepped onto a podium at the far end of the coliseum. His presence commanded attention, and the boys around me stilled.

"Welcome, brave souls, to the Trials of the Forge!" His voice boomed, echoing through the arena. "Today, five of these valiant young men will earn their place among us, becoming wards of the Forge and securing a brighter future in service to our queen. This is no ordinary trial. This is a test of courage, strength, and sheer will."

The crowd murmured with anticipation. He raised his hands for silence. "The rules are simple. Five wild boars will be released into the arena. Capture or kill one, and you secure your place here. But beware—one of these boars is a deviant, a beast of cunning and ferocity. The one who captures it will be granted the honour to compete for the rank of officer!"

A thrill of excitement and fear rippled through the crowd. The gates creaked open, and four wild boars charged into the arena, their tusks gleaming, eyes wild. A fifth boar emerged from another gate, its fur an unusual, mottled colour.

Hugo jabbed a finger toward it. "That one's the deviant. You can tell by the weird colouring."

"Wonder what it can do," Illiam mused, eyes wide with curiosity.

"We will just have to see!" Hugo replied.

A horn blared, sharp and commanding, signalling the start of the trial. The arena erupted into chaos as the twenty boys lunged into action, each determined to capture or kill a boar. I watched, heart pounding, as they spread out, weapons drawn. One boy hurled a spear, missing a charging boar by inches. The animal veered, tusks slashing through the air, and caught another boy's leg, sending him sprawling with a scream.

The wild boars were fierce, their eyes blazed with primal fury. Two boys managed to corner one near the wall, wrestling it down with ropes and sheer muscle. The boar thrashed violently, but they held on, finally binding its legs. As they secured the animal, a scuffle broke out between them. One boy, desperate to claim the victory, shoved the other aside and drove his knee into his rival's ribs, the sharp crack of bone barely audible over the boar's squeals. The injured boy crumpled, clutching his side in agony while the victor stood tall, triumphant over the captured beast. The crowd roared in approval.

"Did you see that?" Quisten shouted, eyes gleaming with excitement. "That's how it's done!"

Amid the frenzy, a boy struggled to wrestle the deviant boar, his hands slipping off its sleek, glistening fur. The creature moved as if friction didn't exist, sliding effortlessly out of his grasp. A second tried to loop a rope around its neck, but the rope slipped off as if the boar were coated in oil. The deviant boar was a terrifying sight, its fluid movements masking lethal intent as it weaved through the chaos of the arena.

As I watched the futile attempts, my eyes locked onto the boy from the barge. He stood his ground, facing the deviant boar as the creature chose him for its next target. The creature's fur shimmered unnaturally, making it seem almost ethereal as it glided across the dirt, an eerie elegance hiding its deadly nature.

"Look at that one!" Hugo exclaimed. "That's the deviant! It's got some kind of resonance trick."

Illiam leaned forward, eyes fixed on the deviant. "Watch closely. This is going to be interesting."

The boy from the barge tightened his grip on a makeshift spear, eyes narrowing. The deviant charged, a glistening blur. At the last second, the boy dodged, but the boar's tusks still grazed his side, tearing through cloth and skin. Blood spattered the ground, but he didn't falter.

"He's done for," Quisten muttered, a hint of satisfaction in his voice.

The boy circled, trying to anticipate the boar's next move. The deviant boar turned, its eyes gleaming with intelligence. It lunged again, slickening itself to slide across the ground. The boy barely avoided a direct hit, his movements growing desperate and more precise.

Another challenger wasn't as lucky. A wild boar gored him, its tusks digging deep into his thigh. He collapsed, screaming, as the boar trampled him. The crowd's roar grew louder, a mix of excitement and bloodlust.

Back in the centre of the arena, the boy from the barge made his move. As the deviant boar slid toward him, he threw a handful of sand into its eyes, blinding it momentarily as it skidded across the sand and into a rock.

Seizing the moment, he plunged his spear into its side. The boar's slick skin couldn't deflect the blow, and it let out a guttural roar, thrashing wildly.

"Yes! That's it!" Hugo shouted, his voice rising above the din. "He's got it!"

The boy held on, his face set in grim determination. With a final, powerful thrust, he drove the spear deeper, and the deviant boar collapsed, its movements slowed until it lay still. The boy stood over it, chest heaving, blood and sweat mingling on his skin.

"Yes!," I jumped up raising a fist into the air only to be met by Quisten's dark look.

The arena fell silent for a moment, the tension taut. Then the crowd erupted into deafening applause and cheers.

"Unbelievable," Illiam muttered, shaking his head. "He actually did it."

The trial continued around them, but my focus was fixed on the boy from the barge. His chest heaved with exertion, sweat and blood streaked his face. Our eyes locked, and for a moment, the chaos of the arena faded. He held my gaze with an intensity that sent a shiver down my spine, a silent acknowledgment passed between us.

Quisten leaned over, his voice cutting through the noise. "Enjoying the show, Fayle? Your father was a challenger too, you know. He defeated a deviant just like that one."

I nodded, unable to tear my eyes away from the boy in the arena. Thoughts of Banar filled my mind, a new respect blossoming for the man who had faced these same trials and emerged victorious. Yet, he never really shared these stories with me or Serah, as far as I could tell, I'd have to ask him.

Chapter 18 - Into the Forge

That first night in the barracks, the same night of the trial, I struggled to sleep. The thin mattress offered little comfort, and the low murmur of the other wards filled the dimly lit room. I lay in my bunk, feeling more alone than I had since my first night at the Fayle manor.

I hadn't realised how much Banar, Elara, and especially Serah had come to mean to me. The thought of them made me solemn, yet it was the guilt that creeped in when I thought about my mother and sister, Liv that haunted my dreams. Now, separated from everyone, I felt a void I hadn't anticipated.

Good, a voice growled in my mind, low and feral. *She is strong. And you? You are weak. You cling to her strength like a crutch. Pathetic. You lean on her too much. Find your own strength or be swallowed by your weakness.*

"Who are you?" I demanded into the dreamscape, the void where my consciousness wandered. The darkness around me seemed to pulse, heavy with unseen presence.

I am Nix, the voice replied, dripping with malice. I caught a vivid image of a crimson wolf, its eyes gleamed with a sinister intelligence, fangs bared in a menacing grin. The image lingered, haunting and powerful, as I stood in the void, grappling with the fear and determination that warred within me.

I woke with a start, sweat on my brow. The darkness still clung to the room, the sun hadn't even begun its ascent. Boys around me were groggily getting off their bunks, rubbing their eyes and pulling on clothes. I did the same, tugging on the worn clothes I had travelled in, and stepped outside into the dark morning.

The chill hit me immediately, the remnants of the previous day's rain still evident in the puddles scattered across the courtyard. At least it wasn't raining today, I thought, taking a deep breath of the crisp air.

Boys from the other barracks began to emerge, their figures silhouetted against the faint glow of the courtyard lamps. They were led by older boys, clearly more experienced. I recognized Keird at the front of his group, his voice carried over the hushed murmurs of the morning assembly.

I followed the stream of boys into the courtyard, the squelch of our boots in the wet ground the only sound breaking the quiet. My pace quickened as I caught up to Keird. "What's going on?" I asked, my voice low but urgent.

He glanced at me, momentarily confused, then recognition lit his eyes. "Oh, you're the boy from yesterday. Where's your mocks? Didn't you pick a set up from the quartermaster?"

I looked around, noticing most of the boys were already dressed in The Forge's uniform: dark tunics with silver trim, sturdy trousers, and boots built for endurance. Each uniform bore the insignia of The Forge, a crossed hammer and anvil.

"No matter," Keird continued, shaking his head. "Do so after the ceremony before the Masters catch you. This is initiation. The Masters will talk to the new recruits—split you into squads and put you on the docket."

I clenched my jaw, seething silently. It was Keird's job to take me to the quartermaster, and I had asked him yesterday. But I bit back the angry words and let him continue.

"We don't form squads with our barracks?" I asked, frowning. "There must be twenty of us per barrack, right?"

Keird smirked. "Didn't I tell you yesterday? If you rank up, you move sleeping quarters. Doesn't make sense to organise by bunkmate. Besides, this is part of the test."

"Test?" I echoed, a mix of curiosity and dread tightening in my chest.

"You'll see," Keird replied, leading us into a section of the courtyard. He lined us up with the other boys. There must have been over a hundred of us standing there, the air thick with anticipation and the faint smell of sweat.

In the dim morning light, I saw a podium set up at the front of the courtyard. I turned to ask Keird another question, but he hushed me, pointing to the stage. Seven men stepped onto it, their presence commanding immediate attention.

One of them moved to the forefront, his very short grey hair and pronounced lines on his face hinting at experience. Yet, despite his weathered appearance, he couldn't have been past middle age. His broad shoulders and the way he carried himself spoke of a lifetime of battles.

"I am Master Kegg," he announced, his voice booming across the courtyard. "Welcome to The Forge. Here, we will shape you into something the Kingdom can use."

The courtyard fell silent. "Some of you will become officers in the regular army. Others will have the honour of being Black Guard. The best among you will be officers of the Black." His words made me think of Banar and Lord Caine, both men who carried the weight of their titles with undeniable presence. Albeit they held it very differently.

"It will be tough," Kegg continued, his eyes scanning the crowd. "We will break each and everyone of you before you are reforged. You are our wards, and we your masters."

He gestured to the men behind him. "Allow me to introduce the men who will be training you."

One by one, the men stepped forward.

"Altar Mores, Master of the Fist," Kegg said. Mores was a hulking figure with a perpetual scowl, his muscles rippled under his uniform. His eyes were cold, assessing us like prey. I for one did not want to be introduced to that man's fists.

"Carmac Breen, Master of Strategy." Breen was lean and sharp-eyed.

"William Kinrade, Master of Arms." Kinrade carried a long sword at his side and his hands were calloused.

"Gilcalm Quark, Master of Beasts." Quark had a rugged look, his eyes fierce and wild, a man who looked to have spent more time with animals than people.

"Godred Owle, Master of Knowledge." Owle appeared older, with a scholarly air. His gaze was piercing, as if he could see through any facade.

"Drystan Veil, Master of Shadows." Veil stepped forward last, his presence eerie. His dark eyes bore into us, and a shiver ran down my spine. There was something unsettling about him, an aura of mystery and fear.

Kegg concluded, "These men will be your guides, your mentors, and your challengers. Prepare yourselves to be pushed beyond your limits, to face trials that will forge you into warriors worthy of our Kingdom."

As he spoke, a sense of foreboding settled over me. This was no ordinary training. This was a crucible, and only the strongest would emerge whole. I did find it strange that there was no mention of the Witch Queen in a place designed to forge her armies. What did that say about the man leading it?

As Kegg finished his speech, the first light of dawn began to creep over the horizon, casting a golden glow behind him. "You have until the sun reaches the top of the podium to sort yourselves into squads of ten," he declared, his voice cutting through the morning air. "Anyone not in a squad will be punished and placed into one, putting them at a disadvantage."

The words had barely left his mouth when the crowd erupted into chaos. Wards darted around, voices overlapping in a cacophony of urgency and desperation. Boys who already knew each other, likely from noble families or shared histories, gravitated together quickly, forming tight knots. Others looked around anxiously, trying to gauge potential allies or threats. The air buzzed with frantic whispers and hurried negotiations.

I stood amidst the chaos, my eyes scanning the crowd. A few boys had already formed solid groups, standing confidently together. Quisten, of course, was already surrounded by a clique of familiar faces. Some boys jostled and argued, their voices rising in frustration.

One group of taller boys, their faces sharp and eyes cold, seemed to operate with an unspoken understanding. Led by a boy with long dark hair that draped down his back like a cloak, they nodded to each other and formed ranks without a word, their movements almost military in precision. In contrast, another cluster was a chaotic tangle of shouted orders and flailing limbs, less composed as they bickered and jostled to pull in the strongest-looking recruits. Their voices rose in frustration, every attempt at organisation dissolving into further disarray.

I felt a pang of uncertainty. My mind raced. No family ties, no alliances, just the fading connections from the barge and the refectory. I caught sight of a couple of boys from my bunk, but they were already being pulled into other groups.

Time was slipping away, and the sun climbed steadily, the pressure mounting with each passing second.

The courtyard buzzed with frantic energy, boys pushing and shoving as they scrambled to form squads. My eyes darted around, searching for a familiar face or a promising ally. Amid the confusion, I spotted the boy who had won the trial yesterday, the one who felled the deviant. His demeanour was calm, confident, his stance firm. He was already in his uniform, standing out among the chaos.

I made my way towards him, the noise of the crowd fading as I focused on my goal. As I approached, his eyes narrowed warily. I extended my hand. "I watched you in the trial yesterday. You fought well."

The boy hesitated, then took my hand with a firm grip. "Thanks. I'm Lear, I'm from the south."

"Karn, from House Fayle," I replied.

Lear shook his head, his brows furrowing highlighting the dark circles under his eyes. "I never thought I'd actually see a deviant. Always figured they were just tales to scare kids."

"Yeah, well, tales have a funny way of becoming real when you're not looking," I said with a wry smile; thinking of my own encounter with the deviant caracal.

He chuckled, and for a moment, we were just two boys in the middle of chaos. "True. Better to face them head-on than be caught off guard."

"True," I echoed. "You fought like a demon out there. Not many could take down a deviant like that." I said as I tried to avoid looking directly at the scar on his cheek.

"Thanks," Lear said, pride and a hint of defiance in his voice. "Had to prove myself somehow. Some of us don't have titles to hide behind."

"It's not about the title, it's—"

Before I could finish, a voice cut through the noise. "There he is!"

Quisten, accompanied by Hugo, Illiam, and several other boys, swaggered over. Quisten, too, wasn't in his mocks, still flaunting his fine clothes and ornate sword, a stark contrast to the uniforms around us or even my own travel attire. Lear's expression darkened, his grip on my hand loosening. "Highborn, huh? Too good for a uniform?"

I shook my head, starting to explain, "No, it's not that—"

Quisten cut me off, his voice dripped with arrogance. "Karn, what are you doing over here? We need you with us." His gaze shifted to Lear, recognition sparking. "Ah, the lowborn who wrestled the pig yesterday. Quite the show."

Illiam nodded. "We could use him."

Hugo snickered. "He'd make a good mascot."

Quisten smirked, extending his hand toward Lear. "What do you say? Want to step up and join the elite?"

Lear's face contorted with disgust. His upper lip curled, and his eyes flashed with contempt as he slapped Quisten's outstretched hand away. The forceful gesture sent a ripple of tension through the air. He turned his gaze toward me, no longer friendly but filled with betrayal and disappointment. The look cut deep, more piercing than any blade

"I'd rather wrestle another boar," Lear spat, his voice dripping with disdain. Without waiting for a response, he turned on his heel, his departure sharp and resolute. The crowd around us seemed to part in deference to his fury, and I watched as his figure receded into the chaos of the courtyard.

"Lowborn filth," Quisten muttered under his breath, venom coated his words. He turned to me, a grin spread across his face as if nothing of consequence had occurred. His hand clapped heavily on my shoulder, the force of it meant to convey camaraderie or dominance, I couldn't quite tell.

"Ah well. To hell with him. This is going to be fun," he declared, his tone unsettlingly gleeful.

The sun was edging closer to the top of the podium, casting a long shadow across the wet ground. Time was running out. I glanced around, noting the hurried movements of the other boys as

207

they scrambled to form their squads. Despite my conflicted feelings, I stayed with the group I knew. Banar's words echoed in my mind: Quisten could make a good ally.

What was I going to say to the boy, Lear, anyway? That I too came from a low birth?

I stood with Quisten, Hugo, Illiam, and the others we had picked out, our newly formed squad casting long shadows in the growing daylight. The sun reached the top of the podium just as the last boy scrambled to find a place in a group, desperation evident in the frantic search.

Kegg's voice boomed across the courtyard, sharp as a blade, "Any not in a squad, come forward."

Lear was among them. My chest tightened as he walked to the front, his head held high despite the grim expectation hanging over him. He stood firm with eight others, their faces a mix of defiance and dread.

Master Kegg lined them up, commanding, "Left hand out!"

The boys extended their hands. The courtyard fell silent except for the murmur of shifting feet and nervous breaths. Kegg's cane sliced through the air with a whistle, landing with a brutal crack on the first boy's hand. He cried out, pulling his hand back instinctively, but a guard forced it forward again.

"If you cannot ally yourselves with the strong," Kegg growled, stepping to the next boy, "then you'll be bonded by blood."

Another lash, another cry. The brutal sound of the cane meeting flesh echoed, sending shivers down my spine. When Kegg reached Lear, silence fell like an iron weight. The cane whipped down, searing red across Lear's knuckles. He didn't flinch, not a sound escaped his lips.

My admiration flared, intense and unbidden. His defiance was a silent scream, louder than any of the cries before. I clenched my fists, feeling the anger smoulder within me. I had to make this right.

"I'll give him that," Hugo muttered beside me, "lowborn's got grit."

Quisten smirked, "Hope it serves him well."

I watched as Kegg finished the punishment, each boy marked and humiliated. Lear's expression remained stoic, his eyes met mine briefly before he turned away, back straight. I vowed silently, determined. Somehow, I would make it up to him.

Master Kegg's voice cut through the air again, "Each squad must appoint a prime. Primes, come to me in the next five minutes."

Whispers and shouts filled the courtyard, boys jostling and arguing, their voices a mix of urgency and pride. Fists flew in some groups, scuffles breaking out as they fought for leadership.

In our squad, there was no contest. Quisten stood tall, self-assured smirk plastered on his face. "Guess I'm the prime, then," he declared, no one daring to challenge him. I felt a pang of annoyance but kept my face neutral.

I knew better than to waste energy on petty disputes. I had a purpose here, something far more significant than the daily squabbles. I needed to hone my skills, to become stronger for the sake of my village, my people, and my sister. These boys, they weren't my friends. They were a means to an end.

Weak. The voice inside my head growled but I just clenched my teeth and ignored it, focusing on my breath instead.

The designated primes moved to the front as the rest of us watched in silence. Kegg organised us into larger groups, his commands curt and efficient. We were shaped into units, the foundation of whatever tests lay ahead. To my surprise, our group also included the long-haired boy's squad and, unexpectedly, Lear's makeshift one.

"Get your breakfast," Kegg barked once he'd finished. "The docket will be arranged while you eat. Lessons with your assigned master start after breakfast."

Quisten and the group strode toward the breakfast hall, their laughter and banter cutting through the morning chill. The sound grated on my nerves, a constant reminder of the facade I had to maintain. I turned in the opposite direction, my steps purposeful and deliberate.

"Where are you off to?" Quisten called out, already expecting me to fall in line.

"I need to head to the quartermaster, get my mocks," I replied, not breaking stride.

Quisten's laugh rang out, sharp and mocking. "Don't get lost, Fayle! We wouldn't want you getting lost in this rabble. It would be a shame for someone of your... modest stature."

I ignored him, pushing through the throng of boys until I found Keird, who was busy talking with his friends. I didn't care. I pushed my way in and locked eyes with him.

"I need directions to the quartermaster," I said, my voice cutting through the din.

Keird glanced at me, recognition flickering briefly in his eyes before he pointed to a small building off to the side of the courtyard. "Over there. Ask for Master Raknor."

I nodded my thanks and made my way to the building. Inside, the dim light revealed a cluttered desk and rows of shelves packed with uniforms and gear. Behind the desk sat a man with round glasses perched on his nose, engrossed in a ledger.

Master Raknor?" I asked, stepping forward.

He looked up, his gaze sharp but somehow kind. "Yes, and you are?"

"Karn Fayle. I need my mocks."

Raknor's eyes flashed with recognition. "Fayle, huh? Banar's boy? I knew your father. He'd always make excuses for his missing buttons." He chuckled, the sound warm and calming, breaking through my tension. "Did everyone know of Banar?" I asked, curiosity getting the better of me.

Raknor nodded. "He was quite accomplished. Raised from lowborn, he earned his place through sheer determination and skill. Everyone around here knows his story."

I couldn't help but smile. "That sounds like him."

"Well, let's get you suited up," Raknor said, standing and moving to the shelves. He rummaged through piles, checking labels and sizes, his movements precise and practised. "Ah, here we go. Try these on."

It took some time, with Raknor cheerfully recounting my adopted father's antics as he adjusted the fit, finding different sizes until everything was just right.

"Perfect. Now you look like you belong here," he said with a grin, handing over the rest of the uniform.

"Thanks, Master Raknor. You've been a great help."

"Hurry up now, don't want to miss breakfast," he said.

I sprinted back to the barracks and quickly changed into my new mocks. Stepping outside, a sinking feeling hit me—the mess hall was empty. My stomach growled, a clear reminder of the missed meal. I spotted my squad heading towards the training grounds, Quisten's obnoxious swagger leading the way. I joined them, the missed breakfast a small sacrifice. The day had just begun, and I couldn't afford any more distractions.

Chapter 19 - Drills

We marched to the hall next to the forges, the clang of metal and roar of fires echoed in the morning air. The smell of heated steel and coal smoke filled my nostrils, a harsh reminder of the world we had stepped into. Other wards joined us, including the long-haired boy and his squad, as well as Lear's ragtag group. The tension between us was palpable, an undercurrent of rivalry and unspoken grudges.

Master Kinrade stood waiting, his sword in hand. He was a solid figure, every inch of him exuded a hardened, battle-tested authority. His eyes, sharp and unyielding, surveyed us as we filed in and lined up. The hall was spacious, its stone walls lined with racks of weapons. The flickering torchlight cast long shadows, adding a sense of foreboding to the air.

Kinrade's voice cut through the murmurs, sharp and clear. "Today, we begin your real training. Forget what you think you know about combat. Here, you will learn to wield a weapon as an extension of your body. You will learn discipline, precision, and above all, control."

His gaze swept over us, settling momentarily on each boy before moving on. When his eyes met mine, a chill ran down my spine. I could feel his scrutiny, as if he was weighing my worth in that instant. I clenched my fists, determined not to flinch under his gaze. Next to me, Quisten shifted, his usual arrogance replaced by a flicker of apprehension.

Kinrade raised his sword, the steel gleamed in the dim light. "By the end of your time here, this will become your lifeline. Treat it with respect, and it will serve you well. Disrespect it, and it will become your downfall."

Master Kinrade's eyes flicked to Quisten, a predatory glint in them. "Lord Cowle, am I correct?" he asked, his voice deceptively calm.

Quisten's chest puffed up, clearly expecting praise. "Yes, sir," he replied, a smug smile crept across his face.

Kinrade's gaze dropped to the ornate sword at Quisten's belt. "That sword of yours," he said, his tone turning icy, "is it a family heirloom?"

Quisten beamed with pride. "Yes, sir. It belonged to my great-grandfather. He carried it during the Siege of Dúnmara. It's been passed down through generations."

Kinrade's lips curled into a smile that held no warmth. "All well and good, boy. But if I catch you with another weapon not made from the forge here, I will flog you. Now, go. Return that sword to your barracks and get a proper uniform on. Once you're in your mocks, run the courtyard for the rest of the morning."

Quisten's face fell. He opened his mouth to protest, a protest poised on his tongue, but Kinrade cut him off with a look that could have shattered stone. "I'll see you again tomorrow, Lord Cowle. We can start again. If I hear you've not run the courtyard, I'll flog you anyway, your family name won't save you. Understand?"

Quisten's jaw tightened, and he nodded, the earlier confidence drained from his face. He turned and stalked off towards the barracks, his posture rigid with suppressed anger.

I couldn't help but smile a little at the sight. From the corner of my eye, I saw Lear's lips twitch into a similar grin. He didn't notice me watching, but the brief moment of shared amusement felt like a small victory.

Master Kinrade then turned to the rest of us. "All right, boys, run around the hall. I drew the short end of the stick and have a

213

unit with three squads instead of the typical two, so you'll work twice as hard."

I couldn't figure out how that logic worked, but I started running with the others. The hall echoed with the sound of boots hitting the floor, a rhythm of exertion and determination.

As we ran, Kinrade stood in the centre, his eyes sharp and calculating. He pointed at random boys, calling them over. Each one sprinted to him, breathless and eager to prove themselves.

"You, what drills do you know?" Kinrade barked at the first boy, a well-built lad with broad shoulders.

"Hammer, Chisel, and Saw drills, sir," the boy puffed out his chest as he announced.

"Good, get back to running", Master Kinrade said with a flick of his wrist.

The next boy, smaller but wiry, stepped forward. "Plough, Harrow, and Flail drills, Master Kinrade."

Kinrade nodded, making a mental note.

I recognized the first two drills and was working on learning the Flail with Banar before we left for The Forge.

Then he called the long-haired boy. The boy's stride was confident, his expression calm. "Plough, Sickle, Scythe, Hammer, Auger, Anvil, Forge," he listed, and the names kept coming.

Kinrade's eyes widened with each drill named, a spark of excitement lighting up his face. "Name?" he asked, his voice betraying a rare enthusiasm.

"Aspallan, sir," the boy replied, his voice steady. "Of House Goldesmyth."

Kinrade nodded, clearly impressed. "I expect great things from you, Aspallan."

From where I was running, I watched Aspallan. His long hair was tied back neatly, revealing a face both youthful and serious. His movements were fluid, his posture impeccable. He carried an air of quiet confidence, the kind that came from rigorous training and high expectations. His eyes, sharp and observant, seemed to take in everything around him.

As I continued to run, my chest tightened with a fierce blend of awe and resolve. Aspallan's skill loomed large, a clear benchmark of the heights I needed to reach. Each step I took around the hall stoked the fire of competition within me, my desire to prove myself igniting into a blazing inferno.

Master Kinrade then pointed at me. "You, next. What drills do you know?"

I jogged over, feeling the weight of the question. "Plough, Sickle, Scythe, Harrow, and I was learning Flail, sir," I answered, trying to keep my voice steady.

Kinrade nodded approvingly. "Good, you know most of the Farm Drills. Back in line."

I rejoined the running, my heart pounding. The next boy Kinrade called was Lear. He approached with a look of resignation.

"And you? What drills do you know?" Kinrade asked.

Lear hesitated before speaking. "None, sir."

Kinrade's eyes widened in surprise. "None? Where do you come from, boy?"

Lear squared his shoulders. "The army, sir. Common foot soldier."

Kinrade rubbed his chin thoughtfully. "Ah yes, I saw you in the trial. That explains it. No formal training, then. You'll need to work twice as hard to catch up with the rest."

Lear nodded, a determined glint in his eye. As we continued to run, Kinrade called more boys, evaluating their skills. My breaths came harder, and my limbs grew heavier with each lap. The hall echoed with the sound of pounding feet and Kinrade's sharp voice.

By the time Kinrade had spoken to most of the boys, I was gasping for air, my muscles burning. Yet, I could feel a strange sense of resolve building within me. This was just the beginning, and I would have to push through every challenge if I wanted to survive and thrive at The Forge.

Master Kinrade called us over, forming a line once more. He scanned our faces, the weight of his scrutiny palpable. "You are all from different parts of the kingdom," he began, his voice carrying authority and a hint of weariness. "This is clear from the drills you know. Drills are a leftover from the time the kingdom was controlled by the tyrant, when those from common trades had to learn to fight and developed their own forms. We call them sets, and there are three of them: The Farmer, The Carpenter, and The Blacksmith"

Kinrade gestured towards us, his eyes sharp and unyielding. "The Farmer, also known as Farmers Drill, include Plough, Sickle, Scythe, Harrow, and Flail. These drills are all about using the body like the tools your ancestors grew up with."

He walked along the line, his presence imposing. "The Plough drill is powerful and sweeping, like turning over soil. Sickle uses rapid, circular slashes for agility and precision. Scythe drill is characterised by wide, arcing strikes and smooth transitions. Harrow is all about breaking up and disrupting with jabs and strikes. And Flail is dynamic and unpredictable, with flexible, whip-like strikes."

Kinrade paused, letting the information sink in. "Then we have the Carpenter drills. Hammer Form focuses on heavy, impactful strikes. Chisel Form emphasises pinpoint accuracy and finesse. Adze Form combines elements of an axe and hammer with sweeping motions. Saw Form uses back-and-forth, sawing motions for sustained attacks. And Auger Form involves drilling and

216

twisting techniques to pierce defences."

His gaze settled on each of us in turn, measuring our reactions. "Lastly, the Blacksmith drills. Anvil Form is defensive, absorbing and countering attacks. Forge Form emphasises generating and controlling internal energy, like the heat of a forge. Tong's Form is about grappling and controlling opponents. Bellows Form focuses on breath control and explosive movements. And Hammer Form, similar to the Carpenter's, but with an emphasis on forging and shaping mid-combat."

Kinrade's voice grew more intense as he concluded, "If you want to know more, ask Master Owle. He loves his history and books."

"Master Kinrade," one boy piped up from the line, his voice tinged with curiosity, "what about the fourth set, the Courtesan Flames?"

Kinrade turned to him, a wicked grin spread across his face. "Are you a whore, boy?" he asked, his tone dripping with mock seriousness.

The boy's face turned a deep shade of red, and the class erupted into laughter. I couldn't help but join in, the tension of the morning eased just a little. But as the laughter died down, I caught a serious look from Aspallan, a flicker of something I couldn't quite place.

Kinrade let the laughter subside before he continued, his voice regaining its authoritative edge. "The Courtesan Flames were created by prostitutes to defend themselves. They have no place in the art of war."

Aspallan's serious look lingered, but before I could dwell on it, Kinrade clapped his hands. "Alright, enough fun. We'll start with drills. Between these drills, you'll spar with different weapons from the training rack. From there, we'll figure out which weapon suits each of you best. Eventually, you'll forge that weapon yourself."

He paused, surveying us with a critical eye. "Form up and pick a wooden weapon from the rack. Create some space. We'll start with the Plough form."

I moved quickly, choosing a wooden sword. It felt familiar in my hand, a comforting weight. We spread out across the hall, the boys around me selecting various weapons: staves, hammers, and daggers.

Kinrade began demonstrating the Plough form, his movements slow and deliberate. I mimicked his actions, the wooden sword slicing through the air in a wide, sweeping arc. The Plough form was all about powerful, grounded movements, leveraging the body's weight to drive the weapon forward.

As I moved, I couldn't help but compare Kinrade's teaching to Banar's. Banar's style had been more fluid, adapting to the situation and the terrain. Kinrade, on the other hand, was precise and meticulous, each motion measured and exact. It was a different kind of discipline, one that demanded unwavering focus and control.

"Focus!" Kinrade barked, catching me mid-thought. I snapped back to attention, adjusting my stance to match his exactly.

The slow, repetitive movements began to take their toll, muscles burning with the effort of maintaining perfect form. Around me, the other boys struggled too, their breaths came in laboured gasps.

"Remember," Kinrade called out, "each movement must be exact. You're not just swinging a weapon; you're controlling it, mastering it. Precision is key."

I felt a bead of sweat trickle down my forehead, the effort of maintaining the stance and motion pushing my body to its limits. But there was a strange satisfaction in the challenge, a sense of purpose that drove me to push through the discomfort.

As we continued, the hall echoed with the sound of wooden weapons slicing through the air, the collective effort of our training filling the space. Each movement brought a sharper focus, a deeper understanding of the form.

After an excruciating round of drills, Master Kinrade called us to form a circle. His eyes scanned the group, a hint of annoyance flickering across his face. "Too many of you," he muttered under his breath. "Fine, let's see what you've got. You and you," he barked, pointing at two boys at random.

The chosen boys stepped into the circle, each holding a wooden sword. They circled each other warily, the tension palpable. The first boy lunged, his attack wild and unrefined. His opponent sidestepped smoothly, bringing his sword down in a controlled arc that connected with the other boy's shoulder. The fight continued with a series of clashes, each strike sounding like thunder in the hall. Finally, with a deft twist, the second boy disarmed his opponent, sending the wooden sword clattering to the ground.

"Good," Kinrade said with a curt nod. "Next, Aspallan and Hugo."

Aspallan stepped forward, his long, slender wooden sword held confidently. Hugo followed, gripping a typical short training sword, a sneer of determination on his face. They faced each other, the air between them thick with anticipation. Aspallan moved first, a blur of motion. His sword flashed through the air, a graceful arc that Hugo barely blocked. Aspallan pressed his advantage, his strikes fluid and relentless. In three swift moves, he disarmed Hugo and had the tip of his sword at Hugo's throat.

The class was silent, stunned by the display. Even I couldn't hide my amazement at Aspallan's skill. The ease with which he had

219

dispatched Hugo was both impressive and intimidating.

"Impressive," Kinrade acknowledged. "Next, Illiam and you," he pointed at another boy.

Illiam stepped forward, two short wooden daggers in hand. His opponent, a stocky boy with a determined look, gripped his own wooden sword tightly. They squared off, and without warning, Illiam sprang into action.

His movements were a whirlwind of precision and speed, the twin daggers darting like vipers. He employed the sickle drills, each strike calculated and efficient. The stocky boy tried to keep up, but Illiam was relentless, his calm demeanour contrasting sharply with the ferocity of his attacks. Within moments, Illiam had his opponent on the defensive, and with a final, decisive strike, he disarmed him, the wooden sword flying from his grip.

I watched, taken aback by Illiam's prowess. The cool, collected boy had transformed into a formidable fighter, his sickle drills executed with deadly efficiency. Kinrade nodded approvingly, a flicker of satisfaction in his eyes.
"Well done," he said, his voice carrying a hint of grudging respect. "The rest of you, take note. This is the level of skill you need to aspire to."

Master Kinrade scanned the circle, his eyes sharp as a hawk's. "Karn and Lear, step forward," he commanded.
My heart thundered as I stepped into the circle, gripping the wooden short sword. Across from me, Lear hefted a one-handed wooden axe, his knuckles white. His eyes locked onto mine, fiery with a blend of determination and fury. The air between us crackled with tension.
"Begin," Kinrade barked.

Lear lunged first, his attack fast and furious. The axe came down in a powerful arc, and I barely managed to sidestep, feeling the rush of air as it passed. I countered with a quick thrust, but Lear deflected it with a grunt, swinging his axe in a wide sweep.

I fell back on my training, recalling the drills Banar had, quite literally, drilled into me. My movements were precise, controlled. Lear, however, fought like a wild beast, his strikes filled with raw power and battlefield cunning. He aimed for my legs, trying to sweep me off my feet, but I danced back, my sword ready.

Every move Lear made was a challenge to keep my own anger in check. The memory of his disdainful look, the way he had dismissed me, fueled a smouldering rage within. I gritted my teeth, focusing on my breathing to maintain control.

Lear's next move was unexpected. He faked a high strike, then kicked at my knee. Pain shot up my leg, but I managed to stay on my feet, swinging my sword in a desperate parry. The wooden blades clashed, the impact jarred my arms.

"You've got spirit," I grunted, deflecting another blow, struggling to keep my anger from spilling over. I could feel it just behind my eyes.

Lear growled, pressing his attack. "And you've got nothing but drills," he spat back, his voice dripping with resentment.

His subsequent attack came low and fast. I saw the opening and took it, my training kicking in. With a swift, practised motion, I stepped inside his guard, deflecting his axe with my sword and landing a solid hit to his side. My rage simmered just below the surface, but I kept it in check, determined to win with skill, not anger.

Lear stumbled back, rage and frustration contorting his features. He roared, coming at me with renewed fury. But I was ready. He swung wide, and I ducked under his arm, driving my shoulder into his chest and sending him sprawling. Lear scrambled to his feet, eyes blazing. He came at me again, but I was in the zone now, my movements fluid and deliberate. He tried another trick, feinting left then right, but I anticipated it, countering with a sharp strike that disarmed him.

His wooden axe clattered to the ground, and he stood there, chest heaving, fists clenched. The fight was over. I had won. Lear's face twisted with fury and humiliation, the scar on his cheek looked ever more fierce for it. Without a word, he turned and stormed out of the circle, his shoulders tense with anger.

Master Kinrade stepped forward, his gaze sweeping over the assembled boys. "That's the difference between knowing how to fight and knowing your drills," he said, his voice carrying over the murmurs. "Drill them into your body until they become second nature. That's how you survive. That's how you win."

At the end of the lesson, Master Kinrade dismissed us for lunch. The boys scattered, their collective sigh of relief echoing through the hall. I hurried to the refectory, my stomach growling in anticipation. Hugo and Illiam fell in step beside me, both looking just as eager for food.

Inside, the smell of roasted meat and fresh bread filled the air, making my mouth water. We grabbed trays and joined the line. I couldn't help but glance at the courtyard, spotting Quisten still running laps, his face red and glistening with sweat.

"Looks like Quisten's getting his workout," Hugo remarked, chuckling.

"Serves him right," Illiam said, smirking. "Maybe he'll think twice before flaunting that sword again."

It surprised me as neither of them had said a bad word about Quisten when he was around.

We found a spot and sat down to dig into our food. The meat was tender, the bread fresh. I hadn't realised how hungry I was until the first bite. The refectory buzzed with chatter, boys exchanging stories of their morning.

"I heard Master Kegg's group had to run the entire perimeter," Hugo said between mouthfuls.

"Good thing we got Kinrade first then," Illiam replied. "At least we got to spar."

I nodded, savouring the food. It was a moment of peace amid the chaos. As I looked around, my eyes landed on Lear, who had just entered the refectory. He grabbed his food and sat down alone at a table in the corner, his face still dark with anger. It looked as though the other boys were ignoring his presence.

"Where are you going?" Hugo asked as I stood up.

"Be right back," I muttered, walking over to Lear.

Lear glanced up as I approached, his expression guarded. "What do you want?" he asked, his tone flat.

I sat down across from him. "You fought well earlier. You've got real talent."

Lear snorted, looking away. "Talent doesn't matter when you're beaten by some noble who's never seen a real fight. Why are you fawning over me anyway?"

I frowned, ignoring the jibe as I tried to bridge the gap. "Sparring is different, sure, but you've got battlefield experience. That's something most of these boys don't have."

Lear's eyes flashed with a mix of frustration and resentment. "And yet, here I am, beaten by someone who's only practised. Sparring isn't the same as a real fight. You can't just rely on knowing your drills."

I opened my mouth to argue, to explain, but the words stuck. He didn't know that I'd fought and killed men and I didn't know how to explain that without sounding like I was boasting. Lear's walls were up, and nothing I said would break through. I nodded, standing up slowly. "Alright. But if you ever need a sparring partner, you know where to find me."

Lear didn't respond, his focus already back on his food. I walked back to Hugo and Illiam, the conversation weighing heavily on my mind. Lear was a fierce fighter, but his anger was a barrier that seemed impossible to break. I knew what that was like first hand.

Lear stood up abruptly, his chair scraped loudly against the stone floor. As he turned, he walked straight into Quisten, nearly knocking his tray out of his hands. Food spilled, and the refectory fell silent, all eyes on the unfolding scene.

Quisten's face twisted in anger. "Watch it, lowborn."

Lear squared his shoulders, eyes blazing. "Maybe you should watch where you stand."

Quisten stepped closer, his voice low and dangerous. "You think you're tough because you survived a few battles? Wrestled a pig? Here, you're nothing. Remember that."

Lear held his ground, the tension palpable. Quisten's sneer deepened as he shoved Lear aside. "Get out of my sight."

Lear glared at him before walking away, fingers dug into his tray. Quisten grabbed a fresh tray of food and made his way over to our table, his mood sour.

"Master Kinrade took my families sword," he grumbled, dropping his tray with a clatter. "And that idiot just had to get in my way. It's his fault."

"Quisten, let it go. It's not worth it," I tried to calm him down.

Quisten scoffed, his arrogance unshaken. "Can't do anything to Kinrade, but that lowborn filth? He's fair game. I'll make sure he knows his place."

"Don't," I said firmly. "This isn't the place for grudges. We're all here to train."

Quisten's eyes narrowed. "You don't get it, Karn. People like him need to be reminded of their place. Don't make me remind you of yours."

Hugo and Illiam exchanged uneasy glances but remained silent. I could see the determination in Quisten's eyes, and I knew he wouldn't be swayed easily. The rest of lunch passed in tense silence, the shadow of Quisten's vendetta hung over us all.

Chapter 20 - Body & Mind

The next few days were a blur of arduous training and relentless drills. The Forge's harsh regimen tested every limit, every ounce of strength and willpower. Each dawn brought new challenges, leaving us battered but more resolute.

One morning, we gathered in a large, dimly lit hall for our session with Master Owle. The air was thick with the scent of old parchment and ink, the room lined with shelves crammed full of dusty tomes. Master Owle stood before us, his sharp eyes glinting behind wire-rimmed glasses, his presence commanding silence.

"Today, we delve into the knowledge of the realm," he began, his voice both soft and penetrating. "History, logistics, intelligence—all crucial for a warrior's mind."

He started with a tale of Dúnmara, the city of stone and iron, its history etched in blood and rebellion. "Dúnmara was wrested free from the Tyrant's grip long ago," he said, his words painting vivid images of battle and liberation. "The city stands as a symbol of resilience, a testament to the indomitable spirit of our people."

I found myself leaning forward, engrossed in the story. Owle's voice carried the weight of centuries, each word resonating with the struggles and triumphs of those who had come before us. His tale painted vivid pictures of battles fought and cities freed. If they had wrestled the city free of the Tyrant, then what did that make the Witch Queen? By all accounts from Elara and Banar, she was just as bad. But the people I'd seen so far did not look enslaved. Yet, I hated her and what her Black Guard had done to my village, my people. The conflicting thoughts swirled in my mind.

"The importance of Ironhold to Dúnmara cannot be overstated," he continued. "It is the backbone of our strength, the repository where we get the ore for our finest weapons as well as a strong garrison of soldiers under Lady Arwen of house Sable. Without Ironhold, Dúnmara would be vulnerable, its heart exposed."

The room was silent, every ward hung on his words. Owle spoke of logistics and supply chains, of how the flow of resources could determine the outcome of battles. He delved into the intricacies of intelligence gathering and reconnaissance, the subtle art of warfare that went beyond brute strength.

"Knowledge is as vital as steel," he said, his eyes sweeping over us. "Understanding the enemy, knowing their movements and their weaknesses, is what turns the tide of war."

As he spoke, I felt a newfound respect for the complexities of warfare. It wasn't just about physical prowess; it was a game of wits, a battle of minds. Quite like Skirmish I realised. The realisation was both humbling and invigorating. I thought of Elara and the many hours I had spent in her study, where she had patiently taught me the importance of strategy and the value of a keen mind. Her lessons, rich with history and tactical insight, had laid the groundwork for this moment.

Owle's lecture drew to a close, the silence in the hall now charged with a deeper understanding. We had been given a glimpse into the vast expanse of knowledge that underpinned every conflict, every strategic decision.

"Remember, wards," Owle concluded, his voice a low rumble, "the mind is a weapon. Sharpen it, wield it with precision, and it will serve you as faithfully as any blade."

One thing that quickly became clear was Master Owle's unique method of rewarding those who answered his questions correctly.

He would toss small sweets to those who got the right answers, a rare treat in the harsh environment of The Forge. The wards would hoard these sweets like precious treasures, trading them like currency in the dorms. A single sweet could be exchanged for chores done, secrets shared, or alliances formed. It added a layer of competition and camaraderie, each ward vying not just for knowledge, but for the sweet reward that came with it.

After class, I approached Master Owle with a question that had been nagging at me. "Master Owle," I began hesitantly, "I've been reading one of the Seeker's books."

His eyebrows shot up in surprise. "Oh? Which book, specifically?"

"The one about self-control," I replied, hoping I wasn't overstepping.

Master Owle's expression shifted to one of curiosity. "Interesting choice. The Seekers are known for their pursuit of knowledge and self-mastery. They believe that true power comes from understanding and mastery of one's inner self."

I nodded, absorbing his words. "What more can you tell me about them?"

He glanced around, as if ensuring no one else was listening. "The Seekers are an ancient order. Their teachings are not widely known here, but they focus on balance, control, and understanding the deeper aspects of the mind and spirit. It's said they can perform feats that border on the mystical, but such stories are often shrouded in exaggeration and mystery. I believe they sought transcendence. It's rare to find someone with a genuine interest in their works."

Master Owle's words lingered in my mind, he didn't mention the Ashen, my people. I had led to believe they had written the book, or at least contributed? I filed out of the hall with the others, the morning light filtering through narrow windows, casting long shadows on the stone floor. The Forge was shaping us, not just in body, but in mind and spirit. Stepping into the courtyard, I felt a steely resolve harden within me. The days ahead would be brutal, but we would emerge stronger, sharper, ready for whatever the future held.

In the afternoon, we gathered in the courtyard for our next session. The sun hung high, casting a harsh light that bounced off the stones. Master Mores, the Master of Fists, stood before us with a stern expression. He was a mountain of a man, muscles bulging under his tunic, his eyes hard as flint.

"Forget drills," Mores barked. "Fighting is about two things: physical fitness and experience. You build strength, you learn through pain."

We started with a jog around the grounds, the pace punishing. Sweat poured down my face, my legs burned, but Mores showed no mercy. Next, we lifted logs, their rough bark scraped at our skin, and threw stones until our arms felt like lead. The obstacle course was a beast of its own.

First, we scrambled up a series of wooden walls, each one higher than the last, our fingers clutched at the rough wood as we hauled ourselves over. The next challenge forced us to crawl under a net strung barely a foot off the ground. The ropes dug into our backs, and the gravel below scraped our elbows and knees.

We leaped over ditches filled with muddy water, the cold splash a brief respite from the heat of exertion. Next, there was a balance beam, narrow and wobbling under our weight, that we had to cross without falling off. My heart pounded in my ears as I concentrated on each step, the beam slick with the mud from our shoes.

Then came the rope climb. Thick, coarse ropes hung from a

high wooden frame, and we had to pull ourselves up using nothing but our arms and sheer determination. My muscles burned, and my grip threatened to slip, but the shouts of Mores pushed us onward.

Finally, we had to weave through a series of hanging sandbags, their heavy weight swinging toward us as we dodged and ducked. Each collision sent a jarring shock through my body, testing my agility and reflexes to the limit. Every muscle screamed in protest.

By the time we finished the course, we were drenched in sweat and covered in mud, our bodies exhausted but our spirits fiercely determined. Mores's brutal regimen left no room for weakness; he kept pushing us, his voice a relentless whip.

"Move! Faster! Don't you dare slow down!"

After what felt like an eternity, he herded us into a makeshift ring drawn in the dirt. "Bare knuckles," he announced. "No drills, no forms. Just fight."

My heart pounded as I stepped into the ring, facing Lear. His eyes were dark, simmering with barely contained rage. This was his chance for revenge, and he wasn't going to let it slip away. I raised my fists, trying to remember any useful lessons from Banar, but bare knuckles was a different beast. The drills I knew were for swords, not fists.

Mores's voice cut through the tension. "Begin!"

Lear came at me fast, his fists a blur. I tried to deflect, to counter, but his attacks were relentless. A fist connected with my ribs, and I gasped, the pain sharp and immediate. Lear's face twisted with a savage grin, sensing his advantage. He moved with the confidence of someone who'd seen real combat, his strikes wild but effective.

"Come on, Fayle," he growled, landing a blow to my jaw that made my vision blur. "Where's your fancy training now?"

I tried to respond, swinging clumsily, but he dodged easily, his fist slamming into my stomach. I doubled over, gasping for breath. Lear didn't let up, driving me back with a flurry of punches. I stumbled, barely keeping my footing. Each hit was a reminder of my inexperience, the drills I clung to useless in the face of his raw aggression.

The final blow sent me sprawling to the ground, my nose gushing blood. Mores stepped in, his voice cutting through the haze of pain. "Enough."

I lay there, the dirt cool against my cheek, struggling to catch my breath. Lear stood over me, his chest heaving, eyes blazing with satisfaction. As I got to my feet, every part of me ached. Mores looked at me, his gaze hard but not unkind.

"This is where you learn," he said. "Pain is the best teacher."

I nodded, swallowing my pride and the bitter taste of defeat. As I limped away from the ring, blood still trickling from my nose, Mores pointed towards the far end of the courtyard.

"Go to the Refuge," he instructed. "Get that nose looked at before it gets worse."

The Refuge was a sanctuary of sorts, a place where soldiers sought healing. But as I approached, a haunting melody began to echo through the stone halls. It was faint at first, a distant hum that grew louder with each step. The song seeped into my bones, cold and invasive, filling me with a fear I couldn't shake. I knew this. I remembered it all too well. My heart pounded in my chest, each beat echoing the eerie tune.

The healer, an older woman with kind eyes, noticed my discomfort. "It's the song of the witches," she explained softly.

"This place is close to their side of The Forge. You're feeling its effects."

I nodded, trying to shake off the unease. "Feels like it's burrowing into my head."

She gave me a sympathetic smile as she tended to my bloody nose. "You'll get used to it. Everyone does."

But the song had put me in a foul mood. As I left the Refuge, the melody still echoing in my mind, I rejoined my squad. Lear was waiting, his expression conflicted.

"Hey, Karn," he began, hesitating. "About earlier... I just wanted to say—"

"Save it," I snapped, the fear and anger bubbling over. "I don't need your excuses, Lear. You think landing a few lucky hits makes you a warrior? You're just a commoner who got lucky."

I'm not sure why I said it. I was as low born as they came but maybe I had been around Quisten and his cronies for too long. Either way it is what I said and I could not take it back, especially with the fear of the witches song stuck in my head.

Lear's face hardened, his eyes flashing with hurt and anger. Without another word, he turned and walked away, shoulders tense.

Quisten, who had been watching the exchange, sidled up to me with a grin. "Good, put him in his place. We should really teach him a lesson, you know? Show him what happens when you mess with us."

I shook my head, trying to push down the rage. "No, Quisten. It's done. Let it go."

Quisten's grin widened, a malicious glint in his eyes. "You're too soft, Karn. Someone like Lear needs to be reminded of their place."

I met his gaze, my own anger simmering just below the surface. "And what, make it worse? We don't need to stoop to that level."

Quisten shrugged, the grin never leaving his face. "Your call. But don't say I didn't warn you when he tries something again."

As he walked away, I took a deep breath, trying to calm the storm inside me. The witch's song still lingered in my ears, a reminder of the darkness that was never far away.

That night, sleep came reluctantly. I tossed and turned, the remnants of the witches' song still echoing in my ears, a haunting melody that twisted through my mind. When I finally drifted off, the nightmares gripped me immediately.

I was back in my village. The sky was dark, the air thick with smoke. Flames licked at the wooden houses, consuming everything in their path. Screams filled the air, a cacophony of terror that tore at my soul. I ran through the chaos, my heart pounding in my chest.

I turned a corner and saw her. Liv. She lay beneath a pile of rubble, her eyes staring up at me, hollow and lifeless. The sight rooted me to the spot, my breath caught in my throat. I reached out, my fingers trembling, but I couldn't move, couldn't save her.

The scene shifted. The ruins of my village faded, replaced by the dark, oppressive halls of The Forge. Shadows lurked at the edges of my vision, whispers and murmurs slithering through the air. The witches' song grew louder, more insistent, wrapping around me like a vice.

I found myself in the refuge again, the walls closing in. The song was everywhere, seeping into my very bones. I tried to scream, but no sound came out. Panic surged, my pulse a frantic drumbeat in my ears.

Liv's eyes haunted me, staring, accusing. The flames from the village melded with the shadows of The Forge, creating a nightmarish tapestry of fear and sorrow. I was trapped, helpless, the weight of my failures pressing down on me.

I jolted awake, drenched in sweat, my heart racing. The room was silent, the other boys still asleep, their breaths soft and steady. The fear lingered, a dark cloud that refused to dissipate.

I sat up, trying to calm my breathing, but the images wouldn't fade. Liv's lifeless eyes, the haunting song, the flames—everything melded into a suffocating mass of dread. I clenched my fists, willing the terror to subside, but it clung to me, a relentless shadow.

Morning couldn't come soon enough.

As the first light of dawn crept through the narrow windows, bringing with it a tentative hope, I felt a renewed sense of purpose. The next day, a pattern began to emerge. Each day balanced physical training with mental discipline. That morning, Master Quark, the Master of Beasts, led us outside The Forge for horse riding along the river.

As we saddled up, I felt a rare moment of peace. Sköll, my horse, nickered softly as I approached. I stroked his mane, feeling the bond between us strengthen. "Ready for a ride, boy?" I whispered, receiving a nudge in response.

Illiam, riding beside me, glanced at Sköll. "Interesting name," he remarked, his eyes curious. "Where'd you get it?"

"Read it in a book once," I replied, a half-truth. "It stuck with me."

Illiam nodded, seemingly satisfied. We set off, the river's gentle murmur and the rhythm of hoofbeats creating a serene accompaniment. We skirted the edges of Dúnmara, a sprawling city mostly made up of one-story buildings. From our path, we could see the outskirts: modest homes and patches of green where the city met the wild. The river we followed was a lifeline, its waters reflecting the morning sun in sparkling ripples.

The countryside around Dúnmara was lush and vibrant, a stark contrast to the harsh stone of The Forge. Tall grasses swayed in the breeze, wildflowers added splashes of colour, and birds flitted about, their songs mingling with the sound of flowing water. The air was fresh and cool, carrying the scents of earth and greenery.

However, the peace was short-lived. It was clear that Lear struggled with riding, his movements awkward and unsteady. Quisten seized the opportunity, his voice loud and mocking. "Careful, Lear! The horse isn't a pig you can wrestle!"

Lear's face darkened, but he remained silent, gripping the reins tighter. The tension between them crackled like a live wire.

As the spring rains returned, our ride was cut short. The downpour slicked the ground, turning it into a treacherous path. Lear's horse stumbled, and he tumbled into the mud with a wet thud. Quisten laughed loudly, pointing. "Look at the mud-born! Right at home, aren't you?"

The fire in Lear's eyes blazed hotter, and for a brief moment, I could almost see a flicker of red. I shook my head, dismissing it as a trick of the light or my imagination playing tricks from lack of sleep and the haunting dreams of the night before. The witches' song still echoed faintly in my mind, a lingering ghost that wouldn't let go.

The ride back was tense, the rain soaking us to the bone. When we returned, I spent extra time with Sköll, brushing and cleaning him, savouring the simple, calming tasks.

Hugo, unusually quiet, was doing the same with his own mount. He glanced over, a rare smile on his face. "You really care for him, don't you?"

I nodded. "Sköll's a good horse. Deserves good care."

Hugo continued brushing, his movements gentle. "My father liked to breed horses. He always said a well-bred horse was a reflection of its owner."

I looked at him, intrigued. "Your father bred this one?"

Hugo nodded. "Yeah, his name's Storm. My father used to say he had the spirit of a storm in him, wild and untamed. Took a lot to break him in, but once he did, he was loyal as they come."

I glanced at Sköll, feeling a deeper connection. "Sounds like your father knew his horses."

Hugo's eyes softened, a hint of pride in his voice. "He did. Spent his whole life around them. Taught me everything I know."

We worked in companionable silence, the storm outside mirroring the brewing tensions within our group. But for those moments, it was just me, Sköll, and the simple, honest labour of caring for a loyal companion. Hugo's presence, his quiet dedication to Storm, felt like a rare moment of calm in the chaos of The Forge.

The afternoon brought a shift in focus, turning from the physical to the mental as we attended Master Breen's session. Master of Strategy, Breen stood before us, not with books, scrolls, or maps, but with a stack of polished wooden boards and a set of intricately carved game pieces.

"Today, we'll be engaging in Skirmish," Breen announced, his voice commanding and clear. "For those unfamiliar, it's a strategy game. Learn quickly, because on the battlefield, hesitation can mean death."

To my surprise, there were a few who had never played, their eyes wide with confusion. Lear being one of them. But I was not one of them. Lucas had taught me Skirmish back at the Silver Stag

Tavern in Eldewood, his patient guidance turning me into a formidable player. I felt a spark of excitement amidst the usual tension.

Breen paired us off, moving through the room to ensure everyone was set up. The clatter of game pieces echoed as we arranged our boards. When Quisten sauntered over, a smug grin plastered on his face, I knew this match would be anything but friendly.

"Ready to lose, Fayle?" Quisten sneered, his arrogance manifested.

"We'll see," I replied evenly, keeping my tone calm.

The game began, each move a calculated risk, each piece a potential sacrifice. Quisten played aggressively, pushing his pieces forward with reckless confidence. I countered with precision, anticipating his bold moves with strategic retreats and careful strikes.

Tension thickened the air as the match progressed. Quisten's brow furrowed, his eyes narrowed with concentration. Despite his arrogance, he was skilled, forcing me to stay sharp. The room faded away, the clatter of other matches dimming to a distant murmur as we locked into our battle of wits.

But then, in a swift, ruthless move, Quisten toppled my defences. His piece slid across the board, taking my flag. He leaned back, a victorious gleam in his eyes.

"Checkmate, Fayle," he said, his voice dripping with satisfaction. "Looks like the noble blood runs true."

I clenched my fists under the table, anger simmering just below the surface. His gloating smile was insufferable, his victory a bitter pill to swallow.

"Good game," I forced out, the words tasting like ash.

Quisten laughed, a cold, mocking sound. "Better luck next time. If there is a next time."

As he walked away, chest puffed out in triumph, I felt a surge of determination. This wasn't over. No one was spared Quisten's arrogance, but next time, I'd be ready.

The last class in the cycle was spent under the stern guidance of Prime Master Kegg, the Prime of the Forge and Master of Leadership. His presence was imposing, his sharp eyes scrutinised every move we made. He wielded his cane with an iron fist, ready to punish any who broke the rules or seemed not to be learning. The slightest misstep was met with a sharp crack against our knuckles or the back of our legs, a painful reminder to stay focused.

Today's lesson was about leadership, critical thinking, and command. Kegg had set up a maze in the training grounds, a labyrinth of wooden walls and barriers. At the centre of the activity were the squad primes, each positioned on an elevated platform overlooking the maze. The task was for the primes to guide three of their blindfolded squad mates through the maze while another squad did the same. The twist was that we could block each other and "knock" opposing squads out of the competition.

Kegg's voice boomed across the field as he explained the rules. "This exercise is about trust, communication, and strategy. You must guide your team through the maze while preventing the opposing team from doing the same. You can tap an enemy combatant on the shoulder to knock them out. Any contact other than a tap on the shoulder results in disqualification. The winning squad will be the first to get all three members to the end of the maze."

As we lined up, Quisten, our prime, stood on the platform, eyes gleaming with determination. I was one of the blindfolded members, my senses heightened as the world went dark.

"Remember, boys," Kegg added with a stern tone, "I'll be watching closely. Mistakes will be punished."

The match began. Quisten's voice rang out, directing us through the maze. "Karn, two steps forward. Hugo, turn left." His instructions were precise, but I could sense the tension in his voice. The sound of other squads moving echoed around us, creating a disorienting symphony of shuffling feet and whispered commands.

"Left, Karn, now!" Quisten's urgency pushed me to move faster. I could hear Hugo stumbling ahead, his steps unsure. The maze was a confounding mess of twists and turns, each step a gamble.

Amidst the confusion, I heard Aspallan's voice clear and steady, guiding his squad with confidence. "Move forward, slow and steady. Turn right now. Perfect." His commands were calm, a stark contrast to Quisten's growing frustration.

"Right, Karn! Watch out!" Quisten's shout came too late. I collided with another blindfolded boy, the impact sending us both sprawling. A sharp pain shot through my side as I hit the ground, the cane's strike following swiftly. "Careless!" Kegg's reprimand stung as much as the blow.

Aspallan's squad moved swiftly, his calm demeanour a testament to his leadership. "Keep going, you're almost there," he encouraged, his voice unwavering. Within moments, Aspallan's squad emerged from the maze victorious, their blindfolds removed amidst cheers of triumph.

Quisten's face was a mask of frustration and anger as we regrouped. He glared at us, his eyes burned with fury. "Pathetic," he spat, his voice dripped with disdain. "You call that teamwork?

I've seen shit shovellers with more coordination."

Hugo flinched, and even Illiam looked uncomfortable under Quisten's searing glare. "If you all weren't so pathetic, we might have stood a chance. Next time, try not to trip over your own damn feet."

I clenched my jaw, the sting of his words adding to the frustration of our loss. It wasn't entirely our fault, but there was no point arguing with him. His arrogance was like a wall, impenetrable and unwavering.

As we moved away from the maze, I couldn't shake the anger simmering beneath the surface. The sting of Quisten's insults mixed with the ache of Kegg's cane, a bitter reminder of our failures.

The days fell into a routine, each master pushing us to our limits with their unique lessons. We grew stronger, keener, and more resilient. However, one master remained elusive—Master Veil, the Master of Shadows. Whispers about his methods spread rapidly among us; rumours swirled that he could vanish into thin air or appear right behind you without a sound. Some said he trained with poison-tipped daggers and conducted lessons in total darkness. Others claimed to have seen him conversing with ravens or hanging upside down from the rafters, his cloak blending seamlessly into the shadows. The stories grew more outlandish by the day, but they only heightened our anticipation and dread.

At the end of the seventh day, as the sun dipped below the horizon, the masters gathered us in the courtyard. Prime Master Kegg stepped forward, his gaze sweeping over us. "You've all done well this week. Tomorrow, you will have a day of rest. Use it wisely. Reflect on what you've learned and prepare for what's to come."

A collective sigh of relief passed through the ranks. The promise of rest was a beacon of hope, a chance to gather our strength for the trials that lay ahead.

Chapter 21 - Seventh Day

On the seventh day, I tried to stay in my bunk past dawn. My body, conditioned to the gruelling schedule of the past week, rebelled against the idea of rest. The thin mattress felt like a slab of stone beneath me, offering no comfort. The air was heavy with the sounds of boys still sleeping, their breaths even and undisturbed. It seemed staying asleep wasn't a challenge for them.

As I lay there, staring at the ceiling, I could hear the faint rustling of leaves outside, the distant call of a morning bird. The urge to rise and begin the day gnawed at me until I could stand it no longer. With a sigh, I swung my legs over the edge of the bunk and quietly dressed, my movements careful not to wake the others. The chill of the early morning air prickled my skin and I wanted to jump back into my bunk. Alas I did not.

I slipped out of the dorm, each step measured and soft. The corridor outside was empty, the silence almost oppressive. I didn't share a living space with my "friends." Quisten, Hugo, and Illiam were housed in different barracks, a fact that had kept me isolated from the camaraderie that might have developed in another setting. The boys in my barracks were strangers, their faces familiar but names unknown. All we did was sleep here, our interactions limited to the brief moments before exhaustion claimed us each night.

As I stepped into the cool morning, the air felt fresher, cleaner. The sun was just beginning to rise, casting long shadows across the courtyard. The peace of the moment was a stark contrast to the constant tension and competition that defined our days. It was a rare and precious silence, one I could only find before the chaos of training began.

The first thing I did was head to the baths. They were located to one side of the courtyard, near the dorms. As I approached, the faint scent of lavender and eucalyptus filled the air, a welcoming change from the usual scent of sweat and grime that clung to the training grounds. The large wooden doors creaked open, releasing a billow of steam that obscured my vision.

Inside, the baths were a marvel of stone and tile, a series of large, communal pools filled with steaming water. The ceiling was high, with wooden beams crisscrossing overhead, and the walls were lined with hooks holding neatly folded towels. The steam hung thick in the air, creating a hazy, dreamlike atmosphere. Marble benches lined the walls, and the sound of dripping water echoed softly, adding to the serene ambiance.

I had expected the baths to be crowded, but to my surprise, they looked completely empty. The stillness was a stark contrast to the usual hustle and noise of The Forge. I stripped off my clothes and grabbed one of the towels provided, wrapping it around my waist before stepping into the hot bath. The silence and the warmth enveloped me, offering a rare moment of solitude and peace.

The water was blissfully hot, and as I sank into it, I felt the tension of the past week begin to melt away. The heat seeped into my muscles, soothing the aches and pains that had accumulated from the relentless training. For the first time since we began the journey to The Forge, I felt like I had a chance to truly relax. I let out a long breath, leaning back against the smooth edge of the pool, my eyes closing as the steam enveloped me.

My thoughts drifted to Serah. How was she faring on the other side of The Forge? The side where girls learned to become... witches. The thought of her training, her struggles, and her strength filled my mind. I hoped she was holding up well, that she was as determined and resilient as I knew she could be. The memory of her smile, her unwavering support, warmed me even more than the bathwater.

But I pushed those thoughts to the back of my mind, not wanting to ruin the rare moment of peace. I focused on the present, on the feeling of the hot water, the quiet murmur of the few boys around me, and the soothing atmosphere of the baths. It had been a tough week, and this was only the beginning. For now, I allowed myself to enjoy this brief respite, letting the water wash away the weariness of the past days.

I settled deeper into the water, letting the warmth seep into my bones. The steam thickened around me, blurring the edges of my vision and creating a cocoon of tranquillity. That's when I heard a soft breath and the gentle trickle of water.

The steam cleared a little, revealing a figure in the corner. Aspallan sat there, his long dark hair now wet and draped over his shoulders. His face, smooth and serene, showed a rare moment of peace. If it weren't for the lean muscle evident beneath his skin, I might have mistaken him for a girl given his fair complexion.

Aspallan's eyes remained closed for a moment, then one eye opened, locking onto me with a calm, assessing gaze. The quiet acknowledgment between us hung in the humid air, the silence of the baths amplified the moment.

The steam swirled around us, wrapping the room in a thick haze. I glanced at Aspallan, his lean frame relaxed, the water trickling down his shoulders. His calm demeanour contrasted sharply with the cool intensity he displayed during training.
"Your weapon forms are pretty damn impressive," I began, breaking the silence. "And the way you translate that precision to fists... it's something else."
Aspallan opened his eyes fully, a hint of a smile on his lips.

"Karn, isn't it? You show promise too, but you need to relax more. Tension will only slow you down. Try doing the drills without a weapon first, then with a partner. It helps to understand the movements better." He paused, then added, "I'll practise with you if you want."

"Thanks, Aspallan. I'll take you up on that," I replied, appreciating his offer.

Aspallan's eyes narrowed, curiosity and something else in his gaze. "Why do you hang around Quisten, Karn? You've got your own strength, but you ride his coattails. Is it because he's a Warden's son? Arrogant as he is."

My first thought was, *aren't you too, a Warden's son?* But instead I shrugged, the hot water easing some of the tension in my shoulders. "My father said The Forge is as much about making alliances as it is about enduring hard training."

Aspallan scoffed, a rare flash of emotion crossing his face. "The Forge is tame compared to my grandfather's training. He used to have me fight his guards blindfolded and on uneven ground. Said it would teach me to expect the unexpected."

I raised an eyebrow, impressed and slightly taken aback. "What about your father?"

Aspallan's face darkened, his voice turning cold. "He was weak. He died for it… At the Battle of Black Rock Hollow." He looked at me with a knowing gaze.

The same battle that Banar was known for as a hero.

In the back of my mind, I heard the voice. *This one is strong.*

Aspallan's usual calm expression returned, his tone more reflective. "The only thing that worries me here are the trials. No one will tell me what they entail."

"Trials?" I asked, curious and a bit anxious.

"They determine how you rank up," Aspallan explained. "You need to rank up at least once in three trials, or you're thrown out of

The Forge."

"My father never mentioned them," I said, the realisation that Banar had kept something from me settled uneasily in my stomach.

Our conversation grew more subdued after that, the looming uncertainty of the trials cast a shadow over us. The steam continued to swirl, the hot water offering a brief respite from the relentless training, but the anticipation of what lay ahead lingered, refusing to be ignored.

Aspallan rose from the water first, his movements fluid and unhurried. This was a boy who did not care who saw him because he was confident in body and mind. As the steam parted, I took in his lean physique, the defined muscles that spoke of rigorous training. His long hair, now wet, clung to his back, highlighting the fairness of his complexion. He draped a towel over his shoulders and nodded to me before leaving.

I stayed in the bath a little longer, savouring the heat that seeped into my muscles, easing the week's tension. The tranquil silence was a rare luxury. But soon, the door creaked open, and the sound of other boys' chatter broke the calm. Reluctantly, I climbed out, grabbing a towel and drying off quickly. Unlike Aspallan I still felt vulnerable when exposed. I had too much to hide.

The bathhouse filled with the murmur of morning routines. I dressed swiftly, pulling on my clothes and stepping out into the crisp morning air. The path to the refectory was familiar now, and I walked it with a newfound appreciation for the rare moments of social connection. When we weren't battering each other with training swords.

Inside, the refectory buzzed with activity. Boys clustered around tables, the clatter of plates and hum of conversation filled the room. I grabbed a tray and loaded it with fruit, cheese, and some sausage. Finding a seat near the corner, I settled in, the warmth of the food a comforting contrast to the cool morning.

As I ate, I noticed Lear sitting alone at a table across the room. Not for the first time. He hunched over his food, his expression closed off, lost in thought. The tension between us still lingered, a tangible reminder of the clash of wills and tempers. I considered approaching him, but the memory of our last interaction held me back. We had had enough friction for one week.

I focused on my meal, letting the simple act of eating ground me. The room's noise faded into the background, a dull hum that underscored the quiet resolve I felt. It was just the beginning of our time at The Forge, and there were still many battles—both physical and mental—yet to be fought.

After breakfast, I scanned the crowded courtyard for Keird. I had questions and he had answers, as well as being the most approachable, even if a bit unreliable. But he was nowhere to be found, his usual laid-back presence absent.

With a sigh, I headed to the registry offices, a building on the far side of the courtyard. The office was quieter than I expected, a contrast to the chaos outside. Behind the desk, Rhys sat with a quill in hand, scribbling away. He looked up as I entered, a smile spread across his face.

"Karn! How's the training treating you?" he asked, setting his quill aside.

I walked over, trying to keep my frustration hidden. "It's been... intense," I replied, leaving out the details of the hate triangle between Lear, Quisten, and myself.

Rhys leaned back in his chair, studying me with a knowing look. "It's meant to be. Separates the weak from the strong."

I nodded, the words weighing heavier than they should. "Rhys,

I wanted to ask you something."

He raised an eyebrow, curiosity piqued. "Go on."

"Is it possible to go to the witches' side of The Forge?" I asked, trying to sound casual. Rhys's eyes widened slightly, and a smirk tugged at the corner of his mouth.

"Ah, wanting to sneak a peek at the girls, are we?" he teased.

I shook my head quickly. "No, it's not that. It's just... Serah is over there, and I was wondering if there's any way to see her."

Recognition dawned in Rhys's eyes. "Serah, right. Unfortunately, it's not possible. The witches' side is off-limits. But later in the year, there will be events where you'll get to see them. Patience, boy. You'll get to see your sister yet."

I sighed, the answer not what I'd hoped for. "What about the trials? Can you tell me anything about them?"

Rhys's expression turned serious. "That, I'm afraid, I cannot discuss. The trials are something you'll have to face when the time comes."

Disappointment gnawed at me, but I nodded in understanding. "Alright."

Rhys leaned forward, his smile returning. "Enjoy the rest of your day off. Maybe take a trip into Dúnmara. Clear your head a bit."

I hadn't thought about that. The idea of exploring the sprawling city, even just the outskirts, sounded appealing. "Thanks, Rhys. I might just do that."

He gave me a friendly nod as I turned to leave. "Take care, little lord Fayle. See you around."

I wandered The Forge, feeling aimless. Boys were everywhere, absorbed in their activities. Some trained rigorously, their grunts of effort punctuating the air. Others were hunched over books and scrolls, faces etched with concentration. On the benches in the courtyard, groups engaged in heated games of Skirmish. The temptation to join them flickered, but I shook it off. A few wards were kicking a leather ball around, their laughter echoing.

I just wasn't sure what to do with myself. My steps eventually led me to the stables, seeking the comfort of familiar company. Sköll greeted me with a nicker, his dark eyes brightening as I approached. I spent some time with him, walking him around the paddocks, feeling the tension of the week ease with each step. His coat gleamed under the sun as I brushed him down, the rhythmic strokes calming us both.

Just as I was settling into the routine, I heard a faint sound of crying. Frowning, I followed the sound down the row of stalls. In Storm's stall, I found Hugo. His face was red and puffy, tears streaking down his cheeks. The moment he saw me, he hurriedly wiped his eyes, trying to put on a brave face.

"Hey, Hugo," I said gently, stepping closer. "What's going on?"
Hugo hesitated, his eyes darting away as he wiped at his face. "I'm just... not used to being away from home," he finally sighed. "And the training here... it's so damn hard. Everything feels like it's crumbling around me."
I thought of Aspallan, thriving effortlessly, and the stark contrast between him and Hugo. I leaned against the stall door, my voice softening. "Yeah, it's tough. But you know what? We need to stick together, right? We'll get through this as a team."
Hugo looked up, his usual jovial demeanour cracked and fragile. "Quisten keeps berating me. And he's my liege Lord... It's... it's just a lot. He makes me feel like I'll never measure up."
I nodded, feeling his pain. "Quisten can be a right bastard, but remember, we're all equals here. You and I, we're both sons of vassal lords. Don't let him get to you. He's just one voice in a sea of many."
Hugo's face brightened with a small, tentative smile. "Thanks, Karn. That actually helps. I just... sometimes I feel so alone."
I clapped him on the shoulder, trying to infuse some strength

into my touch. "We all have our struggles, Hugo. You're not alone in this. Just keep pushing, keep fighting. We'll get through this together, alright?"

Hugo nodded, visibly cheered. "Hey, a bunch of us are heading into Dúnmara. I was just checking on Storm before I joined the others. You should come with us."

I hesitated, glancing back at Sköll. "I don't know, Hugo. I'm not sure if I should—"

"Come on, Karn," Hugo interrupted, his voice more insistent now. "You've been working harder than anyone. You deserve a break. Plus, I could use someone to have my back."

I smiled, feeling a bit of relief myself. "Sounds like a plan. I'll join you guys."

"Great! Give me a second to clean up," Hugo said, wiping the last of the tears from his face and fixing his hair.

I waited, watching as he splashed some water on his face and straightened his clothes. He looked more like the Hugo I was coming to know—jovial, resilient, and ready for anything. When he was done, I offered him a hand.

"Ready?" I asked.

"Ready," Hugo replied, taking my hand and standing up. "Let's go see what Dúnmara has to offer."

We headed towards the docks, the idea of a break from the relentless training lifting our spirits. For the first time since arriving at The Forge, I felt a bit of hope. The chance to explore Dúnmara was a welcome distraction from the challenges that lay ahead.

Chapter 22 - Dúnmara

Hugo and I made our way to the docks, the noon sun cast stunted shadows over the cobblestone path. The river glinted in the light, a stark contrast to the muted, grey buildings of The Forge behind us. As we approached, I spotted Quisten and a few other boys from our squad lounging by the water's edge.

Hugo glanced around and then back at Quisten, his voice hesitant. "Where's Illiam?"

Quisten didn't even look up from the knife he was fiddling with. "The hell if I know. I'm not his keeper," he replied, his tone dripping with indifference.

We boarded the boat, the wooden planks creaked under our weight. The barge wasn't large, just enough to fit about a dozen boys comfortably. The air was thick with the scent of algae and damp wood, the gentle lapping of the water a constant backdrop.

As we pushed off from the dock, the conversation turned to the day ahead. "Finally, a day free," one of the boys, Ivor, said, his voice filled with relief.

"What should we do?" another Edrin asked, looking around.

Quisten didn't miss a beat. "We're going to my favourite tavern. Best mead in Dúnmara," he announced, as if the decision was already made.

Hugo frowned, clearly not thrilled about being ordered around on their day off. "Couldn't we... I don't know, take the long way there? Maybe see some sights?"

Quisten gave him a withering look but then shrugged. "Sure, whatever. Long way it is. But we're ending at the tavern."

The barge glided smoothly over the water, the journey to Dúnmara not long. The city soon came into view, sprawling and alive with activity. The ride would've taken just over an hour on horseback, but mounts were off-limits without explicit permission from The Forge.

The barge slid into a designated berth with a soft thud, the ropes creaking as they were secured. We disembarked, the wooden planks of the dock groaning underfoot. As we walked up the stone steps into Dúnmara, I couldn't help but feel a sense of awe.

The city was sprawling, with wide streets lined with timber-framed houses, their thatched roofs peeking out like uneven rows of teeth. Market stalls cluttered the main thoroughfare, hawkers shouting their wares in a cacophony of voices. The air was filled with the rich scents of fresh bread, roasting meats, and the tang of the river.

Dúnmara was nothing like Ironhold. Here, the buildings had room to breathe, with green spaces and open plazas breaking up the dense clusters of shops and homes. Ironhold, built precariously on a cliff, was a maze of narrow alleys and towering structures squeezed tight by the unforgiving rock.

Stone bridges arched over winding canals, their reflections dancing in the clear water below. People moved with a leisurely pace, a stark contrast to the frantic hustle I was used to. Children played in the streets, their laughter mingled with the distant thud of a woodworker's mallet and the rhythmic clatter of horse hooves on cobblestones. It was hard to reconcile this serene, almost idyllic scene with the horrors I remembered. These were the people whose armies had burned my village and slaughtered my family. The juxtaposition gnawed at me, a bitter reminder of the brutality lurking beneath the surface of this peaceful facade.

As we wound through the bustling streets of Dúnmara, the boys' excited chatter swirled around us, each word dripping with anticipation. The city pulsed with energy, vendors calling out their wares, and colourful banners fluttering in the breeze. I couldn't help but feel a strange mix of envy and exhilaration as I soaked in the vibrant life around me, the lively atmosphere sparking a sense of wonder and longing deep within.

In the heart of the city, where every road seemed to converge, stood an imposing fortress. Its dark stone walls loomed high, distinctly different from the low, timber-framed buildings that surrounded it. Several smaller towers bristled from its sides, but it was the central tower that dominated the skyline, overseeing the entire city with an austere, watchful presence.

I couldn't help but comment, "That place looks like it doesn't belong here. It's so different from the rest of the city."

Quisten turned, a smug look on his face. "That's the Queen's palace. She had the old dun torn down and built her own. A show of power. I would do the same, I suppose."

I nodded, my eyes traced the sharp lines and dark shadows of the fortress. It was a reminder of the Queen's reach, her influence woven into the very fabric of the city.

We wandered into the market, and the boys quickly scattered, each drawn to different stalls. Quisten stood off to the side, his impatience radiating like heat off a forge. Ignoring him, I ventured deeper into the market, taking in the vibrant sights and sounds.

Vendors shouted out their wares, offering everything from exotic spices to finely woven fabrics. The air was thick with the scent of roasting meat and fresh bread, mingled with the more pungent aroma of tanned leather and the sharp tang of metal from a blacksmith's forge nearby. Brightly coloured tapestries fluttered in the breeze, and the chatter of haggling customers filled the air.

One stall caught my eye, displaying an array of jewellery.

Among the silver rings and gem-encrusted bracelets, a knotted necklace with an intricate design stood out. It reminded me of something Serah would like. I picked it up, feeling the cool metal against my fingers.

"How much for this?" I asked the merchant, a wiry man with a keen eye.

"Three silver," he replied, watching me closely.

I handed over the coins and took the necklace, slipping it into my pocket. As I turned, I found Hugo standing nearby, a curious look on his face.

"Who's that for, Karn?" Hugo teased, his tone light. "Got a secret sweetheart you're not telling us about?"

I shook my head, feeling a bit awkward. "No, it's for my sister," I said, then hesitated before adding, "And no, it's nothing like that. She's... training at The Forge too, as a witch."

Hugo's eyes widened, and he fell silent, clearly taken aback. "Your sister's an acolyte?"

"Yeah," I said, glancing away, not wanting to elaborate. "It's complicated."

Hugo nodded, the surprise still evident on his face, but he didn't press further. He simply accompanied me as we continued to explore the market, the unspoken weight of my confession hung in the air between us.

As the sun began its descent, casting a warm, golden hue over the plaza, Quisten gathered us up, his impatience now a sharp edge in his voice. "Come on, enough dawdling. We're going to a real place now."

He led us through a maze of side streets until we arrived at an upscale tavern. The building stood apart from the lively market, its exterior boasting polished wood and stained glass windows that caught the last light of the day. The sign above the door, painted in gold leaf, proclaimed it as "The Golden Hall."

A hulking bouncer stood at the entrance, arms crossed over his chest. His eyes narrowed as he took us in, but his expression softened when he recognized Quisten. "Ah, Lord Cowle. Good to see you again," the bouncer rumbled. "Just remember, we want no trouble," he added, his gaze shifting to the rest of us.

Quisten gave him a confident smirk. "No trouble, I promise."

As we stepped inside, the tavern's opulence hit me. The floors were covered in rich, dark wood, polished to a gleaming shine. Ornate chandeliers hung from the ceiling, casting a warm, inviting light. The walls were adorned with intricate tapestries depicting grand hunting scenes and heroic battles. Plush, velvet-covered chairs surrounded tables of polished oak, and a grand piano stood in one corner, its player filling the room with soft, melodic tunes.

Quisten strutted to the bar, his chest puffed out with arrogance. "Drinks are on me, boys," he announced loudly, turning heads. "We're drinking mead tonight. None of that piss-water ale."

I glanced at Hugo, who shrugged. "Never had mead before," I admitted.

Quisten turned, a smug grin on his face. "Well, Karn, that's because mead is the drink of the gods. Far superior to ale in every way. It's smooth, sweet, and strong."

Hugo snorted. "Yeah, and it has nothing to do with your family producing most of the Kingdom's mead, right?"

Quisten shot him a withering look. "Shut up and enjoy your free drink, scrounger."

Despite myself, I felt a flicker of appreciation for Quisten. He was still a prick, but at least he was being friendly, in his own twisted way.

Quisten then nudged me, pointing to a section of the tavern where rows of people were intently focused on Skirmish boards. "This is what this place is known for," he said, his voice carrying a note of pride. "They run tournaments here all the time. We're too late to enter today, but I thought we could have a drink and size up the competition."

We found a table near the Skirmish players and settled in with our mead. The drink was as Quisten had described – sweet, smooth, and deceptively strong. I took a sip, feeling the warmth spread through me, and watched the players manoeuvre their pieces with strategic precision.

Quisten leaned back in his chair, observing the room with a critical eye. "See that guy over there?" he pointed to a tall, thin elderly man with a hawk-like nose. "He's the current champion. Smart as a whip. And that woman next to him? She's ranked second. They're both deadly on the board."

Hugo leaned in, curiosity piqued. "Think we stand a chance?"

Quisten smirked. "Of course. But it's not just about skill; it's about knowing your opponent, anticipating their moves." He took another swig of his mead, eyes glinting with determination. "We'll come back and show them what we're made of. For now, enjoy the drink and the show."

I nodded, sipping my mead thoughtfully. The night stretched ahead, full of possibilities.

We continued to drink and talk, the atmosphere growing more relaxed as the mead flowed.

"So, what do you think the witches are like?" asked Ivor, a lanky boy with a mop of curly hair. He leaned forward, his eyes wide with curiosity. "Think they're good-looking?"

Quisten snorted, nearly choking on his drink. "You? Hoping a witch will look your way? No woman, witch or not, would touch a rat like you," he jeered, drawing laughter from the table.

Ivor flushed, a sheepish grin on his face. "Just curious," he muttered.

"You shouldn't bad mouth them," said Edrin, a quiet boy with sharp features. His voice was low, almost a whisper. "They'll hear you and take you away."

The boys laughed, but there was a nervous edge to it. Quisten waved his hand dismissively. "Superstitions. Witches have better things to do than worry about our chatter."

Laughter erupted around the table. Hugo rolled his eyes but grinned, raising his mug in a mock toast. "To avoiding the witch's curse."

Quisten raised his own mug. "To finding a way to make even the witches swoon."

I laughed with them despite one of those witches being my adopted sister.

We all took a deep drink, the mead's warmth spread through me. The room seemed to spin, the edges of my vision blurring.

Quisten leaned closer to me, pointing out a Skirmish game where two older men were locked in a fierce battle. "See that move?" he whispered, nodding towards one of the players. "Classic ploy to bait his opponent into overextending."

I nodded, trying to focus. "Yeah, but it looks like the other guy isn't falling for it. See how he's holding back?"

Quisten's eyes gleamed with approval. "You've got a good eye, Karn. Not many can see that."

We continued to discuss the finer points of the game, our conversation weaving through various strategies and memorable matches. Despite his arrogance, Quisten's passion for Skirmish was infectious, and I found myself genuinely enjoying the exchange. The camaraderie between us felt genuine, a rare moment of connection. I took another swig of mead, feeling the warmth spread through me. The alcohol was stronger than the watered-down ale I was used to, and it was starting to show. My movements became looser, my laughter louder.

"Hey, Karn," Hugo slurred, nudging me with an elbow. "How are you holding up? This mead is no joke, huh?"

I grinned, my head pleasantly fuzzy. "It's good. Stronger than I thought."

Quisten chuckled. "Mead's not for the faint of heart. But it's fitting for warriors like us."

We continued talking, our conversations weaving through topics from The Forge's gruelling training to speculations about the witches. The room buzzed with the energy of a hundred different stories, laughter, and the clinking of mugs. The atmosphere was intoxicating, a blend of fellowship and competition.

I glanced around, feeling a sense of belonging that had been missing since I arrived at The Forge. For now, the weight of training, the tension with Lear, and the ever-looming trials faded into the background. Here, amidst the laughter and the mead, I could just be another boy, enjoying a rare moment of peace.

Quisten leaned in, his eyes glinted with a cruel edge. "I've been thinking. We need to teach Lear a real lesson. Make him understand he's not welcome here."

The other boys leaned closer, the noise of the tavern fading into the background. "What do you have in mind?" I asked, though I could feel a knot tightening in my stomach.

Quisten's smile was cold. "We'll wait until he's asleep. Sneak into his bunk, drag him out into the courtyard. Strip him naked and tie him to the flagpole. Let him freeze until morning."

I frowned, the harshness of the plan making my skin crawl. "That's too far, Quisten. We shouldn't let this feud continue. It'll only get worse."

Quisten's gaze hardened. "Lear hurt you, Karn. He embarrassed you in front of everyone. Don't you want revenge?"

Hugo, sitting next to me, shook his head. "Quisten, this isn't right. We're better than this."

Quisten's lips curled into a sneer. "Fine. Be weak if you want. But don't expect me to show mercy next time he crosses us." He stood abruptly, his chair scraping against the floor. "I have other business to attend to."

As Quisten left, the tension at the table lingered. Hugo turned to me, his expression serious. "He's out of control, Karn. We need to be careful around him."

I nodded, the weight of Quisten's plan still heavy on my mind. "Yeah. Thanks for backing me up, Hugo."

We talked for a bit longer, our conversation drifting to lighter topics in an attempt to shake off the lingering unease. When Quisten returned, his cheeks were flushed, and he rejoined the group with a forced casualness. His eyes, bloodshot and narrowed, locked onto me.

"Hey, Karn," Quisten slurred, his tone carrying a drunken edge. "There's a Skirmish competition soon called The Three Moons Tournament. You and I should sign up together."

I frowned, feeling the tension from our earlier disagreement about Lear. "I'm not sure, Quisten. I've got a lot on my plate already."

Quisten's smile turned into a sneer, his arrogance shining through. "Come on, Karn. Don't be a coward. I'm a Warden's son, and I say we're signing up. You think you can just say no to me? Besides, there's a special piece you can only get from the tournament—the Moon Rider."

I could feel the underlying anger in his words, his posture aggressive. He didn't give me much of a choice, his insistence bordered on a challenge. Sighing, I nodded reluctantly. "Alright, fine. I'll sign up with you."

Quisten's expression softened, but the tension between us remained. "Good," he muttered, his anger still simmering beneath the surface.

The mead continued to flow, the warmth in my veins battling the cold dread of Quisten's proposal about Lear. After a while, the pressure on my bladder became impossible to ignore. I stood, swaying slightly. "I need to take a piss," I announced, making my way to the bar.

A girl with dark hair and bright eyes stood behind the counter, her smile polite but weary. I admired her a bit too blatantly before clearing my throat. "Where's the privy?"
She pointed to a door at the back. "Through there, to the left."
"Thanks," I said, giving her a smile that I hoped wasn't too drunkenly awkward.

I made my way through the tavern, feeling the mead swirling in my veins. The barmaid's directions were clear, but my unsteady steps made the journey to the privy seem longer. Inside, the air was musty, the floor damp. I untied my hose, relieving myself with a sigh. The sound of urine hitting the basin echoed in the small space. I leaned against the wall, letting the momentary relief wash over me.

After finishing, I retied my hose and splashed some water on my face, hoping to clear my head a bit. As I exited the privy, the light of the tavern seemed brighter compared to the dimness of the small room. I started walking back to our table, my mind still buzzing from the mead.

I rounded a corner and collided with someone. The man halted abruptly, his hat, rimmed with a feather on top, falling to the floor. Instinctively, I bent down to pick it up, my fingers brushing the polished wood of the floor.

When I straightened, I found myself face-to-face with none

other than Lucas. His long, messy hair framed a face that hadn't changed since our last encounter. His narrowed nose and long coat were unmistakable. Lucas smiled at me, a charming, almost roguish smile. "Karn, what a pleasant surprise."

"Lucas," I slurred, blinking rapidly. "What are you doing here? I thought you were heading up river?"

Lucas chuckled, taking his hat from my outstretched hand. "That was Lord Fayle's request. I did indeed have business in Dúnmara. Selling some important and very rare merchandise." He nodded towards the shoulder bag he carried, his eyes twinkling with mischief.

I glanced around, then leaned closer, trying to lower my voice but likely failing. "Those men... were they after you?"

Lucas's smile faltered for a moment. "Hush, Karn." He pulled me to a quieter corner of the tavern. "Yes, unfortunately so."

"Why?" I asked, struggling to keep my thoughts coherent.

Lucas sighed, glancing around as if to ensure we weren't overheard. "Some of my goods aren't strictly... legal. Important people from other kingdoms may not approve. Best leave it at that."

My head swam, the alcohol making it hard to process his words. "But... why?" was all I could manage.

Lucas patted my shoulder, his touch firm but gentle. "It's good seeing you, Karn, but I really must go." He glanced over my shoulder. "It looks like your friends are leaving."

I turned, seeing Quisten and the others making their way towards the door. "Next time we meet, we'll play a game, alright?" Lucas's voice brought my attention back to him.

I nodded, a slow smile spread across my face. "Yeah, that sounds good."

With a final, reassuring pat, Lucas disappeared into the crowd, leaving me with a head full of questions and a heart a slight lighter. I stumbled back towards my friends, the warmth of the tavern and the promise of another meeting with Lucas buoying my spirits.

I caught up with my friends just as they were heading out of the tavern, the cool night air hitting my face like a splash of water. We stumbled along the streets, the mead warming our blood and loosening our tongues.

Hugo, ever the cheerful one, started singing a well-known tavern song, his voice carrying through the night.

"Here's to the Tinker, who travels afar,
With pots and pans and a battered old jar,
He'll fix your kettle, your plough, and your cart,
And with a wink and a grin, he'll mend your heart!"

We all joined in, our voices a ragged chorus, laughing and bumping into each other as we made our way to the docks. The city's lights twinkled in the distance, and the river reflected the moon's pale glow.

My steps were unsteady, and I knew I'd regret the drinking come morning. But for now, the camaraderie and the simple joy of the moment drowned out the worries and rivalries of The Forge.

"Here's to the Tinker, with tales and with lore,
He'll drink and he'll laugh till he's flat on the floor,
But don't you trust him, with coin or with cheer,
For he'll disappear, when your purse is near!"

We reached the docks, the last barge waiting to take us back. Hugo's singing grew louder, more boisterous, and I couldn't help but laugh, despite the nagging thought of the hangover awaiting me.

As we boarded the barge, the song continued, echoing over the water.

"To the Tinker, to the Tinker,
With his hat and his pack,
He'll mend and he'll fix,
Then he'll never look back!"

The barge pushed off, the city slowly fading from view. The night was calm, the river's gentle sway lulling some of the boys to a drowsy silence. I leaned against the rail, the cold metal a sharp reminder of the warmth of the mead still coursing through me.

Chapter 23 - The Expanse

The next morning hit me like a hammer. My head pounded with a relentless, throbbing ache, each beat echoed through my skull. My mouth felt dry as sand, and the sour taste of stale mead lingered on my tongue. Rolling over, I groaned, a sharp wave of nausea twisting my gut. Leaning over the edge of my bunk, I retched, vomit splattered onto the floor.

The other wards in the dorm groaned and muttered, disgust clear on their faces. "What the hell is that smell," one boy grumbled, his voice thick with sleep. "Did you bathe in rancid wine?"

"Nice, Fayle. Real nice," another spat. "Smells like a brewery in here."

I forced myself upright which only caused the room to spin. My muscles ached, my joints protested with every movement. Swallowing back another wave of nausea, I stumbled to the nearest rag and began cleaning the mess. The sharp, acrid stench of vomit stung my nostrils, making my eyes water.

Halfway through wiping up, my stomach lurched again, and I barely made it to the bucket in time. The retching left me trembling, sweat beading on my forehead. I finished cleaning, my hands shaking, the smell clinging to me like a curse.

As I straightened up, another boy wrinkled his nose, glaring at me. "You better clean yourself up too. You smell like a pigsty."

I nodded weakly, too drained to argue. The aftermath of yesterday's drinking had me in its claws, and it wasn't letting go anytime soon.

Thankfully, I didn't miss breakfast, but I was damn close.

Stumbling into the refectory, the smell of food hit me like a punch to the gut. My stomach churned, and I swallowed hard, forcing the bile back down.

Hugo sat at our usual table, looking as miserable as I felt. His head was cradled in his hands, eyes bloodshot and half-closed. Quisten, on the other hand, sat there looking infuriatingly fresh, a smirk plastered on his face.

"Morning, gentlemen," Quisten greeted, his voice annoyingly chipper. "Sleep well?"

Hugo groaned, barely lifting his head. "Shut up, Quisten."

Quisten laughed, a rich, mocking sound. "Come now, Hugo. Can't handle a little mead?"

I dropped into a seat next to Hugo, wincing as my head pounded. "How are you not feeling like death?" I muttered, glaring at Quisten.

He shrugged, taking a leisurely sip of water. "Practice, my dear Karn. Practice." His eyes gleamed with amusement. "You two look like you've been run over by a cart."

Illiam joined us, dropping into a seat across from Quisten. "Morning," he mumbled, his face etched with fatigue. "What did I miss?"

Quisten smirked. "Where were you? You missed all the fun." Hugo and I just groaned in unison.

Illiam shrugged, "had other things to attend to."

Ignoring his jibes, I reached for some bread and cheese. The food helped, though every bite was a struggle. I forced myself to chew slowly, willing my stomach to keep it down. The water was a different story. I drank it in desperate gulps, each swallow a soothing balm against the dryness in my mouth and throat.

Hugo managed to eat a little, but his face was a mask of misery.

"I swear, never drinking mead again," he mumbled, pushing his plate away.

Quisten chuckled, shaking his head. "Amateurs. Just enjoy your free drinks next time, scroungers." He glanced at me. "And you, Karn. Maybe learn to hold your liquor a bit better."

I wanted to snap back, but I didn't have the energy. Instead, I focused on the food, hoping it would help me survive the day.

The first lesson of the morning, mercifully, was with Master Owle. My head pounded with each step, and my stomach churned ominously. The classroom was a haven of dim light and relative quiet, but it was still hard to focus.

Master Owle began his lesson by firing off questions. "Who can tell me the three main supply routes into Dúnmara?"

A boy to my left, Davin, raised his hand confidently. "The Northern Road, the River Way, and the Southern Pass."

"Correct," Owle nodded approvingly, tossing a small sweet his way. "And what was the decisive battle that led to the reclaiming of Ironhold?"

Illiam, always quick with an answer, replied, "The Battle of Broken Cliffs."

"Very good," Owle said, smiling as he handed over another sweet. "Now, can anyone explain the significance of Ironhold to the defence of the kingdom?"

I struggled to keep my eyes open, my head throbbed too much to think straight. Another boy answered, but I barely registered the words. I just wanted the lesson to end.

When it finally did, I joined the line of boys filing out of the classroom. Master Owle's knowing smile met my gaze. "First night in Dúnmara?" he asked, amusement in his tone.

Sheepishly, I nodded. "Yes, sir."

Owle chuckled softly. "I'm not going to punish you, Karn. It's a life lesson. Happens to wards every year. The aftereffects and

265

hangover are punishment enough in this case, but good luck with your next master."

His laughter echoed in my ears as I walked out, dread pooling in my stomach at the thought of facing the rest of the day.

Master Owle had been right, of course. Despite shoving more food and water into me at lunch, I still stumbled around feeling weak and hazy. The next drill was with Prime Master Kegg, and my stomach churned at the thought.

Hugo had feigned illness and hadn't shown up. Smart one, I thought, despite his usual jovial nature. Kegg had us running the maze blindfolded again. With Quisten's squad already down a man, Kegg's anger simmered just below the surface. When I couldn't hold back and vomited against one of the walls, that anger erupted.

"Fayle!" Kegg's voice cut through the maze, harsh and unforgiving. He stormed over, ripping me out of the maze himself. "A soldier needs grit and forbearance!" he roared, his grip like iron on my arm.

"I... I'm sorry, Master," I stammered, my voice weak.

"Sorry? Sorry doesn't cut it, boy. You're a disgrace to The Forge!"

I expected a lash on the wrist, something I'd felt before. Painful but temporary. Instead, Kegg dragged me across the training grounds, past curious eyes, to the wall that separated the wards' side from the witches' side of The Forge.

"This is The Expanse," Kegg explained, his voice echoing ominously as he opened a door to a small, dark box embedded in the wall, like a closet. "Any who break the rules, as you have, will spend the night here."

Before I could protest, he shoved me inside. The door slammed shut, plunging me into darkness. "Master, please—"

"Silence!" Kegg barked. "A night in The Expanse will teach you more than I ever could. Consider it a lesson in discipline."

The lock clicked, sealing me in. A small act of mercy caught my eye—a water skin left on the floor. The faint light from outside cast eerie shadows, heightening the sense of isolation.

I didn't know how long I had been in the Expanse. A cool, dark place with a water skin felt like exactly what I needed. My head pounded less, and the nausea had subsided leaving me feeling marginally better. I managed to get some rest, the stone floor surprisingly comfortable after the hell of the day that I had. I figured I had missed supper, but my stomach wasn't ready for food anyway.

The only thing I craved was a bath; I still reeked of last night's excesses, sweat, mead, and vomit. I could practically taste the grime on my skin, but I took solace in the darkness. No one could see my shame. All in all, I was almost enjoying my stay.

Then the song started.

A haunting melody that seemed to crawl into my ears and wrap itself around my brain. Harsh notes cut through the air like blades, sharp and unforgiving. The sound was overwhelming, filling the small space of the Expanse with an eerie, otherworldly resonance.

This wasn't like the faint echoes in the Refuge. This was like being back in my village, the night it was attacked. The song had echoed off the walls then too, creating a cacophony of pain and fear. I covered my ears, but it did little to muffle the sound. It vibrated through the stone, through my bones, making it impossible to escape.

I curled into a ball, trying to shut it out, but the song seemed to grow louder, more insistent. Each note was a reminder of the horrors I had witnessed, of the helplessness I had felt. It was as if the witches themselves were around me, singing just for me, reminding me of their power and my insignificance.

I panicked, my fingers jammed into my ears, trying to block out the song. It did nothing. The melody, twisted and cruel, vibrated through the stone and into my bones. I couldn't escape it.

My vision blurred, and I started to see things. Soldiers tearing through my village, their faces twisted into monstrous visages. They cut down my family and friends, leaving a river of blood in their wake. Then Liv appeared, her blank eyes staring into nothingness. Serah next, her eyes mirrored my sister's, empty and hollow. Elara's face, usually so stern, was lifeless. Banar, Lucas— they all stared with dead eyes.

I screamed, tears streaming down my face, my voice raw and desperate. The Expanse echoed my cries back at me, the sound bouncing off the walls, mocking my helplessness. Everything went black. For a moment, I thought I had found peace, but then I heard the hoofbeats.

A horse galloped towards me. It was Sköll, but his eyes glowed red, flames licking at his mane. His breath steamed in the cool air. A man rode him, clad in the same dark armour as those who had attacked my village. No, not just any man—Lord Caine in his black and gold armour. He raised his sword and thrust it down. I looked down to see myself impaled, blood pouring from the wound.

"Help me," I pleaded, my voice weak.

Quisten appeared, then Hugo, then Lear. They circled me, passing me around like a ragdoll, mocking me, stabbing me with their wooden training weapons. Each stab left splinters, pain radiating through my body. Their eyes were red and aflame, just like Sköll's... just like mine.

Serah stood there, singing the haunting melody. Her voice was beautiful yet terrible all at the same time, she was the source of my torment. I stumbled towards her, desperate for comfort, for anything that would make the pain stop. When I reached her, she smiled, a cold, cruel leer, and slid a dagger into my gut.

I screamed one final time, the sound tearing through the Expanse, a cry of pain, betrayal, and despair.

Weak, the voice hissed, low and sinister. *Weak,* it repeated, louder this time, reverberating in my skull. *Weak,* it roared, a deafening chorus of disdain. *You are weak, boy. You are my kin, you are meant to be wraith.*
"You..." I stammered, my voice barely a whisper. "Nix?"
I am.
"What are you?" I managed to ask, my voice trembling with fear and desperation.
A relic of a bloodier age, the wolf replied, its voice dripping with malice. *When our people hunted. When our people fought.*
"Help me," I pleaded, the words choking out through the tightness in my throat.
Help yourself, runt, the wolf snarled. *Show me your strength.*
"I... I can't..."
Darkness took me.

Daylight filtered into The Expanse, piercing the darkness like a blade. The next morning had come, indifferent to my suffering. I was covered in my own fluids—drool, piss, vomit. The stench was overwhelming, but I was too exhausted to feel anything more than a dull, throbbing pain throughout my body. My limbs felt like lead, my head a mass of fog and aches.

Rough hands grabbed me, hauling me out of the cramped

space. I recognized Keird among the boys dragging me into the light. The courtyard was filled with more than just the three squads from my unit; curious eyes watched my humiliation. Faces blurred together, their expressions a mix of curiosity and horror.

I couldn't stand. My legs were jelly, my body convulsed with involuntary shakes. Words tumbled from my lips, incoherent and pitiful. My mouth was dry, throat raw from screaming, and every muscle screeched in agony.

Kegg leaned in close, his stern face inches from my own. "You'll thank me for this later," he said, his voice like cold iron, his breath hot against my ear. The words cut through my haze, but only just.

The Prime Master straightened and addressed the gathered wards. "Let this be a lesson to you all. He is the first, but he shall not be the last."

He then turned to the boys holding me up. "Get him cleaned up and to the Refuge."

As they dragged me away, my feet dragging uselessly on the ground, I managed to lift my head one last time. My gaze met Lear's. There was no anger in his eyes, only pity. His face was a mask of sorrow, making me feel even more shattered and defeated. Darkness clawed at the edges of my vision, and I let it take me, the world slipping away into a merciful black void.

Chapter 24 - Night's Lesson

It took several days to recover from my ordeal in The Expanse. Each morning, I awoke feeling as if my limbs were made of lead, my mind a foggy mess of fear and exhaustion. Every sudden noise made me jump, every shadow seemed to hide a lurking threat.

The masters gave me space, their stern faces softened with pity. Even the other wards, usually so quick to tease, held back, their eyes filled with a mix of curiosity and sympathy. Quisten, of course, couldn't resist mocking me, but I saw the fear in his eyes whenever he glanced at that cursed room in the wall.

"Survived your little nap in the box, did you?" Quisten sneered one morning, his voice dripping with forced bravado.

I didn't bother replying. His words were hollow, and we both knew it. He kept his distance, the mocking tone unable to mask his unease. The ordeal had changed the dynamic between us, a shift I couldn't quite put into words.

Physically, I slowly regained my strength. Each day, the weakness ebbed as my muscles remembered their old strength, and my steps grew firmer. I forced myself through the drills, focusing on each movement, each breath, pushing the memories aside.

But the memories and visions haunted me. They crept into my mind unbidden, flashes of horror that sent my heart racing and left me gasping for breath. It wasn't the first time I'd faced such darkness. Back in my village, I'd seen things, felt the weight of despair and terror.

One afternoon, during a strategy lesson with Master Breen, I found myself drifting, my mind replaying the nightmare images of soldiers tearing through my village, transforming into monsters, the blood, the blank eyes of Liv and Serah, the betrayals. I clenched my fists, nails digging into my palms, grounding myself in the pain.

"Karn, are you with us?" Master Breen's voice cut through the fog, pulling me back to the present.

"Yes, sir," I replied, my voice steady despite the turmoil inside.

"Good," he said, nodding. "Focus is essential. Strategy isn't just about the mind, it's about the heart. You must remain clear-headed, no matter the distraction."

I nodded, swallowing hard. The lesson resumed, but the words felt distant, a background murmur to the storm raging in my mind.

As the days passed, I forced myself to engage more, pushing through the haze, fighting the remnants of the terror that lingered. Each drill, each lesson became a battle, not just against the physical challenges, but against the ghosts that haunted my thoughts. I fought the remnants of terror with every swing, every step, determined to reclaim my mind.

Drills continued relentlessly, a gruelling balance of mind and body. Each day, I felt my muscles forge themselves anew, the strength returning, harder and more enduring. New drills became second nature—Hammer, Anvil, Saw, Auger, and Adze, each one a step towards mastering the art of combat. Master Kinrade's voice drilled into my head, each instruction a hammer strike on the anvil of my will.

Strategy lessons with Master Breen sharpened my mind. I learned the intricacies of warfare, the delicate balance of supply lines, the subtleties of reconnaissance and intelligence. My riding improved under Master Quark's stern eye, each session with Sköll building a bond between horse and rider that felt unbreakable that even Serah would have approved of.

Weeks turned into a blur of training and learning. Every seventh day, we were given off to rest and recuperate. At first, I swore off

272

drinking like Hugo, the memory of my hangover a vivid reminder of my limits. But by the next seventh day, I found myself at The Golden Mead Hall with Quisten, Illiam and indeed Hugo, the allure of camaraderie and mead too strong to resist.

I cannot say that I never drank to excess again, but I did tame my drinking, mindful of the lesson learned. Yet, I still enjoyed the evenings. Quisten and I practised Skirmish diligently for the upcoming Three Moons tournament. The games revealed that I wasn't as skilled as I had thought. The experienced players there, their strategies honed by countless matches, exposed my weaknesses and forced me to adapt. Each game was a lesson, each loss a step towards improvement.

A few weeks later, on one of these outings, I finally met Lucas again. He stood at the bar, his familiar long coat draped over a stool, his hat tipped jauntily to one side. My heart leapt at the sight of him, a mix of relief and excitement bubbling up.

I introduced Lucas to my new friends from the Forge. To my surprise, Quisten spoke up first. "We've met," he said, offering no further details. The ambiguity hung in the air, but I let it slide, curiosity tugging at the back of my mind.

"Lucas taught me Skirmish back at the Silver Stag in Eldewood," I mentioned, glancing at Quisten.

Quisten's eyes flickered with surprise before settling into a calculating gaze as he sized Lucas up. "Is that so?" he murmured.

I set up the board, the familiar pieces clicking into place. "Ready?" I asked, looking between the two of them.

The game began in silence, the tension between Lucas and Quisten almost visible. Quisten, confident and strategic, played aggressively. Lucas, ever the enigma, countered with moves so fluid and unexpected that they seemed almost casual. The game progressed, pieces clashing and retreating, until Lucas emerged victorious.

Lucas didn't gloat. Instead, he offered Quisten a small, respectful nod. Then he turned to me, his eyes twinkling with a hint of mischief. "I visited Eldewood," he said, taking a sip of his drink. "All is looking good."

He paused, leaning in slightly. "Though, I must admit, I didn't show my face to Lord Fayle." I thanked him for that, knowing the unspoken animosity between Lucas and my adopted father was a delicate thread best left unpulled.

Lucas then leaned back and, with a roguish grin, began to spin a small tavern tale. "You lads remind me of a night in Graycliff. There was a barmaid there, a fiery redhead with a temper to match. She had every man in the room wrapped around her finger, but she only had eyes for the quietest lad in the corner. Turns out, the quiet ones always have the best stories—and sometimes, the boldest moves." He winked, his grin widening as he took another sip. "So, remember, it's not always the loudest who win the game."

The other wards around us listened, captivated by the charm and subtle heat of his story. It was a small encouragement, a nudge to find their own confidence in unexpected places.

I wanted to speak to Lucas in private, to ask him about the men who had pursued him and to clear up the lingering questions that gnawed at me. But the opportunity never presented itself. The evening slipped away, the conversation flowing around us like the mead in our cups. I did not overindulge that night, thankfully.

True to Master Kegg's word, others got to experience the horrors of The Expanse. Lear was next. Quisten had instigated a fight during Master Breen's class. Although Quisten had started it, Lear threw the first punch, sealing his fate. He was dragged to The Expanse, his protests echoing down the halls.

When Lear emerged, he looked as broken as I had felt. Seeing his state, I volunteered to help him out, and Illiam joined me, offering his arm as well. I do not think Illiam approved of what Quisten had done to the boy. Together, we took Lear's shoulders, supporting his unsteady steps. He was drenched in sweat, trembling with a fear that I knew all too well. The haunted look in his eyes mirrored my own.

"Thanks," he muttered afterward, his voice rough and unsteady. That simple word held a weight that bridged the gap between us. Since then, we'd been more civil, though the tension between him and Quisten remained, a simmering grudge that refused to die.

Two more wards were thrown into The Expanse in the following weeks. One of them, a frail boy named Alden, was gone the next day. His bunk was empty, his presence erased. Keird told me that it was just how things happened—the weak were filtered out.

Training continued and ramped up, each day more arduous than the last. Master Owle's questions grew harder, twisting our minds into knots as we struggled to keep up. Each session with him was a battle of wits, the promise of sweets a small reward for those who could decipher his riddles.

Master Kinrade drilled us relentlessly, adding more complexity to the drills. The Farm Drills, once familiar, now blended with the Carpenter and Blacksmith sets, each movement demanding precision and strength. My muscles ached, but I could feel myself growing stronger, more adept.

Strategy lessons with Master Breen were no less demanding. He had us playing Skirmish, each game a lesson in tactics and foresight. We shared knowledge, dissecting past battles and hypothetical scenarios. The room buzzed with discussions, each of us eager to prove our understanding.

Master Mores decided it was time to show us how real fighters handled themselves in the ring. His fists were like iron, and he moved with a fluidity that left us all in awe. A few spirited wards tried to challenge him, but each was defeated soundly. I was grateful for Aspallan's advice; the drills I had practised bare-knuckled helped me hold my own when it was my turn to face Lear again. Lear was still fragile from his time in The Expanse, and while I didn't win outright, I managed to avoid a beating.

Master Quark introduced us to mounted warfare, the thrill of riding combined with the strategy of battle. Sköll responded well to the training, and our bond deepened. Each session on horseback was exhilarating, the rush of wind and the power beneath me a reminder of the freedom I had both lost and regained.

Prime Master Kegg's lessons in command were the most daunting. He rotated the leaders of each squad, those commanding the blind through the maze, making it clear that after the trials, squad primes would change. The weight of responsibility pressed on us all, the thought of the upcoming trials sent a shiver down my spine. Each exercise in command was a test of our ability to lead under pressure, to make decisions quickly and effectively.

Days blurred into one another, a relentless cycle of training and learning. The Forge was shaping us, each lesson a hammer blow on the anvil of our determination. We were becoming something more, something stronger, each of us fighting our own battles within and without.

Then finally, as spring changed to summer, the days grew hot and dry, the air heavy with the scent of blooming flowers and sunbaked earth. It was during this sweltering season that we were introduced to the last Master.

One evening, after supper, Prime Master Kegg stood before us, his presence commanding as always. "Tonight," he announced, "you will meet Master Veil, the Master of Shadows. Report to the same classroom where you have your lessons with Master Owle. But this session will be at night."

The announcement sent a ripple of excitement and apprehension through our ranks. Whispers buzzed among us as we filed out of the dining hall, the weight of the unknown hanging over us.

We gathered outside the classroom, the night air cooler but still tinged with the heat of the day. The moon cast long shadows across the courtyard, and the stars twinkled above, indifferent to our nerves. Inside, the room was dimly lit by a few flickering candles. The familiar setting felt different under the cloak of night, the shadows played tricks on our eyes. The usual order and structure seemed to fade, replaced by an eerie anticipation.

We walked into the dimly lit classroom, the usual air of academia was replaced by an unsettling anticipation. Sitting atop the desk usually occupied by Master Owle was a man draped in a cloak, its fabric dark and flowing, almost blending with the shadows themselves. He sat casually, one leg dangling off the edge, the other bent at the knee, his posture relaxed yet commanding. His eyes were sharp, glittering with a strange intensity, and his hair, dark and wild, framed a face that was both intriguing and unsettling.

As we took our seats, a tense silence filled the room. Quisten, ever the opportunist, attempted to break it. "Master Veil, it's an honour to—"
"Spare me the flattery, boy," Master Veil interrupted with a

sharp, mocking grin. "Unless you're planning to sweep me off my feet, let's skip the courtship."

A ripple of uneasy laughter moved through the room. Quisten's face flushed with embarrassment, his attempt at ingratiation thwarted.

"I am Master Veil," the man continued, his voice smooth and captivating. "Or Drystan, if you prefer. Titles are tedious, don't you think? Now, what do you think I will teach you?"

Silence. Then, one boy tentatively spoke up. "Stealth?"

Hugo, never one to shy away from boldness, added, "Assassination?"

Drystan chuckled, a sound both amused and dismissive. "You've been reading too many bad novels, Hugo. But nice try."

I felt a strange compulsion to speak up. "Resonance."

Drystan's gaze snapped to me, a smile spreading across his face. "Interesting. And why do you think that?"

I hesitated, then gathered my thoughts. "It doesn't make sense to split the school in two, especially when we're supposed to join the Black Guard. We're meant to work with the witches."

Drystan's smile widened, a glint of approval in his eyes. "Very astute, Karn. Yes, indeed. I will be teaching you about Resonance, the witches, and even deviants. So, what are we training for?"

Quisten, eager to redeem himself, parroted my reasoning. "To fight with the witches."

Drystan laughed, a sharp, almost maniacal sound that echoed off the walls. "No, not at all. It's in the name, boys. We are here to guard them. They wield the power, the resonance, the songs that turn the tide of battle. And us? We guard them. Or rather, you do. Sure, there'll be a bit of bloodshed, maybe a few men to stick. But let's be honest, what real effort is it when our enemies are stumbling around, confused, terrified, and practically pissing themselves with fear?"

My stomach churned at the memory of my village but I pushed it down, I was starting to grow tired of that feeling, of the fear.

Drystan's voice cut through my thoughts. "This is not about glory or heroics. This is about understanding our role, our purpose. The witches are the spear, and we are the shield. Fail to understand that, and you fail entirely."

Drystan then straightened up, his quirky demeanour giving way to a more intense seriousness. "Resonance comes in all shapes and forms, boys, but fundamentally, it affects a person's body and mind internally. No one grows horns or an extra limb." His eyes darted around the room, gauging our reactions.

"In the Kingdom of Eirithia, under our beloved Witch Queen, our witches use their songs to instil fear in our enemies." He paused, letting the weight of his words settle in. Hugo's, curiosity piqued, raised a hand.

"Is Resonance just a song then?" Hugo asked.

Drystan shook his head, a wry smile on his lips. "The song is merely the medium through which Resonance is delivered. It could be a chant, a spoken spell, or even a tattoo upon the skin like the Rhudoria warriors use." His words struck a chord in me, echoing what Lucas had hinted at.

"The important thing to understand," Drystan continued, his gaze intense, "is that Resonance only affects living things. It's internal. No fireballs, no conjuring lights out of thin air. It's about altering the mind, the body, the essence of a person."

Quisten scoffed. "So, it's not magic?"

Drystan's eyes sparkled with amusement. "Magic is for fairy tales, my boy. Resonance is real. It's how people resonate with each other." He leaned forward, eyes sharp. "You do it every day—when you make someone happy with a joke or upset by throwing a punch." He glanced pointedly at Lear, the jibe not lost on anyone.

"It's all about the medium, the resonance, and the intent behind it," Drystan continued, his voice growing more animated. "Think of it as a way to influence others, to change their state of mind or body through specific means."

I furrowed my brow, struggling to wrap my head around the concept. Evidently so was the rest of the class. Drystan noticed and waved a hand dismissively. "I'm getting ahead of myself. Don't worry, you'll all experience it firsthand soon enough."

He paused, his gaze sweeping across the room. "You're in this class because the Trials start next week. I will educate you in between. Unlike the other Masters, we'll only meet once a fortnight."

Lear raised his hand. "Is there anything we can do to prepare for the Trials? Anything we can be told?"

Drystan's expression shifted, a flicker of anticipatory guilt crossing his face. "No, I'm afraid not. Only that the Trials will be next week, and I will see those that remain the week after."

"Class dismissed until then," Drystan announced, his voice echoing through the room. The other wards began to shuffle out, murmuring amongst themselves.

As I made my way toward the door, curiosity gnawed at me. I turned back to Drystan. "Master Veil, are there really women in Seraphel who use Resonance to cause men to lust after them?"

Drystan laughed, a sound both sharp and genuine. "Be more wary of men who charm using the same tactic." With a wink, he dismissed me with a wave, leaving me to ponder his words.

Outside, I spotted Quisten talking with Hugo and Illiam in the courtyard. Quisten saw me and called out, "Karn, over here!"

I joined them, feeling the tension in the air. "We need to know more about the Trials," Quisten said, frustration edging his voice. "None of our fathers or siblings told us anything."

"Same here," I replied, crossing my arms.

Illiam's eyes brightened with an idea. "Since the Trials seem related to Master Veil, we should investigate him. Maybe we can find some clues about what they entail."

Quisten nodded, a smirk forming on his lips. "That's a good idea. It's seventh day tomorrow. We can do it then."

A voice from the shadows interrupted us. "I'm joining you." Lear stepped forward, his face set with determination.

Quisten's expression darkened. "Like hell you are."

Lear's eyes flashed with defiance. "Unless you want me to go straight to the Master and see you end up in the Expanse, you'll let me come."

Fear flickered in Quisten's eyes at the mention of the Expanse. He clenched his jaw, then nodded reluctantly. "Fine. We'll meet here tomorrow morning."

As we dispersed, the weight of what lay ahead pressed heavily on my mind. The Trials loomed like a dark cloud, and the unease in my gut grew with each passing moment.

Chapter 25 - Master of Shadows

Meeting at dawn, the air was still cool from the night, a
welcome respite from the relentless summer heat. Quisten, Hugo,
Illiam, and myself gathered in the courtyard, the first light of day
casting long shadows on the cobblestones. We exchanged nervous
glances, each of us feeling the weight of what we were about to do.

Quisten, as usual, couldn't resist a jibe when Lear joined us.
"Surprised you showed up, Lear. Thought you might be too scared
after your last trip to The Expanse."

Lear's eyes flashed with anger, but he kept his voice level. "I'm
here, aren't I?"

Hugo tried to lighten the mood, giving Lear a friendly pat on
the shoulder. "Let's just get this over with, eh? No point in biting
each other's heads off."

Illiam, cool and composed as ever, simply nodded. "Let's go."

We approached the classroom cautiously, though I'm not sure
why, we were allowed to be there but the intent of what we were
doing is what put me on edge. The wooden door creaked as
Quisten pushed it open, the dim light cast eerie shadows on the
walls. The room was empty because of course no one worked on
the seventh. Master Veil was nowhere to be seen.

"Spread out," Quisten ordered, his tone sharp. "Check
everything. There has to be something here."

We fanned out, checking desks, cabinets, and corners for any
clues. Hugo rummaged through the drawers, his movements
uncharacteristically serious. Illiam examined the shelves, running
his fingers along the dusty spines of old books. Lear and I searched
the back of the room, lifting chairs and peering behind them.

"Anything?" Quisten asked, frustration creeping into his voice.

"Nothing," Hugo replied, slamming a drawer shut.

"Empty," Illiam confirmed, shaking his head.

I glanced at Lear, who was silently fuming. "No luck here either."

Quisten muttered under his breath, his eyes narrowing. "He has to have left something."

"Maybe we're looking in the wrong place," Lear suggested, his tone challenging. "You think you're so clever, Quisten, but maybe we need to think differently."

Quisten bristled, but before he could retort, Illiam stepped between them. "Focus, both of you. This isn't helping."

A tense silence filled the room as we continued our search, the weight of the unknown pressed down on us. The empty classroom seemed to mock our efforts, each shadow hiding secrets we couldn't uncover. We were running out of time. The trial was approaching, and we were no closer to understanding what lay ahead. The frustration and fear gnawed at me, but I knew we couldn't give up. Not now.

Finding nothing in the classroom, we slumped into the desks, defeated. The quiet settled over us like a thick fog, each of us lost in our own thoughts.

"We're missing something," I muttered, rubbing my temples.

Illiam, snapped his fingers. "The Master's Quarters."

Lear looked up sharply. "You realise if we get caught in there we'll all be heading to The Expanse right?"

Quisten leaned back, his face set with determination. "I'm not failing this trial. Let's do it."

We moved quickly and quietly across the courtyard, the dawn light slowly giving way to morning. We passed the wards' barracks, the empty forges, each step taking us closer to the Master's Quarters. The building loomed, an imposing structure of stone and iron, a place that Keird had told me that we were forbidden unless in an emergency. Not knowing what the trial's entailed was an emergency, right?

The Master's Quarters stood apart from the rest of The Forge. The stone walls were polished and adorned with intricate carvings, casting long, dignified shadows that seemed to watch our every move. The windows, though narrow, were filled with stained glass depicting historical scenes, casting fragmented light in vibrant hues. The corridors were silent, their opulence imposing, and the air carried a weight of authority and secrets.

Illiam led the way, his movements cautious and deliberate. We crept along the corridors, the silence amplifying every creak and rustle. Hugo went to one door, reaching for the handle.

"No, that's Master Owle's," Illiam hissed, pulling him back.

We continued down the hall, our eyes scanning each door. Finally, Illiam stopped, pointing to a door ajar. "That's it. I've seen most of the Masters go in and out. This has to be Drystan's."

Illiam knelt by the door, producing a set of slender tools from his coat. His fingers worked deftly, the picks dancing inside the mechanism with practised precision. The soft click of the lock as it yielded was barely audible. He glanced up, catching my astonished expression, and shrugged nonchalantly as if to say, "No big deal."

We slipped inside, careful to close the door silently behind us. Hugo stayed by the entrance, his eyes darting nervously, every sound making him flinch.

The room was a treasure trove of oddities. On one wall hung a series of masks, each more grotesque than the last, their hollow eyes seeming to follow our every move. Shelves were crammed with jars containing bizarre specimens—pickled eyeballs, twisted roots, and small creatures suspended in amber liquid. A faint, herbal scent wafted through the air, mixing with the musty smell of old parchment.

Scrolls were scattered across a large desk, their edges frayed and stained. A brass astrolabe, intricately detailed, sat beside an ancient globe marked with unfamiliar constellations. Strange trinkets cluttered the room—a clockwork bird frozen in mid-song, a box of multicoloured stones that glowed faintly, and a collection of feathers from birds I couldn't identify.

As we spread out to search, I whispered to Illiam, "How did you know about Owle and the other Master's rooms?"

Without pausing in his search, Illiam replied, "I've been sneaking in for a while now. Getting the answers to Owle's tests."
Lear, rifling through a desk drawer, looked up sharply. "Why?"
Illiam's voice was matter-of-fact. "I figured they would mean something eventually. Wanted to get ahead."
I'm not sure if I believed Illiam or if he could tell a lie so smoothly.

Suddenly, Lear's hand brushed against a hidden compartment in the desk. With a click, it popped open, revealing personal notes and a strange, intricately carved gem. The gem was dark, almost black, with deep red veins running through it, pulsating faintly as if alive. The notes were written in a language none of us recognized, filled with symbols and diagrams that hinted at something far more complex than we could decipher on the spot.

Quisten, eyes wide with fascination, leaned in to get a closer look. "What do you think it is?" he whispered.
I shook my head, my mind racing with possibilities. "I don't know, but it's definitely important."
Lear stared at the stone, his face pale. "We shouldn't touch it. Something about it feels... wrong."

I felt a growl of the voice in the back of my head, the feeling was repulsive, pushing me away. Lear's refusal to touch it, his instinctive fear, gave me pause.

"Let's leave it," I said, the growl of the voice subsiding as I forced myself to turn away. "We don't need more trouble than we've already got."

Illiam stared at the stone for a moment too long and then nodded my way, closing the compartment and wiping his hands on his trousers. "Let's get out of here before we're caught."

Hugo burst in, his eyes wide with panic. "Someone's coming!"

Quisten rounded on him, his face twisted in frustration. "Why didn't you tell us sooner, idiot?"

Before Hugo could reply, we heard footsteps echoing down the hall. Panic gripped us, hearts pounding in our chests. We each scrambled to find hiding spots, ducking behind furniture and pressing ourselves into shadows. The footsteps grew louder, each one a hammer blow to my nerves.

As the footsteps drew near, I held my breath, the sound of my heartbeat thunderous in my ears. The door creaked open slightly, and I froze, every muscle tensed.

"Must have left it open again, the fool," a gruff voice muttered, followed by the sound of the door as it slammed shut.

I waited in silence for what felt like an eternity, the only sound the fading footsteps of the intruder. The moment I was sure the coast was clear, I joined the others in our careful retreat. Quisten led the way, his eyes darting around like a hawk's. Every creak of the floorboards under our feet felt like a thunderclap.

Hugo crept out first, peering around the corner before waving us forward. We moved as one, a silent shadow slipping through the dimly lit corridors. Illiam paused at a corner, checking for any signs of life, before motioning us to follow.

The tension was obvious, each step measured and deliberate. My heart hammered in my chest, the fear of being caught heightened my senses. The Master's Quarters, with its cold stone walls and narrow windows, felt like a labyrinth designed to ensnare us.

I reached the exit, where Hugo held the door open just enough for me to slip through. The fresh air outside was a welcome relief, the oppressive atmosphere of the quarters left behind. We didn't stop, our movements quick and silent as we made our way past the wards' barracks.

Behind one of the forges, we finally stopped, the heat from the lingering embers a comforting contrast to the cool morning air. We gathered in a tight circle, our breaths still heavy from the adrenaline.

Quisten was the first to speak, his voice low but intense. "That was too close. Next time, Hugo, be quicker with the warning."

Hugo nodded, looking chastened but relieved. "I know, I know. I'm sorry."

Illiam glanced around, ensuring our privacy. "we need to be more careful," he paused then with his eyes sparkling with fascination as he spoke, "that stone... it's something significant. I wish we could've taken it. We can't afford to get caught, but I can't stop thinking about what it could be."

Quisten scoffed, rolling his eyes. "Oh, stop dreaming, Illiam. You think you're the only one who noticed its importance? We leave it, end of story. We don't need you getting us thrown into The Expanse because you can't control your curiosity."

Lear, still pale from the encounter, looked at each of us in turn. "We shouldn't have gone in there. But we need to be ready for the trials. We need every advantage."

Hugo's eyes widened as he spotted Drystan striding through the courtyard. "There he is," he whispered urgently, pointing towards the enigmatic Master. "Let's tail him."

I moved cautiously with the others as we kept our distance, using the back of the forges as cover. The forges stood silent and empty, their fires quenched on the seventh. The usual clanging of metal on metal was absent, replaced by the quiet murmur of the few who still roamed the grounds.

Drystan's peculiar cloak fluttered with each step, his gait purposeful yet relaxed. As we shadowed him, darting from one forge to the next, he suddenly halted. Master Owle approached, his demeanour wise and composed, a stark contrast to Drystan's quirky energy.

"Master Veil," Owle greeted with utmost respect, inclining his head slightly. "A pleasant day for a stroll, it seems. Have you noticed, the wards are particularly educated this year."

Drystan's lips curled into a mischievous smile. "Indeed, Master Owle. They actually manage to string a sentence together without drooling. It's quite the achievement."

Owle chuckled softly. "Credit to your unique teaching methods, no doubt."

Drystan waved a hand dismissively. "Oh, I just give them a bit of chaos and watch them squirm. Keeps them on their toes."

"Chaos has its place," Owle replied, nodding. "But structure and knowledge are the foundations of their future."

Drystan's eyes twinkled with amusement. "And what a future it will be. Full of surprises, I'm sure."

Owle leaned in slightly, lowering his voice. "Speaking of surprises, I was caught off guard by one of the wards, asking me about the Seekers. Turns out the boy has a copy of one of their books."

Drystan raised an eyebrow, his interest piqued. "Oh, is that so?"

"Yes," Owle confirmed, a hint of curiosity in his tone. "Are you going to say anything to the boy?"

Drystan's smile widened, a gleam of intrigue in his eyes. "No, not really. Let me have at least some secrets. It makes the game more interesting."

Their exchange was brief but courteous, the kind of interaction that hinted at a deeper understanding between them. Just as we started to relax, a smithy's apprentice emerged from one of the nearby buildings, his eyes scanning the area. I couldn't help but feel a spark of curiosity at the mention of the Seekers' book. What did Drystan know about it, and why didn't he seem concerned?

Hugo muttered under his breath, "Who works on the seventh?"

The smithy's apprentice's gaze swept dangerously close to our hiding spot. My heart pounded in my chest. Illiam, quick on his feet, stepped out from behind the forge and called out, "Hey, need a hand with anything?"

The apprentice shook his head, "Oh I thought I heard something. I was just finishing up."

"Need help? I was just stretching my legs," Illiam said.

"Nah, I'm heading to the refectory now once I get this soot washed off," the apprentice replied.

"Me too, I'm hungry," Illiam said, his quick thinking covering for us as he wandered off with the apprentice. His diversion saved stopped our group from being discovered, but now we had to continue following Drystan without him.

My nerves were on edge as we tailed Drystan through the courtyard. The risk of getting caught added a layer of tension to our pursuit, but the need to uncover any hint about the trials kept me going. Drystan moved with a casual grace, seemingly unaware of our presence. I kept my breaths shallow and my steps light, blending into the shadows. Quisten followed close behind, his eyes darting around, while Hugo and Lear moved with similar caution. The sound of our footsteps was muffled by the soft dirt paths, and the stillness of the seventh day gave the empty grounds an eerie calm.

Ahead, I saw Master Kegg striding purposefully towards Master Veil. His face darkened as he approached Drystan. "Master Veil," Kegg greeted, his voice dripped with barely concealed disdain. "I took the liberty of shutting your door. Again."

Drystan's lips curved into a smirk. "Ah, Prime Master Kegg, always so diligent. How can I possibly repay your vigilance?"

Kegg's eyes narrowed. "By learning to close your damn door, perhaps. It's a simple enough task, even for you."

Drystan chuckled, the sound light and careless. "I'll make a note of it. Thank you for your concern." He continued on his way, his demeanour unchanged, as if Kegg's words had merely been a passing breeze. I watched with the others in silence as Kegg marched off, his shoulders tense with annoyance. Drystan, on the other hand, walked with a carefree air, oblivious or indifferent to the scorn that followed him.

Following Drystan felt like walking a tightrope over a pit of flames. Each step toward the Grand Hall intensified the sense of foreboding, the shadows of the empty forges seemed to stretch longer, darker. Hugo, Quisten, Lear, and I exchanged tense glances, the silence between us heavy as we continued with our misdeed.

As Drystan reached the entrance of the Grand Hall, he paused, speaking to a figure shrouded in the shadows. "Is the Grand Hall ready?" Drystan's voice was low but carried an edge of anticipation.

The figure nodded, their reply confident. "Yes, Master Veil. Everything is prepared."

Quisten leaned in, his whisper barely audible. "He's talking about the trials."

Quisten signalled for us to move closer but then Drystan turned sharply, his eyes locking onto ours with a predatory glint. "Ah, my eager young wards," he called out, a smirk playing on his lips. "Your sneaking skills are about as subtle as a drunk bear in a library. Can't wait for the trials, can you?"

My heart skipped a beat, panic surged through me. Quisten, usually so quick with a retort, was struck silent, his face paling. Hugo and Lear both froze, their eyes wide with dread.

Drystan's smile widened, a gleam of malicious delight in his eyes. "Don't fret, lads. You've just volunteered to be the first ones to dance the trials, you'll be glad to hear they start next week. Should be quite the show!"

The weight of his words hit me like a blow. There was no backing out now. The trials were an unknown, looming ahead, ready to test us in ways we couldn't even imagine.

Chapter 26 - First Trial

The pressure built over the next few days. I kept my head down, muscles aching from endless drills, sweat stinging my eyes. Each swing of the sword felt heavier, each morning run longer. The trials that loomed gnawed at my nerves, making my hands shake, my heart raced. Despite all our efforts, we still had no clue what the trial entailed. The uncertainty was a constant, nagging weight.

Finally, the night arrived. The air was thick with anticipation, each breath felt like inhaling smoke. Prime Master Kegg stood in front of the massive, iron-banded door, his stern face illuminated by the flicker of torchlight. The other six masters flanked him, their faces unreadable except for the occasional raised eyebrow and slight tilt of the head. Master Veil, with his peculiar smirk and unpredictable demeanour, stood slightly apart, his eyes glinting with mischief.

Kegg's voice cut through the tension, low and commanding. "Wards," he began, his tone brooking no nonsense, "The Forge exists to mould you to serve the Black Guard, the elite defenders of our witches, servants to our Queen. This trial is your next step. You will face it three times. Today is the first. The second in two weeks. The third in a month. You must pass at least one of these trials, or you risk being thrown out of the Forge." His tone serious.

I could feel the eyes of my fellow wards on me, each of us trying to read the fear in the other. My breath was shallow, a metallic taste in my mouth from the stress. I focused on the feel of the rough hilt of my sword, grounding myself.

Kegg's disdain for Master Veil was palpable, a sneer curling his lip as he gestured for him to take over. "Master Veil," he said, barely masking his contempt.

Veil stepped forward, his smirk widening. His eyes danced with a kind of mad glee as he surveyed us. The silence stretched, the night growing darker, the air colder. We were on the brink, waiting for his words, our fates hanging in the balance.

Master Veil, or Drystan as he preferred to be called, stepped forward, his eyes glinting in the torchlight. "Behind me is the Grand Hall," he said, his voice smooth and laced with a hint of amusement. The massive building loomed, its stone facade merging into the great wall that split the Forge in two. One side for wards, the other for witches.

"All you have to do," he continued, his smile wide, "is get from the wards' end to the witches' end."
The torches flickered, casting long shadows across our faces. He pointed to the path of torches. "These will mark your progress. Use them to gauge how far you get, so you'll know for next time." His tone dripped with expectation of our failure.

Whispers erupted among the boys. Hugo, beside me, leaned in. "Is that it?" he murmured, his voice tinged with disbelief.

Drystan's eyes snapped to us, cutting through the whispers like a blade. "A group of boys have bravely volunteered to go first," he said, his sarcasm biting. He untied a scroll with a flourish, letting the moment hang.
"Karn Fayle," he announced as his eyes locked onto mine.

The world narrowed, the sounds of the other boys fading into a dull roar. I gulped and stepped forward. The masters parted, and the massive doors creaked open, revealing the Grand Hall, a yawning black void. Master Veil's voice, smooth as silk, cut through the tension. "Step inside, Karn."

The moment I crossed the threshold, the doors slammed shut behind me with a resounding boom, plunging me into near darkness other than the torches that flared, their flames bright and steady, marking a path ahead. I squinted, trying to figure out how they managed that effect.

I took a hesitant step forward. The silence was thick, almost suffocating. Then, a sound sliced through the stillness, a haunting melody. It was like nothing I had words for, like a voice rising and falling in a language I couldn't understand but felt deep in my bones. I'd heard it before—during the attack on my village, in The Expanse. The witches' song grew louder, enveloping me.

I knew this was coming. Deep down, I'd felt it, a gnawing sense of dread bubbling up inside me. The torchlight flickered, casting long, writhing shadows that twisted into monstrous shapes, dark figures that lurked, waiting to strike. Fear clawed at my insides, making my legs heavy and my breaths shallow.

I forced myself to take a step, my body trembling with the urge to turn and run. Each movement felt like wading through thick mud. I made it to the first set of torches, their light casting eerie glows on the stone floor. Then, out of the corner of my eye, I saw them—the men I'd killed in the forest. Poachers, their skin grey and decaying, their eyes hollow. They lunged at me, hands grasping.

"Get away!" I kicked at them, my foot connecting with nothing but air. I stumbled, hitting the ground hard, the impact jarring. I scrambled backward, the cold stone biting into my palms, my breaths coming hard and fast.

The men faded, leaving only the oppressive darkness and the relentless song. A chime rang out, clear and haunting. Then, from the void, a voice—Liv's voice.

"Leif!" she called, her voice sharp with accusation and pain. "You left me to die! The Leif I knew would never have done that. How could you abandon me?"

The accusation cut deep, the guilt wrapping around me like a vice. The song grew louder, echoing off unseen walls, each note a stab to my heart.

Hands grabbed me, yanking me down into the shadows. My sister stood above me, her dead eyes piercing through the darkness.

Weak! The wolf inside growled.

I looked up at her, heart pounding. It wasn't her. It couldn't be. Liv died when the building fell, crushed beneath the rubble. Her death created her cairn, and in that moment, Leif's cairn too.

Three realisations hit me like a punch to the gut. First, I was done with fear, done with this damn song and what it did to me. Second, I was no longer Leif, the scared little boy from the village. I was Karn, and my anger was building, a fire I could no longer control. Ignoring the breathing exercises drilled into me, I let the rage flood my veins.

The third realisation was that in the darkness, no one would see my eyes turn red. I allowed my fury to consume me, my rage burning brighter than the torches lighting the Grand Hall. The power of the song broke, shattering like glass. My eyes blazed like the torches, and the grip of fear vanished.

Good, Nix rumbled within me. *Be fierce, use what I have given you, become wrath.*

The song still cut through the darkness, harsh and piercing, each note like a blade slicing the air. But now, I heard it for what it was—a twisted melody without the power to instil fear. I pushed myself up, the shadows slinking away as I moved.

Step by step, I walked past the third set of torches, their light cast long, flickering shadows. Then the fifth, sixth, and finally, the seventh set came into view.

I let my anger fade, feeling my eyes return to normal, the heat behind them dissipate. The strength within me ebbed with it but didn't vanish completely. The song's grip tightened again, but I could bear it. The flickering shadows clawed at me, but I ignored them, my focus on the path ahead.

I passed the seventh torch, reaching the far end of the hall. Another pair of grand doors loomed before me. They creaked open, revealing the other side of the Forge.

I stumbled out into the open air, the clear sky and full moon casting a cold light over the scene. A group of girls stood there, their faces etched with shock, their whispers filling the night. I took a few steps past the doors before my legs gave out, and I fell to my knees, breathing heavily. Sweat dripped from my brow onto the dry dirt below, each drop a vivid reminder of the struggle I had endured.

"Silence," an older woman commanded, her voice cutting through the murmurs. The girls fell silent instantly.

I looked up, taking in their faces. They all wore dark cloaks, their makeup stark against their varying skin tones. Their hair was pulled back and greased, their eyes made sharp with dark lines of makeup. Among them, one pair of eyes locked onto mine.

Serah.

Her lips were a thin line, her dark, piercing eyes never leaving mine. Her black hair, greased and bound tightly, contrasted sharply with her pale skin, making her presence even more striking. But it was the sorrow in her eyes that hit me hardest.

In that moment, the weight of everything seemed to crash down on me, reflected back in her gaze

Footsteps approached from behind, and a girl in a cloak stepped out. I turned to look at her. She was slender, with chestnut hair pulled back tight, her face framed by sharp lines of makeup that accentuated her hazel eyes. She glanced at the older woman, and her calm composure faltered.

"Mistress Aufrica," she began, her voice trembling. "I had him until the third torch. He was crumbling, and then suddenly he stood."

Panic gripped me, but I forced my face to remain impassive. The singing had to have come from somewhere, and now I knew it was her. I hoped she hadn't seen my eyes.

The older woman, Mistress Aufrica, gave a small nod. "You did fine, Acolyte Nancy," she said, her voice soothing yet firm. Then she turned her gaze to me. "Boy, have you taken a trip to The Expanse?"

I nodded, struggling to find my voice. "Yes."

Mistress Aufrica smiled, a hint of satisfaction in her eyes. "See, girl? He's already endured much. He must be strong. As was your use of resonance."

The girl bent her knee to bow to the woman.

She waved to two of other the girls. One of them was Serah. She leaned in as they helped me up, her voice a soft whisper. "You did well."

They brought me to a bench and handed me a flask of water. As I gulped it down, Serah and the other girl returned to the group. Mistress Aufrica watched me with a critical eye. She was tall, her grey hair pulled back into a severe bun, her face lined with age but still striking. Her eyes, cold and calculating, seemed to see right through me.

"You'll sit there until the trial is over," she said, her voice leaving no room for argument.

I just nodded, grateful for the chance to catch my breath. Prime Master Kegg's words about being thankful for my time in The Expanse echoed in my mind. He was right. It had given me a cover, a way to hide my power. I could only hope it was enough.

The girl who came out after me rejoined the group of witches, and another stepped forward, disappearing into the Grand Hall. The doors closed with a heavy thud, leaving me waiting on the bench. The girls stood so still, it was eerie. My eyes kept drifting to Serah, and I noticed her glancing at me too before quickly looking away. Their cloaks were similar to our ward mocks—dark grey and blue, with hints of purple and the emblem of the hammer and anvil stitched on them.

Time dragged on. The doors opened again, but no boy stepped out. Instead, two girls went in and dragged Hugo through the doorway. The usually talkative and jovial boy was dead quiet, shaking as if he had the chills. The acolyte who had gone into the Grand Hall spoke as she emerged. "Third torch."

Mistress Aufrica's expression remained unchanged. "Take him to the Refuge," she instructed. "Tell the healer to expect more before the night is done."

I sat there, the weight of what I had endured pressing down on me, watching as Hugo was taken away.

The witches swapped again, another stepping forward. This time it was Serah. She gave me a look, something unspoken passing between us, before she stepped into the Grand Hall. The doors closed with their usual ominous finality.

More time passed. I watched the girls, the eerie stillness of them, the occasional flicker of eyes towards the door. My gaze kept wandering to Serah's empty spot. The wait stretched, heavy and silent, until finally, the doors creaked open again.

Lear strode out. His blue eyes were red and puffy, but he held his head high, stepping out on his own. The reaction from the witches was immediate. Mutters spread through the group, whispers of "Two on the first trial?"

Mistress Aufrica approached Lear, her face a mask of stern curiosity. "Have you, too, endured The Expanse?" she asked.

Lear nodded, his expression stoic.

"Sit down," she instructed, though I caught a flicker of surprise in her eyes.

Lear walked over and sat next to me, a smug smile curled his lips. He didn't say a word, just sat there, basking in his accomplishment.

That just leaves Quisten, I thought, watching the witches swap again.

Their dark cloaks swirled as they moved, the fabric catching the moonlight. The doors closed with a heavy thud, and the wait began anew. This time, it wasn't long before they opened back up, and the witch walking out called for help.

Screams echoed from the void of the hall, high-pitched and filled with terror. Two girls rushed in, their footsteps echoing off the stone floor. Together with the first witch, they half-dragged, half-carried Quisten out. As he came into the light of the moon, his face was pale and twisted with fear. He saw the girls and began to cry, his sobs broke the stillness of the night.

A dark stain spread through his breeches, glistening in the moonlight. Lear snorted, his voice dripping with disdain. "Pissed himself. Pathetic."

Quisten barely reacted, his sobs growing louder, his shoulders shaking. Mistress Aufrica's glare cut through the night like a knife. "One more word, boy, and you're going back in."

Lear shut up, his smugness evaporating in an instant.

"Take him to the Refuge with the other boy," Mistress Aufrica ordered, her tone leaving no room for argument. The girl assisting her nodded and added, "He only made it to the second torch."

Quisten's cries echoed in my ears as they carried him away, the sound of his anguish mingled with the night's silence.

It was a long night after that, following the same grim pattern. The door would open, a girl would go in, and the witches would drag a boy out afterward. Each time, the scene repeated with slight variations of horror and despair.

Boys emerged in different states—some shaking uncontrollably, others muttering incoherently, all in shock from what they had endured. One by one, they were taken to the Refuge.

Illiam, usually clever and quiet, was a shell of his former self. He muttered to himself, his eyes darting around, searching for phantoms only he could see. He had made it to the fifth torch, one of the best any of us had heard all night. But his haunted look said it all.

The only other boy to come out of the Grand Hall and sit beside Lear and I was Aspallan. The cool and collected high born boy, Aspallan shook as he lowered himself onto the bench, his composure shattered. He sat next to Lear, silent, his eyes fixed on the doors as the rest of the trial continued. We watched together, the three of us, each enduring our private hells while the night dragged on.

Hours passed, and when the trials finally ended, the last boy was sent to the Refuge. Mistress Aufrica sent her girls to their dorms. Serah and I locked eyes one last time, and I saw her mouth "good luck" before she disappeared into the shadows.

Mistress Aufrica turned to us. "You three, follow me."

We walked through a narrow hallway between the Grand Hall

and The Expanse. The corridor was well lit, the brightness stabbed at my eyes, which had grown accustomed to the darkness of the night. The light revealed every tired line and grimy detail on our faces.

In the middle of the hallway, we met Prime Master Kegg and Master Veil. Kegg's eyes widened when he saw us. "Three boys? Impossible."

Mistress Aufrica nodded, equally surprised. "Two of them have already faced The Expanse."

Master Veil leaned in, a curious smirk on his lips. "Well, well, looks like the shadows couldn't keep you. Most intriguing."

Kegg's lips thinned with disdain. "Still, I've not seen more than one boy pass the first trial in nearly a decade."

Mistress Aufrica straightened. "I need to get back to my girls."

Kegg nodded. "Likewise, I have a mess to clean up."

He turned to us. "Master Veil will get you a strong glass of wine. You've earned it tonight. All boys get it on trial nights. Afterward, head to bed. The others who failed are likely already asleep. Best not to disturb them, got it? Tomorrow, I'll explain what happens next."

We nodded, the promise of wine a small comfort after the night's ordeals.

Master Veil led us to his quarters, the same ones Lear and I had snuck into before. The room was dimly lit by a few flickering candles, casting shadows that danced on the walls. He poured a dark amber liquid into small glasses, the strong scent hitting my nose immediately.

Aspallan sniffed his glass and wrinkled his own nose. "What is this? It doesn't smell like wine."

Drystan, with his ever-present smirk, winked. "Tonight, you've earned a real reward. This is whiskey. Trust me, you'll need it."

As I took a sip, the whiskey hit my tongue with a fiery bite, its smoky flavour deep and rich. The burn travelled down my throat, leaving a trail of warmth that spread through my chest, easing the tension in my muscles. My eyes drifted to the compartment where we had found the veined gem, and I caught Master Veil's gaze. He raised an eyebrow, a knowing smile playing on his lips.

"Interesting, isn't it, how some places seem more familiar than they should?" he said, his tone casual yet pointed.

The words sent a jolt through me, but I kept my face impassive. Master Veil watched us with a curious glint in his eye as we drank, then led us to our dorms. We parted ways silently, each lost in our own thoughts.

I entered the dorm to the sound of weeping, crying, and the occasional wail. Shadows of boys were curled up in their bunks, some shaking, some staring blankly at the ceiling. The air was thick with despair.

Climbing into my bunk, I struggled to sleep. The weight of the night's trials pressed down on me, but I refused to let fear take hold. I wouldn't be burdened by it, not any more.

That night, dreams of the red wolf filled my mind, vivid and intense, its eyes burned like fire.

Chapter 27 - Aftermath

The next day was the seventh. I figured the Trials must have been strategically planned to give us time to recover, and we needed it. The other wards shuffled around, eyes bloodshot and hollow, faces pale, their movements sluggish. It was clear none of them had gotten any real sleep, tormented by nightmares that refused to let go. It was eerily quiet, the usual banter replaced by the sounds of muffled groans and the creak or bunks.

I had my own nightmares, flashes of red and the haunting melody still lingering. But they barely held sway over me. The resolve I'd found, combined with the whiskey from the night before, kept them at bay. I could still feel the warmth of the drink in my chest, a reminder of the small victory I'd earned.

As I left the dorms that morning, I almost collided with Keird. His face was serious, but there was a hint of something else in his eyes—curiosity, maybe respect.

"Karn," he said, his voice steady, "I've been asked to bring you to Prime Master Kegg."

I nodded, not surprised. Kegg had mentioned it the night before. I fell in step with Keird, the silence between us thick until he broke it.

"Impressive that you passed the Trial on your first attempt," he said, glancing at me. "I barely made it on my third."

I looked at him, noting the honesty in his tone. "Keird, have you really been here for more than a year? Isn't the academy only supposed to last a year?"

He sighed, a faint smile tugged at his lips. "The masters need people with experience to assist them. Those of us who passed but... didn't excel, we can stay on as prefects. It helps bump up our position when we leave The Forge."

I raised an eyebrow, genuinely curious. "How many boys drop

out after the first attempt?"

Keird's face darkened. "More than you'd think. The first trial breaks a lot of them. The fear, the failure... it gets into their heads. I'd say about half don't make it to the second attempt. And by the third... well, if you don't pass by then, you're out. No exceptions."

I nodded, understanding the unspoken part. The Forge wasn't just about survival; it was about proving yourself, earning a place in the hierarchy.

He continued, his tone softer. "It's tough, watching them go. Some are good lads, but this place... it's unforgiving."

We continued through the corridors, the air heavy with the scent of burnt wood and steel, until we reached the Master's Quarters and stood before Prime Master Kegg's office.

As we arrived at the office I saw that Lear and Aspallan were already waiting with their prefects. Keird knocked on the door and announced, "They're all here."

Kegg's voice came through the door, firm and authoritative. "Send them in."

Keird and the other prefects left, and we stepped inside. Kegg sat behind a large wooden desk, stern but with a hint of pride in his eyes. Master Kinrade stood to one side, his muscular frame imposing. Next to him was a burly, bald man I hadn't seen before. On the other side was Quarter Master Raknor.

"Congratulations," Kegg began, his voice steady. "It's a great achievement to pass the trial on your first attempt. It's rare for more than one boy to do it, let alone all three of you. Passing the trial means you've ranked up from Iron to Steel."

Lear, ever curious, asked, "Does that mean we no longer have to compete in the trials?"

Kegg shook his head. "No. While you've earned your spot, everyone continues to do the trials to determine where they'll land in the Queen's army."

He continued, "Earning a spot means you've been granted two of the Queen's blessings." He gestured to Master Kinrade. "The first is; you'll be spending part of your seventh day with Master Kinrade and Forge Master Paton." He introduced the big, burly man next to Kinrade. "Together, you'll work on forging your own weapon."

For a moment, I felt a twinge of irritation at losing part of my only day off, but then excitement sparked in me at the news. I saw the same look in Lear's eyes, and even Aspallan showed a glint of enthusiasm.

Master Kinrade stepped forward. "Over our drills in the next week, we'll decide together what weapons you'll forge."

Prime Master Kegg spoke again. "The second blessing is more private quarters. You'll be sharing, but it's a step up from a room full of bunks. Since there are three of you, I've taken the liberty of splitting you up. Karn and Lear, you'll be sharing a room."

I felt a mix of emotions. Sharing with Lear was better than most options, but still, the idea of sharing any small space with the fierce boy was a little unsettling.

"Aspallan," Kegg continued, "you'll have a room to yourself until the next trial, at the very least."

He congratulated us once more. "Master Raknor will see you to your new chambers. Go get your belongings and report to him. Dismissed."

Raknor nodded. "I'll meet you outside the dorms in an hour."

We filed out, each of us processing the news in our own way. I left the Master's Quarters and headed back to the dorm. Inside, most of the boys were still in their bunks, their faces pale, eyes bloodshot. The room felt like a morgue. Usually, on the seventh, they'd be up and out by now, but the trials had drained them completely.

I moved quietly, collecting my few possessions: The Seeker's guide I had gotten from Serah, a small knife, a half-empty journal. I stuffed them into my trunk, the wood creaking under the added weight. As I looked around, I realised I hadn't made any real friends in this dorm. No farewells, no goodbyes. Just a sense of relief at leaving behind the restless nights and shared misery.

More privacy was welcome, but sharing a room with Lear was another matter. His constant need to prove himself, his sharp tongue... could be a problem. I sighed, hoisting my trunk, ready to face whatever came next.

I met Quarter Master Raknor and the other boys outside. The chill morning air stung my skin, but it was a welcome change from the oppressive atmosphere of the dorms. Raknor led us to a building nestled between our original dorms and the Master's Quarter, with one more building in between—likely the private accommodation, I guessed.

We followed Raknor down a dimly lit corridor. As we passed one open door, Keird waved at me. I wasn't surprised to see that the prefects got more privacy from the start. It made sense; they had earned their place here.

Raknor stopped at a door and gestured to Aspallan. "This is your room." Aspallan nodded, slipping inside without a word.

Lear and I followed Raknor to the next. Lear couldn't resist a jab. "Bet he got his own room because he's a Warden's son."

I shot back, "Actually, his father's dead."

Lear snorted, his disdain clear. "Lucky for him. Still a noble, though, isn't he?"

Raknor interrupted, opening the door to our room. "This is yours. I won't have any squabbling over whose bed is whose. Sort it out yourselves." With that, he left us to it.

I stepped inside, taking in the two small beds, each with a rough-hewn chest at the foot, perfect for storing our belongings.

The single shared desk was cramped, its surface marred with scratches and ink stains from previous occupants. The walls were bare stone, cold and unwelcoming, with only a single narrow window letting in a sliver of light. The floor was also bare, and the ceiling low, making the space feel even more cramped. Lear and I exchanged glances, a silent agreement hanging in the air. This was our new reality. We'd have to make it work.

Lear tossed his trunk onto the bed on the right without a word. I took the bed on the left, setting my own trunk down with a thud. The silence was thick, and I felt the need to break it.

"Looks like we're in for some real luxury," I said, failing to inject some humour into the situation.

Lear shot me a look. "Don't think we're friends. I've not forgotten you're a witch loving lordling as well."

I nodded, accepting the rebuff. If only he knew just how much I, too, hated them. We both started unpacking, the sound of trunks opening and items being moved filling the space. I stashed most of my belongings in the chest, keeping only the necessities within reach.

As Lear unpacked, I noticed him pull out something that caught my eye. It was a small wooden carving of a wolf, intricately detailed with fierce eyes and sharp teeth, its fur painstakingly etched into the wood. I felt like I had looked into those fierce eyes before.

"That looks familiar," I ventured, "where are you from?"

Lear's eyes narrowed. "Southwest," he said curtly, shoving the carving into his chest.

I let it go, but the image stuck in my mind.

Eventually, I decided I'd rather find my own friends than suffer Lear's cold shoulder. I made my way to the refectory, where Illiam and Hugo were picking at their breakfasts. The room was filled with boys eating slowly and methodically, their eyes dull and their conversations minimal. The aftermath of the trial hung heavy in the air.

I slid onto the bench across from Illiam and Hugo. "Mind if I join you?"

They nodded their heads, and I started to eat. "Rough night," I said, trying to break the silence.

"Yeah," Hugo muttered, his eyes distant and haunted. "Saw things I never want to see again. Horses, my father's stable burning, and... them. Shadows, tearing everything apart." His hands shook as he gripped his spoon, the knuckles white.

Illiam nodded, his face pale and gaunt. "Same here. It felt like I was back in the alleyways, hiding from those who would string me up for the slightest wrong step. But this time, there was no escape. The darkness just closed in." He rubbed his temples, his eyes darting around the room as if expecting the shadows to materialise.

Hugo looked at me, his curiosity piqued but his face still etched with fear. "Is that what you saw in The Expanse?"

I nodded, swallowing a piece of bread. "Yeah, but in The Expanse, there's no room to run. Nowhere to go."

Hugo's face paled further, his eyes wide with terror. "A few boys have already left this morning. Can't blame them."

Illiam, usually the calm one, snapped, his voice tinged with desperation. "You thinking of leaving, Hugo?"

Hugo shook his head, his jaw set but his eyes betraying his fear. "No. If I fail here, I've got nowhere else to go."

Illiam's anger softened, a flicker of fear crossing his own expression. "Same here."

They both turned to me, gazes searching, desperate for some kind of reassurance. "How'd you do it, Karn? How'd you get past the trial?"

I shrugged. "The Expanse toughened me up. It was still hard, but I just kept putting one foot in front of the other." I took a breath, thinking of something to lighten the mood. "But there are some boons to it. We get to forge our own weapons now. That's something to look forward to." I paused, glancing around the room, then added, "Oh, and I got a new room and it comes with its own brooding roommate. Lear."

Hugo snorted. "Don't tell Quisten. He'll love that."

I raised an eyebrow. "Seen him around?"

Both shook their heads. "No sign," Illiam said.

"I'm gonna check on him," I decided, pushing my plate away.

Illiam frowned. "Why bother?"

"He may be a bastard at times, but he's our friend, right?"

They both shrugged, but I could see a flicker of agreement in their eyes.

I headed over to Quisten's dorm. I'd always figured the boy, being a Warden's son like Aspallan, had a room to himself. But that wasn't the case; he was just in a different dorm, the same one as Illiam.

Entering the dorm, I found it similar to my previous one, with rows of bunk beds. Most of the boys had already risen or left, leaving the place eerily quiet. Quisten's bunk was closest to the hearth. He didn't have a private room, but he had the best spot in the house, refusing to let anyone share it with him. He sat on the edge of that bunk, staring into the fire.

It struck me as odd to see a fire lit in summer, but I assumed it was Quisten's doing. He sat there with a haunted expression, tears rolled silently down his cheeks. I approached him, trying to speak.

"Quisten," I began, my voice gentle, "are you alright?"

There was no response, just the crackling of the fire and his shallow breaths. I reached out, placing a hand on his shoulder.

Quisten jerked back, eyes wide with fear. The stench of urine clung to him. Obviously he'd yet to take a bath. His voice rose, shrill and defensive. "Get away from me, you low-born swine! I don't need your pity or your help! Just leave me alone!"

The raw terror in his eyes, the trembling in his voice, and the way he recoiled told me everything. This wasn't the arrogant noble I knew. He was broken, terrified. The trial had shattered something inside him.

Just as I turned to go, a thought struck me. I hesitated, then faced him again. "Hey, Quisten," I said softly, "do you want to practise for the Three Moons Tournament? It might help to get your mind off things."

For a moment, his eyes flickered with something other than fear, but it quickly vanished. He shook his head, refusing to look at me. "Just leave me alone," he muttered.

I stepped back, hands up in surrender. "Alright, Quisten. I'm leaving."

Without another word, I turned and walked out, leaving him to his haunted silence and the flickering flames.

I spent the rest of my seventh practising drills. The yard was quiet, most boys too exhausted from the trials to bother. I started with wooden weapons, my movements precise and deliberate. Each swing, each block, each thrust—repeating the patterns drilled into us since the first day. The weight of the wooden sword felt reassuring, the rhythm of the practice grounding me.

After a while, I switched to bare-fisted drills. My fists thudded against the training dummy, each strike a release of pent-up frustration. The coarse sackcloth split under my knuckles, the sound of tearing fabric mingling with my heavy breaths. Sweat dripped from my brow, but I welcomed the burn in my muscles, the ache in my bones. It reminded me I was alive, that I could still fight.

When my arms felt like lead, I made my way to the stables. Sköll greeted me with a soft whinny, his dark eyes calm and knowing. I brushed him down, the repetitive motion soothing. His coat shone under the dim stable light, each stroke of the brush easing some of the tension from my body.

"Hey there, boy," I murmured, running the brush along his flank. "You wouldn't believe the day I had."

Sköll snorted softly, his ears flicking as if he understood every word.

"Quisten's being an even bigger pain than usual," I continued, working the brush through a knot in his mane. "And then there's Lear. He's got this anger, you know? Like he hates everything."

Sköll nudged me gently with his nose, a silent reassurance.

"I just don't get it," I said, feeding him an apple. "How do you stay so calm, Sköll? Wish I could be more like you."

He munched contentedly, his eyes never leaving mine.

I sighed, resting my forehead against his neck for a moment. "At least you're here. You're the one thing that makes sense in all this madness."

I fed him, letting the simple task clear my mind. "Thanks for listening, boy," I whispered, giving him a final pat. "Let's hope tomorrow is a bit easier, yeah?"

Sköll's soft whinny seemed to agree, and I smiled despite myself.

I considered heading into Dúnmara but dismissed the thought. I didn't have the energy, and the idea of wandering the streets alone didn't appeal. Instead, I found a quiet corner in the forge and rested, the heat from the smelting furnaces a comforting presence. I stretched out, letting my thoughts drift. The sounds of the forge—metal striking metal, the hiss of steam—lulled me into a state of weary contentment. I closed my eyes.

That night, I lay in my new bed, staring at the ceiling. The room was dark, the only light coming from a sliver of moonlight peeking through the narrow window. Sleep eluded me, my mind raced with the day's events.

From the other side of the room, Lear's voice cut through the silence. "I saw her," he said, his tone flat yet tinged with anger. "The witch in my trial. She didn't see me, but I saw her."

I turned my head slightly, though I didn't respond. Lear continued, his voice growing harsher. "She had dark eyes, pale skin, and her hair was greased back. The look in her eyes... after what she made me see, I wanted to kill her. Strangle her with my own hands."

A chill ran down my spine. He was describing Serah. She had been the one to perform his trial. The anger in his voice was clear, and for a moment, I imagined his hands around her neck, his fingers tightening.

I kept silent, knowing I should respond, but the words wouldn't come. Couldn't come. Shouldn't come.

That night, as I lay there, I heard the witch's song again. It was distant, a haunting melody that seemed to seep through the walls. I wasn't sure if it was real or just a figment of my exhausted mind. The eerie notes lingered, a reminder of the darkness that surrounded me.

Chapter 28 - Forging a Weapon

Before drills the next day, Prime Master Kegg gathered the remaining wards. The courtyard felt emptier, and I was surprised to see that at least a quarter of our original group of around a hundred had fled. Kegg's presence was commanding, his voice cutting through the morning air.

"Wards," he began, his tone stern. "Those who wish to join the Black Guard must be able to face the witches' song. There is no question about it. To that end, there will be two more of the initial trials." His emphasis on "initial" wasn't lost on me. "You must pass these trials or leave The Forge, where you will likely become officers in the regular forces."

The crowd shifted uneasily. Kegg continued, "To help you prepare, we are implementing two measures. First, we will allow anyone who wishes to brave The Expanse to do so." He gestured towards me and Lear. "Karn and Lear are prime examples of how it helps overcome fear."

I felt a mixture of pride and discomfort. Turning a punishment into a method of training was clever, but I knew I wouldn't like to do it again myself.

"Second," Kegg went on, "the witches will sing at night. It will not be potent, but through extended exposure to the song, we hope to build your resistance."

He finished his speech by gesturing towards me, Lear, and Aspallan. "These three have proven themselves. This is what you should hope to achieve."

I didn't like being put on display like that. I could feel the eyes of the other wards on me, their gazes heavy and varied. Some looked at me with narrowed eyes, their resentment almost tangible.

Others watched with wide-eyed admiration, and a few with a tight-lipped envy that made their expressions hard. Kegg knew it would draw attention and possibly ire, but the bastard did it anyway. My eyes met Quisten's in the crowd. He looked broken, a shadow of his former self. Kegg's words lingered in the air as we prepared for the day's drills, the reality of our situation sinking in deeper with each passing moment.

After Kegg's speech, we returned to our regular drills. The morning session was with Master Owle, who drilled us on the rising tensions with the Kingdom of Rhudoria in the western peaks. Known for their ability to harden their own skin, Rhudoria's warriors were a formidable force. Master Owle's voice echoed through the room, detailing the strategic importance of their capital city, Stonehaven.

"The Ironclad Council," he intoned, "a coalition of powerful mining families and warrior chieftains, rules Rhudoria. Their control over the mining operations grants them immense power and influence."

My mind wandered as he continued, but I forced myself to focus. The information was vital. "Rhudoria's warriors are some of the toughest you'll face," Owle warned, his eyes scanning the room. "Their tactics and resilience in battle are unmatched."

Names and events flashed through my mind, each one a piece of a larger, intricate puzzle. The rising tensions between our kingdom and Rhudoria were more than just background noise—they were the prelude to a potential conflict that could shape our future.

In the afternoon, Master Kinrade took me, Lear, and Aspallan aside while the others continued with their physical drills. His gaze was intense, his voice firm. "Focus on what weapon you think suits you best. What feels right when you fight. The Forge has a range of wooden replicas for you to practise with."

I approached the racks filled with the training weapons, each neatly organised. I picked up a short sword first, feeling its weight in my hand. The grip was familiar, almost comforting, a reminder of the countless hours I'd spent training with Banar. But as I swung it, something felt off. The balance wasn't right, the blade too light for the strength I'd built.

Next, I tried a broadsword. It was heavier, requiring more effort to wield. The broad blade cut through the air with a satisfying whoosh, but it lacked the agility I craved. I moved to the two-handers, their massive forms imposing. The power behind each swing was undeniable, but they felt cumbersome, too slow for my liking.

My eyes landed on a messer, its single-edged blade sleek and deadly. I picked it up, testing its weight. The grip felt good, the blade responsive. I swung it in a wide arc, the edge whistling through the air. It was close to what I wanted, but still, something felt missing.

Aspallan, meanwhile, was examining the stoc, rapier, and longsword. His movements were precise, almost surgical. He tested each weapon with a fencer's grace, his eyes focused and calculating. The Stoc seemed to hold his interest the longest, its straight, thrusting design matching his measured style.

Lear gravitated towards the axes. He hefted a battle axe first, then a smaller hand axe, testing their balance and weight. His swings were powerful, each strike delivered with brute force that suited his build and temperament. He had a similar short but muscular frame to my own, and I could see why the axes appealed to him.

I continued to practise swings with each blade, my frustration growing. The short sword, once an extension of myself, now felt like a child's toy. The broadsword was powerful but unwieldy. The two-handers were simply too cumbersome. The messer came closest, but still, it didn't feel right.

I paused, sweat dripping down my brow, my muscles aching from the repeated motions. I looked at the racks again, considering my options. The right weapon was here somewhere, waiting for me to find it. I just had to keep searching.

The second half of Master Kinrade's drills had us gathered around the sparring circle. This time, Lear was pitted against Quisten. Quisten wielded the weapon of the day, a wooden broadsword, while Lear had chosen the short axe. The tension was clear to see for anyone. Despite our many lessons, they'd never been pitted against each other, and everyone sensed the brewing storm.

Quisten still bore the haunted look of someone suffering the aftereffects of the trial. His movements were sluggish, his eyes darting nervously. In contrast, Lear was a coiled spring, his short, muscular frame radiating aggression. He looked a little like a one toothed snake with that short axe. Both kept their mouths shut, knowing that jibes would only earn them trouble with Master Kinrade.

The fight began. Lear charged forward, axe swinging with brutal efficiency. Quisten parried, but the force of Lear's attack drove him back.

Quisten sneered, his eyes darting to the scar on Lear's cheek. "That scar suits you, Lear. A permanent reminder of how useless you are."

I could hear Quisten's insults and I was certain Master Kinrade could too but nothing was done about it. The clang of wood echoed in the training yard, each blow sending vibrations up the shafts of their weapons.

Quisten's defence was shaky. His broadsword was unwieldy in his hands, and it was clear he wasn't at his best. Lear pressed his advantage, his strikes relentless. He ducked under a sloppy swing from Quisten and brought the axe up in a vicious uppercut. The wooden edge of the axe caught Quisten's nose, and he staggered back, blood streaming down his face.

Lear didn't gloat verbally, but the smug look on his face was enough. He stepped back, eyes locked on Quisten, daring him to retaliate. Quisten, humiliated and angry, lashed out wildly. Lear sidestepped the attack and whispered just loud enough for those close to hear, "Careful, Lordling. Don't want another piss stain on your trousers."

The words hit their mark. Quisten's eyes blazed with hate. He swung the broadsword with all his might, but Lear easily deflected the blow. Before the fight could escalate further, Master Kinrade stepped in, his voice a whip-crack in the air.
"Enough!" he barked. "Both of you, back in line."
Lear smirked, wiping Quisten's blood from his axe, while Quisten shot him a murderous glare. The hate in Quisten's eyes was unmistakable. It was clear this fight wasn't over, not by a long shot.

True to Prime Master Kegg's word, the witches sang that night. The haunting melody seeped through the walls of The Forge, weaving its way into our dreams. Both Lear and I tossed and turned in our bunks, the song pulling at the edges of our minds. It wasn't like being in the Expanse or the Grand Hall, but it still affected us, a subtle, insidious presence.

I lay on my back, staring at the ceiling, listening to Lear's restless movements. "You feel that?" I whispered into the darkness.

Lear's voice came back, tense. "Yeah. It's like a whisper in my head. Not as bad as the trial, but still... unsettling."

I nodded, even though he couldn't see me. "Guess it's supposed to help us build resistance."

"Supposed to," Lear muttered. "Doesn't mean I have to like it."

We fell into silence again, each of us wrestling with the remnants of the song in our minds.

A week passed, and the wards started to recover from the trials. I noticed that each day the haunted look faded from their eyes, replaced by a cautious determination. Whether they'd pass the next trial was unknown, but there was a noticeable shift in the air.

I felt more confident. The Expanse had hardened me, and the nights of subtle singing were becoming easier to endure. I knew I could always rely on my abilities to negate the Resonance, though I was careful not to get caught doing that. For now, I played the part, enduring like the rest, keeping my secrets close.

The next lesson with Master Kinrade arrived, and he gathered us around. His sharp eyes scanned us, assessing our readiness. "Have you chosen your weapons?" he asked, voice steady and authoritative.

I stepped forward first. "The messer," I said, feeling the weight of my decision. It was a versatile weapon, and its balance suited my fighting style.

Aspallan was next. "The stoc," he declared, his voice calm and sure. The weapon's reach complemented his lanky frame and graceful movements.

Lear stepped up last. "The bearded axe," he said, a fierce grin on his lips. It fit him perfectly, his aggressive fighting style demanding something... brutal.

Master Kinrade nodded, satisfaction glinted in his eyes. "Good choices," he said. "Now, to The Forges."

We followed him to The Forges, the air grew hotter and thicker with the scent of molten metal and burning coal. Inside, Forge Master Paton, a burly man with arms like tree trunks, greeted us. He assigned each of us a journeyman to work with.

To my surprise, my blacksmith was a girl named Rein. She was shorter than me, with strong arms and calloused hands. Her auburn hair was tied back in a messy bun, and her green eyes sparkled with determination.

"So, you're Karn," she said, sizing me up. "You ready to get your hands dirty?"

I nodded, feeling a surge of anticipation. "Let's do this."

Rein grinned, her smile infectious. "Good. Let's make a weapon you can be proud of."

Over the next week, I was ordered to miss drills to work on forming my sword. Rein was confident and had a bone to pick with anyone who doubted her skills. Rein looked at me, eyebrow raised. "So, what kind of sword are we making and why?"

I took a moment to gather my thoughts. "A messer, but straight. I need something versatile, with a good balance between cutting and thrusting. The straight blade will give me more control and precision in tight situations. Plus, it feels right in my hand, like an extension of myself."

"Alright, don't go falling in love yet young ward with your fancy words," she said with a mock grin.

The first day, she led me to the back of the forge, where stacks of metal ingots were piled high. "First things first," she said, hands on her hips. "We need to choose the right metal. It's got to be strong but flexible. Ever heard of pattern welding?"

I shook my head. "No, but I'm ready to learn."

She smirked. "Good. We're going to layer different steels together to make a blade that's tough and holds an edge. Start by picking out these ingots." She pointed to a few specific piles. "Hard and soft steels. We'll forge-weld them together."

As I hefted the metal, she scrutinised my choices, occasionally nodding or shaking her head. When satisfied, she led me to the forge. "Now, watch closely," she instructed, her tone commanding yet encouraging.

The heat of the forge was intense, sweat beaded on my forehead almost instantly. Rein worked the bellows, bringing the fire to a white-hot intensity. "Place the metals in and keep an eye on the temperature. Too hot and we'll ruin the steel."

I followed her instructions, watching the metal glow and spark. She took over, hammering the glowing pieces together with rhythmic precision. "Your turn," she said, stepping aside.

The hammer was heavy, but I swung it with determination. "Not bad," she commented, guiding my hands to ensure even strikes. "Keep at it."

We repeated the process over the next few days, heating, hammering, and folding the steel until it was a single, cohesive billet. Each day, Rein pushed me harder, her critiques sharp but fair. "You've got a good arm, Karn. Use it."

Once the blade was formed, we moved on to the guard and hilt. "What do you want?" Rein asked, sketching rough designs on a piece of parchment.

I thought for a moment, Banar's emblem of the stag flashing in my mind but that was his. I needed something of my own. "Something simple but sturdy. A crossguard that can catch an opponent's blade. The hilt... wrapped in leather for a firm grip. And," I hesitated, "could we incorporate a wolf surrounded by stars? It would pay homage to my lord father's emblem."

She considered this, her charcoal piece pausing. "The hilt would be too fancy for that, but I can put the design on the pommel."

A growl of approval rumbled inside my head. I nodded. "That works."

Her charcoal flew across the paper, and she held up a detailed sketch. "Like this?"

I grinned. "Exactly."

The next step was shaping the guard and hilt. Rein showed me how to heat and bend the metal, then attach it securely to the blade. "Every piece has to fit perfectly," she explained. "No room for error."

By the end of the week, the messer was taking shape. I admired the balance and weight of the nearly finished weapon. "It's incredible," I said, genuinely impressed.

Rein smiled, a rare softness in her eyes. "We're not done yet. We need to quench it, then sharpen it to a razor edge."

As we finished the final steps, I found myself respecting Rein more each day. Her skill, her confidence, and her determination were contagious. "You're good at this," I said one evening as we cleaned up.

"Thanks," she replied, wiping sweat from her brow. "I've worked hard to get here. You're not bad yourself, Karn. You'll be a force to be reckoned with on the field with one of my blades."

At the end of the second week, all three of us—Lear, Aspallan, and I—had our new weapons. We were allowed to carry them around, though forbidden to use them outside of Master Kinrade's sessions. "No sparring with them without my say," Kinrade had warned. "Break those rules, and you'll face expulsion from The Forge and martial law."

Despite the restrictions, we were allowed to show them off. And show them off we did. The other boys gathered around, marvelling at the weapons we'd forged.

I stood in the courtyard, holding my messer with pride. The sleek, straight blade gleamed in the sunlight, the wolf emblem on the pommel catching the light. Hugo, Illiam, Ivor, and Edrin crowded around, their eyes wide with admiration.

"That's a beauty," Hugo said, reaching out but stopping short of touching it. "You can tell it's top-notch craftsmanship."

"Rein would appreciate you saying that," I said.

Illiam nodded, his usual cool demeanour giving way to genuine interest. "The balance looks perfect. How does it handle?"

I gave it a few practice swings, the blade cutting through the air with a satisfying whoosh. "It feels like an extension of my arm," I said, unable to hide the pride in my voice.

Ivor and Edrin exchanged glances, clearly impressed. "Bet it'll serve you well in real battle," Edrin said.

Just then, Quisten sauntered over, his gaze fixed on my messer. A sneer curled his lips. "Nice toy," he said, voice dripping with sarcasm. "But it's not as good as my family's sword. Can't wait to get it back after I pass the trial."

I shot him a level look. "We'll see, Quisten."

Quisten's eyes narrowed, but he didn't retort. Instead, he turned and walked away, leaving a tense silence in his wake. The other boys exchanged uneasy glances but didn't comment.

Two weeks passed in a blur of training, drills, and restless nights. Before I knew it, it was time for the next trial.

The Grand Hall loomed ahead, dark and foreboding. The air was thick with tension as we lined up, ready to face the next test. The torches continued to mark my progress, each one a challenge. I moved forward, my heart pounding in my chest. The song of the witches echoed through the hall, a haunting melody that clawed at my sanity.

When I reached the fifth torch, I felt the familiar fear clawing at me, a cold hand squeezing my heart. But I dug deep, letting the red haze of my anger surge through me. The fear melted away, replaced by a burning determination. The song lost its grip on me, and I took a deep breath, stepping forward with renewed strength.

Illiam passed as well, his face pale and drawn but resolute. Hugo, however, only managed to get to the sixth torch before collapsing, his body trembling with exhaustion and fear. Lear, unsurprisingly, passed with a grim determination etched into his features. Aspallan also succeeded. At least ten other boys managed to pass that night, their relief masked only by their exhaustion.

Afterwards, Illiam approached me, his usual calm replaced by a haunted look. "I sent myself to The Expanse for a couple of nights," he admitted quietly, his voice barely above a whisper. "It helped. Barely."

Quisten, however, didn't pass. It was revealed he only got to the third torch before collapsing. Seeing him defeated and broken, tears streaming down his face, was a stark reminder of the trial's brutality.

Despite the tension, the ceremony afterwards offered a brief respite. I got to see Serah again, her presence a small comfort amidst the chaos. Her dark, piercing eyes met mine across the gathered crowd of witches and wards crowd, a silent connection that spoke volumes. We didn't get a chance to talk, but the brief moment of eye contact was enough. I noticed Lear staring at her too, his eyes filled with a burning hatred that made my skin crawl.

The next day, the eleven wards who had passed were celebrated. The Forge felt emptier, a stark contrast to the bustling chaos it had been. More boys had left, reducing our numbers to half of the original hundred or so. Not far off Keird's predictions. Those who passed were granted the privilege of forging their own weapons, a rite of passage that filled the air with the sound of hammers and the heat of the forges. Each ward also gained more privacy with shared rooms, a welcome respite from the crowded dormitories. I, however, was still stuck with Lear.

Lear and I talked more, a reluctant camaraderie forming between us. Each night, we proudly left our weapons on top of our chests, a testament to our hard work and survival.

On one of those nights, Lear seemed particularly stressed. He lay on his bed, staring at the ceiling, his brow furrowed in frustration. "I just can't get the hang of Skirmish," he muttered. "Master Breen's strategy class is driving me to the brink."

I looked over at him, considering my next words. "I could teach you," I offered. "I've been visiting The Golden Hall in Dúnmara. There's a tournament next week I planned to join, but Quisten hasn't been right since the trial."

Lear hesitated, clearly remembering Quisten's bitter words and demeanour. "I don't know, Karn," he said slowly. "Quisten's a prick. Always has been."

I shrugged. "True, but this isn't about him. It's about you. And Skirmish isn't as hard as it seems once you get the basics."

Lear sighed as he rubbed at his temples. "Alright, show me."

We sat down at the small desk, the game board between us. I laid out the pieces, explaining each one. "Foot Soldiers move one square at a time in any direction," I said, placing a piece on the board. "Knights move in an L-shape, like this." I demonstrated with a quick flick of my wrist.

Lear nodded, watching intently. "Okay, I get that. What about the others?"

"Archers move in straight lines, any number of squares, but can't jump over other pieces," I continued. "Cavalry move up to three squares in a straight line and can jump over one piece. Siege Engines are powerful—they can't move but they can destroy an adjacent piece without moving into its square."

He seemed to be catching on, his earlier frustration giving way to curiosity. "And these special pieces?"

"Witches move one square in any direction and can immobilise an adjacent enemy piece for a turn. Assassins move up to three squares diagonally, bypassing the first piece they encounter and capturing the second. Spies move diagonally any number of squares and can reveal your opponent's next move once per game. The objective is to capture the opponent's flag, which is placed in the back row."

Lear's jaw tightened at the mention of witches, his knuckles turning white as he gripped the edge of the desk. "Witches," he spat, his voice laced with anger. "Of course, they have the power to immobilise. Just like in real life, always messing with us."

He leaned forward, examining the pieces with a fierce determination. "Alright, let's play."

As we played, I explained strategies, showing him how to balance offence and defence, how to set ambushes and anticipate moves. Lear was a quick study, and despite his initial hesitation, he began to enjoy the game.

After a few rounds, Lear leaned back, a rare, reluctant smile on his face. "Thanks, Karn. This helps... a lot."

"No problem," I replied. "It's a good game. Helps with thinking ahead. Plus, it's a break from everything else."

I glanced at Lear. "I was planning to join a tournament at The Golden Hall in Dúnmara next week. But with Quisten acting the way he is... I'm not so sure."

Lear's expression darkened. "Quisten's becoming more bitter every day. He's getting on my nerves."

I nodded. "Yeah, I noticed. The trials are hitting everyone hard."

Lear sighed. "I just need to get through this. We all do."

As I packed up the game, unease settled deep within me. The final trial loomed, its shadow darkening our every thought and action. The weight of it pressed down on all of us, but especially on Hugo and Quisten. For them, this could be the end of the road.

I thought about Quisten, his haunted eyes, the fear that had replaced his usual arrogance. He hadn't been the same since the last trial. The Three Moons Tournament was just a week away, and I hoped it would give him the strength and focus he needed to get through. But doubt gnawed at me. Would he rise to the challenge, or would his fear consume him?

The room felt colder, the silence more oppressive. The stakes were higher than ever, and the tension was clear. The final trial was coming, and with it, a reckoning that none of us could avoid.

Chapter 29 - Three Moons Tournament

The Three Moons Tournament was on the next seventh day. I spent the morning searching for Quisten at The Forge and the docks, but he was nowhere to be found. Frustration gnawed at me, but I had to push it aside.

I travelled to the Three Moons Tournament in Dúnmara at The Golden Hall with Hugo, Illiam, Ivor, Edrin, and surprisingly, Lear. The others were reluctant at first but eventually agreed to let him join.

The Golden Hall was alive with energy, the kind that thrummed in your veins and made the air seem wild. Laughter and shouting filled the space, mingling with the clink of mugs and the rich, sweet smell of mead. People crowded around tables, their faces lit with anticipation and excitement.

The tournament had drawn quite a crowd. Soldiers, merchants, and townsfolk mingled, their animated conversations creating a vibrant tapestry of sound. Candles flickered in iron sconces, casting a warm, golden glow over the wooden beams and stone walls.

As we entered, Hugo elbowed me, a grin stretching across his face. "This is going to be something, Karn."
I nodded, feeling a rush of adrenaline. The room was a sea of eager faces, each one a potential opponent. The tournament was more than just a game—it was a proving ground.

I pushed through the throng of people as I searched for a familiar face. My eyes scanned the room, landing on Quisten in a dimly lit corner. His dark hair fell in waves around his face, framing his piercing green eyes that seemed to catch every flicker of light. There was a noble look to him if I had ever seen one, an air of arrogance and confidence that set him apart from the rest. He was speaking with Lucas, their conversation hushed and intense. I saw Lucas hand Quisten something small, a leather pouch, and Quisten slipped him more than a handful of coin in return, much more.

"Quisten," I called out, trying to sound casual. "You ready for the tournament?"

He glared at me, his eyes narrowing with annoyance, a shadow flickering behind them that hinted at something darker.

"Karn," he said, his tone guarded. "I was thinking about it, but now..." His gaze shifted to Lear, and his face twisted in anger. "What's he doing here?"

Lear stepped forward, fists clenched. "I'm here to watch, just like everyone else."

Quisten sneered, shaking his head. "I should have known. You all betray me." His voice rose, drawing a few glances from nearby tables. "First you, Karn, then Hugo, Illiam, and now you bring him along?" He spat the last word like a curse.

"Quisten, what are you talking about? it's not like that," I tried to reason with him. "What about all those nights we spent preparing for this?"

His laugh was cold and bitter. "Prepare? For what? Another chance to watch me fail? You all just want to see me broken."

"That's not true," Hugo interjected, stepping beside me. "We want you with us, Quisten."

I thought about the hours I had spent practising Skirmish with the arrogant noble, enduring his arrogance because I thought it might help him. The tournament was the only reason I spent so much time with the prick. But now, all that effort seemed wasted.

Quisten's eyes darted around, his face a mask of hurt and rage. "Stay away from me. All of you." He turned sharply, pushing through the crowd towards the exit.

"Quisten, wait!" I called after him, but he didn't stop. His figure disappeared into the sea of people, leaving us standing there in stunned silence.

Lear muttered under his breath, "Let him go. He's a liability anyway."

I shot him a look, biting back a retort. The tension between us was blatant, but I forced myself to focus on the task at hand. The tournament was about to begin, and I couldn't afford any more distractions.

"Look at this crowd," Hugo said, leaning in. "Never seen so many people so eager to play a board game."

"Must be the stakes," Illiam added, his eyes darting around. "And the chance to show off."

We found a table near the edge of the room, and I left the others to secure seats while I headed to join the other players. The Golden Hall was packed with people, the air thick with excitement and anticipation.

"Good luck," Hugo called out, giving me a thumbs up.

From my spot at the players' area, I checked out the room, taking in the mix of faces. Soldiers, merchants, and townsfolk mingled, their conversations a vibrant hum in the background. The flickering candlelight cast warm shadows over the wooden beams, adorned with gold leaf, and stone walls covered with tapestries, adding to the hall's elegant charm.

The tournament began with a flurry of activity. The first round paired me against a soldier with a rough demeanour. His calloused hands moved his pieces with adept ease. We exchanged nods, and the game commenced.

I opened with a cautious strategy, placing my Foot Soldiers to secure key positions. The soldier responded aggressively, pushing his Knights and Archers forward. Remembering Lucas's advice, I focused on controlling the centre of the board. My Siege Engine managed to take out one of his Knights, giving me a crucial advantage. The game turned into a battle of attrition, but my patience paid off. I cornered his Flag with a combination of Archers and a Cavalry charge, securing my first victory.

"Nice one, Karn!" Hugo cheered as I walked back to the table for a brief break.

The second game was against a wiry merchant with sharp eyes and quick fingers. He played with a deceptive calm, setting traps and feints to lure me into mistakes. I nearly fell for one of his tricks, but my time with Master Breen had taught me to read my opponent's intentions. I used my Spy to reveal his next move, thwarting his plan. The Spy doesn't really reveal the next move of course but whatever move your opponent tells you they'll make they have to, locking them in.

"He's trying to lure you in," Lear mouthed, watching the game intently. As if I hadn't only recently taught him how to play.

The game became a tense back-and-forth, each of us trying to outmanoeuvre the other. In the end, a well-timed move with my Knight sealed his fate, and I won my second game.

"Two for two," Hugo shouted, grinning. "Keep it up!"

Feeling confident, I approached the third game. My opponent was an older man with a stoic expression, his eyes betrayed years of experience. As we set up our pieces, he looked up and met my gaze.

"Been playing long, boy?" he asked, his voice gravelly.

"Long enough," I replied, trying to match his calm demeanour. "But there's always more to learn."

He chuckled softly. "That's the right attitude. Let's see what you've got."

The game started slowly, each of us probing for weaknesses. He played defensively, fortifying his positions with Earthworks and strategically placed Archers. I tried to break through his lines with a coordinated assault, but his defence was impenetrable.

"He's good," I muttered to myself, feeling the pressure mount.

The old man caught my eye and grinned. "Patience, lad. This game is as much about endurance as it is about strategy."

As the game progressed, I realised he was baiting me, using my own aggression against me. My Siege Engine was caught in a trap, and he immobilised it with his Witch.

"Didn't see that coming, did you?" he said, a glint of amusement in his eyes.

"No, I didn't," I admitted, trying to regroup. "But it's not over yet."

"That's the spirit," he said, nodding. "Always fight to the end."

From there, his counterattack was relentless. I struggled to regroup, but it was too late. His Cavalry swept through my weakened defences, capturing my Flag with a final, decisive move.

I sat back, the sting of defeat sharp but familiar. I had learned much from Quisten, Master Breen, and Lucas, but there was always more to learn. The older man gave me a respectful nod.

"Well played," he said, extending his hand. "You've got potential, boy. Keep honing your skills."

I shook his hand, acknowledging his own skill. "Thanks. I will."

He smiled, a glimmer of respect in his eyes. "Remember, every loss is just a step toward becoming better. Learn from it and come back stronger."

"I will," I said, determined. "I'll see you next time."

Returning to our table, I found the boys waiting eagerly. "How'd it go?" Hugo asked, his eyes bright with curiosity.

"Two wins, one loss," I replied, shrugging. "Learned a lot,

though."

Illiam clapped me on the back. "Not bad, Karn. Not bad at all."

"That last guy was something else," I said, shaking my head. "He knew every trick in the book. I'm just disappointed I couldn't win the Moon Rider."

We gathered around our table, mugs of mead in hand, the energy of the tournament still buzzing in my veins. The room was alive with laughter and shouts, the air thick with the smell of roasted meat and spilled beer.

Hugo took his opportunity to copy Illiam and slapped me on the back, a wide grin on his face. "Not bad, Karn! You held your own out there. That last guy was tough, though."

"Yeah, he was something else," I replied, taking a sip of my drink. "Learned a lot from him." I repeated what I had said earlier.

Illiam, cool and composed as always, leaned in. "Speaking of learning, what do you think of these?" He pulled out his new weapons, two long dirks, the blades gleamed under the candlelight.

I examined them closely, appreciating the craftsmanship. "Those look deadly, Illiam. You planning to juggle them or just scare the piss out of everyone?"

Illiam smirked. "A bit of both, maybe."

Hugo laughed, his eyes twinkling with amusement. "Well, I'd rather face Illiam's knives than deal with this new horse. Damn thing nearly bit my hand off this morning."

"Still having trouble with him?" Ivor asked, shaking his head.

"Yeah, it's a Windsteed," Hugo replied, grinning. "Fastest breed there is, but temperamental as hell. He's giving me a run for my money."

Edrin, usually quiet, spoke up, his voice tinged with uncertainty. "I've been thinking… maybe The Forge isn't for me. It's been… tough."

Lear, serious and focused, fixed Edrin with a steady gaze.

332

"What do you mean, you can't just quit now."

Edrin shrugged, looking down at his drink. "It's not just the training. It's everything. The trials, the constant pressure. I don't know if I can handle it."

"None of us knew if we could handle it," I said, my voice firm. "But we're still here, aren't we? You've got to push through."

Hugo nodded. "Karn's right. Besides, who else would we have to boast about catching up to? We need you, Edrin."

Edrin smiled weakly. "Maybe you're right. I'll think about it."

Illiam raised his mug. "To surviving The Forge. And to making it to the other side, together."

We all clinked our mugs together, the sound ringing out like a promise. The conversation turned lighter, filled with boasts and banter.

"I bet I could take you all on with these knives," Illiam said, a playful glint in his eye.

"Please, you'd trip over your own feet before you got close," Hugo retorted, laughing.

"You talk a lot for a guy who's got a Windsteed biting at his heels," Ivor teased, earning a round of laughter from the group.

The night wore on, and I finally found a moment to speak with Lucas. He stood by the bar, his coat draped over a stool and his hat tipped to one side, as always.

"You did a good job out there, Karn," Lucas said, his eyes twinkling with mischief.

"Thanks," I replied, feeling a swell of pride. "But why didn't you play? You'd have wiped the floor with them."

Lucas leaned in closer, his voice dropping to a conspiratorial whisper. "Ah, my young friend, sometimes the greatest victories are the ones unseen. Too much attention can be... problematic for someone like me."

I frowned, curiosity gnawing at me. "What about Quisten? I

saw you two earlier. What was that about?"

Lucas's expression shifted, a shadow passing over his face. "Quisten and I have our dealings. That's all you need to know."

I pressed on, my frustration mounting. "Come on, Lucas. What's going on? Is he in trouble?"

Lucas's smile turned sharp, almost dangerous. "Karn, some mysteries are best left unsolved. You've got enough on your plate without sticking your nose where it doesn't belong."

I opened my mouth to argue, but his piercing gaze silenced me. The conversation was over before it even began.

Then Lucas's sharp gaze softened, a knowing glint in his eye. "Alright, Karn, you look like you need a good story to take your mind off things."

I raised an eyebrow, intrigued. "Go on then, enlighten me."

Lucas leaned against the bar, his voice taking on a storyteller's cadence. "There's a gem I've been searching for, a rare thing with deep red veins running through it. They say it holds incredible power, hidden away for centuries. This gem, it's said to be able to amplify a person's deepest desires or fears, bringing them to the forefront of their being. Imagine the chaos or the control it could bring."

I couldn't help but think of the gem I'd seen in Master Veil's quarters, the one with those same crimson streaks. The memory of its eerie glow and the strange pull it had on me lingered, but I kept my mouth shut, letting Lucas weave his tale.

"Thing is," Lucas continued, swirling the drink in his hand, "I'm not the only one after it. Those men you saw, they think I have it. But I don't. Not yet, anyway." He winked, the twinkle in his eye unmistakable. "They've been chasing shadows, always a step behind. They think they can outsmart me, but they underestimate the lengths I'll go to find it first."

The bar was filled with the low hum of conversation and the clinking of mugs. The warm glow of the candles cast flickering

334

shadows, adding to the mysterious aura surrounding Lucas's story. I leaned in closer, the noise of the tavern fading into the background.

I was about to ask more, I wanted to know what the gem was and tell Lucas about the one I'd seen in Master Veil's quarters, when my friends returned. Hugo, Illiam, Ivor, Edrin, and Lear all crowded around, their boisterous energy filled the space. Hugo slapped me on the back, a wide grin on his face.

"There you are, Karn! We've been looking for you," Hugo exclaimed, his eyes bright with excitement.

The chance for privacy was gone. Lucas straightened, the storyteller's mask slipping back into place. "Looks like your friends are here to drag you back into the fray."

I nodded, a small smile playing on my lips. "Seems so. Thanks for the story, Lucas."

"Anytime, Karn. Keep your wits about you," Lucas replied, his tone carrying a hint of seriousness beneath the light-hearted facade.

The night continued, the story left hanging in the air, a mystery I knew I had to unravel. But right then, the camaraderie and laughter of my friends took precedence. We found a table, the conversation shifting to lighter topics, the tension of the day melted away in the warmth of The Golden Hall and its golden mead.

Chapter 30 - The Third Trial

The day of the third trial came sooner than expected, as summer began to give way to autumn. The leaves on the trees that covered The Forge's courtyard had turned vibrant shades of red and gold, creating a multilayered carpet that crunched underfoot. The air was crisp, a reminder of the changing seasons.

I sat with Quisten, Hugo, and Illiam in Master Kegg's drill yard. We watched intently as the six remaining members of Aspallan's squad faced off against the five remaining members of Lear's. Lear had been promoted to Prime of his squad since the previous Prime had dropped out of The Forge.

The courtyard was alive with tension and anticipation. The remaining members of each squad were blindfolded, navigating a complex maze designed to test their teamwork and trust. The Primes, Lear and Aspallan, stood at strategic points around the maze, shouting instructions to their blindfolded comrades.

"Left, left! No, your other left!" Lear's voice was sharp and commanding, cutting through the crisp autumn air.

Aspallan's, in contrast, was calm and measured. "Slow down, listen to my voice. One step to the right, now forward."

I glanced at Quisten, who was unusually quiet, his green eyes focused intently on the scene before us. Hugo, ever jovial, muttered under his breath, "I bet Lear's going to lose his tongue before they get through this."

Illiam, cool and collected as always, smirked. "If he doesn't lose his mind first. The maze is designed to frustrate even the best of us."

As the blindfolded boys stumbled and hesitated, I could see the strain on Lear's face. He was relentless, barking orders, his muscular frame tense with the effort of guiding his squad through the labyrinth. The leaves rustled around us, adding a whispering backdrop to the shouts and commands.

Aspallan's squad moved more fluidly, their trust in his calm directions evident. They were ahead, but Lear's squad was not far behind, driven by his fierce determination.

"He's got them running like headless chickens," Hugo chuckled, shaking his head.

Quisten, finally breaking his silence, sneered, "Lear's always been good at barking orders. Let's see if the loudmouth can actually lead them out for once."

I watched Lear closely, noticing the fire in his eyes. He was a fierce leader, driven and uncompromising. The trial was more than just a test of skill; it was a battle of wills, a fight to prove who could lead and who would follow.

Since the night at the tournament, Quisten had returned to near enough normal. Noble arrogance with a dash of bastard. Though, surprisingly, he even came to apologise to me for not being there. That would have been strange enough for someone like Quisten, but he seemed genuine.

Either way, Hugo and Illiam had taken him back, and in a way, so had I. "Lear as Prime, what a joke," Quisten sneered, his voice dripping with disdain. "The only thing he can lead is a parade of fools."

Despite the apology, we still had to tread carefully when Lear was around. The animosity between him and Quisten was still a simmering pot ready to boil over.

The boys and I sat together, watching the squads navigate the maze. The atmosphere was tense, but Hugo broke the silence with a determined smile. "I'm going to make it this time. I can feel it."

I noticed Hugo's eyes dart briefly to Quisten, who remained

silent. Instead, Illiam chimed in, "What weapon are you thinking of forging once you pass?"

Hugo's face lit up with enthusiasm. "Ideally, a bow. A short bow would be perfect for horseback. But since it has to be a hand weapon, I'm thinking of a Longseax. Something versatile that I can use in different situations."

He glanced at the sword on my side and added, "Something like your messer, Karn, but with a longer reach and a bit of a curve."

I nodded, intrigued. "A Longseax sounds practical. It's got the versatility you need."

Illiam leaned in, curiosity piqued. "Why not just go with the bow if that's your first choice?"

Hugo shrugged. "Rules are rules. Besides, a Longseax will still give me an edge. I can always get my bow later. Plus, the thought of forging a blade that's both urbane looking and deadly is pretty appealing."

Quisten, finally breaking his silence, smirked, "Careful, Hugo. You might hurt yourself with that."

I turned to him, my voice firm. "Knock it off, Quisten. We're supposed to have each other's backs."

Quisten rolled his eyes but kept quiet.

Hugo, unfazed, continued, "I've been practising with the short bow in my spare time. But a good hand weapon will give me the edge in close combat I need."

I nodded in agreement. "Sounds like a solid plan, Hugo. Just remember, it's not just about the weapon, it's about how you use it."

Quisten, his voice dripping with arrogance, broke the silence. "I can't wait to get my family's sword back."

I raised an eyebrow, genuinely curious. "Why not craft your own? Make a name for yourself?"

Quisten scoffed, a condescending smirk on his face. "My family's name is enough. We've earned it over the years. One of the first families to pledge fealty to the Queen."

I fought the urge to roll my eyes. The disdain I felt for Quisten's self-importance was clear. Yet, I thought about Banar's advice. Making alliances, even with those I despised, was part of the plan. Illiam and Hugo weren't too bad, but Quisten was a different story. When would my revenge come? I was starting to forget about it, finding myself unexpectedly enjoying my time at The Forge.

The third trial loomed, and with it, the promise of returning home for the Harvest Festival. The first half of our year at The Forge would soon be over. It was time to confront Banar and Lord Caine about their plans for the future. I couldn't lose sight of my revenge. I had grown too complacent, too comfortable.

I turned back to Quisten, nodding curtly. "Sure, Quisten. Whatever you say."

His eyes narrowed at me. He did not like that response.

The evening air was thick with tension as we all gathered in the refectory. The usual chatter and laughter were replaced by sombre faces and hushed whispers. The looming third trial hung over us like a storm cloud, and everyone knew that those who failed would be leaving The Forge for good.

We sat together at our usual spot. The smell of stew and freshly baked bread filled the air, but it did little to lift the mood. I glanced around the table at Quisten, Hugo, and Illiam, their faces drawn and serious.

Quisten was trying to put on a brave face, but I could see the agitation in his eyes. His jaw clenched and unclenched as he picked at his food. The brown leather bag that Lucas had given him was now a permanent fixture on his belt, and I hadn't had a chance to ask him about it.

Hugo broke the silence first, his voice unusually quiet. "Tonight's the night. I can feel it. I'm going to make it through."

Illiam nodded, his cool demeanour masking whatever nerves he might have been feeling. "Just keep your head clear, Hugo. You've got this."

I looked at Quisten, who was staring into his bowl, lost in thought. "Quisten, you ready?"

He snapped out of his reverie, forcing a confident smirk. "Of course. I am Lord Cowle, after all."

I couldn't help but notice the tension in his voice. "You've got the strength to do this," I said, trying to offer some encouragement but hated myself for saying it to such a bastard.

Quisten's eyes flicked to me, a hint of anger flashing before he quickly masked it. "I know what I'm doing, Karn."

We fell into an uneasy silence, the weight of the upcoming trial pressing down on us. I had no doubt I could pass, but I was determined to do it without relying on the wolf's abilities. I needed to prove to myself that I could do it on my own.

Illiam's voice broke through my thoughts. "Just remember, we've all come this far. We can do this. We have to."

Hugo nodded, a steely resolve in his eyes. "Yeah. We can."

I caught Quisten's eye again. He gave a slight nod, but the uncertainty was still there. Whatever was in that bag, it was clearly weighing on him. I made a mental note to ask him about it when I had the chance.

For now, we had to focus on the trial ahead. It was the only thing that mattered.

Eventually, the doors to the refectory opened, and a prefect called out, "wards, it's time for the Third Trial." The room fell silent, the weight of those words sinking in. Just under half of the original number of recruits remained. I wondered just how many of us would continue on after tonight.

The tension in the air had manifested as we lined up. Those who had failed the previous trials were to go first. Hugo stepped forward, glancing back at us. I caught his eye and mouthed, "Good luck." He nodded with a determined expression, before the doors closed behind him. Once he entered, I wouldn't see him, or the others again until we all reached the other side, whether we passed or failed.

Time seemed to stretch. Quisten was next. He walked with a confidence that bordered on pretension, his strides purposeful and steady. Gone was the overwhelming fear he'd shown in the previous trials. The doors closed behind him, and I held my breath, knowing I wouldn't see him again until the trial's end.

Illiam was called next. His usual cool demeanour was in place, but I saw the tension in his shoulders as he stepped forward. The doors shut, leaving us in anxious anticipation.

Finally, it was Lear's turn. He gave a nod to me before disappearing behind the heavy doors. I watched as the doors closed, knowing the next time I saw him, it would be on the other side.

Then it was my turn. I took a deep breath, steeling myself for what lay ahead. The Third Trial awaited, and I was determined to face it on my own terms. I stepped forward, the heavy doors closing behind me, sealing me into the darkness.

The third trial awaited me, the final hurdle to prove my worth. The darkness loomed ahead, a familiar yet daunting challenge. This time, I resolved to face it without relying on my abilities. I would conquer the fear on my own terms.

I stepped into the grand hall, and the oppressive blackness

swallowed me whole once again. The torches flickered weakly, their feeble light barely piercing the thick shadows. The song began, an eerie melody that seeped into my bones. The fear it brought was visceral, a cold, creeping sensation that threatened to consume me. But this time, it was muted compared to my first encounter, tempered by the scars of my previous trials.

Each step was a battle. The shadows twisted into grotesque forms, reaching for me with clawed hands. I forced myself to breathe, to focus on the path ahead. The first torch, then the second. Each flicker of light marked a victory, a small triumph over the terror that had gnawed at my resolve. My heart pounded like a war drum, each beat a reminder that I was still alive, still fighting.

Halfway through, the hallucinations began. Men I had killed in the forest, their decaying faces twisted in pain, lunged at me from the darkness. I kicked and fought, my heart pounding in my chest. But I kept moving, one foot in front of the other, refusing to give in.

As I neared the end, a new vision emerged. The silhouette of the Witch Queen, a dark and twisted figure, loomed before me. Her presence was suffocating, a black aura radiating malevolence. She held Serah by the throat, her long, spike-like fingers piercing through her flesh, blood trickling down Serah's neck. Serah's eyes, wide with terror, pleaded for help, her mouth forming silent screams that tore at my soul. Rage surged through me, boiling away the fear. My resolve hardened. I would end the Witch Queen's reign. For Serah, for everyone.

I took three deep breaths to calm myself, pushing through the final stretch. The song's power waned, unable to hold me back any longer. I reached the last torch and the doors ahead swung open, revealing the faint light of the outside. I stepped through, breathing heavily, but triumphant. I had faced the trial without my abilities, relying solely on my strength and resolve. The fear was still there, but it no longer controlled me.

Outside, under the crescent moon, the scene was as I expected. To one side stood the group of witches, their numbers also greatly reduced. My eyes immediately sought out Serah, and I felt a surge of relief seeing her there, unharmed. Her presence was a small comfort amidst the tension. I made a mental note to ask her about the other girls when I had the chance.

On our side, only a third of the original hundred or so boys remained. Aspallan, Illiam, Lear, and Quisten stood with me. Quisten's face was smug with satisfaction, his eyes gleaming with an almost predatory pride.

But as I scanned the group, a pang of sadness hit me. Hugo was not there. His absence was a heavy weight on my chest. We had bonded over our love for horses, and I had genuinely come to see him as a friend. The realisation that he had not made it through the trial hit me harder than I expected. I caught Serah's eye across the courtyard, her face unreadable in the moonlight. We had all endured so much, and yet, the trials had taken their toll.

That night, the remaining wards celebrated. The refectory was filled with laughter and the clinking of wine cups. The tension from the trials had lifted, replaced by a sense of camaraderie and relief. Candles flickered, casting warm light on the worn wooden tables, and the rich scent of roasted meat and fresh bread filled the air.

I sat with Illiam, Quisten, and Lear. Illiam was congratulating Quisten, who couldn't help but boast. "I told you I'd make it through," Quisten said, leaning back in his chair with a smug grin. "My family's name means something, after all."

I sipped my wine, trying to ignore Quisten's bragging. My thoughts kept drifting to Hugo. We didn't even get to say goodbye.

The wards who failed had their belongings packed and were on a barge out of The Forge before we even returned from the trial.

"Don't worry, Illiam," Quisten said with a dismissive wave. "I'll make a better roommate than Hugo anyway."

The casual cruelty of his words snapped something inside me. "You don't have to be such a prick about it," I said, my voice sharper than I intended. But the energy drained out of me just as quickly. I felt exhausted from it all, the trials, the losses. It was surprising Quisten didn't feel the same.

Quisten's eyes narrowed. "Watch it, Karn. Just because you got lucky doesn't mean you're better than me."

Lear, who had been silently drinking, looked up, his eyes cold. "Luck had nothing to do with it. We all earned our place here."

Quisten sneered. "Is that so, Lear? You think you're some kind of leader now? Don't forget, you were nothing before The Forge."

Lear's hand tightened around his cup, the tension evident. "Better than a pompous fool who thinks his family name will save him."

Quisten stood, his face a mask of anger. "Say that again, I dare you."

Before things could escalate further, Illiam stepped between them, his hands up in a placating gesture. "Enough. We've all been through hell. This isn't the time for fighting."

The room went silent, all eyes on our table. Quisten's jaw clenched, but he sat back down, glaring at Lear. Lear didn't look away, the challenge still in his eyes.

I sighed, feeling the weight of the night. The third trial was over, the first major obstacle done, but the path ahead was still uncertain, fraught with tension and unspoken conflicts.

Chapter 31 - Autumn's Grace Promenade

The courtyard of The Forge buzzed with life; eager whispers and lively chatter filled the air. The remaining wards, now promoted to Steel Novices, gathered for Prime Master Kegg's ceremony. The crisp autumn air carried the scent of fallen leaves, mingling with the faint tang of metal and sweat that clung to our uniforms. The courtyard, usually a place of rigorous drills and relentless training, now felt almost festive, with lanterns hanging from the trees and casting a warm glow over the assembled crowd.

Prime Master Kegg stood at the forefront, his presence commanding and authoritative. He wore his masterful attire, a blend of regal blue and stern black, adorned with the emblems of his rank. As he stepped forward, the cheering wards fell silent, their eyes fixed on him with a mix of respect and awe.

"Steel Novices," Kegg began, his voice resonating through the courtyard, "congratulations on your promotion from Iron Initiates. You've endured the trials, faced your fears, and emerged stronger for it. This is no small feat, and it speaks to your hard work and perseverance."

The crowd responded with a round of applause, the clapping echoed off the stone walls. I glanced around, catching sight of familiar faces—Illiam, Quisten, Lear—all wearing expressions of pride and determination.

Kegg continued, "Soon, you will forge your own weapons, a symbol of your journey and your growth. But before that, we have a tradition to uphold, one that you may not have heard of yet—the Autumn's Grace Promenade."

Whispers rippled through the crowd. I turned to Illiam, who shrugged, his cool demeanour actually betrayed a hint of curiosity.

"The promenade," Kegg explained, "is an opportunity for wards and witches to interact and celebrate your achievements. It is a night of camaraderie and celebration before we break for winter. This is a time to enjoy the company of your peers and to reflect on how far you've come."

The idea of seeing Serah after the last half year was appealing, but I wasn't sure how I would feel facing the rest of the witches. The memories of those who burned my village still haunted me. I hated the very idea of them.

Kegg's gaze swept over us, his eyes hardening. "Remember, this celebration is also a test of your character. Conduct yourselves with honour and respect. The partnerships and alliances you build here will carry you forward in ways you may not yet understand."

The applause still echoed in my ears as I returned to the small, cramped room I shared with Lear. The anticipation of the promenade was clear, a mix of excitement and tension that buzzed in the air. I could hear Lear rummaging through his trunk. Our mocks, freshly washed, lay neatly on our beds, the simple fabric a stark contrast to the significance of the evening.

I picked up my family crest, running my fingers over the embroidered stag antlers and stars of Lord Fayle's emblem. The stitching was intricate, a sign of Banar's pride and heritage. The dark blue and grey fabric felt sturdy under my touch. As I fastened it to my shoulder, I noticed Lear staring at his own, plain mock, a flicker of uncertainty in his eyes.

"What's wrong?" I asked, fastening the last button.

Lear shrugged, his shoulders tense. "Nothing. Just feels... strange not having a house emblem. Makes me feel like an outsider."

I glanced at his tunic, the fabric bare where an emblem should be. An idea sparked. "Here," I said, pulling out a piece of cloth and a needle from my trunk. "Let's make you one."

Lear raised an eyebrow, a sceptical look on his face. "You serious?"

"Dead serious," I replied, already threading the needle. "What's something that represents you?"

He hesitated, then his gaze drifted to the emblem on my tunic. "How about a wolf and an axe?"

I nodded, starting to stitch a simple design. "A wolf and a bearded axe. That works."

Lear watched as I worked, his expression softening. "You didn't have to do this, Karn."

I glanced up, a small smile on my face. "It's no big deal. We need to stick together. Especially now we've passed the third trial."

The mention of the trial seemed to jolt him. He nodded, but his gaze turned distant, a shadow crossing his face. "Right, the trials. It's just... these trials, everything we've been through. I hate the witches, Karn. Really hate them."

I looked up, taken aback by the vehemence in his voice. The last thing I wanted was for him to figure out my sister was one of those witches, the very one who'd conducted his trial. Desperate to change the subject, my eyes shifted to the lightning bolt scar on his cheek, a jagged line that seemed out of place. "How did you get that scar, anyway?"

Lear's face darkened, and he looked away for a moment. "From my fa—," he started, then quickly changed course. "From my time in the army." He went quiet, the room filling with the unspoken weight of his words.

As I finished the emblem with a smile as I handed it over.

"Here you go. Pin it on your tunic and let's make it official."

Lear's eyes shone with gratitude. "Thank you, Karn. This... means a lot. You've got some real skill with that needle, maybe you should put down the sword?" He said, flashing me a cheeky grin.

He pinned it to his tunic, standing a little taller. The room felt less cramped, the air less stifling, as we prepared to face the promenade together.

Lear and I stepped out of our cramped room, mock uniforms pristine and adorned with our freshly added emblems. We walked through the corridors, the anticipation of the promenade thrumming in the air. We met up with Quisten, Illiam, and Ivor in the main hall.

Quisten stood tall, his dark hair meticulously styled, and his piercing green eyes glinting with pride. His emblem, a silver gryphon clutching a golden shield, stood out brilliantly against his dark blue and grey uniform. The ornate sword strapped to his side, with its hilt adorned in intricate designs, caught the light. Hanging from his belt was the brown bag he had received from Lucas. That mystery still gnawed at me.

Illiam, always too composed for my liking, had an emblem of a coiled serpent, symbolising agility and cunning. His sharp features and dark eyes gave him an enigmatic air that made me wary.

Ivor, a lanky boy with a mop of curly hair, wore an emblem of crossed arrows, representing his family's expertise in archery. His thin frame and wiry build gave him a deceptively fragile appearance, but his sharp eyes and quick reflexes hinted at a formidable skill set.

We exchanged nods, feeling more of a squad of our own. Quisten, such a peacock, couldn't resist showing off his sword.

"Got your sword back, huh?" I said, smirking as Quisten ran a finger along the hilt of his ornate weapon.

Quisten nodded, his eyes gleaming with pride. "An heirloom. A reminder of what true nobility looks like," he said, puffing his chest out.

I couldn't help but roll my eyes. "Hope you remember how to use it," I teased.

Quisten shot me a look, half amused, half annoyed. "You worry about your own skills, Karn. I'm more than ready."

Illiam, ever the pragmatist, chimed in. "Let's just make sure we all enjoy the night without any incidents, alright?" His eyes flicked to Quisten, who gave a noncommittal shrug.

We approached the large doors of the Grand Hall, the imposing wooden barriers now a symbol of celebration instead of dread. Prefects stood at the entrance, their faces softened by the glow of the lanterns.

As the doors swung open, the Grand Hall was revealed in all its glory. The space was magnificently lit, distinctly different to the shadowy depths we had faced during the trials. Murals covered the walls, depicting wards and witches in battle, their dark armour and black cloaks painted with fierce precision. The scenes told stories of valour and sacrifice, the weight of history in every brushstroke.

Sophisticated lighting enhanced the hall's majestic atmosphere, casting a warm glow over the polished marble floors and high vaulted ceilings. Chandeliers hung like constellations, their light reflecting off the intricate artwork and gilded decorations.

"Impressive, isn't it?" Illiam remarked, his eyes studying the hall.

"More than I expected," I admitted, taking in the grandeur of the setting. The hall felt alive, a living testament to the legacy we were now a part of.

Quisten, back to full confidence, strutted ahead with his chin held high. "Let's make this night unforgettable."

We followed, stepping into the heart of the celebration, the echoes of our footsteps swallowed by the murmurs and laughter of those already inside. The Autumn's Grace Promenade had begun, and we were ready to embrace it.

We stood on one side of the room, dressed in our sharpest uniforms, the dark blue and grey fabric crisply pressed, with weapons hanging proudly at our sides. The stag emblem on my shoulder gleamed under the soft light. Across from us, the witches wore elegant gowns in subtle colours, their flowing dresses a striking contrast to their usual dark cloaks. Each gown shimmered faintly in the lantern light, adding an ethereal quality to their presence.

Both groups eyed each other warily, the unease between us almost tangible. We, the wards, couldn't shake the lingering fear of the witches, who had put us through their gruelling trials. Their power was undeniable, and their role in our trials had left us on edge. On the other hand, the witches seemed equally unsure, their eyes flitting between us with cautious curiosity. They were used to commanding respect and fear, but tonight was different; tonight, we stood on more equal ground.

Lear stood beside me, his jaw clenched and eyes burning with barely concealed hatred. His gaze flickered over the witches, a mix of disdain and anger tightening his features. His white-knuckled grip on the hilt of his weapon spoke volumes, a silent witness to his loathing. The intense reaction seemed more than just the result of the trials; it was a deep-seated animosity that simmered just below the surface. I could understand that. I hated them too but refrained from letting it show.

The air was thick with tension and nerves. Every movement seemed louder, every glance full of meaning. It was a delicate balance of wariness and cautious steps towards understanding, shaped by the trials we had faced.

Masters filled the room, their presence commanding. Prime Master Kegg, Masters Mores, Breen, Kinrade, Quark, Owle, and Master Veil all stood in their finest uniforms, each one a symbol of their authority and pride. Mistress Aufrica led the witches, flanked by other Mistresses, whom I knew not their names, their expressions unreadable.

"This place is incredible," Illiam murmured, his eyes wide as he took in the splendour of the hall.

I nodded, unable to suppress my own awe. "They really went all out."

Quisten, however, was unimpressed. He smirked, leaning in with a dismissive air. "My father's auditorium puts this to shame."

I rolled my eyes. "Of course it does, Quisten."

Lear, standing beside me, glanced around with a mix of curiosity and caution. "Still, it's impressive. They've really transformed it."

I couldn't help but feel a pang of sadness. "I wish Hugo could be here to see this."

The music began, lively and joyous, setting a celebratory tone that cut through the tension in the room. Prime Master Kegg, usually so stern and imposing, stepped forward with Mistress Aufrica. Together, they led the first dance, their movements elegant and fluid. I found it odd, almost surreal, to see Kegg glide across the floor with such grace, but it had the intended effect. The room's atmosphere softened, the wary glances easing into something more tentative and curious.

I surveyed the room, my eyes landing on Serah. She looked stunning, her gown a soft shade of blue that complemented her eyes. Lord Fayle's colours of course. Her dark hair cascaded in waves, framing her face perfectly. She also wore the emblem of

House Fayle, the stag and stars, pinned proudly on her shoulder. When she saw me, her lips curled into a warm smile, and for a moment, the trials and the tension melted away.

Gathering my nerve, I walked over to her. "May I have this dance?" I asked, extending my hand.

She raised an eyebrow, her smile turning mischievous. "Think you can keep up?"

"Only one way to find out," I replied, grinning as I took her hand.

We moved onto the dance floor as the music swirled around us. I took her hand, and we began to dance. The connection between us was undeniable, our movements in sync as if we'd been dancing together for years. Yet it was our first.

"It's been so long," I said, my voice barely above a whisper. "So many trials."

"Too many," she replied, her gaze locking onto mine. "And yet here we are, still standing. Well, dancing."

I nodded, trying to keep my focus on the steps. "There's so much I want to talk about, but maybe not here."

She laughed softly, a musical sound that blended with the melody. "Oh, you mean you don't want to discuss our deepest fears in the middle of a ballroom? Scandalous."

The thought of home brought a mix of emotions: relief, nostalgia, and a touch of apprehension. But with Serah in my arms, it felt manageable. The dance continued, each step reflecting our shared history and unspoken bond.

"You're a good dancer," she teased, her eyes sparkling. "Who knew you had rhythm?"

"Only because I have a good partner," I replied, grinning.

As we moved across the floor, I couldn't help but feel a sense of rightness. This was where I was meant to be, and Serah was a part of that.

Around us, other boys began to move forward, asking the other acolytes to dance. Illiam approached a tall witch in a deep green gown, his usual cool demeanour softened by a genuine smile. Quisten, stepping with a noble grace onto the floor, confidently asked a girl with striking red hair, his pomposity barely masked the nerves beneath. Even Ivor, with his unassuming nature, found himself on the dance floor, trying his best to keep up with his partner's graceful steps.

As the music continued, I caught sight of Lear standing on the sidelines. His eyes were locked onto Serah and I, his hatred for the witches clear in his tense stance and clenched jaw. I pushed the thought aside, focusing on the warmth of Serah's hand in mine and the rhythm of our dance. When the music finally slowed to a stop, we lingered, caught in the glow of the moment.

Reluctantly, we stepped apart. Before leading her to my friends, I reached into my pocket and pulled out the knotted necklace with an intricate design I had bought in the market in Dúnmara.

"Got you something," I said, holding it out to her.

Serah raised an eyebrow, her trademark wit flashing in her eyes. "Oh, really? Is this a bribe for all the trouble you've caused?"

I chuckled, shaking my head. "Just a token. I saw it and thought of you."

She took the necklace, examining the intricate knots and patterns with genuine appreciation. "It's beautiful, Karn. You've got an eye for these things. Or maybe just a knack for stumbling upon them."

"Maybe a bit of both," I admitted, feeling a bit of pride.

Serah slipped the necklace over her head, the delicate design contrasting with her gown. "Thank you," she said softly, her sarcasm melting into sincerity for a moment. "It means a lot."

I nodded, smiling. "Glad you like it."

"Now, shall we go meet your friends? Or are you going to keep me all to yourself?" Serah teased, her playful tone returning.

"I suppose I can share you for a bit," I replied, leading her towards the group gathered nearby.

"Serah, I'd like you to meet my friends," I said, gesturing to the group. Illiam, Quisten, and Ivor stood together, their eyes glinting with curiosity and anticipation.

Quisten, never one to miss a chance to assert his confidence, stepped forward. "Serah," he said, his tone dripping with forced charm. "Long time no see."

Serah raised an eyebrow, her expression unimpressed. "Not long enough, Quisten was it?" she replied smoothly, her sharp tongue as quick as ever.

Quisten's smile faltered for a moment before he regained his composure. "Always a pleasure," he said, though his eyes flickered with a hint of annoyance.

I saw Illiam step forward, a smile clear on his lips. I gestured towards Serah. "Serah, this is Illiam. Illiam, Serah."

Illiam nodded in greeting and turned to introduce the girl beside him. "And this is Kiara," he said. Kiara was tall and graceful, her auburn hair cascading down her back in loose waves. It matched the dark green of her gown. She had an air of quiet confidence about her.

Serah's face lit up with recognition and genuine warmth. "Kiara!" she said, hugging her friend. "I see you've met Illiam."

Kiara smiled, her eyes sparkling. "Yes, he's been quite the gentleman."

Illiam glanced between Serah and me, "So, Karn, how's it feel to dance with such a beauty?"

I chuckled, shaking my head. "Feels pretty great, considering she's my sister."

Serah laughed softly. "You did fine, Karn."

As we talked, I couldn't shake the feeling of Lear's eyes upon us. I glanced over and saw him still standing alone, his expression dark and brooding. The anger in his eyes was intense, but I turned away, refusing to let it ruin the night.

"Let's get some drinks," I suggested, leading the group towards the refreshment table. The hall was alive with laughter and conversation, the tension from earlier now a distant memory.

We gathered around the table, filling our cups and toasting to our successes and the night ahead. The atmosphere was light, and for a moment, it felt like we were just a group of friends enjoying a celebration, the weight of our trials and the uncertainty of the future temporarily forgotten.

As we clinked our cups together, I glanced at Serah, her presence a steadying force amidst the chaos. It made me realise just how much I had missed her the last six moons.

Master Kegg and Mistress Aufrica stepped onto a raised platform at the far end of the hall. The room fell silent, all eyes turned towards them. The light from the lanterns and chandeliers focused upon them, making the moment feel almost sacred. Kegg, with his imposing presence, began to speak, his voice commanding yet warm.

"Steel Novices, wards, and witches," he began, his tone resonating through the hall. Myself and the other wards stood tall, their freshly washed uniforms crisp and neat, weapons gleaming at their sides. Across from them, the witches, draped in their elegant gowns, watched with a mixture of curiosity and pride.

"You have faced your trials with courage and resilience. Tonight, we celebrate not just your survival, but your growth and the bonds you have formed."

Mistress Aufrica, elegant and poised, continued, "We know the challenges you have faced were not easy. But they have forged you, much like the weapons you now carry. Remember, this is only the beginning. Greater challenges await, but tonight, you have earned the right to enjoy yourselves."

Kegg nodded, adding, "Over the next week, you will return home to winter with your families. But before spring returns, you will be back here, facing further trials. Wards and witches will work together, so keep training, stay strong, and be prepared."

Aufrica's gaze swept the room, her eyes glinting like polished steel, each glance brimming with pride and unwavering determination. "And know this," she said, her voice lowering to a dramatic pitch, "the Queen herself watches with great interest as her loyal servants grow and rise to meet their destinies. Do not disappoint her."

The hall erupted in applause, the combined cheers of wards and witches mingling in a rare moment of unity. I glanced at Serah, who was smiling beside me, and felt a surge of determination. Around us, the faces of my friends reflected the same resolve— Quisten's smug grin, Illiam's cool smile, Lear's intense stare.

The applause died down, and the wards and witches started to mingle again. The festive atmosphere returned, but a subtle tension lingered, a reminder of the challenges still ahead. I was standing with Serah when Lear walked over, his expression hard and questioning.

"Lear," I greeted him, forcing a smile. "Enjoying the night?"

"Why were you dancing with… her?" he asked, his eyes boring into Serah with a look of pure disdain. His voice was low and seething. "I thought you hated them as much as I do."

Serah opened her mouth to apologise, but Lear cut her off with a sharp, dismissive glare.

I sighed, glancing at Serah before turning back to Lear. Her expression was pained, her eyes reflecting the tension.

"Serah is my sister, Lear."

His eyes widened in shock, and he took a step back, jaw

tightening with barely suppressed rage. "Karn, she's the one who sang during my trial. She made me see... those things."

"I know," I admitted, feeling a sharp pang of guilt. "But she's still my sister."

Lear's face twisted in a mixture of fury and betrayal. "And you think that makes it okay? After everything they did to us?"

Serah tried again to speak, but Lear's icy glare silenced her. "I don't want your apologies," he snapped.

He didn't say anything more, just turned and began to walk away, his shoulders rigid with anger.

"Lear, wait—" I started, but he had already moved past the crowd, vanishing into the throng of people. My frustration and concern grew as I watched him go, knowing this unresolved tension would only fester.

To make things worse, I saw Lear bump into Quisten, the collision sent a drink spilling onto Quisten's immaculate attire. Quisten's eyes flashed with irritation as he looked down at the stain spread upon his clothes. Deja Vu, just like the encounter that first sparked their grudge.

"Watch where you're going, lowborn scum," Quisten snapped, his tone cutting like a blade. "Look at my clothes, you worthless piece of filth."

Lear met his gaze with a sneer. "Maybe if you weren't so full of yourself, Quisten, you'd see where you're walking."

Quisten's face darkened, his eyes narrowing. "At least I know my place, Lear. Unlike some gutter rats who think they belong here."

Lear's expression twisted with anger. "Better a gutter rat than a prancing peacock. You think your family's name means something here? It doesn't mean shit."

Quisten's hand clenched into a fist, but before he could retort, Lear strode off, leaving him standing there fuming. I saw Quisten's expression shift to something more dangerous as he followed Lear.

"Oh, hell," I muttered under my breath. "Excuse me," I said to Serah, giving her a quick nod before weaving through the crowd after them.

The grand hall was filled with laughter and conversation, the clinking of glasses mingling with the soft strains of music. But my focus was solely on the two boys ahead. I manoeuvred through the throngs of elegantly dressed witches in their subtle, shimmering gowns and sharply attired wards, each movement a calculated effort to keep Quisten and Lear in sight.

My eyes never left them, tracking every step, every twitch of their shoulders. The tension between them was thick, like a storm cloud ready to burst. I knew I had to intervene before things escalated further.

"Wait, Karn!" Serah's voice called from behind, a note of concern threading through the merriment of the evening.

I didn't stop, weaving between clusters of people. The glances thrown my way barely registered as I pushed past laughing couples and animated conversations. The flickering candlelight cast long shadows on the polished floor, and the air was thick with the mingled scents of perfumes and the faint tang of sweat.

Quisten's posture was rigid, his movements sharp and purposeful. Lear, in contrast, stalked forward with a barely contained fury, his fists clenching and unclenching at his sides. The crowd seemed oblivious to the brewing conflict, but I could see the storm building.

"Quisten, Lear!" I called, my voice firm but not loud enough to draw unnecessary attention. They didn't hear me, or maybe they chose not to.

"Move," I muttered to a pair of witches blocking my path, their eyes widening in surprise as they stepped aside.

I followed them down a side corridor, the noise of the grand hall faded into a distant hum. The light here was dim, casting long shadows that seemed to twist and writhe as I hurried after them. Ahead, I saw Quisten shove Lear against the wall, his face twisted with rage.

"You're nothing but low-born scum," Quisten hissed, his voice low and venomous. "You don't belong here. Go back to the pig-shit farm you came from."

Thankfully both of their weapons remained at their sides.

Lear's response was a swift punch to Quisten's gut. The impact echoed in the narrow space, and Quisten doubled over, gasping. But he recovered quickly, lashing out with a wild swing that caught Lear on the jaw. Lear staggered back, but his eyes burned with defiance.

"I belong here more than you. I earned my place," Lear spat, ducking another swing. "You pissed your breeches and barely passed the trial."

Quisten's face darkened, a furious snarl twisting his features. "Shut up!" he shouted, slamming Lear against the wall again. "You don't know anything about me!"

They grappled, crashing into the walls and knocking over a small table, the sound of splintering wood blended with their grunts and curses.

"Stop it!" I shouted, but my voice was drowned out by the chaos. I lunged forward, trying to pull them apart, but they were too far gone in their fury.

In the midst of their struggle, Quisten's brown leather bag tore from his belt. It hit the ground with a dull thud, and something rolled out, catching the faint light. My eyes widened as I saw it—a pair of red pupils, glowing with a subdued, crimson light.

The eyes seemed to stare directly at Lear, then at me, freezing us both in place. Lear's fist hung in the air, inches from Quisten's face, as we both stared at the eyes. The room grew colder, the shadows pressing in around us.

I felt a sudden, gut-wrenching connection to those eyes—eyes that belonged to my people, taken from my village. A wave of horror and sorrow crashed over me, nearly knocking me to my knees. Those two little orbs, full of pain and terror, bore into my soul, reminding me of everything I had lost.

Lear's face drained of colour, his body trembled.

The room seemed to shrink, the walls pressing in as dread thickened the air. The red pupils flared brighter, casting a furious, pulsing light that drowned out everything else. The fight between Quisten and Lear became a distant murmur, overshadowed by the oppressive presence of my own smouldering rage.

The red eyes whispered dark promises of vengeance, echoing the pain of my people. The weight of their suffering crushed down on me, fueling my resolve. Anger surged through me like a wildfire, burning away any lingering fear. My fists clenched, my jaw tightened, and in that moment, vengeance wasn't just a thought—it was a roaring, undeniable call.

Chapter 32 - Crimson Tears

Frozen, I just stared at those eyes, feeling a wave of anger and sorrow crash over me. Beside me, Lear's voice broke through the haze. "This is how you managed it, how you beat the trials?" he spat, his voice trembling with fury. "With these!?"

It felt like the scar on his cheek had lit up with a torrent of rage as his eyes flashed with anger.

I stepped toward Quisten, my vision narrowing to his terrified face. He saw the hate in my eyes and tried to speak, but his words were drowned out by the roar in my ears. He raised his arms to defend himself, knocking my hand away to land a punch, but I felt nothing. Nothing. Grabbing Quisten by the throat, I slammed him into the wall, as I felt the satisfying impact that resonated through my bones as he hit the stone. He crumpled to the ground, gasping for breath.

Desperately, Quisten raised his arms again in a futile attempt to defend himself. My fists moved on their own, swinging wildly, fueled by the rage that coursed through me. My knuckles connected with his face, the sickening crunch of bone and the warmth of his blood splattering against my skin. Each strike was a release, a cathartic explosion of everything I had held back over the last few months.

Quisten's shouts and screams were muffled, drowned out by white hot rage. His face became a canvas of blood and bruises, his eyes wide with terror and pain. But I didn't stop. I couldn't stop. The anger, the sorrow, the need for vengeance—it all poured out in a torrent of violence.

I felt the heat of my own fury wash over me, each blow landing with a sickening thud. Suddenly, from the corner of my vision, I saw Lear beside me, his own fists flew with the same brutal intensity. I turned my head, catching a glimpse of my own crimson red eyes reflected in his. Lear... Lear was Ashen, like me.

My blows slowed as the realisation hit. Quisten's attempts to shield himself grew weaker with each hit. His arms dropped limply to his sides, his body slumped against the wall, barely conscious. Lear and I stood over him, our chests heaving, fists clenched, staring down at the ruin we had made of him.

The wolf inside me growled, urging me to continue, to unleash all my fury. But instead, I took one deep breath and grabbed Lear's hand, stopping him from landing one more blow on an already battered and beaten Quisten.

Lear looked at me, his eyes glowing with the same furious red light. He growled, the sound low and menacing. We both jumped back, circling each other in the dimly lit hallway, our breaths coming in ragged gasps. The fury still raged through my veins, and I could see the same wildness in Lear's eyes.

"You... you were never in our village, were you?" I said, my voice rough with anger and confusion.

Lear's reply was feral, rabid. "Grew up with my father away from it. Heard what the witches did. Wanted revenge. You should want revenge too. Let's kill him!"

"No," I said, shaking my head. "We can't. I want more than this, more than just to take my anger out on one spoiled noble. I want my true revenge, on the Witch Queen."

Lear was too far gone. With a snarl, he lunged at me, and we clashed in a frenzy of fists and fury. Our rage fueled us, making us stronger, faster, more aggressive. The hallway turned into a battleground as we fought like animals, all our training, all of those drills lost in the heat of our rage.

Lear's blows were relentless, each one a hammering force. I blocked, countered, swung wildly, our movements a blur of violence. My fist connected with his jaw, sending him staggering back, but he recovered with a ferocious roar as he charged at me again.

We grappled, crashing into the stone walls, knocking over a table, the sounds of the Grand Hall muted and distant. The only thing that mattered was the fight, the primal need to dominate, to survive. Lear's eyes blazed, his teeth bared in a snarl. I felt the same savage hunger burning in my chest, the wolf inside me urging me on, driving me to tear him apart.

But even as we fought, a part of me knew this wasn't the way. Knew we couldn't let this fury consume us. Yet in that moment, with Lear's hands around my throat and my own fists pounding into his ribs, it was hard to care. Hard to think of anything but the rage and the blood and the need to win.

Lear's growl was cut short by a piercing scream. We both turned to see an acolyte standing in the hallway, her eyes wide with terror. She clutched her throat, then forced herself to steady, her training taking over. Her voice wavered for a split second before she managed to let out a single, clear note. The sound was intended to be a weapon, a way to subdue and control, but instead, it seemed to fuel Lear's rage further. His eyes flared with even more intensity, and the guttural cry that erupted from him was savage and unrestrained. The note hung in the air for a heartbeat before dissolving into chaos.

With a feral snarl, Lear shoved me aside and lunged for the girl. "No!" I shouted as I chased after him. I managed to push him just as he reached her, sending him sprawling to the floor. The horror on the girl's face was visible as she stared at me, eyes wide, recognizing the monster inside.

Lear didn't stay down. He scrambled up, moving almost on all fours, his fury driving him forward. The girl's scream echoed through the corridor, grabbing the attention of everyone nearby. My heart pounded with a mix of fear and desperation. All our efforts, all the secrets, and now we were exposed.

I bolted after Lear, my feet pounding against the stone floor. We nearly collided with other wards and witches, their faces blurring past in a whirl of confusion and alarm. My breath came in ragged gasps as I pushed myself to keep up with him, the corridor twisting and turning, the chase growing more frantic with each step.

Lear's movements were wild and unpredictable, crashing into walls, knocking over anything in his path. I dodged a toppled candelabra, barely keeping my footing. The sound of the girl's scream faded, replaced by the shouts and footsteps of those now in pursuit.

"Stop!" I shouted, but Lear was beyond reason, his only thoughts were fight or flight. He turned a corner sharply, nearly taking out a pair of startled wards. I followed, my mind racing, knowing that everything was falling apart. The chase seemed endless, the hallways a blur of stone and shadow, our breaths ragged and desperate. And as we ran, I couldn't shake the feeling that we had crossed a line from which there was no return.

I lost sight of Lear for a moment, the dim hallways twisted and turned, obscuring him from view. Footsteps and shouts echoed through the corridor, each sound reverberated off the stone walls. Panic clawed at me as I ran, the words of the pursuers catching my ear. They spoke of red eyes and orders from the Witch Queen. Then, cutting through the chaos, I heard Master Kegg's voice, stern and commanding.

I rounded a corner just in time to see Lear bolt towards a set of stairs. I pushed myself harder, my breath coming in ragged gasps as I followed him. The stairs wound tightly, each step echoing like a drumbeat in the enclosed space. We exchanged a blow or two on the narrow steps, fists connecting with flesh, knuckles scraping against the rough stone walls. I stumbled, catching myself on the railing, but surged forward again. Lear's foot slipped on a wet step, and I seized the moment, landing a punch that sent him sprawling against the wall. But he recovered quickly, lashing out with a wild kick, his boot grazed my cheek. The fight was a blur of motion and anger, our bodies crashing into the walls, but neither of us slowed. We were both too far gone to think clearly, driven by a primal fury that refused to be quenched.

The stairs led us to the first-floor balcony of the Grand Hall. Rain lashed against the stone, the night sky dark and foreboding. We continued up, the path narrowing as it led to the roof. The rain drenched us both, turning the stone slick under our feet. The roof was also the wall separating the wards' half of The Forge from the witches'. It was a precarious place to fight, but there was no turning back now.

I heard the footsteps behind me, the pursuers grew close. The only way to go was forward. Lear and I ran along the roof, the edge dangerously close, the river far below a dark, churning threat. The rain beat down on us, masking the sounds of the chase.

"Lear, we're both blood of the Ashen!" I pleaded, my voice barely audible over the storm. "We can still find a way out of this!"

Lear looked back at me, his eyes wild and desperate. "It's too late, Karn! We're discovered. We'll both die."

I felt the fury receding, leaving a hollow despair in its wake. I didn't know what to do. The steps behind us were closer now, shouts mingling with the rain. We reached the end of the wall, the river below roaring like a beast.

The footsteps grew louder, many of them, and the shouts became clearer. We were out of time.

The rain plastered my hair to my face, the cold rivulets dripping down my nose. I looked at Lear, desperation clawing at my throat. "Lear, please, don't do this," I pleaded, my voice barely audible over the storm's roar.

Lear's eyes glowed a fierce crimson in the night. "They won't take me, Karn. They won't take my eyes." His voice was wild, defiant. Before I could react, he jumped.

"No!" I screamed, lunging forward. I reached out, but my fingers grasped only air. I watched in horror as Lear's body plummeted, hitting the water below with a sickening splash.

Footsteps thundered behind me, and suddenly people were there. Master Kegg's strong grip hauled me up as others peered over the edge. Two men with bows began firing into the water, their arrows slicing through the storm.

Kegg's face loomed close to mine, rainwater running down his stern features. "Is it true?" he demanded, his voice cut through the chaos.

I stared at him, my mind reeling. His gaze locked onto mine, unyielding.

"Is it true?" he repeated, shaking me. "The boy, did he have red eyes? Was he the one to do that to Lord Cowle?"

My breath caught in my throat. The scene played over in my mind—Lear's wild eyes, the horror on Quisten's face. I felt the weight of it all crashing down on me. "Yes," I choked out, barely able to form the words. "I couldn't stop him."

Kegg's expression hardened, and he released his grip, enough for me to breathe but not enough to let me go. The exhaustion hit me then, like a tidal wave. My vision blurred, the edges darkened. The last thing I thought of was Lear, his defiant eyes burning red in the night. Then, the world faded to black.

Epilogue

I woke up in a bed in the Refuge, the light filtered through the narrow windows casting a soft glow on the room. I felt the familiar stiffness of exhaustion in my muscles, but otherwise, I seemed to be in one piece. On the bed next to me lay Quisten, bandaged and breathing heavily, his face a mess of bruises. The sight stirred a mix of emotions—anger, pity, and more than a sliver of guilt.

The door creaked open, and Serah walked in, her presence bringing a sense of calm to the room. I tried to speak, but she quickly put a finger to her lips, silencing me. She moved gracefully to my side, her expression both stern and gentle.

"It's alright," she whispered. "The boy, the one that they're calling a deviant, got away. But thanks to you, the acolyte Helia was saved, and possibly your friend, Quisten too. The healers don't know yet if he'll fully recover."

Her words hit me hard. They were calling Lear a deviant, like some kind of animal. The boy who shared my anger and pain, now hunted like a beast.

Serah sat next to me, pulling out an apple and a small knife. She sliced it with precision, offering me a piece. "You need to eat," she said softly, her eyes never leaving mine. "You've been through a lot."

I accepted the apple, chewing slowly as I absorbed her words. I wasn't too injured, just exhausted. Despite this, they insisted I stay in the Refuge for several days. Quisten never woke up during that time, his condition unchanged. I wondered if he ever would and, if he did, whether he'd remember what happened. Would he tell them that Karn too was a Deviant?

One morning, Master Kegg arrived with Master Veil to ask

questions. The animosity between them was evident, their mutual loathing clear in their stiff interactions. Kegg's questions were direct and probing, each one feeling like a hammer striking an anvil. Veil watched silently, his gaze piercing, as if trying to see through me.

"Tell me again what happened with the boy, Lear," Kegg demanded, his voice cold and unyielding.

I took a deep breath, trying to keep my answers clear and steady. "He snapped, Master. He couldn't handle the trials. He...changed."

Veil's eyes narrowed, but he remained silent, his presence a constant, oppressive force.

"What exactly did he say?" Kegg pressed, leaning in closer.

"He said he wouldn't be taken. He...he wanted revenge," I replied, my voice barely above a whisper. The memory of Lear's red eyes haunted me, but I couldn't show fear now.

Kegg's jaw tightened, and he exchanged a brief, tense look with Veil. The two Masters stood in stark contrast—Kegg, the stern enforcer, and Veil, the silent observer. The room felt colder with each passing moment, the air thick with unspoken tension.

"Anything else?" Veil finally spoke, his tone light and almost whimsical, as if he found the entire situation amusing.

I shook my head. "No, Master Veil. That's all he said."

Kegg nodded curtly, signalling the end of the interrogation. "You're dismissed."

As they turned to leave, I couldn't help but feel relieved. The confrontation with the Masters had left me drained, and the lingering tension between Kegg and Veil made my skin crawl.

Later, Illiam and Ivor showed up to check on me and Quisten, their concern evident in their eyes. Even Aspallan made a brief appearance, though he didn't say much. The camaraderie was a small comfort in the midst of uncertainty.

Eventually, I was allowed to leave. Drills had been suspended for the autumn and winter break, and also because of the recent events. The Forge seemed quieter, the usual buzz of activity replaced by a tense silence.

Finally, the day arrived. Banar appeared at the threshold, Serah in tow, his arrival like a cool draught in a stifling room. His eyes, brimming with a complex dance of pride and worry, met mine. Without a word, he stepped forward and rested his hand on my shoulder, the weight of it grounding.

"We're taking you home," he said, his voice steady and comforting.

Together, Banar, Serah, and I left the Refuge. The weight of recent events lingered but softened by the promise of home.

As we set out, the haunting visage of Lear—the boy with eyes like smouldering embers and a soul ablaze with the same fury as my own—clung to my mind. His desperate leap into the churning river replayed in my head, a chilling echo of our shared darkness.

The End

SKIRMISH

Overview: Skirmish is a tactical board game where two players command battalions to capture the opponent's flag. The game involves strategy, bluffing, and quick thinking. It's played on a larger-than-checkerboard grid with various pieces representing different military units.

Game Components:

1. **Board:** A grid of alternating coloured squares, larger than a typical checkerboard (e.g., 12x12 or 24x24).

2. **Standard Pieces:**
   - **Foot Soldiers (Cost: 1):** Move one square at a time in any direction.
   - **Knights (Cost: 3):** Move in an L-shape (two squares in one direction and one square perpendicular, or vice versa).
   - **Archers (Cost: 2):** Move in straight lines, any number of squares, but cannot jump over other pieces.
   - **Cavalry (Cost: 3):** Move up to three squares in a straight line, horizontally or vertically, and can jump over one piece.
   - **Siege Engines (Cost: 4):** Cannot move. But can destroy an adjacent piece without moving into its square.
   - **Earthwork (Cost: 2):** Cannot move. Can fortify a square and only be destroyed by siege engines. Cannot enclose a flag.

3. **Special Pieces:**
   - **Witch (Cost: 5):** Moves one square in any direction. Can "cast a spell" to immobilise an adjacent enemy piece for one turn.
   - **Assassin (Cost: 4):** Moves up to three squares diagonally. Can bypass the first piece it encounters

(even earthworks) and capture the second, making it ideal for penetrating defences.

- o **Spy (Cost: 3):** Moves diagonally any number of squares. Can reveal the opponent's next move once per game. Opponent must tell the user what their next move is and stick to it.

4. **Flag (Cost: 0):** The objective is to capture this piece.

Setup:

- Each player arranges their pieces within the first three rows of their side of the board.
- The flag is placed in a designated area at the centre of each player's back row.
- Players can have as many pieces as they want, as long as the total cost is within the game's resource allotment (e.g., 12 for a 12x12 game and 24 for a 24x24 game).

Objective: Capture the opponent's flag while protecting your own.

Basic Rules:

1. **Movement:**
   - o Foot Soldiers move one square in any direction.
   - o Knights move in an L-shape.
   - o Archers move any number of squares in straight lines but cannot jump over pieces.
   - o Cavalry move up to three squares in a straight line and can jump over one piece.
   - o Siege Engines move two squares in any direction and can destroy an adjacent piece without moving into its square.
   - o Earthwork moves one square in any direction and can fortify an adjacent piece, giving it one extra move to avoid capture.

2. **Capturing Pieces:**
   - o A piece captures an opponent's piece by moving into its square.
   - o Siege Engines destroy an adjacent piece without

moving into its square.

- o Capturing is mandatory if possible, simulating the inevitability of conflict in battle.

3. **Winning the Game:**
   - o The game ends when a player's flag is captured. By having a piece step into the flag's square.
   - o The player who captures the opponent's flag is the winner.

Advanced Tactics:

1. **Bluffing and Sacrifices:**
   - o Players may bluff by positioning pieces to mislead their opponent about their true intentions.
   - o Sacrificing pieces can be a strategic move to lure opponents into traps or to open a path to the flag.

2. **Defence and Offense:**
   - o Balancing offensive manoeuvres with defensive strategies is crucial.
   - o Protect the flag by positioning stronger pieces around it while probing the opponent's defences with other pieces.

3. **Ambushes:**
   - o Set up ambushes using archers and knights to surprise the opponent.
   - o Anticipate the opponent's moves and position pieces to counter their strategy.

Example Gameplay Scenario:

Resource Allocation (12x12 game with 12 points):

- Player 1 (Elara) chooses:
  - o 2 Knights (6 points)
  - o 1 Archer (2 points)
  - o 1 Cavalry (3 points)
  - o 1 Foot Soldier (1 point)
- Player 2 (Banar) chooses:
  - o 1 Witch (5 points)
  - o 1 Assassin (4 points)

- o 1 Earthwork (2 points)
- o 1 Foot Soldier (1 point)

Opening Moves:
- Elara advances a knight and a foot soldier to probe Banar's defences.
- Banar positions his Earthwork to fortify his Witch, giving it extra protection.

Mid-Game:
- Elara sacrifices her foot soldier to lure Banar's Assassin out of position.
- Banar uses his Assassin to bypass one of Elara's pieces and capture another, creating a gap in her defence.

Special Piece Maneuver:
- Elara uses her Archer to move across the board, threatening Banar's key pieces.
- Banar's Witch immobilises Elara's advancing Cavalry for one turn, buying time for repositioning.

Endgame:
- Elara executes a bold manoeuvre, sending her knight deep into Banar's territory.
- Banar attempts to block with his remaining pieces, but Elara's knight breaks through, capturing Banar's flag.

Winning Strategy:
- Elara's combination of bluffing, sacrifices, and a well-timed offensive push secures her victory.

Final Tips:
- Always watch for potential traps and ambushes.
- Use each piece's strengths to your advantage.
- Adapt your strategy based on the opponent's moves and the changing dynamics of the game.

Skirmish is a game that combines strategy, foresight, and psychological acumen, offering a unique challenge with every match. Enjoy the battle of wits and may the best strategist win!

DISCOVER MORE

If you enjoyed this book, please consider leaving a review.

If you'd like to be kept up-to-date on the status of the final book and new releases by Simon Shugar then please consider joining my newsletter!

www.simonshugar.co.uk/newsletter

ABOUT THE AUTHOR

Simon Shugar, a native of Oxfordshire, England, currently resides in North Carolina, United States, with his awesome young son, Thomas and adored dog, Jasper. As a voracious reader, Simon found inspiration in the captivating works of Robin Hobb, Brandon Sanderson, and Patrick Rothfuss throughout his childhood.

Originally pursuing a degree in game design at the University of Wolverhampton, Simon was drawn to the art of world-building and the endless possibilities it offered. However, he later transitioned to a career in software engineering, seeking stability and practicality.

This change of direction ignited a new creative spark within Simon, kindling a passion for writing. It wasn't until years later, with some spare time and unwavering determination, that he began translating his vivid imagination into words on paper. With every story, Simon continues to enthrall readers as he brings his unique worlds to life.

www.simonshugar.co.uk
www.facebook.com/simon.shugar.author

Made in the USA
Middletown, DE
26 August 2024

59233592R00227